STA
S

EXILE

DANIEL cast a surreptitious glance at his captor and wondered whether he'd seen the creature before. It was difficult to tell with such alien features, but he thought he recognized the tattoo on the side of the Wraith's face. Could it be one of the Wraith who'd held them captive in the pods?

"Now where?" Jack said from up front. He'd stopped in a slight clearing, the undergrowth thinning out but with no obvious path ahead.

Without releasing Daniel's arm, the Wraith stalked past Jack and started clearing away branches and leaves to reveal the foundations of a brick wall and a flight of stone stairs that led to an underground doorway. He gestured for the others to precede him down the steps.

"I don't think so," Jack said. It was subtle, but Daniel noticed the way his weight moved forward onto the balls of his feet, how his grip on his weapon shifted. He was getting ready for a fight and Daniel did the same; they all knew that he'd be the first victim if things got ugly and he didn't plan to make it easy.

Teal'c's staff sprung into life and Sam thumbed off the safety on her MP5.

Daniel braced himself, waiting in hope for the mistake that would let him free himself and run.

But it didn't happen. Instead, the Wraith spoke. "Trust me or you will die," he said, baring teeth in a way that didn't exactly encourage trust.

"Don't you mean 'Trust me and you will die?'" Jack said.

"This area will be swept by darts within moments. If you are above ground, you will be culled."

Jack lifted his eyebrows. "And you're helping us because…?"

"Because you are of use, Lantean."

To Colin
Thanks for reading
Laura Harper :)

For Colin
Watch out for the cliff hanger!
Sally Malcolm

STARGATE
SG·1

EXILE
Book two of the Apocalypse series

**SALLY MALCOLM &
LAURA HARPER**

FANDEMONIUM BOOKS

An original publication of Fandemonium Ltd, produced under license from MGM Consumer Products.

Fandemonium Books, PO Box 795A, Surbiton, Surrey KT5 8YB, United Kingdom

Visit our website: www.stargatenovels.com

STARGATE
SG·1

METRO-GOLDWYN-MAYER Presents
RICHARD DEAN ANDERSON
in
STARGATE SG-1™
MICHAEL SHANKS AMANDA TAPPING CHRISTOPHER JUDGE DON S. DAVIS
Executive Producers JONATHAN GLASSNER BRAD WRIGHT
MICHAEL GREENBURG RICHARD DEAN ANDERSON
Developed for Television by BRAD WRIGHT & JONATHAN GLASSNER

STARGATE SG-1 is a trademark of Metro-Goldwyn-Mayer Studios Inc. © 1997-2015 MGM Television Entertainment Inc. and MGM Global Holdings Inc. All Rights Reserved.

METRO-GOLDWYN-MAYER is a trademark of Metro-Goldwyn-Mayer Lion Corp. © 2015 Metro-Goldwyn-Mayer Studios Inc. All Rights Reserved.

Photography and cover art: Copyright © 2015 Metro-Goldwyn-Mayer Studios Inc. All Rights Reserved.

WWW.MGM.COM

No part of this publication may be reproduced, stored in or introduced into a retrieval system, or transmitted, in any form, or by any means (electronic, mechanical, photocopying, recording or otherwise) without the prior written consent of the publisher. Any person who does any unauthorized act in relation to this publication may be liable to criminal prosecution and civil claims for damages. If you purchase this book without a cover, you should be aware that this book is stolen property. It was reported as "unsold and destroyed" to the publisher and neither the author nor the publisher has received any payment for this "stripped book".

ISBN: 978-1-905586-71-4 Printed in the USA

For Mia — kid, you'll move mountains — L.H.

For Jess and Ben, as always — S.M.

Acknowledgement
We're indebted to Melissa Scott, Jo Graham and Amy Griswold for the fantastic Wraith culture they developed in the STARGATE ATLANTIS Legacy series, from which we have borrowed many terms and concepts in this book.

Historical note:
This story is set in season three of STARGATE SG-1,
between the episodes
One Hundred Days and Shades of Grey.

"We live in the age of the refugee, the age of the exile."
Ariel Dorfman

CHAPTER ONE

Evacuation Site — April 2000: The world was made from heat and noise and dust. The arid landscape threw up its crimson sand, as if in protest at the two thousand pairs of boots that now trod across its desolate plains. Janet Fraiser wiped her brow on her sweat-damp forearm and shouted directions for the raising of the surgical tent. To her left, the sun's glare reflected off a lake of pristine water — in this scorched terrain, it was the colony's best hope of survival.

The trek to the camp had been hard going. The new world's population of just over two thousand was about forty percent military personnel, who were accustomed to periods of arduous physical activity and deprivation. It was the other sixty percent who had slowed their progress: the soft palmed politicians, the policy makers, the spin doctors, the speech writers, those used to air conditioned sedans and single malts. Though Maybourne's base had been relatively well stocked and sophisticated, technology-wise, there weren't enough boots and BDUs to go around, and so some were forced to negotiate the rough and rocky terrain in Italian loafers and tailored suits. It was the most bizarre band of refugees Janet had ever seen.

Nevertheless, here they were, less than two weeks after their world had ended, breaking new ground like the western settlers who'd made their home on Colorado's dirt. Of course, those frontiersmen had set out on their journeys with the future in their eyes, seeking the uncharted and the undiscovered in the spirit of hope. They hadn't been running from the destruction of their world.

She was struck then, as she often was, with hideous imaginings of what had become of Colorado and her old life. Her house, Cassie's school, her favorite deli: what were the chances that anything was left? Janet doused the thought and ran to catch the tarp that was collapsing on one side of the tent.

"Ma'am?" She glanced over her shoulder at the young nurse who approached. Janet struggled to remember her name. The woman had only been at the SGC for about a week before the evacuation. Lucky for her, thought Janet wryly. All medical personnel on base automatically had a place on the evac list.

"Yes… De Sousa?" The name came to her at the last second and she hoped the nurse didn't notice the slight pause.

"We need you in triage, ma'am. There are two more showing symptoms."

Janet took a breath and closed her eyes. As if having to flee for their lives wasn't enough, they now faced another threat in the form of a virulent flu that had laid low fifteen of their number so far. Dehydration was the worst of it and the soaring temperatures were not helping. "There's saline in one of those crates. Get them on an IV and I'll be there in five."

What they needed was an antiviral, but supplies of Tamiflu were limited and they could only afford to administer them in the worst cases; they needed to ration meds in case this thing got worse. De Sousa nodded, collecting the supplies, and headed back to the triage tent, which had been set up as a priority when they'd arrived at the lake. But then everything was a priority — if only they had the time and the resources they needed.

"You look like you need a hand, Doctor."

The voice set her immediately on edge, and she swiped the tarp away from her face to find Maybourne surveying the assembly with a look of absent derision on his face. He was no longer dressed in the leather bomber jacket and slacks he'd been wearing when he'd stumbled, terrified, into the base, and had changed into desert BDUs. The jacket and pants still held the creases from being packed in a supply crate, and the boots shone, having not yet been marked by the red dust of the valley. It didn't surprise her that he'd been one of those to get hold of the prized gear.

"I can manage," she said, securing the tarp with a half hitch. She gritted her teeth and gave the line a harder tug than was necessary. A trickle of sweat ran down her back, sticking her tank top to her skin.

Maybourne ignored her refusal of help and picked up the other side of the tarp, fastening it to the pole. She caught him glancing around at the chaos of the camp. The grimy faces, the stacks of military crates, the ramshackle tents that would offer them shelter were all that remained of an entire planet. It was gratifying to see a trace of guilt in his expression. *You did this*, she thought. *You brought us here.* But she said nothing; she'd voiced enough accusations when they'd first come through the gate and all she'd gotten was shut down.

"You know, there are bunks up at the base, Janet. We have personnel living up there out of this heat. I'm sure I could arrange—"

"My patients are here," she said. She wouldn't let him assuage whatever guilt he was feeling by offering her a few home comforts. Besides, it was true that she needed to be near her patients while this flu raged. "There isn't enough room for them at your base and there aren't any resources nearby. As for the rest of us, we need water and we need land that's fit for farming. We won't get that at the top of a cliff." She finished off her line and looked him in the eye. "It isn't exactly the most hospitable of environments."

Maybourne gave a tight smile, not missing her meaning. It wasn't only the lack of resources that made the ruins housing the Stargate unsuitable for settling the survivors. There was another unspoken, uglier truth that prevented them from staying there; it was NID territory, and she didn't mean the legitimate branch of that organization. There were factions that went further into the dark, and higher up the ranks of power, than even Maybourne and, like cockroaches, they'd managed to survive the apocalypse.

Others were crawling out of the woodwork now, emerging

from the shadows in which they'd operated while on Earth. They had claimed the clifftop base under the guise of bringing their rogue element under control and anyone remaining there would no doubt have to accede to their rules. They'd sneaked in the back door and now controlled the greatest source of power left to humanity, simply by virtue of calling first dibs. It left the sourest of tastes in her mouth.

Maybourne glanced around the camp. "You find this environment more to your liking?"

"I find it easier to breathe here."

He snorted. "I find it stifling, and I don't just mean the heat."

The last thread of her patience began to unravel. "I think I get that. It must be difficult to witness the outcome of all those plans you made."

He froze in the middle of kicking a tent peg into the ground and his jaw tensed. "Have a care, Dr. Fraiser. Don't let misguided loyalties give you ideas. All of this came about for one reason."

She raised her eyebrows in question.

"We spent too long pandering to the whims of alien races that had nothing but contempt for us. We were trying to make friends when we should've been looking after ourselves. *That's* why we're here. President Turner gave his ear too readily to General Hammond and he sold him a pup."

That was too much. "Don't you dare—"

"Be realistic, Dr. Fraiser. There's a lot you can achieve here, but you'll never do it trying to honor the memory of a dead man. Hammond got his priorities wrong and that's why he's dead. Don't make the same mistake."

"And what about your mistakes, Colonel? Are you still insisting you didn't make any?"

He grinned and turned away, as if bored, but the expression looked forced. "I'd be careful about making those ludicrous claims about my part in those thefts again, Doctor. Let's just say there are others in our little society who share my philosophy. You'd be wise not to rattle any cages."

Janet pressed her lips together, refusing to be baited. The claims she'd made were nothing but the truth — she knew it, Maybourne knew it, and she guessed that most of the NID people here knew it too — but she didn't doubt that there were certain people who'd been on the evac list because of the power they wielded. They'd managed to spin a story that painted Maybourne as the one who'd uncovered the truth about the entire plot to steal alien technology and, in the end, it was Robert Makepeace, for his sins, who'd borne the full weight of the blame. There was, Janet supposed, no patsy like a dead patsy.

"I wouldn't waste my breath, Colonel. You know people. I get that. It's the only explanation I can think of for you making it this far. You can say what you want about George Hammond, but there isn't a man or woman down here who wouldn't agree that he was worth fifty of you." She took a step toward him and allowed herself a moment of satisfaction at seeing him flinch. It was in that twitch of his teeth that she saw it; he understood the truth of what he'd done, and his arrogance was nothing but an attempt to hide his guilt, even from himself.

Maybourne glanced around, but Janet knew no one was paying them any heed. Behind her, voices were raised in a dispute over where the crates containing the medical supplies should be stored. She resented this petty little man for distracting her from her more important concerns. She resented him standing there in immaculate BDUs while the rest of them sweated in the dirt. She wanted rid of him. Apparently, though, he wasn't quite ready to leave. When he spoke, his voice was almost a hiss. "My loyalty has always been to Earth, Doctor. If it wasn't for me, most of these people would still be back there under Apophis's yoke — or worse. If it had been left to Turner's administration, there would have been no evacuation, and that's the truth. *I* made this possible."

Janet laughed in disbelief. "*You* did? Please, Colonel. You're a puppet, letting someone else pull the strings. I've seen you with them. Don't overestimate your power here."

"It's you who shouldn't *under*estimate it, Dr. Fraiser."

She crouched and pulled the lid off a plastic supply crate, wanting to draw a close to this conversation. She had triage to get to. At least there she could serve a real purpose, rather than be left feeling helpless and frustrated. "Why are you here, Colonel?" she asked, counting through the packets of antivirals inside the crate. "Wouldn't you prefer the company up at the gate?"

He drew himself upright. "*Novus ordo seclorum*, Dr. Fraiser. The time for change is upon us. You would do well to choose the right side."

CHAPTER TWO

Earth — 2098: Daniel had often mused that the reason archaeology was considered a science and not a liberal art was because it was based on evidence, on the physical remains of the past. Each unearthed artifact told a story and it was the job of the archaeologist to decipher those stories and, by telling them, to lift the veil on history.

But standing in the ruins of his own past, looking up at the shattered windows of the control room, at the half-buried Stargate through which he'd stepped only days earlier, Daniel felt the mental acuity needed to uncover this story start to slip away.

The truth was simply too much to comprehend. It was impossible. And yet the evidence was right before his eyes, horrible and incontrovertible.

"This is the SGC…" Sam was the first to speak in a long time.

"It's a trick," Jack said, more in hope than conviction. "It's some Goa'uld trick."

He glared at Daniel, looking for agreement, but Daniel could only shake his head. "I don't think so." Crouching down, he ran his fingers over a scrap of red paint on the floor. The same red paint they'd followed through the warren of half-excavated tunnels, the same red paint that had led the way to the gate room through the labyrinthine corridors of the SGC.

"How has this happened?" said Teal'c, cutting straight to the point.

Daniel glanced up at their companions: Dix, who claimed to be Rya'c, and the woman, Zuri. There was a tight expression on Dix's face, akin to pity, but Zuri only looked suspicious. They exchanged a glance. "How can it be that they do not know?" she said.

Dix didn't answer her, turning instead to Teal'c. "Much in

the galaxy has changed in your absence, Father."

"I have not been absent," Teal'c said, and there was a heat in his voice that Daniel understood. *I did not abandon you*, was the subtext.

If Dix heard it too, he didn't respond. "Zuri," he said, "have food and drink brought to my quarters. We have much to discuss."

Zuri didn't seem happy with the order but she didn't argue, just turned on her heel and headed down another shadowy corridor. Dix gestured along the passageway from which they'd entered the ruined gate room. "Come," he said, "and I will tell you all that I know. There is some great mystery here."

"No kidding," said Sam.

But no one moved; all eyes were on Jack to give the order. He sighed in defeat. "Okay, let's go listen to the story," he said, because, really, what choice did they have? Everything they thought they knew had changed; their universe was upside down.

Even with ropes, it was a hard climb up what Daniel now knew to be the walls of the missile silo that housed the Stargate. The lower levels were uninhabitable, Rya'c said. They were too unstable and dangerous.

"Ground zero," Jack guessed as they climbed. When Daniel lifted a questioning eyebrow, he expanded the point. "It looks like they had to use the self-destruct. It would have brought down the lower levels."

Daniel shivered. It was impossible not to imagine General Hammond standing in the control room and giving that order; it was impossible not to imagine him dying there. He would have stayed until the end.

Once they were back on a habitable level, Dix guided them through another rubble-filled corridor until they found themselves outside a small room. The walls had been whitewashed and there were unlit candles neatly placed on the makeshift table pushed against the far wall. Cushions dotted the floor and a sleeping pallet lay against another of the walls. Daniel tried to place the room, to figure out where they were, but, whatever it had once been used for, there were no clues left to find.

"There is not much space," Dix said as he dropped down onto the pallet and gestured for the others to seat themselves on the cushions. "You should leave your packs and weapons outside."

"Oh, I don't think so," Jack said, cradling his MP5.

Dix lifted an eyebrow. "Still you do not trust me, Colonel O'Neill?"

"Still I don't *know* you."

"But you do," Dix said. "You taught me to catch a baseball, Colonel, do you recall? I still have the glove you gave me, though I no longer wear it as a hat."

Jack opened his mouth and snapped it shut again, cast a glance at Teal'c. "That was just last year."

Daniel remembered it well: the day Teal'c took his family to safety in the Land of Light after Apophis had brainwashed Rya'c, and the catching mitt Jack had given the bemused boy to take with him. He also remembered Rya'c's anger at his father, his furious accusations of abandonment.

"That was almost one hundred years ago," Dix said. "Tuplo and his kin are all dead now." His gaze settled on Teal'c. "As is my mother."

Jack cursed softly beneath his breath. Teal'c remained silent.

After a pause, Dix carried on. "Keep your weapon if you wish, Colonel. It does not threaten me, though I think you will find it uncomfortable." Then he gestured to the cushions. "Please, sit. Here is Zuri with food and drink."

Zuri pushed past Jack, who still loitered on the threshold, and she was followed by two men carrying trays of food. She crouched close to Dix to help set the plates on the floor. "Do not be misled by what you wish to be true," she warned him in a whisper designed to carry. "Do not tell them more than is wise."

Daniel registered the exchange, but the food looked enticing and distracted him; he was hungry and tired after the largely sleepless night and the long trek down to Dix's secret hideout. Dumping his pack outside, he sank gratefully onto one of the cushions and perused the feast. There was cheese and dark, heavy bread, as well as a kind of dried fruit he didn't recognize and a sweet, warm drink not unlike spiced cider. It was more and better food than he'd seen anyone topside eating. He offered Zuri a grateful smile. "Thanks," he said. "This looks good."

"Hecate provides," she said, then returned her attention to Dix. "I wish to stay."

He gave an indifferent shrug and gestured to one of the cushions. "It is your right."

Teal'c took a seat directly opposite Dix, sitting with his customary fluid grace and ramrod straight back.

Sam dropped down next to Daniel and reached immediately for the bread, while Jack eased himself to the floor with a sigh and a complaint about his knees. He unslung his weapon, but kept it within reach. "I don't suppose Hecate provides La-Z-boys, does she?" he said.

Zuri ignored him, but Dix smiled and it was hard not to see Rya'c in the expression.

When they had all helped themselves to food and drink, Dix said, "I shall tell you all that I know about what happened here, and perhaps you can tell me more."

"Don't count on it," Jack muttered, giving one of the dried fruits a tentative sniff; he wasn't exactly adventurous about eating off-world.

"When I was a boy," Dix said, "living with my mother in the Land of Light, I received a visit from General Hammond and Dr. Fraiser."

"Janet?" Sam exchanged a look with Daniel. It was rare for their Chief Medical Officer to venture off world, yet every detail lent plausibility to the story.

Dix nodded. "They came to tell me that you," he encompassed them all with a sweep of his arm, but his eyes were fixed on Teal'c, "had disappeared on a Goa'uld world." He frowned for a moment, trying to recall something. "General Hammond said you were 'Missing…'"

"…in Action?" Jack supplied. "Missing in Action."

Dix shook his head. "No, Missing and Presumed Dead. Those were his words." He locked gazes with Teal'c. "I was angry. I told General Hammond that I did not believe him. I told him that my father would come back. But you did not."

Teal'c said nothing.

Dix shrugged and reached for a fruit, biting into it and chewing. "Many said that SG-1 would return to save us, but you did not. Until now."

Zuri made a dismissive sound deep in her throat and Dix cast an irritated look in her direction.

"Save you from what?" Jack said.

Dix looked at him as if he were stupid. "From the Wraith."

"Um, you've mentioned them before," Daniel said. "Are they the creatures people on the surface call Amam?"

Dix nodded. "Amam, Devourers, Snatchers — they have many names. Wraith is one they brought with them from their own galaxy."

"Their own *galaxy*?" Sam said, her eyes going wide. "Really?"

"Dix, you talk too much," Zuri said, getting to her feet. "You should speak less and ask more questions."

"Such as what?"

"Such as, if these people are really SG-1, how do they come to be here at all? Humans cannot live so long and even your father would be aged, yet he appears younger than you."

Dix nodded. "Zuri asks good questions. How do you answer, Father?"

"I have no answer," Teal'c said. "I can only set before you the facts. Three months ago, Colonel O'Neill and I visited Rya'c and Drey'auc in the Land of Light. O'Neill did indeed teach my son to catch a baseball."

"That was the last time I saw you," Dix said, and Daniel could hear a break in his voice. Through it, he glimpsed the boy this man had once been. It tugged at something in Daniel's heart; he knew what it was to lose a father.

Teal'c's jaw clenched and it took a moment before he said, "Three months after that visit — several days ago now — we came under Goa'uld attack on P5X-104. We retreated through the Stargate under heavy fire and arrived here. Since then we have been seeking a way to return to Earth. Those are the facts as I know them. And I know this also to be true, Rya'c: I did not abandon you."

Daniel caught Jack's eye. It seemed that Teal'c was accepting his story and, in truth, Daniel was having a hard time doubting him too. Crazy as it was, this man appeared to be the boy they'd once known. Reluctant agreement edged the skepticism from Jack's face; Rya'c had got to him with the baseball glove, Daniel suspected.

"Well," Jack said with an expansive sigh, "looks like someone finally made a monkey outa me."

Sam smiled at the reference and Daniel felt his tension ease a fraction. But Dix — Rya'c — simply bowed his head and Zuri took a step toward him, putting a protective hand on his shoulder. Teal'c didn't move, perhaps respecting the privacy of the moment, or perhaps simply struggling with the impossibility of comforting a son who was now a man older than himself. A son who had lived a lifetime without his father.

After a pause, Jack said, "So, let's just say it's all true. 'Dix' is Rya'c and we're stuck in some post-apocalyptic zombie future. How do we get home?"

Sam's expression darkened and she shook her head. "I don't know, sir."

"Wrong answer, Carter."

"Colonel, think about it. When the wormhole intersected a solar flare and we ended up in 1969, we only got home because of the note General Hammond had passed to us before we left — with the exact date and time of a solar flare we could use. And even then we needed Cassie's help. But we have no idea when another solar flare is going to occur and we have no way to predict one with the level of accuracy we'd need. Not to mention the fact that we don't even have a working Stargate, or a DHD, or a—"

"Whoa!" Jack held up a hand to stop her. "Enough of the boundless optimism, Major."

Sam winced. "Sorry, sir, it's just—"

"I know," he said, more gently. "One step at a time, Carter. First we find a working gate."

Sam blew out a long breath and gave a little nod, pulling herself together.

Daniel used the pause to say, "Dix—" He stopped himself. "Actually, may I call you Rya'c?"

"You may," Dix said with a small smile. "But it has been many years since I have gone by that name."

"Okay, Rya'c." Daniel returned his smile. "You still haven't told us what happened to Earth. When did the Wraith come?"

"The Wraith came some sixty years ago," Rya'c said, with a glance at Zuri. "We know little about them, but it seems they were brought to the Tau'ri world by technology beyond our own." He shifted where he sat, scratched a hand over his graying hair. "Earth, however, was in no position to defend itself when the Wraith attacked. Its people were already weak, enslaved as they were by Apophis."

For the second time in less than an hour, Daniel felt his jaw drop. "*What?*"

"Some say," Zuri added, before Rya'c could answer, "that SG-1 betrayed Earth to Apophis. They say that is why they did not return to defend their home."

"That is a lie!" Teal'c said, moving as if to get to his feet.

Jack stopped him with a hand on his shoulder. His expression was stark, locked down. "What about the Protected Planets Treaty?" he said. "Where were the Asgard?"

It was an odd question, Daniel thought. Diplomatic relations had never been Jack's first port of call in a crisis.

"The Asgard are gone," Rya'c said. "The Protected Planets Treaty failed and the Asgard left our galaxy, never to return. Earth stood alone against Apophis, but it did not stand for long."

Jack closed his eyes and went very still, his hand still gripping Teal'c's shoulder. Daniel glanced from him to Sam, but her anxious shrug told him she didn't know much more than he did.

"There were some human refugees," Rya'c continued. "Their colony is still on the world they call Arbella, but they have turned their back on Earth. This –" He gestured around, encompassing the whole base — "is the only resistance to the Wraith on your world. It is led by Hecate."

"A Goa'uld?" Sam said. "Fighting for Earth?"

"Fighting for us all," Rya'c said. "The Wraith threaten the whole galaxy, Major Carter. Their hunger is insatiable."

"Oh I get it," Daniel said, with sudden, bitter understanding. "The Wraith are killing the humans that the Goa'uld want to use for slaves and hosts."

"Nice to be popular," Jack said.

Daniel just shook his head. "I figure, in the end, all wars are over finite resources. I just never thought that humans would be one of them."

Rya'c spread his hands. "Is not my enemy's enemy my friend, Daniel Jackson?"

"Not always."

After a pause, Sam said, "This human colony, do they have a Stargate? And technology? I mean more than what's left on Earth?"

"Yes they have a Stargate," Rya'c said, "although they do not like to use it. And I believe they possess some technology they brought with them from Earth, or gathered from other worlds. It is many years, however, since I have been permitted to visit Arbella."

Jack raised an eyebrow at that, but kept silent.

"What about records?" Daniel asked. "They must have

recorded what happened here."

"Yes." Sam nodded with enthusiasm. "We'll need to know exactly what happened if we're going to stop it." She turned to Jack. "Sir, I think we have to go there. It's got to be our best shot at getting home. I mean, *home*-home."

Jack held her gaze for a moment, his own expression inscrutable. Then he nodded toward Rya'c. "Can you get us there?"

Rya'c frowned, rubbed a hand over his mouth. "Travelling to Arbella is possible — our ha'tak is in orbit and possesses a Stargate. But it is not as simple as you believe."

"Sure it is," said Jack. "Get us up to the hat'ak and send us through the gate."

"Hecate is fighting a war," Zuri objected. It was more out of principle than real opposition, Daniel thought; she clearly didn't trust, or like them. "She has more to concern her than your petty needs, Colonel O'Neill."

Jack's answering smile was false, bright and dangerous. "Hecate doesn't need to know. In fact, I'd rather she didn't."

"She *will* know," said Rya'c.

Teal'c fixed his son with a firm look. "And how will she know, Rya'c? Because she is a god? Have you forgotten all that you knew of the Goa'uld?"

It was strange to see the older man look chagrined at the stern words from his father, but Teal'c had clearly struck a chord. "I have forgotten nothing," Rya'c said, with heat. "But you were not here, Father. If you had been, you would know why we have made these choices. Hecate has wisdom and power: without her, our fight here would be hopeless."

"So now you fight on the side of the vain and the cruel? I did not raise you so."

"*You* did not raise me at all."

Now it was Teal'c who looked chastened. He dropped his gaze and merely said, "If you are truly my son, then you will help us leave this place."

"And if I do, you may not thank me for it. The people of

Arbella are not what the Tau'ri once were."

Daniel ran his fingers through his unwashed hair and wondered, briefly, if the people of Arbella had showers. "I guess the real question is: where else can we go? We can't stay here."

"Why not?" said Rya'c. "You have seen how matters are on the surface, what the Wraith have done to your home. Why not stay here? Stay and help us drive them from our galaxy."

"Rya'c, we have to find our own people."

Zuri sorted angrily. "Are these not your people, Daniel Jackson?" She flung Rya'c a look full of challenge. "If they truly were the great 'SG-1', would they not fight for their world rather than run away like cowards?"

"No one's running away," Jack said evenly, although Daniel heard a spike of anger beneath the calm surface.

"You have to understand," Sam added, "that there are other ways to stop this, Zuri. We shouldn't be here, none of this should have happened, and if we can find a way to go back and fix things…"

Zuri folded her arms, eyebrows raised, and Sam trailed to a halt. Telling these people that she wanted to delete their timeline probably wasn't the most diplomatic approach, Daniel thought.

"Look, Rya'c," he said, trying a different tack. "We probably knew most of the people who left Earth. The colony they created is the closest thing to home we have left, and their descendants are the only people who can tell us what happened to our friends and families." He paused, glanced at Sam. "We have to go there; it's where we belong."

For a long while, Rya'c said nothing. He simply sat in contemplation, much like Teal'c often did. Zuri stood sentinel at his side, her watchful gaze on SG-1, and into the silence flooded the distant chink-chink sound of Rya'c's men excavating the Stargate.

Daniel exchanged a glance with Jack, but his edgy expression did nothing to ease Daniel's tension. Sam sat chewing her lip, deep in thoughts of her own, while Teal'c simply regarded his son with an expression too subtle to interpret.

The moment felt eternal but at last Rya'c rose to his feet. "Very well," he said. "If you wish to travel to Arbella, then you may use Hecate's Stargate to do so."

Zuri hissed her protest, but a swift look from Rya'c silenced her.

"But I warn you," he said, sweeping SG-1 with an imperious look, "do not expect to be welcomed as heroes. The Tau'ri lost much more than people when Earth fell to Apophis. You will find them a changed race, and no friends to those beyond the Stargate."

CHAPTER THREE

Evacuation Site — May 2000: Hiking up to the ruins and the Stargate was a long and arduous climb. Narrow steps had been cut into the side of the cliff, but age had made them crumbly and there was nothing but a narrow strip of rock between them and the sheer drop. Not that it made any difference to Janet. She was determined to be there when they dialed out, no matter the difficulty. She owed that much to General Hammond.

It was dusk when she started the climb, leaving behind the noise of the makeshift camp to make this pilgrimage. Burnt orange sunlight skimmed over the rocks, casting heavy shadows, but at least the heat had abated for the day. At noon, the climb was impossible and she supposed that had been the intention of whatever alien race had built their temple on the top of the mountain. It was a difficult place to reach, the ascent a struggle of endurance. Enlightenment for them had come, perhaps, in the journey and not at the destination.

But Janet didn't feel enlightened. As she forced her tired body to carry her up the mountain, back to the gate room that sat in the center of the alien base, she just felt exhausted. They all did. But how could they feel otherwise? They'd lost everything. The trauma of the last three weeks had been unbearable.

The truth was that she still hoped it wouldn't be necessary to make this nameless planet their home. She still hoped that a miracle had happened, that General Hammond and the SGC had somehow been spared. That SG-1 had come home and saved the world at the last moment, just like they always did.

And if they had, the refugees wouldn't know about it yet. No one at the SGC knew the address to Maybourne's base. Hammond had insisted that only those leaving Earth be given the address of their refuge. It was too big of a risk to let anyone else have that information in case it fell into enemy hands. All of which meant that it was still possible that, when they dialed Earth, the SGC would still be standing and they could go home. Until she knew otherwise, that was the hope to which Janet was determined to cling.

The first alien stars were starting to peer through the hazy sky by the time she reached the top. Catching her breath, she began to make her way through the ruins to the base that housed the Stargate. Yellow, artificial light streamed out of its windows and across the plateau, and she found herself drawn to it like a moth. Not to the light, per se, but to the semblance of civilization it represented. She slowed and stopped before she went inside, taking a breath of warm, dusty air, taking a moment to compose herself. Realistically, she knew the odds. She'd been there at the end; she'd heard the Jaffa enter the base. She'd seen the self-destruct ticking down to zero. Nevertheless, there was still hope. There had to be.

"Dr. Fraiser?" The low voice made her jump and she spun around.

Colonel Albert Reynolds appeared out of the shadows of the ruins, one hand lifted in reassurance. "Sorry to startle you, Doctor."

"It's okay, sir. I was miles away." She relaxed enough to give him a smile, but then noticed his tense expression. "Everything okay, Colonel?"

Given the situation, it was a ridiculous question, but Reynolds ignored the irony and gave a non-committal shrug. "You were pretty tight with General Hammond, right?" he said.

Not entirely sure where this was leading, she just said, "We were friends, sir, yes."

Reynolds lowered his voice and paced closer. "Did he tell you about this place? About what Maybourne had done?"

"Ah," she said, with a quick glance at the doors to the base. They remained shut. "Yes he did, and about Colonel O'Neill's mission to uncover the mole at the SGC."

Reynolds blew out a long breath. "I thought he had." He

rubbed a hand over his stubbly chin. "And yet Maybourne's in there right now, schmoozing with the President and the Chiefs of Staff. I mean, don't they realize what he did?"

"I think there are other powers at play here, Colonel."

Reynolds said nothing, but she could tell by his expression that he suspected the same — and he wasn't happy about it.

Reynolds gave a grunt of agreement and kicked irritably at the ornate base of an ancient column. A chip of stone fell away and Janet found herself thinking, 'Good job Daniel's not here to see that!' Then she remembered why he wasn't there and the hollow ache in her chest grew sharper. She still held out hope that 'Missing, presumed dead' would turn out to be a false call.

A sharp wind picked up, winding through the ruins with a low, desolate moan. It tugged at Janet's hair. She'd washed it in the lake, but the water, though safe to drink, was tainted with some mineral that left a residue. It made her head itch, and she scratched her fingers over her scalp.

"There's a lot of them," Reynold's said into the silence. "Have you noticed? There's a lot of NID here."

"Yes, I noticed that."

"Funny that they all got to be top of the evacuation list, huh?"

She gave a grim smile. "Yes. Funny."

Brow drawn down in thought, Reynolds was quiet again for a while. Then he glanced at her, and in a cautious voice said, "There's been talk that maybe we should do something about that."

Janet felt a sharp beat of fear. "What kind of something?"

"Take control," he said. "This should be an SGC base, not run by the NID."

"Colonel…"

"They don't have the right to command here."

"And you do?" she said. "You have the right to take command? The President of the United States is in there, Colonel. He's the civilian authority here, and he gets to run things, sir. Even now. Even here."

"But *is* he running things? He's surrounded by NID."

Janet shook her head, as if that would help dispel the frightening idea. "All I know," she said, "is that the last thing we need to do is start fighting among ourselves. If we're stuck here…" She gestured toward the lights of the camp below. "If we can't contact Earth, then all we have is each other. There's no NID anymore, no SGC — we're all just people, sir. We have to get along or we'll die here. All of us."

Reynolds didn't answer, just glared out across the barren mountains. "I don't want to die in this place," he said eventually. "I want to go home."

"I know. We all do."

Ahead of them, one of the doors to the base opened and a pool of light splashed across the rock. She could see people moving about inside and checked her watch. It was nearly time.

"Come on," she said, heading toward the base. "Let's go."

But she'd only taken a couple steps before Reynolds caught her arm, stopping her. "We need to stick together, Doctor," he said. "Whatever happens today, the SGC needs to stick together. We don't know enough about the NID yet, and until we do we can only trust each other."

She nodded. Reynolds' assessment of the situation was bleak, but not unrealistic, and it always paid to plan for the worst. She just hoped it wouldn't come to that; she didn't think she could bear to live in a world of such mistrust. Pulling her arm out from beneath his hand, she said, "Well, maybe SG-1 are out there ready to pull off another Hail Mary pass, sir."

Reynolds gave a thin smile. "Yeah," he said. "Maybe."

There was no more to say, so they walked into the base in silence.

It was much smaller than the SGC, made up of a warren of prefabricated huts and a few makeshift rooms excavated out of the alien ruins. In truth, the place made Janet feel deeply uncomfortable. All around them was a plethora of alien tech, evidence of the base's true nature. Janet didn't need Daniel's expert knowledge to deduce that the artifacts came from a range of different cultures, most likely stolen. But it was the object balanced on a stand in the corner of the room that made the hairs prickle on the back of her neck. The Goa'uld communication device squatted there, dormant for now, the room's reflection distorted on its convex surface. It made her wonder how far the rogue team's thievery had gone.

The Stargate itself was at the installation's heart and the familiar sight went someway to alleviate Janet's disquiet and restore her hope. While they had the Stargate, they could get home. They could go anywhere, maybe contact old friends and allies.

The room was already full when they arrived. Maybourne was there, of course, standing next to a tall man with hard eyes she'd come to know as Colonel Frank Simmons. He was NID, apparently, although she'd never met him before the evacuation. Major Newman stood a little in front of them both, his restless gaze immediately finding Reynolds. But there was no smile of greeting, just a bald-faced assessment of each other. There was no love lost there.

Formerly Special Forces, Newman had been running the NID base since before the evacuation and he didn't seem willing to stop now. His people huddled close to him, their attention fixed on the Stargate. They looked nervous, but Janet knew it wasn't for the same reason that her stomach was screwing itself into knots.

If the SGC, and Earth, had survived, then a lot of questions would be asked of Harry Maybourne and his rogue team.

Janet and Reynolds pushed their way through the small crush of personnel just as a kerfuffle of shuffling feet behind them announced the arrival of President Bill Turner and his close protection team. Everyone came to attention as he walked briskly into the room, still presidential despite his rumpled clothing and day's growth of beard. He gave a nod to Reynolds and Janet, then to Simmons and Maybourne, before turning to address the crowd.

"We all know why we're here," he said, "so let's get on with it."

Janet appreciated his brevity; no one was in the mood for speeches.

At least, almost no one.

"Mr. President." Colonel Simmons stepped forward. "For the record, I would like to restate my objection to this reckless course of action one final time."

"Colonel—"

"Sir, by opening a wormhole to Earth under Goa'uld occupation, we risk giving away our location. Not to mention the power wasted in this pointless—"

"Enough!" Turner barked. "Your objection has already been noted, Colonel. Repeatedly. And I'll repeat what I've already told you: I will not turn my back on those left behind. Not now, not ever." He gave a curt nod to Newman. "Major, dial home."

Newman glanced at Simmons, almost as if asking for his approval, before he made his way over to the DHD. Simmons said no more, but neither did he hide his displeasure and stood with his arms folded, glaring at the Stargate.

Janet glanced at Reynolds to see if he'd noticed. He simply shrugged. Three weeks ago Simmons' open insubordination could never have been tolerated, but everything was different now. She could feel power shifting like sand in the tide.

Swallowing her unease, she fixed her eyes and her hope on the Stargate as it started to turn.

An eternity passed before the first chevron locked, the whole room watching with bated breath. She caught sight of Harriman at one of the computer terminals, waiting in silence like the rest of them as one by one the chevrons lit. Occasionally he glanced down at the screen, as if confirming what his eyes had told him.

Finally, the seventh chevron locked into place and for a moment the event horizon fizzed across the gate, bathing the room in its familiar, watery light. Janet's heart leaped with a hope that flared as bright as the wormhole — and then collapsed.

The event horizon sputtered out of existence. The light was gone and they were alone.

Silence stretched taut until, from behind his computer screen, Harriman spoke in a muted, broken voice. "Connection failure. Earth's Stargate is not responding, sir."

Janet closed her eyes. For the gate to not even respond meant that the destruction of the SGC must have been complete. It also had one other implication — the beta gate had been rendered inoperable too. Hammond's last gambit, his final order for Colonel Dixon to save the beta gate and use it to continue the evacuation, had failed. There was no way back to Earth, no way for its suffering population to escape. When she opened her eyes again, she caught the guarded look Simmons shared with Maybourne. Was it satisfaction? Relief? Triumph, even?

She felt sick, felt the world begin to sway beneath the weight of their defeat. And then everyone was talking at once in a rising wave of despair, and she thought it might drown her until a strong hand touched her back, lending support. She opened her eyes to find Reynolds watching her. His face was ashen, his eyes brimming with the grief they all shared.

"Remember," he said, so quiet that only she could hear, "the SGC sticks together."

They had no one to trust but each other.

CHAPTER FOUR

Earth — 2098: "Stay sharp," Jack warned, bringing his weapon up as the Goa'uld rings descended around them in the tunnel beneath Cheyenne Mountain.

The last thing he saw before the flare of golden light was Carter's brief nod. A fractured moment of dislocation followed and then the rings shot up past his ears and he was… elsewhere.

Immediately he registered the hum of engines through the deck plates beneath his feet and the slightly altered gravity that told him he was in orbit. The air was dry and pungent, dusty with the incense favored by the Goa'uld.

Weapon raised, Jack checked his quadrant. They were in a circular room of overblown Goa'uld décor, a number of arched doorways leading away into empty corridors. "Clear," he said.

"Clear," Carter confirmed to his left.

"Looks like a ha'tak to me," Daniel said — his approximation of 'No one's trying to shoot us.'

But Teal'c said, "We are not alone."

Turning, Jack saw two Jaffa standing in one of the arched doorways behind him, staffs resting on the ground. He recognized the mark on their foreheads; it was the same one Hunter had worn. The same one the Jaffa on P5X-104 had worn too, he remembered, way back before all this insanity had started.

Interesting.

Rya'c stepped away from the ring platform and spoke to the Jaffa. Although he was speaking in Goa'uld, Jack heard the words 'SG-1' and watched the Jaffa's eyes widen and their gazes dart past Rya'c's shoulder to where Jack stood with his team. He resisted the urge to wave, instead nudging Teal'c with his elbow.

"What's he saying?"

"Nothing of concern," Teal'c assured him.

"He told them who we are."

"He did. He told them we were his guests."

"Hmmm," Jack said, lowering his weapon to port arms but not relaxing. Not even when the two Jaffa bowed to Rya'c and left the room.

Rya'c turned around, spreading his arms in a gesture of greeting. "As First Prime to the Lady Hecate, I bid you welcome to her ship."

Teal'c twitched at 'First Prime', but didn't comment.

Jack just said, "I won't ask you to take me to your leader."

"That is wise, because she would not admit you to her presence. The Lady Hecate sees none but me."

"A little shy?"

"You are quite safe here, Colonel O'Neill," Rya'c said. "Hecate is allied to the Tau'ri in the war with the Wraith. My Jaffa are not your foe; you will come to no harm aboard my ship."

"Your ship?" Teal'c said. "Is this not the ship of your mistress?"

"The Lady Hecate has absolute trust in me, Father. " Rya'c lifted his chin, defiant as a teenager. "It is a pity that you do not."

"I trust none who serve the Goa'uld."

Rya'c didn't respond and the two men just stared at each other across a deepening silence.

"I hate to break up this little… moment," Jack said, when it seemed that neither of them would blink, "but how about we get moving? The sooner we leave the better."

The whole father/son thing aside, Jack understood exactly where Teal'c was coming from; an alliance with the Goa'uld, with any Goa'uld, put his hackles up. And as friendly as Rya'c might seem, they were still on a Goa'uld mother ship and entirely at Hecate's mercy. Situations like this could turn on a dime.

With a curt nod, Rya'c turned away from Teal'c. "Follow me," he said and led them from the room.

Jack glanced at Teal'c. "Cover our six," he murmured as he followed Rya'c. Whatever was ahead, he wanted to face it first — and, he figured, the bigger the distance between Teal'c and his son the better.

After an interminable trek through soulless Goa'uld corridors, they approached a large set of double doors even more ornate than usual. Rya'c didn't pause as he approached and the doors swept open ahead of him. Beyond them stood the Stargate, elevated on a low dais at the end of a long colonnade. To the left, behind the columns, a large bank of windows looked out onto a starscape.

"I like what you've done with the place," Jack said, cautious as he led his team inside. "Minimalist."

Rya'c smiled. "We captured this ha'tak after Osiris fell to the Wraith — his taste was always ostentatious."

"And for a Goa'uld, that's saying something," Jack said. But what he was thinking was, 'Osiris fell to the Wraith?'

"Um," said Daniel, unable to keep his mouth shut. "Did you say Osiris fell to the Wraith?"

"Many System Lords have fallen," Rya'c said. "Apophis was the first, others have followed. The Wraith have no honor and no mercy. They feed on humans and Jaffa alike, as if we were cattle, and they do not die easily. You cannot fight them as you would a natural enemy."

Jack couldn't argue with that. He and Teal'c had taken down a couple of the things in the Shacks, but only just, and if they came at you in numbers... It wouldn't be pretty.

But Daniel's mind was clearly elsewhere. "Apophis?" he said. "Apophis is dead?"

"He died when the Wraith first attacked Earth." Rya'c paused, a sudden flash of understanding brightening his expression. "Ah, I am sorry, Daniel. I remember, now, that Apophis took your wife from you."

"Yeah," Daniel said, frowning down at the floor. "Yeah, he did."

There was a silence and Jack jumped into it before Daniel was forced to say more. "You wanna dial us up, buddy?" he said to Ry'ac. "Time's a wasting."

Rya'c looked from Daniel to Jack, his expression puzzled, but said only, "In due course, Colonel. First, I must contact Arbella and ask them to deactivate their Stargate shield."

"Stargate shield?" Carter sounded interested. "You mean, like an iris?"

"Not precisely the same," Rya'c said. "The shield is of Ancient design and cannot be penetrated by incoming travelers or weapons."

"But it allows radio signals to pass through?"

"It does. But Arbella prefers an alternative means of communication." Rya'c turned to a table half hidden behind the pillars. "You have seen a long range communication device before?" he said, gesturing to the globe that sat on the table.

"I guess you guys really must be close," Jack said, "if you're giving them your number."

Rya'c looked uncomfortable. "I did not give Arbella this device," he said after a pause. "They possessed one already."

Jack felt something turn in the pit of his stomach, a suspicion he prayed wasn't true. There could be any number of ways the human colony had gotten hold of Goa'uld technology in the years since they left Earth. And yet the Protected Planets Treaty had collapsed and Earth had fallen to the Goa'uld: this whole screwed-up future had Harry Maybourne's thieving fingerprints all over it...

Walking to the table, Rya'c initiated the device and the globe sprang to life, its misty surface swirling with color. "I wish to speak with General Bailey," he said. "It is a matter of importance."

It took several minutes before a face appeared in the globe, distorted but clear enough to make out long curly hair and a woman's features. "Dix," she said. "It's good to hear from you."

"General Bailey." Rya'c bowed. "It is an honor, as always."

"Has he woken up?"

"That is not for now, General."

Daniel's eyebrows rose and he mouthed, *Woken up?* Jack just shrugged.

"But I have other news," Rya'c continued. "There are friends here who wish to travel to Arbella."

In the misty surface of the globe, the woman — Bailey — frowned. "You know that's difficult right now."

"Indeed," Rya'c said. "However, I believe these are visitors that even President Jones will want to admit."

"Why? Who are they?"

"By some quirk of fate or science they are long lost citizens of your world."

"Of Arbella?"

"Of Earth."

"Dix, Jones won't allow refugees—"

"It is SG-1," Rya'c said. "I swear it on the life of the goddess. My father is among them."

There was a long silence and Jack supposed it must be a little like Amelia Earhart showing up in the skies over Oakland and asking for permission to land. "Did you say SG-1?" General Bailey said at last. "From before the evacuation?"

"That is correct. I cannot explain how they come to be here, and neither can they. But they are here and wish to travel to Arbella."

Another pause, and then the general laughed. "Jones will never believe it. To be honest, I'm not sure I do."

"You will, if you see them with your own eyes. So will President Jones."

"I'll have to speak to him. I'll contact you shortly. Arbella out."

Turning away from the communication device, Rya'c said, "As I warned you, the people of Arbella are not like the Tau'ri."

"In fairness, I can see why they'd be suspicious," Daniel said. "I mean, it's pretty hard to believe that we're here."

"Especially for us," Jack said.

Rya'c lifted an eyebrow, a gesture painfully similar to his father. "Do you still not believe what I have told you?"

"No, it's not that," Daniel said. "We believe you; it's just a lot to take in."

"Then perhaps you should see for yourselves." Rya'c walked past the communication device, through the pillars, and toward the vast window. "When the Wraith entered our galaxy, Earth became the battle ground between the Goa'uld and the invaders," he said in a voice taut with pity. "Your world paid a heavy price."

Jack made no move to follow; he wasn't sure he wanted to look.

Daniel's expression was grim. "We have to see."

Carter was already moving, her curiosity getting the better of her, but she stumbled to a halt as she approached the window. Her hand shot to her mouth. "Oh my God."

"Crap," Jack muttered and forced himself to join her.

In retrospect, he wished he hadn't. The dead, brown planet below, wreathed in ashy cloud, couldn't be Earth. Yet his treacherous eyes traced the faint outline of a continent through the swirling haze — the tip of South America — and he knew that it was true. His last shred of doubt, of hope, blew away like dust.

CHAPTER FIVE

Earth — 2098: Smoke still lingered in the aftermath of the attack, its stench seeping into the flesh of the hive ship. Almost all the humans had fled when the Lantean and his people had detonated their explosives, and those left behind were weak and barely worth feeding upon.

It was a disaster.

Had he been here, Sting thought, perhaps he could have prevented it. Leaving Stormfire alone with the Lantean had been a mistake. But they were so few now that he'd had no choice, and the Lantean had proven more resourceful than Sting had expected. He would not make that mistake again.

But this return to the hive was bitter and he moved through her damaged corridors with grief. In truth, the hive had been dying for years, ever since the war with the parasite-gods had damaged her beyond her ability to heal. This assault had only hastened the inevitable and it would not be long before the hive failed entirely. He was glad that Covenant, their old hivemaster, had not survived to see it. Nor Brightstar, the queen they had both served in better days, before they had come to this wretched place.

Soon he would be forced to find an alternative location for Stormfire to work, although where that might be Sting could not imagine. No such place existed on this blasted world, at least not that they could use.

There was, he supposed, the place that was spoken of among Queen Shadow's blades, where her clevermen worked on projects unspeakable. Sting had seen it himself, after much searching: an encampment where humans were brought, not to be fed upon but for some unnatural purpose he had yet to discover. Yet, perhaps, if matters grew desperate, it would be necessary to infiltrate the place so that Stormfire could make use of it to continue his research. His work was, after all, the only means by which they might one day return home.

The doors to the laboratory opened sluggishly at Sting's touch, the hive weary as she drew toward her end. He rested a hand on her, gave what little strength his mind could offer, before he stepped into the laboratory where Stormfire labored.

To look at him, stooped over the devices of the Ancestors, you would not know that half the hive had been blown out into the dusty air of Earth. As always, the cleverman's focus was inward, fixed upon what he was doing. His mind, as damaged as his body by the battle with the parasite-gods, darted here and there like wildfire. Sting could not follow it, so he spoke out loud instead.

"The Lantean escaped."

"I have his blood," Stormfire said, not looking up. "I can taste it."

"Taste it?" Sting looked about the cleverman's laboratory as he spoke. It appeared unscathed, the devices of the Ancestors neatly placed and ordered. Strange that such a disordered mind could be so methodical.

Stormfire turned with his head cocked at its unnatural angle and limped forward. "Taste it," he repeated, reaching for one of the devices on the bench. It was a disk with a dark surface lit by lines in the gray-white light of the Ancestors. A map, Sting realized, of the place where their hive rested. A second light blinked and Stormfire touched it with a broken talon. "There."

"The Lantean?" Sting was surprised; so few of these devices responded to Wraith touch.

"Yes."

"He is in the human encampment? We must send blades."

"Shade, Heartsong, and Reckless went hunting," Stormfire said, with a wild laugh. "They did not return." His laughter ebbed. "No, no, they did not return…"

That was a blow. They were few enough already. "Then I will take a dart myself," he said, turning for the door. "I will bring the Lantean back."

But Stormfire hissed, a feral sound. "Darts will do you no good, Consort. Rock and dust and dirt: darts will not capture him."

Used to Stormfire's ramblings, it was nevertheless frustrating. "Speak more plainly," Sting said. "Is the Lantean in the human camp?"

Stormfire looked at him, dark fire in his eyes. "Beneath it, now. Far beneath it."

"Dead?" Humans often buried their dead to rot beneath the ground.

"Hiding."

He felt a pulse of relief. It was common for humans to live underground. Perhaps some distant ancestor of theirs had been subterranean, or perhaps it was simply the most effective way to hide from their enemies.

Sting regarded the map, filling in its bare detail with his knowledge of the landscape. "He is beneath the mountain the parasite-gods' once used as a landing platform," he realized. "Maybe that is why they landed there, because humans lived in the mountain?"

"Perhaps they still do."

Sting considered that idea. If it was true, it would be difficult to penetrate well-guarded tunnels and fight within them to recapture the Lantean. Below ground, Sting would lack even the meagre support of those few darts that remained to them, and Shadow's blades patrolled the human camp above. It would not do to give Shadow any cause to question the loyalty of those who had once served Brightstar. "Is he worth pursuing?" he said.

Stormfire gave a hiss, his mind too disrupted for Sting to make out his thoughts. "He is Lantean," he said at last. "He is different."

"Yes." That much Sting had seen for himself; the Lantean had intervened to save him from the humans who had hung him up to die like a beast. He was stronger and braver than the kine that huddled in the vast camps waiting to be fed upon. "Then he is the one we seek?" he said.

"His blood will make us fly," Stormfire confirmed, running his broken talon over the Ancestors' device again. "His blood will take us home."

"He is wily," Sting pointed out. "He escaped you. He killed our blades and did great damage to the hive."

But Stormfire shook his head. "Not him," he said. "His queen came for him. *She* did great damage."

"Human's do not have queens," Sting reminded him. He had lived among them long enough to know it was true. Human females were no queens; they were as commonplace as the males. They did not stir the blood like a queen, bright and brilliant and worthy of adoration. Stormfire would know the same if he paid them any attention.

Beneath their feet, the deck shifted. Sting could almost feel the life seeping out of the dying hive. "We will not be able to remain here much longer," he said. "Soon, she will begin to decay. You will need to find a new place for your research."

Stormfire's eyes narrowed and Sting didn't need to touch his mind to feel the eruption of anger. "*She* could save her," he hissed. "If she would come."

Sting bristled at his tone. "Speak with respect of your queen," he warned. Then, with less heat because he understood and shared Stormfire's grief, he said, "Even if the young queen came, she could not save our hive, my friend. If Brightstar could not, then her daughter certainly would fail. You know there is only one way to end this."

Stormfire turned back to the device of the Ancestors. "His blood," he said.

"We could wait for them to leave the tunnels," Sting mused. "They cannot stay beneath the mountain forever. If nothing else, they must eat. When they emerge, I will pilot the dart myself to cull them and—"

Suddenly Stormfire hissed, his whole body jerking as he stared at the Ancestors' device.

The light had disappeared.

"What happened?" Sting said.

Stormfire did not answer, he just watched as the display on the device shivered and reconfigured to show the planet as if from orbit and above it the blinking light that was the Lantean.

"He's aboard Shadow's cruiser," Sting said, heavy with foreboding. It was the only explanation; there were no other ships in orbit. "If Shadow has him…"

He did not complete the thought aloud; they both knew what would happen if Shadow bent the Lantean to her will. All hope of salvation would be over. Unopposed, Shadow's kin would flourish and spread across the feeding grounds of this galaxy until, stronger than all others, she returned to claim dominion over their own galaxy. With her she would bring the gross corruption she had found here and so doom their entire race.

Stormfire's fingers tightened about the disk, as if he would hurl it across the room.

"Don't," Sting said and put his off-hand on Stormfire's arm. "Better that we know." Even if retrieving the Lantean from Shadow's hive would be impossible, it was foolish to cast aside even this scant knowledge. "And perhaps she will return him to Earth. We must be patient."

"Patient?" Stormfire cursed — Sting could hear it in his mind as well as out loud — and flung the disk down, but with enough care that it remained whole and active. "So Brightstar said, before she breathed her last into the dirt of this world."

"Do you doubt her word?"

"How could she *know*?" Stormfire spat, turning with his crooked arms stretched wide and his hair, unkempt, swinging wild. "How could she know what we would become here, gorging on the creatures that infest this world?" He stopped, turned his head and stared. "You would die here, Consort? Bury your bones in this dirt, far from our feeding grounds, if the young queen demanded it?"

"I am hers to command," Sting said. "As are you."

"As am I," Stormfire nodded. "Yes, yes. As am I..."

"And you know that the queen plans to lead us from this place." Sting took a step closer, his hands upturned to offer no threat. "We will return home, my friend, and then your mind will be eased."

For a moment he felt the brush of Stormfire's thoughts, a scorch against his own mind, and then the cleverman hunched away. "This one," he said, gesturing to the device on the bench, "is our best hope."

"Then we will watch him," Sting said, picking up the disk and fixing his eyes on the blinking light. "We will watch him until he returns, and then we will find him."

CHAPTER SIX

Hecate's ha'tak — 2098: It was a couple of hours before General Bailey contacted Rya'c again, and another hour before the agreed time at which Rya'c would dial the gate and Arbella would lower their shield.

Daniel spent most of the long wait staring out at the ravaged planet below, as if by absorbing every detail of its scarred surface he could more easily accept its incomprehensible truth.

Sam had moved away from the window. She was sitting with her back resting against one of the pillars, her eyes closed. Her lips moved a little and Daniel guessed she was making plans in her head to fix this mess. Above all things, Sam was a fixer. She wanted to mend this, erase it like bad programing. Delete. Delete. Delete.

Daniel wasn't sure it was that easy.

He'd been to alternate realities and he'd seen versions of Jack and Sam fighting for their world, a world that he didn't share. But this broken planet below them *was* his world, this was *his* future. Even if they could, did they have the right to change it? There was a reason life didn't come with a backspace button, after all.

"Hey," Jack's voice, close to his ear, made him jump. "Got something for you."

He turned just in time to catch the zat Jack tossed to him. "Thanks," Daniel said, turning it over in his hand.

"Rya'c's given us a half dozen of the things."

"Generous."

"I'd have preferred a couple dozen boxes of ammo, but apparently he doesn't stock that."

"No Kwik-E-Mart here, huh?"

Jack smiled, but the brief humor faded as his eyes were drawn to the sight beyond the window. After a pause he said,

"How many people do you think are down there? Tens of thousands? Hundreds?"

"Impossible to know unless we see more of the planet."

Jack nodded. "I wonder where the gate was, the one we came through. It must have been the beta gate, but that wasn't Nevada."

"No," Daniel said. "I guess they moved it at some point."

"Somewhere remote; they were probably trying to hide it. Canada, maybe? There were trees."

"Maybe." It was all speculation. He cast a sideways glance at Jack — he looked gaunt, haunted. Probably they all did. "I keep thinking about Elspeth," Daniel said. "I promised I'd go back for her if we found a way off the planet."

"The girl in the caves?" Jack shook his head. "You knew you couldn't keep that promise, even when you made it."

"I was dying when I made it," he said, looking back at the planet. Somewhere down there Aaden and Elspeth's people were hiding, scraping a living on that barren hillside. "But now I know they're…" He struggled with the concept. "I don't know, our people, I guess — from Earth. Now I know that, it feels wrong to just leave them out there."

Jack was silent for a long beat. "It feels wrong to leave any of them out there."

It did, Daniel realized: doing nothing to help them felt very, very wrong. He met Jack's troubled gaze and held it. "So much for 'no one gets left behind.'"

Jack didn't reply, his mouth pressed into a thin line of disquiet.

"Colonel O'Neill, Daniel Jackson?"

Daniel turned, feeling oddly guilty, to find Rya'c standing a respectful distance away. "It is time," he said.

Teal'c was already standing before the gate, waiting to go. Sam was shrugging into her pack, adjusting her weapon. Daniel had no pack, having abandoned it at Elspeth's encampment when he was too weak to carry it. He pressed a hand to his side, the memory stirring an echo of pain. But it was only an echo; the Wraith had healed him entirely.

It was strange that such brutal creatures could return life in a gesture of gratitude. It made him wonder how beings who were obviously intelligent and rational could justify feeding on other intelligent, rational beings. Did they have no conscience? Or did they have no choice?

"Here we go then," Sam said, coming to join him. She looked tense and tired, but no less determined than always and Daniel pushed aside his musing to focus on what came next.

"I literally have no idea what to expect," he said, glancing up at the Stargate. Usually the unknown excited him; today, he wasn't so sure.

Sam's eyes strayed briefly to Jack. He stood a little apart from the rest of the team, his attention fixed on Rya'c who began to dial. But Rya'c was careful to shield what he was doing from sight — the address remained a secret. "I think the colonel knows something," Sam said.

"Really? Did he tell you that?"

"Not exactly."

"Not exactly?"

She gave an awkward shrug. "Before, when we were topside with Hunter, he told me there was something wrong at home. On Earth."

"What kind of something?"

"That's all he said. But look at him… He knows something about Arbella. Or he's afraid he does."

Daniel looked again, but couldn't see anything in Jack's expression beyond the tension they all shared. "I guess we'll know soon enough," he said. "But if Jack thought Arbella was dangerous, why would he take us there?"

"Maybe he just thinks it's less dangerous than here?"

"It probably is."

Suddenly, the sound of the gate activating — a sound Daniel had almost despaired of hearing again — filled the empty room, bouncing off the pillars. The Stargate began to spin.

Chevron One, locked. Chevron Two, engaged...

He counted them off in silence, hearing Harriman's voice in his head. Then, with its familiar rush of energy, the wormhole surged through the gate and out into the room, drowning them in watery light. The tang of ozone prickled his nose, static danced across his skin, and, despite everything, Daniel found himself smiling at the familiar sensations. Even though they weren't going home, this felt like the first step on the journey; the Stargate had always given him hope. He glanced at Sam but her eyes were fixed on the event horizon.

"There has to be a way," she said. "There has to be a way to fix this."

His instinct was to reassure her that there was, that she'd find it, but then he thought back to Elspeth and Aedan and found that he didn't know what to say. Would they even exist in Sam's possible future? Would it matter if they didn't?

Jack walked toward the gate and cut off any further opportunity to ponder. "Okay kids," he said, "try to look friendly. Daniel," he beckoned him over, "you do the talking. Carter, Teal'c, give us a slow count of five and then follow." He stopped before the steps that led up to the gate and glanced over his shoulder at Rya'c. "Will we see you again?"

"It is probable," Rya'c said. "There is a matter in which General Bailey and I are both concerned." He gave a formal bow. "Colonel O'Neill, Major Carter, Dr. Jackson... Father." He looked at Teal'c, his face impassive. "Your arrival here is strange and unlooked-for, but I believe it is a sign of hope. There are still those on Arbella who keep faith that SG-1 will return to save them and perhaps they are right." He gave a wry smile. "But there are others who believe the opposite. You will need to walk a narrow path, my friends."

"Oh," Daniel said, "we're pretty good at that." He glanced at Jack and tried not to wince. "Most of the time."

Jack didn't rise to the bait, just threw Rya'c a sloppy salute.

"See you around," he said, then turned to face the event horizon. "Okay, kids, let's see who's out there."

Evacuation Site — 2000: Janet had never been a drinker — the outcome of a marriage to a man who'd never met a bottle of bourbon he didn't like. But the clamor and color of the place that had taken on the role of the local watering hole somehow set her at ease, and she enjoyed spending a half hour there after the chaos of the day. It wasn't a bar as such, more of a common room for military personnel. But the quartermaster, Gus Steiner, had acquired himself some supplies with which to make his own sour mash and, though Janet hadn't tried it personally, it was proving popular with the locals. Gus had found himself a spot on the edge of the camp and set up some upturned crates and planks on barrels in the open air. At night, in the warmth of the evening, with the lanterns strung around the makeshift tables, the place had a certain rustic charm. Sometimes Janet could almost pretend things were normal, if it wasn't for the overhanging feeling of booze-fuelled despondency. The Fu-Bar, she'd heard people calling it, and she couldn't think of a more appropriate name.

"God, this stuff is gutrot." Albert Reynolds swung his leg over the crate across from her and took a seat. He swilled the liquid in his tin mug, before tossing the rest back and slamming it down on the table. "I can feel my insides dissolving," he said, before gesturing to Gus for another. "You want one? On me."

Janet smiled and shook her head. "Thanks but no thanks, I prefer my guts unrotted. And I wouldn't want to leave you out of pocket. How much is he charging anyway?"

"Depends what you've got that he needs. This evening's refreshment is costing me a pack of 3-volt lithium batteries. But hey, you gotta pay for quality." He took a slug of the drink that Gus had just topped up and coughed. From the bleary look in his eyes, Janet realized this wasn't his first.

"How're you doing, Colonel?"

He wiped his mouth and leaned on the table, not looking at her. "That a professional question, Doc?"

"It's a friendly question."

He looked up, and it was a few seconds before he spoke again. "I'm doing about as good as you look. Why don't you tell me about your day, Janet?"

She wasn't sure if the question was genuine or if he was being deliberately sardonic. She hoped for the latter; any real concern for her welfare would likely send her over the edge, and she couldn't deal with that right now. Her fourteen hour day had been spent trying to help the patients, twelve now in total, who had been struck with the flu. She couldn't call it treating, because there was no treatment. No antivirals left, no ventilators, no monitors.

She'd watched a man sit by his wife's bedside that day and pump air into her lungs with a manual respirator for four hours. Janet had called time of death just before she'd finished her shift. She'd said to the husband how sorry she was for his loss, and asked, as gently as she could, if she could have the respirator back.

"My day was fine, thank you for asking."

Reynolds smiled and raised his cup to her. "Liar."

She didn't contradict him and they sat in silence for a while, watching the groups at the other tables. Navy, Air Force, Marine Corps: experience told her it was an unstable mix. A couple of tables across, expressions were sober and the conversation intense. One man — a Marine if Janet had to bet on it — was jabbing his finger towards the chest of an airman whom Janet thought she recognized from the SGC.

"This place is ready to blow," said Reynolds looking round. "We can't stay here."

"Yeah," said Janet. "It's late."

"I don't mean *this* place. I mean this planet. We can't stay here."

"I don't see that we've got much of a choice, Colonel. You were there when we dialed out. Where else would you suggest we go?"

He shrugged and stared into the bottom of his cup. "I don't know. Somewhere. We stay here, we're at their mercy. They make the rules."

Janet didn't need to ask who *they* were. "I think maybe we just have to make the best of it. We make our case heard. This is still a democracy."

Reynolds let go a laugh. "I didn't take you for a fool, Doc. This is no democracy. This is a coup by default. Maybourne's plan might not have worked the way he'd thought it was going to, but whoever's pulling the strings still got their way. With the SGC gone, the door's open. We were the gatekeepers, Janet. Literally. Now though?" He threw his hands out. "It's gone. It's all gone. Except us."

Janet sighed. This was old ground. Old, and painful. "Colonel—"

"No, Janet." Reynolds leaned forward and fixed his bloodshot eyes on her. "We're still the last defense. We have to talk loud, because they're going to keep shouting. And if they are the only ones who people hear, then who do you think they're going to believe? It's down to us, Janet. We have to make a stand–"

A shout from the other table interrupted him. The group that Janet had been watching earlier was on their feet, the Marine still pointing at the airman's chest. "They're goddamned traitors, and what they did screwed us all over."

"You shut your mouth," said the airman through gritted teeth.

"Well, where are they now, huh? Where's your precious SG-1 now? Probably dining out with the snakeheads, that's where."

The airman lunged, smashing the Marine into the table, sending crates and barrels flying. Reynolds raised a knowing eyebrow at Janet, before running to the melee. She followed, pulling others back from joining in the fight while Gus and the colonel separated the two soldiers.

"Stand down, Airman," growled Reynolds, looking suddenly sober.

The airman fell back, but still looked primed for a fight. "Sir, he said –"

"This isn't a damned schoolyard. Now get out of here. Both of you." He cast a threatening glance at the Marine.

"You're not my CO."

Reynolds walked over to stand nose to nose with the Marine. "Maybe not, but I could still hand you your ass and not break a sweat. Now I said get out of here."

The airman and his friends left without further objection, but the Marine took his time, as if trying to prove a point while not wanting to provoke the colonel any further. Once they'd gone, Reynolds looked down at the ground beneath their table. "Well, would you look at that," he said, bending to pick something up from the dirt. He tossed it to Janet, and it glinted silver in the air. She caught it and opened her hand. George Washington's somber face sat in profile on the tarnished quarter.

"You should keep hold of that, Doc," said Reynolds, as he turned to leave. "You never know what it'll be worth one day."

CHAPTER SEVEN

Arbella — 2098: SG-1 was met by two lines of armed men and a frisson of fear that made the hairs on Jack's arms stand to attention.

Trouble.

He didn't recognize the dark uniform of the soldiers, but the expression of unease on their faces was familiar and concerning. Fear made for twitchy trigger fingers.

A quick glance around showed him a small, white gate room with slender lights running from the floor to the high ceiling. A bank of computers huddled against the back wall — he could see the Goa'uld communication globe among them — and a rounded corridor, almost a tunnel, disappeared away to the right of the room.

He glanced at Daniel, who took it as his cue to speak.

"Hello," he said, lifting a hand. "I'm Daniel Jackson. This is Colonel O'Neill."

Behind him Jack felt movement — Carter and Teal'c stepping through the gate. He was beginning to wish he'd told them to wait for his okay before they came through.

"And this," Daniel continued, without missing a beat, "is Major Carter and Teal'c."

A couple of heads turned, quick glances shared. Disbelief? Whatever it was they felt, their reaction showed poor discipline — another reason to be wary of these people.

"Your names are well known to us," said a woman's voice, and a moment later she appeared at the mouth of the tunnel. Short and compact, with a crop of unruly hair tied back, it was the woman Rya'c had spoken to through the communication device. She was dressed in a different uniform to the other soldiers. It looked more Air Force, with a patch on the arm that read 'CMF'. "We have some photographs in our archives," she said as she moved through the ranks to stand before them. "It's incredible to see you standing here in person. Some people might think it's impossible. A trick of the enemy, perhaps?"

"I had the same thought myself," Jack said. "Unfortunately, this all seems to be very real."

The woman quirked her lips in a faint smile that was cautious, but not entirely unfriendly. "My name is General Bailey," she said. "Commander of the Combined Military Force."

There wasn't exactly a protocol for the situation, but even a hundred years into the future Jack figured a general was still a general. He came to attention and offered a salute, "Colonel O'Neill, ma'am."

Behind him, Carter did the same. "Major Carter," she said.

Bailey returned the salute, or a version of it, as her gaze slipped past Jack to where Teal'c stood in silence behind him. Unlike the soldiers, Bailey looked more curious than afraid, her eyes bright with interest. "Mr. Teal'c," she said. "With the exception of Dix, you're the only Jaffa to ever set foot on Arbella."

Teal'c gave a scant bow. "It is my honor."

"You've got Dix's good manners," Bailey said. "But I'm afraid we can't reciprocate."

Jack tensed, his balance shifting forward, ready to act. He didn't like their odds, but instinct was instinct. "Meaning what?" he said, keeping it light.

From the corner of his eye, he saw Carter shift her grip on her gun, watching him and waiting for the order.

Bailey must have noticed the hike in tension because she spread her hands and said, "I only meant that I have to ask for your weapons, Colonel. President Jones— That is, the President would like to meet you and you can't enter his office armed." She appealed to Jack with a frank look. "You understand."

He did. On the other hand he didn't like the idea of giving up his weapons. Again. He glanced at Carter, but she just lifted her eyebrows as if to say *What choice do we have?*

Not much of one, he had to admit.

"We're all friends here, right?" Daniel said. "We can trust each other. We're all refugees from Earth, after all."

"Speak for yourself," said a gruff voice from behind the general. A thick-set soldier with squinty eyes glared at Daniel. "I ain't no refugee."

Bailey flicked him an irritated look and Jack waited for her to hand the guy his ass for the attitude; men like that needed to be kept on a short leash. But she didn't, she just turned back to Jack and said, "Colonel, I'll have to insist. I've got no choice in the matter." There was a silent plea for cooperation in her eyes that was difficult to ignore and it spoke of the kind of intrigue and politicking that Jack hated almost as much as the Goa'uld.

He suppressed a sigh and said, "Daniel's right, we're all friends here." No one was fighting their way out of this anyway. "Carter, Teal'c — hand over your weapons."

Removing the clip from his MP5, Jack passed the gun to one of the unsmiling soldiers. He did the same with his sidearm but didn't touch the zat tucked into his belt, waiting to see if they recognized it as a weapon.

"The zat too, sir."

So much for that plan.

Once they'd been disarmed, Bailey turned to a tall man standing next to her. "Officer Hayden," she said, "the President asked that I accompany our visitors to his office. If you'd be so kind…?"

Hayden nodded and gestured for several of his people to move aside, opening a path to the corridor. "Follow me," he said, and led the way.

Jack cast a quick glance at the rest of his team. Daniel gave a little shrug of agreement, Carter a nod. Teal'c merely lifted an eyebrow, which Jack interpreted as *This is a Bad Idea*. He wasn't entirely sure he disagreed.

Fixing a confident look on his face, he trotted down the steps from the gate. The others followed, their boots echoing against the white stone floor.

"You must understand," General Bailey said, falling in at Jack's side, "we are a cautious people, and with good reason. We don't trust strangers."

"We're not strangers," Jack pointed out. "Although, I admit, our being here might seem a little… strange."

Bailey smiled. "Precisely." After a short silence she added, "President Jones will have some close questions, Colonel. You must be prepared to answer."

Jack wondered if 'close questions' was code for 'interrogation' and felt his anxiety level kick up another notch.

As Hayden led them out of the gate room, other men fell in behind them and to either side so that they were surrounded as they walked along the winding corridor. Rooms branched off to left and right — offices and labs as far as Jack could tell — and in each one people looked back at them through fearful eyes.

Jack supposed they had their reasons to be afraid, but he couldn't help comparing these people to Hunter and the others they'd met back on Earth. They'd been afraid too, but not cowering. They'd been ready to fight.

"How big a command do you have here, General?" he said. "Looks like a sizable base."

Bailey flicked him a look. "It is, but the Stargate complex is under civilian command. The CMF is quartered down in Laketown."

"Civilian," said Jack. Interesting. He took a closer look at the uniformed officers escorting them. These guys were police then, not military. Their weapons he didn't recognize, but they were heavy-duty and certainly weren't of Earth origin. There was a logo on the back of their shirts too, an old square-rigger in full sail. It didn't mean anything to him.

"The President's intelligence officers guard the Stargate complex," Bailey said, obviously noticing the direction of his gaze. "The Founders decided that the Stargate should remain under civilian control."

Jack looked at her, hearing more in her voice than she was

saying. "But?"

"No 'but', Colonel," she said with a static smile. "We have learned from the mistakes made on Earth."

"Which were...?"

"Insufficient civilian oversight of the Stargate program and an unhealthy dependence on a system of weak alliances." It sounded like rote, the way she parroted the explanation. Her gaze dipped to the SGC patch on his jacket. "Too much power in too few hands," she said. "Unaccountable, military hands."

Bullshit. But he swallowed the curse, very aware of the black-clad Intelligence Officers surrounding them, and fixed a bland expression onto his face. He could almost see their ears pricking and he started to understand Rya'c's warning about this place; it was definitely nothing like Stargate Command and he had a nasty suspicion why that might be.

Daniel cleared his throat, breaking the burgeoning silence. "Interesting architecture," he said, craning his neck to peer at the ceiling. "Is it Ancient?"

Bailey seemed relieved by the change of subject. "It's certainly very old," she said.

"No, I meant—"

Jack silenced him with a look. This was the time to be gathering intel, not giving it away; if these people didn't know, or had forgotten, about the Ancients then that was information worth keeping to themselves.

"How many people live here?" Jack asked instead. "In total, I mean."

"At the last head-count," Bailey said, with some pride, "almost sixty-four thousand."

A small town, Jack thought. Earth's last outpost in the galaxy was no bigger than a small town.

Behind him, Carter gave a low whistle. "That's less than a quarter the size of Colorado Springs."

Bailey frowned. "We started from a base population of two thousand, Major," she said. "And only twenty-five percent of the First Generation was female. We consider our population growth program to be a success."

"Yes, ma'am," Carter said. "I meant— Only two thousand people got out?"

"They had two days to evacuate, Major. They did the best they could."

"Yes, ma'am." Carter fell silent, lost in thought.

Jack supposed that, to Bailey, they were talking about history. But to Carter — to all of them — they were talking about yesterday. They were talking about their friends, colleagues, and families. It was almost impossible to accept the reality of what had happened to their world.

"We'd like to find out more about the evacuation," Daniel said. "Do you have any records from that time?"

"Or a list of the people who got out?" Carter added.

"Of course," Bailey said, "we have detailed records of the colony's history. It's one of the things that unite us as a people."

Daniel nodded. "A collective history is powerful. I'd love to take a look at your records, if I may?" He gave a melancholy smile and glanced at Carter. "I guess it doesn't really matter now, but we'd like to know if any of our friends made it out."

Before Bailey could reply, Teal'c said "You are correct, Daniel Jackson. It does not matter."

Daniel frowned, but didn't answer. Neither did Jack, he just threw Teal'c a quelling look. The last thing he needed was a public discussion about their plans to end this timeline before it even began.

If Bailey understood what Teal'c had meant, she didn't say anything and, luckily, at that moment Officer Hayden came to a halt. On the door in front of them were the words 'President Gunnison Jones'. Jack said, "Looks like we're here."

Bailey glanced at Hayden, then at Jack. He had the distinct impression she wanted to say something, but couldn't with Hayden right there. She'd called them the President's intelligence officers earlier, and Jack was starting suspect that they — and the President — were not exactly friendly to the military. Especially, perhaps, to the very military personnel they blamed for having too much control over the Stargate and supporting a 'weak system of alliances'.

Bailey knocked on the door and it was opened a moment later by a tall sharp-faced woman dressed in civvies. "General," she said. "President Jones is ready to see you and your…" She regarded Jack and his team with cold distrust. "… visitors."

"Thank you, Agent Yuma." Bailey stepped inside without looking at the woman.

It wasn't exactly the Oval Office, but the President's office was large enough for it not to feel cramped. The floor was made of the same shiny stone as the rest of the base, but the desk and the five chairs arranged before it looked familiar. Who knew cheap Air Force furniture could last a hundred years?

Yet the most striking feature of the room was the window. It looked out over a plateau of rust-colored sand that sailed above windswept spires of rock, stretching away in all directions beneath a sky of burnt-orange cloud. An alien world indeed.

"Mr. President," Bailey said, jerking Jack's attention away from the view, "may I present Colonel Jack O'Neill, Major Samantha Carter, Dr. Daniel Jackson, and Mr. Teal'c. SG-1."

The President stood up from behind his desk. A young man, he was slim built and athletic, his cropped hair a color not dissimilar to the rocks outside the window. But he was gaunt and regarded Jack through unfriendly eyes, little chips of ice-water glittering in the sun. "You'll forgive me," he said, "if I'm not immediately convinced by your story."

Jack spread his hands. "Sir, I'll be the first to admit that this whole situation is—" He swallowed the first word that sprung to mind. "— messed up."

President Jones remained unsmiling. With a wave of one hand, he gestured for them to take a seat and sat down in his own chair, keeping the desk firmly between himself and everyone else. The woman Bailey had called Agent Yuma remained standing, behind the President and just to the right of the window.

Jones regarded them for a long, silent moment.

Through the thin walls of the office, Jack could hear distant voices, footfalls, and the blustery moan of a strong wind outside. Little clouds of dust kicked up against the window, rattling against the glass. There was a clock somewhere, its slow ticking the only sound inside the room.

At last the President spoke, addressing his words to Bailey. "What evidence did Dix provide regarding the identity of these people?"

Bailey perched on the edge of her seat, hands clenched in her lap. "Only the evidence of his eyes, sir," she said. "He claims that this man is Teal'c, his father. He's given his word."

"His word," Jones repeated, with obvious contempt.

"Dix is Arbella's friend, sir. He has been since before either of us was born. And he's the only person alive who knew SG-1."

"So he says." Jones pressed his hands together, tapping his fingertips against his lips. "And still no news of —" his voice caught and he cleared his throat "— of our missing team."

Bailey let a beat fall before she said, "Dix still has people looking, sir."

The President didn't respond to that and, after a moment, he turned his gaze back to Jack. "You claim to be Colonel O'Neill, the leader of the infamous SG-1."

"Infamous?"

Jones ignored the interruption. "If you're who you say you are," he said, "then there's a question that perhaps you can answer."

Bailey stiffened. "Mr. President—"

"No," Jones said. "If this is Colonel O'Neill, he'll be able to settle the matter. God knows, we've argued about it long enough."

Jack flexed his fingers, easing the tension building through his shoulders. He missed his gun. "What's the question?"

At his side, Daniel shifted anxiously. Carter was literally

on the edge of her seat.

Jones fixed him with a hard look. "Only this: why did SG-1 abandon Earth?"

"We abandoned no one!" Teal'c said, with heat.

Jack lifted a hand to silence him. "He's right," he said. "We didn't abandon anyone. We were on our way back to Earth when something went hinky with the Stargate and we found ourselves a hundred years in the future. That's all we know."

"Which is nothing," the President said. "Are you saying you don't know how you got here?"

"We can only hypothesize at this point, sir," Carter said.

Jones got back to his feet, turned away from them and walked to the window. He pressed his hand to the glass, gazing out over the desert. The woman, Yuma, watched him in silence. "The First Generation built a home on Arbella," Jones said. "A beacon for humanity. They lived through mankind's greatest calamity and they triumphed. Because of them, because of the Founders' foresight in creating this refuge, our culture, our values — our species — have survived."

"It's an admirable achievement," Jack said, although he couldn't help thinking about all those people scavenging for a meager existence on Earth. They'd survived too and what was Arbella doing for them?

"But that doesn't mean we've forgotten how we got here," Jones carried on, "or why our great-grandparents were forced to abandon their homes." He fell silent again, his fingers curling into a fist. "Many people here believe that Stargate Command was responsible for what happened to Earth. At best, they think your failure to prepare for war left us vulnerable, at worst they think that you — that SG-1 — fled and betrayed us to the Goa'uld."

"That's bull," Jack said, keeping his voice even despite his anger.

Bailey shifted where she sat, her jaw working, but she didn't say anything. Perhaps, like him, she was biting her tongue.

"If we knew more about what happened on Earth," Daniel said in those measured tones he deployed so well, "maybe we could understand better?"

Jones turned back to them, his pale eyes fixed on Jack. "Some people say that you, Colonel O'Neill, are the reason our allies abandoned us."

"That's ridiculous," Daniel said. "Jack was—"

"Daniel." A cold weight settled in the pit of Jack's stomach, the same weight he'd been carrying since Hammond had tapped him for the mission. "Why?" he said to Jones, though he was afraid he knew the answer. "Why do they say that?"

"Because you could have saved the treaty if you hadn't abandoned Earth to save yourself. You were the only one who could have saved it and you didn't."

And that sounded like something straight out of Harry Maybourne's book of 'How to Pass the Buck and Get Away with It'. *Sonofabitch.* He closed his eyes, took a breath.

"Jack?" Daniel said. "What's he talking about?"

"It's why I needed to get home so fast," he said. It was a relief, in a way, to be able to explain it at last. "The Protected Planet Treaty was collapsing and I was tapped to go undercover and fix it."

"Undercover?" Daniel said. "Why?"

"Because someone at the SGC was stealing technology from our allies."

Carter's eyes went wide. "Who?"

"That's what I was meant to find out. We suspected Maybourne was running a rogue off-world team, using someone at the SGC to traffic their stolen technology. The Asgard, the Tollan, the Nox — they were pretty pissed."

"I bet," Daniel said. He shared a tense look with Carter. "Were we suspects, Jack? Is that why you couldn't tell us what was going on?"

"Not to me." This was the moment he'd been dreading since the start and he fixed each of his team with a look, willing them to believe him. "Not for a single second."

"And yet…?"

"It was part of the deal, Daniel. They insisted I uncover the mole alone."

"Because you were the only one they trusted."

He shrugged. "Maybe if I'd gotten home in time…" He thought bitterly of everything he'd put his team through in the last week: his attempts to destroy their trust in him, his decision to drive them on without rest, even when Daniel was dying on his feet, his single-minded determination to get home and save the treaty at any cost. All of it had been for nothing; Earth had been dead the whole time. "Too late now."

"Sir, this isn't your fault," Carter said. "They can't blame you — us — for this."

"Major Carter's right, Mr. President." General Bailey stood up, arms behind her back, shoulders straight. "Incredible as it might seem, sir, we now know the answer to your question. SG-1 didn't abandon Earth. In fact they've come back to save it."

"We're just running a little late," Jack said. "Traffic."

No one smiled.

"Our enemies," Jones said, "have ways of raising the dead, of extending life. How do we know you're not spies?"

Jack didn't answer right away. Truth was he had no answer to give, no evidence to prove he hadn't been on ice in some Goa'uld sarcophagus for the past ten decades. "I guess," he said at last, "you're just going to have to trust us."

"Is that so?" This time it wasn't Jones who spoke, it was Agent Yuma. She hadn't moved from her place behind the President, standing with her arms folded next to the window. "Trust is a dangerous policy, Colonel."

"But sometimes," Daniel countered, "trust is all we've got."

Behind them, the officer by the door shifted, his boots scraping on the floor. He could be lifting his weapon, training it on the back of Jack's head, finger on the trigger. Jack's neck prickled but he didn't turn around; he held the President's gaze and wondered if the man was afraid enough to have them killed on the spot.

Jones licked his thin lips and exchanged a glance with Yuma. For a moment, for a fraction of a second, Jack saw something like doubt in Jones' face. In that moment he turned away from Yuma and addressed Bailey. "Take them down to Laketown," he said. "Keep them under watch. They're not to return to the Stargate complex without my express permission. Understood?"

Bailey rose to her feet, offered a salute. "You have my word on it, sir."

From her evident relief, Jack knew he hadn't been imagining the danger.

CHAPTER EIGHT

Despite the yellow clouds shrouding the sun, the heat hit like a hammer blow when they stepped outside. Sam could feel it radiating through the soles of her boots, saw it shimmering around the ruins scattered across the plateau. It was so hot it made her shiver.

Daniel reached for his boonie hat, the colonel for his sunglasses. Sam did the same, impressed that they'd survived the punishment her tac vest had taken over the past week. She slipped them on and pulled her cap low over her eyes. It helped a little.

Teal'c remained bareheaded and angry. "I do not believe it is in our interest to leave this base," he said. He kept his voice low and conspiratorial, but his frustration was evident.

"Jones wasn't going to let us stay in there," Sam said. "At least the general seems friendlier."

"It is not friendship we seek."

She glanced up at him, squinting against the bright sky. "It can't hurt," she pointed out. "We're going to need these people's help to get home."

"So long as that remains our objective."

"Why wouldn't it?"

His gaze moved to the others. "I have noticed many times that Colonel O'Neill and Daniel Jackson have a tendency to become involved in the concerns of others."

"Well, yes, Daniel does, but…" She looked over at the colonel. He was listening closely to whatever Bailey was saying, nodding and gesturing toward the town below. Laketown, she assumed. He often said he didn't want to get involved, but when it came down to it the colonel was usually the first to intervene — especially where he saw injustice or suffering. And there was plenty of that to go around in this messed up reality.

"Colonel O'Neill," Teal'c said, looking at her askance, "believed it was impossible to return to Earth from Edora. Instead, he became involved with… the concerns of others."

Frowning, Sam shook her head. She didn't want to think about Edora. "This is different," she said. "Colonel O'Neill wants to fix this. You heard what he said: he blames himself for what's happened here."

"He does," Teal'c said. "But Colonel O'Neill also believes he is too late to save Earth."

"No, that's not what he meant."

Teal'c was silent for a moment, shifting his feet on the sandy rock. "I believe," he said at last, "that you and I must ensure that our friends do not forget what must be done in order to prevent this future from unfolding."

"They won't forget," Sam said. "But it's going to take time, Teal'c. I can't solve this problem in a day, or a week. Or even a month. I'm sorry, but you're going to have to be patient."

He lifted an eyebrow. "I served Apophis as warrior and First Prime for almost eighty years before the opportunity arose to cast him down." He gave a Jaffa smile. "I understand patience, Major Carter."

It was a long trek down from the plateau. A staircase, worn smooth with time, had been cut into the rock, a crude railing erected along one side to keep you from pitching over the vertical drop. Daniel, Sam noticed with a sympathetic wince, was white-knuckling the railing all the way down and keeping his eyes firmly fixed on the horizon and away from the precipice. He looked immensely relieved when they reached the bottom.

"Laketown was the first of the settlements," Bailey said as she led the way from the base of the cliff toward to the lake. "There are others now, mostly for farm workers who want to live closer to their fields, but this was the first and remains the largest."

It was cooler down here and Sam pulled off her hat to let the breeze from the lake ruffle through her sweaty hair. It felt good. "Your farmland is irrigated?" she guessed as their path cut across a grain field, the crop coming up to her knees and swaying in the wind.

"It is," Bailey said. "Irrigation was one of the first engineering projects the First Gens undertook when they arrived. The land, as you can see, is very dry. But the lake provides enough water to farm and the soil is remarkably rich."

"Lucky," the colonel said, looking beyond the field to where the town spread out along the edge of the lake. "You've got a lot of mouths to feed."

"We do," Bailey said with a smile. "But no one goes hungry."

Laketown was very different from Hunter's sprawling camp back on Earth. The buildings, most a kind of adobe construction, were organized into neat rows, laundry flapped in the onshore breeze, and there were children everywhere. Laughing, playing, and working: they didn't know the fear of the Amam — the Wraith — and they didn't look like they knew hunger. These people, this colony, had succeeded. Somehow, that made Sam proud.

"Lots of kids," Daniel said with a laugh, watching a troop of boys chasing a ball around at the edge of the field.

"Children are a vital resource," Bailey said. "We encourage all women to have at least four, preferably by different fathers."

The colonel twitched his eyebrows. "Sounds like my kinda town."

"Jack…" Daniel protested.

"It's to promote genetic diversity, sir."

"Carter," the colonel said with a twitch of an eyebrow, "you make it sound so clinical."

She swallowed a smile but didn't answer because by then General Bailey had come to a halt. Her expression turned serious. "Colonel," she said, "I think it would be a good idea if you and your team removed the patches from your jackets at this point."

"Expecting trouble?"

"Your presence here is extraordinary," she said, "and will raise strong feelings — both good and bad. It'll be better if we can manage that."

After a moment's consideration the colonel nodded. "Okay, do as she says."

With a rip of Velcro, Sam pulled the SGC patch from the front of her jacket and tucked it into a pocket in her vest. The SG-1 patch on her arm was long gone, left as a marker next to the beta gate back on Earth. The thought of it sitting there made her sigh; no one was ever going to find it now, except perhaps the Wraith. No one was coming after them.

When they were all safely anonymous, Bailey turned her eyes on Teal'c. She gestured at the mark of Apophis on his forehead. "Do you have a hat?" she said.

"I do not."

"Here." Daniel pulled out one of his bandanas and offered it to Teal'c. "That'll work."

They got a lot of curious looks as they made their way through town, but Sam didn't feel the same degree of suspicion or hostility that had pervaded the Stargate complex. General Bailey appeared well-liked and she waved and called greetings as they went.

But what struck Sam most about the town wasn't its neat buildings or the homespun friendliness of its people. It was the alien technology she saw in use almost everywhere — some clearly of Asgard or Goa'uld origin, others completely unfamiliar.

Surprised, she glanced at the colonel to see if he'd noticed. He clearly had; his brow had knitted into a thoughtful frown.

"So I'm guessing you trade with people on other worlds?" Daniel said, taking everything in as they walked along. "For food, technology, weapons?"

That had been Sam's assumption too, so she was surprised when the general shook her head. "No," she said. "The government observes a closed-door policy."

"Really?" Daniel didn't hide his surprise. "But... Where does all this technology come from?"

"It was here when they arrived," the colonel said. His tone was restrained but Sam could hear anger banked beneath the surface. He looked at Bailey, a challenge in his eyes. "Right, General?"

She nodded. "That's correct, Colonel. The Founders had stored all sorts of different technology here before the attack, and it's lucky for us that they had. I doubt the colony would have survived without it — especially without the medical technologies. And the shield, of course."

"The shield across the Stargate?" Sam said.

"Yes. It's kept us safe from the Goa'uld and the Wraith." She cast a questioning look at the colonel, obviously picking up on his attitude, but didn't comment. Instead she gestured toward a large building close to the lake. "Come on, we're nearly at CMF headquarters."

Bailey walked on but the colonel lagged behind and let Sam and Daniel fall in next to him. He was still frowning and after a moment said, "They stole it. That must be what this place was — Maybourne's off-world stash of stolen tech."

"Really?" Sam was astonished.

"What else could it be? We had no Alpha Site, Carter. The Pentagon shut the project down, remember?" He shook his head. "They'd have had nowhere else to go."

"Huh," Daniel said. "I bet Maybourne was crowing."

"A lot more than crowing." The colonel looked back up at the plateau; sunlight was glinting against the roof of the Stargate complex, making it twinkle. "I bet Maybourne was running the joint. I bet this was what he always wanted."

That thought sank them all into grim silence.

"And President Gunnison Jones is his successor," Daniel said after a moment, as if he'd just solved a riddle.

"They seem to share the same paranoid outlook on life," the colonel agreed.

Daniel puffed out a sigh. "So, this is potentially bad."

"Perhaps not," Teal'c said from behind them.

Sam squinted up at him. "What do you mean?"

"There is a great deal of advanced technology on this world," he said. "I suggest we use it."

He had a point. She turned to the colonel. "Sir, he's right. If they have any kind of advanced computer I could use it to try and figure out a way to predict a solar flare that will get us home."

"And why would they let us do that?" Daniel said. "We're planning on destroying their timeline."

"An abhorrent timeline," Teal'c said.

Daniel frowned. "Well, actually, is it?"

"Evidently."

"But from their point of view—"

"Daniel?" the colonel said. "Not now."

Whatever Daniel had been about to say, he swallowed it. But he didn't look happy.

The colonel tugged his ball cap lower and looked over at the general. She'd stopped walking and was watching them from the shade of the CMF headquarters. "I'll ask Bailey if we can access their computers," he said.

"Sir, you can't tell her what we're doing," Sam warned. "Daniel's right, she might not help us if she knows we're planning to change the timeline."

The colonel shared a long look with Daniel before he said, "I know that."

Daniel didn't speak, turning away and plunging his hands into his pockets. But Sam had noted the exchange, the flash of understanding she'd seen pass between them, and it made her uneasy. Was it possible that Teal'c was right? Were Daniel and the colonel getting too drawn into the plight of the people trapped in this terrible future?

"Sir," she said, touching the colonel's arm to get his attention. "I can fix this. You have to trust me."

"Always, Carter." But his expression was troubled and when

he walked off to join Bailey, Daniel at his heels, Sam watched him go with a profound sense of disquiet.

"We must be vigilant," Teal'c said as they followed on behind. "Much rests on our actions here."

Yeah, Sam thought, the entire future of humanity.

Evacuation Site — 2000: The gathering in the gate room took place at night, the large chamber frigid now with the setting of the sun. Maybourne's breath misted in the air and the sweat of the day had dried into something clammy and uncomfortable. He felt out of his element here, unsettled and on edge, and wished he had his dress blues rather than the BDUs that hadn't been washed in four days.

Looking around, he took in the assembled crowd, many of them even more disheveled than he. This was considered a prestigious occasion and the room was filled with dignitaries and leaders, still retaining a claw-like grip on the VIP status that had been worth so much back on Earth. Never mind that most of them were wearing the same suits they'd had on when they made their trip through the gate to this godforsaken corner of the galaxy. There was a reason it had been chosen as a place to hide the rogue base: no one in their right mind would ever want to come here. Yet here they were, the huddled masses of humanity, stinking up what used to be his gate room.

He supposed he'd only himself to blame, but then what choice had there been other than giving up the location of the base? He'd never have been allowed through the Stargate without offering them something.

A hush descended on the room as President Turner took the podium in front of the gate, looking like a battered imitation of the man who had sat in the Oval Office. It was hard to believe that this was a man who'd held countries in the palm of his hand, who'd been nominated for a Nobel Prize three years running and been awarded it for economics on one of those years. Now he was more like some pissant mayor of Nowheresville.

"Good evening fellow citizens," began Turner. His eyes held the room, moving to fix on individuals at various points throughout the room. Maybourne looked at the ceiling in case the man's gaze fell on him. "Tonight we gather to mark the passing of an age in our history. Four weeks ago, our planet was brought to its knees in an act of unprovoked violence and cowardice, a heinous attack by a species that has no concept of humanity, no understanding of peace or compassion. Tonight, we pay tribute to those billions who lost their lives, and we stand united to..."

Maybourne tuned out. The idea of a memorial was noble enough, he supposed, but ultimately worthless. He'd heard such trite platitudes before and he knew they meant squat in the grand scheme of things, especially when the grand scheme was now a planet-sized ball of rubble twenty thousand light years away.

"Inspiring, don't you think?" The low voice came from just behind his left shoulder. No matter his jolt of alarm, experience told Maybourne not to whirl round to face its owner and he let a few seconds pass before casually glancing behind him. Colonel Frank Simmons: he knew the man, of course, though he hadn't spoken to him much this side of the gate. Even back on Earth, his was a face he knew only from shadowy corners in rooms where orders were handed out and not questioned.

When he'd arrived on this planet, Maybourne had taken note of those faces which represented a contingent at odds with the current administration; a contingent responsible for the existence of this base, in fact. Though they hadn't openly acknowledged each other, he'd exchanged glances with those NID operatives whose purpose served a more radical agenda. Those glances had said a lot.

"Inspiring. Without a doubt," Maybourne whispered, making a pretense of listening to the speech. "And I'm sure, if this was an Iowa caucus, at least one person in the room would be impressed."

"I take it you're not?" Simmons moved forward slightly so that he and Maybourne stood shoulder to shoulder. "Impressed, I mean."

"All I'm hearing is the liberal crap that got us into this situation in the first place. Turner hasn't the faintest clue how to lead us through this."

Simmons smiled, not taking his eyes from the President. "You think he's not the man for the job anymore. Maybe something should be done."

Maybourne paused and glanced at Simmons from the corner of his eye. He was suddenly worried that he'd misjudged this man's allegiances and that this was a trap. *He knows what I've done. He's trying to bait me now. Makepeace wasn't enough of a scapegoat for them.*

"You're speaking of a coup, Colonel. That's a dangerous notion."

Simmons pursed his lips. "I'm merely pointing out that just because we've left Earth, doesn't mean we have to accept a dictatorship."

On the podium, Turner was quoting Eleanor Roosevelt, reminding those gathered of the strength needed to do that which we think we cannot. Maybourne took in the intent expressions on their faces. "Doesn't seem like anyone here feels particularly oppressed," he murmured. "They all look pretty enthralled to me."

"For now, yes. They're lost, desperate for a leader. Turner assumed that role before anyone could question it, and everyone here is just going along. But it won't last. The discord will come, Colonel. And when it does, they'll need an alternative."

"And that's where you come in?"

Simmons chuckled. "Oh no, I'm not cut out for the limelight, Maybourne. But there are others. It's just a matter of getting the right people on our side. Make a convincing case. We already hold a significant advantage in the balance of power." He nodded toward the podium, but Maybourne knew he didn't mean Turner. The most powerful object in the room stood behind the man.

The Stargate.

Maybourne had to concede the point, but it raised another issue. "You know, the Stargate could also represent a flaw in your thinking. This planet was chosen as a base because it's unpopulated, and there's a reason for that. It isn't exactly Shangri-la. What's to stop Turner from promising them somewhere better?"

At this, Simmons laughed, drawing a few annoyed glances in their direction. He didn't seem to care. "And where would he take them, Colonel? Some other undefended planet, but without an outpost like this, without established resources? The inhabitable planets not under Goa'uld control are currently protected by the treaty our former allies hold so dear, and I don't know if you noticed, but we Earthlings are something of a *persona non grata* amongst them at the moment. No, Colonel, we're on our own here and it's back to basics. We've just experienced what almost became a mass extinction event. Perhaps the universe is trying to tell us something."

"Tell us what?"

"That it's the strong among us who have to take the lead if the human race has any chance of survival. Look around you, Colonel. This is our kingdom now."

It was then that Maybourne realized he'd been wrong to doubt this man's agenda. Simmons wasn't one to play games, to bait clumsy traps in the hope that Maybourne would incriminate himself. If Frank Simmons wanted Maybourne out of the picture, then he'd already be gone. There was something in the pipeline and for some reason Simmons was letting him in on the secret. The question was, why? Maybourne decided to play along, to find out what was in it for him; then he could decide whether to commit himself to one side or the other. "If a… particular party intended to make a play for power here, they'd need a pretty big carrot to keep the masses in check. Or a pretty big stick."

Simmons' expression was still one of amusement, as if he was one step ahead of everything Maybourne might say. "Easy, Harry. We're not the bad guys. We think we can catch more flies with honey. There's something up our sleeve that will ensure the allegiance of our people."

"Like what?"

"Let's just say there were other projects being worked on here besides the ones you were aware of."

Maybourne felt a bolt of anger that he'd been kept in the dark about what had been going on his base, but then he realized his anger was misplaced. The NID did everything under a veil of secrecy; it shouldn't surprise him that many of those secrets were kept from him. Nonetheless, he wasn't in the mood to play games.

"Just cut the crap, Simmons," he said. "What is it you want from me?"

"We need to cover all bases. Make sure there are no obstacles in our way. And over there stands what could be a considerable obstacle." Maybourne followed his line of sight to the group gathered just to the right of the podium. A woman stood off to one side listening to Turner's speech, almost unrecognizable without her blues and white coat.

"Janet Fraiser? How in the hell can she be an obstacle? She's a doctor. She hasn't been in the field in... I don't know if she's ever been in the field."

Simmons sighed. "Try looking a little further than the end of your nose, Colonel. It's not her combat experience that's worrying. It's what she represents. She's from the SGC, and was at the right hand of George Hammond before he made his great sacrifice. She's a doctor, she's good looking, she's the All-American girl. And if that wasn't enough, she was friends with SG-1, and like it or not, even in their absence, their status borders on legendary. Janet Fraiser is the poster child for everything that threatens us, Colonel. She has to be brought under control."

"And you expect me to do that? If you want to use your 'honey' approach, I'm possibly the worst person for the job. The woman hates me."

Simmons rolled his eyes. "I'm not asking you to woo her, for God's sake. There are other means of bringing a person to their knees. You just need to think outside the box. Let us do the rest, Maybourne. Now, I suggest you listen to the wisdom our Commander in Chief has to impart. It's all very stirring, I'm sure."

Maybourne turned to speak again, but Simmons had already withdrawn into the crowd, and he was left with only the glimpse of his disappearing shoulder. With some effort, he focused his attention on Turner again, who was still droning on, obviously favoring quantity over quality. Someone should remind him that Gettysburg only took two minutes, thought Maybourne.

"And so we pay tribute to our forefathers," Turner said, "who sailed into the unknown with the certainty that a new life awaited them, that a new world was theirs to build. So it is, on this day, that we stake our claim on *this* new world, and call it our own. On behalf of the people of Earth, I hereby name this world 'Arbella'."

There was a moment of silence and then rapturous applause filled the room. Turner spread his hands in a gesture of thanks to his people, but was interrupted by a familiar and terrifying sound. Somewhere in the crowd, a voice rang out as if compelled by whatever purpose he'd served in his past life.

"*Incoming wormhole!*"

Shouts and screams replaced applause, and Maybourne could only watch in dread as the gate spun its way through the address.

They've found us.

The gate room was in a panic as the crowd tried to flee, apparently forgetting that they were 2000 feet up a cliff with only a narrow walkway allowing access to the bottom; whatever was coming through that gate would be on them before they'd made it across the first bridge.

President Turner was being dragged bodily from the podium by his secret service agents, while airmen took position, their weapons trained on the spinning Stargate. He saw Janet Fraiser expertly shoulder an MP5 she'd acquired, her eye focused through the sight; perhaps he'd underestimated her skill with a firearm.

"Activate the iris! *Activate the iris!*" That damn airman had apparently lost his mind, thinking they were back in the SGC. There was no disc of trinium alloy to protect them here. Once that final chevron locked, they were at the mercy of whatever Goa'uld was about to come calling.

It took a few seconds for him to realize that the voice calling for the iris was one he recognized, one he'd just spent the past twenty minutes listening to. Colonel Frank Simmons pushed his way through the crowd, shouting at someone in the center of the room.

Newman?

Major Dean Newman was already running to one of the many consoles that occupied the gate room. When he got there, he began punching in instructions, his expression intent.

The final chevron locked and the blue of the wormhole burst forth into the gate room, but it had only just settled into the rippled blue of the event horizon when something even stranger happened. A translucent film of energy unfurled itself across the gate's inner ring, shimmering in front of the open wormhole.

"Now that is impressive," murmured Maybourne.

"Iris activated, sir," called Newman, who braced his hands on the console, head hanging between his shoulders. "Nothing's getting through that thing."

Maybourne realized it was Simmons whom the major addressed. *Let's just say there were other projects being worked on here.* A gate shield; that was certainly an ace up their sleeve.

A hush had descended on the gate room as people froze in their attempts to flee, transfixed by the shimmering forceshield and the event horizon visible through it. A sense of relief was palpable, but Maybourne wondered how many were as curious as he about what it would look like if anyone tried to get through the gate.

They waited, but nothing appeared.

"Uh sir," said Newman to Simmons, "this wormhole. It… it's from Earth, sir."

A murmur went through the crowd at the news. Across the room, Maybourne saw Fraiser falter, her weapon dropping to her side and her hand going to her mouth. But how could it be Earth?

"Apophis?" said Simmons.

"If it is, he's not trying to get through. I don't—" Newman broke off, scanning the console. "Colonel, we're getting audio."

"Well, let me hear it, dammit!" For someone who didn't like the limelight, Frank Simmons was sure getting his face known. All eyes were trained on the pair, alert for what might happen next.

A few key strokes by Newman and the hiss of radio static filled the gate room. At first, it just sounded like white noise, but then a voice could be heard through the distortion.

"This is a distress call from Colonel David Dixon at Earth's beta site. We have survivors, we have wounded, and we are in need of assistance. Please respond."

"Sir, should I—?"

"Do not touch that iris, Major!"

Newman's surprised gaze darted to Maybourne, apparently not expecting the order to come from his direction. He looked at Simmons again, but the colonel's expression was inscrutable as he slipped back into the crowd.

Janet Fraiser, it seemed, was not so willing to obey Maybourne's orders. "Colonel, those are our people out there. We have to help them!"

"Doctor, those people are on a planet that is now occupied by the Goa'uld and we have no way to verify who's contacting us. You might be willing to throw protocol to the wind and let a Jaffa unit march through the gate to wipe the rest of us out, but I think a little more prudence is called for."

"Mr. President?" Fraiser's tone was desperate as she looked for back-up from Turner, who'd managed to shake off his goons.

The President looked up at the active gate, as if considering his options, but Maybourne knew the man's hands were tied. To open the gate and risk an attack that endangered the rest of humanity would be unconscionable.

"I'm sorry, Dr. Fraiser," Turner said. "We can't risk it. They're on their own."

CHAPTER NINE

Arbella — 2098: They'd been given rooms inside CMF headquarters, although Daniel couldn't shake the feeling that they looked rather more like cells than guest rooms. Nevertheless, he'd been able to bathe and the narrow bed had been comfortable enough. Gate-lag notwithstanding, he'd slept for over twelve hours.

Without his glasses on, the light coming in through the room's small window looked hazy, mellow with either sunset or dawn — he couldn't be sure which — and cast golden shadows across the floor. He didn't exactly feel at ease, given that his mind was still processing the end of the world, but he felt better than he had in days. He felt content to simply lay there and stare at the blurry window, thinking.

But an impatient rap on the door put paid to that plan and he hadn't even had time to call an answer when Jack's head poked into the room. "Hey," he said, "you're awake."

"Kind of?" Daniel struggled to sit up. He reached for his glasses. "What time is it?"

"Uh, I don't know. Sunrise." Jack slipped into the room and closed the door behind him. "We slept."

"We did," Daniel said, cracking a yawn.

Jack paced over to the window and gazed out. "There's food downstairs, apparently."

"A free continental breakfast too, huh?"

Jack gave a slight smile. "I'm hoping for pancakes." He fell silent then, still gazing out the window.

When it looked like he might have drifted away entirely, Daniel said, "Um, as much as I'm enjoying this early morning visit, was there something you wanted?"

"I guess," Jack said. When he turned around his lips were set in that familiar tight line that spoke of worry. He scrubbed a hand through his hair. "This situation," he said. "What do you make of it?"

Okay, so that was a broad question. "You mean the whole Armageddon thing?"

"And us, here in the future."

"I think," Daniel said, choosing his words carefully, "that it's not going to be easy for Sam to find a way home. I'm no astrophysicist, but it seems to me that predicting solar flares with the degree of accuracy we need is…"

"Impossible?" Jack suggested.

Daniel shrugged. "But then, this is Sam we're talking about."

"Yeah." He let out a breath, scowled down at the floor for a moment. "She could drive herself seriously nuts trying to find a way home that doesn't exist."

That was true enough, and Sam wasn't likely to give up even if she *was* chasing the impossible. Swinging his legs off the bed, Daniel set his bare feet on the floor and relished the cool of the floorboards. Even this early in the day, the oppressive heat was building. "There's something else," he said, lowering his voice — not because he thought they'd be overheard, but because what he was about to say felt heretical.

Jack caught his tone, looked up from beneath his brow and waited.

"What Sam and Teal'c want to do," he said, "is hit the reset button, undo this timeline and make it so that none of this ever happened. But, Jack, isn't that acting like God? I mean, who are we to say which timeline's right? And even if we could go back and somehow change this, who's to say the alternative future would be any better?"

"Hard to see how it could be worse."

"That's because we can't imagine every outcome."

Jack frowned again and then nodded. He was tactician enough to understand that it was what you didn't know that usually bit you on the ass. After a pause he said, "I keep thinking about Hunter and his people, back there fighting these

Wraith bastards." He frowned. "And these guys are just sitting here doing nothing to help. It's like they've given up on Earth."

Daniel rubbed a hand over his mouth; he was thirsty. "Sam would say the best way to help Earth is to stop this future from happening in the first place."

"But even if — and it's a big if — she can find a way back, what do we do while we wait? Just sit around cooling our heels and ignore what's happening here?"

"Teal'c thinks nothing happening here matters."

"Teal'c…" Jack shook his head. "Things are pretty black and white for him."

"Can you blame him? He's been cheated out of a hundred years of fatherhood." He grimaced when he realized what he'd just said and glanced at Jack in apology.

"I get that," was all Jack said, and if he'd been reminded of Charlie, of his own lost fatherhood, he didn't comment. "And it means his objectivity is screwed." After a pause he added, less vehemently, "So's Carter's, by the way; she thinks this is her fault." It was his turn to wince. "I made her think this was her fault and now she won't quit until she fixes it."

"On the other hand," Daniel said, because it was impossible not to state the other side, "tens of millions of people must have died on Earth. And if we have a chance to stop that, aren't we morally obliged to take it?"

Jack gave a nod, more an acknowledgment of the conundrum than an answer. "I think that decision's above my pay grade."

"Problem is," Daniel said, "there's no one left above your pay grade."

Jack stared at him for a moment and then turned away, back to the window. Daniel watched his fingers tapping against the sill, his face creasing in thought. "There's no Air Force anymore," Jack said, as if the realization was unfolding before him.

"I guess not. No airplanes."

Jack gave a slight smile, rubbed a hand over the back of his neck. "No Chiefs of Staff, no chain of command, no after-action reports…"

"I guess you and Sam are it now."

He gave Daniel a quick, searching look. "No we're not," he said. "We're not anything. Everything's different here."

"It's a new world," Daniel agreed. "New rules."

Jack didn't reply, his fingers tap-tapping on the windowsill again. Then he turned with an opaque smile that told Daniel the conversation was over. "Put your boots on," he said. "I'm hungry."

Evacuation Site — June 2000: "Sir, with all due respect, this is a no-brainer." Colonel Reynolds leaned across the table in the President's tent, his hands clenched into fists and his impatience on display. "We have to go back. We have to help them."

Three days since Dixon had made contact through the beta gate, and Janet doubted anyone had slept more than a couple of hours. News had spread quickly through the camp, a bright but dangerous hope taking hold among people who had spent weeks mourning their dead.

There was a way home, but no home to go back to. There were survivors, but no one knew who, or where, or how many. They didn't even know where the beta gate was — all Hammond had said was that he'd ordered Colonel Dixon to take it some place safe. Most likely, that was far from Colorado, far from the families people had left behind.

There were more questions than answers and a universal pressure to act, to do *something*, but no consensus about what. And so tension grew in the camp like a weed, winding itself around the frightened, bereft population and choking out their goodwill. Janet had seen it in the bar already. Discussions became arguments and arguments became fights. No one agreed on what they should do to help the people on Earth, and increasingly no one agreed on who had the right to decide.

Janet shifted in her chair, sweat making her shirt cling to her back as she moved. Outside the sun was reaching its zenith and it was hot and sticky inside the tent. They'd been in there since dawn, eating their carefully rationed breakfast at the table as the discussion circled around and around. Janet hadn't seen Cassie since the night before, when she'd come back late and Cassie was already asleep on her narrow cot. Her daughter had stirred, half-waking, and Janet had kissed her forehead and stroked her hair until she'd fallen asleep again.

She wished she could go back there now, to make sure she was okay helping in the makeshift school that had sprung up close to the lakeshore. There were enough families here to make it worthwhile, and enough parents fighting to bring some normalcy to their kids' lives. Janet was more grateful to them than she could express.

The President's loud sigh brought her back to the room. "I don't dispute that, Colonel," he said, rocking back in his chair.

He looked frazzled, Janet thought, weary to the bone. He'd been wracked by indecision since Dixon had made contact, and there was no shame in that. The fate of humanity was too much for any one man to bear and the fact that Bill Turner was struggling under the weight of the decision did him no harm in Janet's eyes. A less thoughtful man may have decided sooner, but would the decision have been right?

Scrubbing his fingers through his hair, Turner said, "The question must be how we can help them without compromising the security of Arbella."

"Your caution is quite correct, Mr. President." Colonel Simmons sat opposite Janet and Reynolds, his cool gaze fixed on Turner. "As you know, we only have enough supplies to feed and house the people on the evacuation list. We simply don't have the capacity to take in refugees. That was the point of having the list in the first place."

"But we can at least help them treat their wounded," said Janet.

"Here?" Simmons said. "Don't be naive, Doctor. Where would you treat them? In our field hospital?"

Unfortunately, that was a good question. She had six beds,

all occupied by people suffering from the flu, and there must be hundreds, thousands, in need of help on Earth. What difference could one doctor make? What difference could any of them make?

Turner ran his fingers over his couple days' growth of stubble. His anxiety was contagious and Janet could feel it building in the pit of her stomach.

"I'm sorry to say it, Mr. President," Simmons insisted, tapping his fingertips on the table, "but we can't show the same reckless disregard for protocol that was endemic at Stargate Command."

"Simmons," Reynolds growled, "you know nothing about—"

"Don't I? Tell me, Colonel, what do you think General Hammond was thinking when he gave Dixon orders to steal the beta gate and evacuate refugees here? Did he consider the danger he was putting us in? What if Dixon is captured by the Goa'uld? What if the next time the gate opens a legion of Jaffa tries to march through?"

Reynolds ground his teeth but was silent. In truth, Janet knew he had no answer to Simmons' accusation. It had been reckless, but it was also brave. A heroic, insane plan that was typical of Stargate Command and all who'd served under General Hammond.

Simmons opened his mouth to continue, but Janet spoke first. She couldn't stop herself because a knot of anger was building in her chest, tightening her throat, and she had to let it out. Struggling to keep her voice even, she said, "Mr. President, I know what General Hammond was thinking. He was thinking that two-thousand survivors aren't nearly enough. He was thinking that we cannot be the future of the entire human race. We're too few." She glanced at Simmons. She'd never been afraid to challenge authority when she knew she was right, and this was no different. "General Hammond was acting with compassion and humanity, Colonel. And *that* is what was endemic at Stargate Command."

Simmons' expression didn't change, although something menacing shifted beneath the frosty surface of his eyes. "The fact remains," he said, turning back to the President, "that we don't have the resources to become a refugee camp for the world."

Across the table, Maybourne sat knotting his fingers together. She watched the way his hands shook, the way his eyes darted around the room with a restless agitation that spoke of an unquiet mind. She wondered what demons haunted his sleep.

Until now, he'd been silent. But he chose this moment to sit forward, unknot his nervous fingers, and say, "The purpose of this base, Mr. President, was always to find new technologies that could help Earth. There are teams here who can go through the gate and bring back what we need." He spread his hands across the table, pressing them flat. "Perhaps if Stargate Command had done that from the start, we wouldn't be sitting here now. But here we are, and I say it's time we use the gate to go get what we need to survive. Perhaps then we'll have the resources to help the refugees from Earth." He threw a glance at Janet, who was left speechless at this unexpected, and unwanted, ally.

Simmons sat forward in his chair and cast an inscrutable look at Maybourne. "Mr. President, I really must insist –"

"You insist, do you, Colonel?" The President raised his eyebrows in a challenge that dared Simmons to continue. "This *is* novel, because I'm used to my advisors *recommending* action and leaving the final decision up to me, their Commander in Chief. Are we doing things differently here?"

Simmons bowed his head in acknowledgment of the rebuke and sat back, though Janet found it hard to believe that he was as chagrined as his demeanor suggested. She hated very few people, but right there and right then she downright despised Colonel Frank Simmons. How could he propose that they just sit there and do nothing while Earth burned, while people died? It was impossible, everything in her soul rebelled against the idea. She simply refused to do it.

"I'll go back, sir."

She said the words almost without thought, and the moment they'd left her mouth she thought of Cassie and her heart dropped like a stone. But even a mother's love couldn't keep her from doing what she knew to be right. In memory of General Hammond and her friends on SG-1, she could do no less. "I'll go back to Earth and treat the wounded if that's the best we can offer them."

President Turner lifted his head from his hands and looked at her. She couldn't interpret the intense expression in his eyes.

"I'll go with her, sir," Reynolds volunteered. "She'll need protection."

Janet smiled her thanks to the colonel, although she suspected it might be better for the colony if he stayed on Arbella and ran interference between President Turner and Simmons. But this wasn't the time for that discussion.

"Alright," said President Turner, in a careful tone that reminded her of General Hammond when a challenging decision had to be made. Turner rose to his feet. "Doctor Frasier, you have permission to return to Earth. Maybourne, if this mission is a success then I'll consider sending your teams offworld. To trade, though, not to steal." He turned to Simmons, shoulders braced as if for a confrontation. "Colonel, I've heard your concerns, and I'm not dismissing them. But a woman called Emma Lazarus once wrote a sonnet, just a few lines, which were inscribed on a statue you may have seen. Those words said, 'Give me your tired, your poor, Your huddled masses yearning to breathe free, The wretched refuse of your teeming shore. Send these, the homeless, tempest-tost to me, I lift my lamp beside the golden door.' We have to lift that lamp, Colonel. We have to lift it high no matter what the danger. We can't change what we believe in just because we're afraid. If Arbella is to be anything, it has to be a beacon of hope. And we need to go out there and hold the torch high for all to see."

Simmons only nodded. "Very well, sir. I've given my... recommendation."

"Yes," Turner said. "You have."

The rest of them sat in tense silence, watching the President. His gaze came to rest on Janet, and she smiled because she saw a spirit in his eyes that had been absent before. *Hope*, she realized. *He has hope.*

"Good luck, Doctor," Turner said with a trace of his own smile. "And Godspeed your return. I think we're going to need you here."

Arbella — 2098: Food was being served in a sort of officers' mess, long rows of tables and people in uniform collecting bowls from the server at the far end. Daniel picked out Sam and Teal'c at a table close to the wall and lifted his hand to wave. Sam waved back with a smile. She looked excited. Perhaps she'd found coffee in this brave new world?

Breakfast turned out to be a kind of cereal-based gloop that looked somewhat like oatmeal, served by a wiry man with a missing front tooth. He watched Daniel with bright eyes as he handed over his bowl. "So you're Dr. Jackson?"

"Ah, yeah, that's right." Given Bailey's warning about their SG-1 patches, Daniel thought it best to tread lightly.

But the man beamed toothlessly and pushed up his sleeve to reveal a familiar tattoo. The Earth glyph, just like Elspeth's back on Earth. A symbol of resistance, she'd called it. Daniel wondered what it meant here. "It's an honor, sir," the man said as his sleeve fell back into place. He nodded to Jack, standing behind Daniel in the line. "Colonel O'Neill. My grandfather always said SG-1 would come back. I wish he was alive to see this day."

Daniel heard Jack's boots scrape on the floor, sensed his unease. "What's your name?" Jack said.

"Lieutenant Jefferson, sir. My grandfather served at Stargate Command."

There was a moment of stillness, and then Jack said, "Marines?"

"Yes sir."

"Major Levi Jefferson?"

The man's eyes went wide, his jaw slack. "You knew him, sir?"

"He was a good man," Jack said. "I'm glad he made it out."

Jefferson let out a laugh, shaking his head. "Man, I can't believe this…" Then he turned serious and in a more controlled voice said, "Colonel, CFS has got your back. Remember that. We never lost faith."

Faith, Daniel thought, was a big word with big implications. He glanced at Jack but his soldier's mask was firmly in place, which meant he sensed trouble too.

"I appreciate that, Lieutenant," was all Jack said, giving a friendly nod. Then he gestured at the stack of bowls. "I'd appreciate breakfast too."

"Yes sir!" Jefferson grinned and spooned a helping of gloop into a bowl, handing it over.

As they made their way toward Sam and Teal'c, Daniel said, "You knew his grandfather?"

"Kinda," Jack said with a shake of his head. "He was just a kid, joined SG-5 a couple months back."

"Give or take a hundred years."

"Right." He sighed. "Give or take."

Sam was watching them approach and her excitement from earlier was still evident. She'd already finished eating and was sitting drumming impatient fingers on the table. "Sir," she said, as Jack took a seat opposite her. "Good news."

"You found *Dunkin' Donuts*?" Jack said, picking up his spoon and prodding his breakfast.

"No sir. Better than that — we've got access to their computer system already." She glanced at Daniel. "And their archives."

"That *is* good news," Daniel said, clambering over the bench and sitting down. There was a jug of water in the center of the table and he poured himself a glass. It tasted odd, full of iron.

"I've already had a peek," Sam said, "and I'm pretty sure they're using an Asgard system, which should mean some impressive computing power."

Jack nodded as he lifted the spoon to his lips and tasted his breakfast. He made a face, but ate it anyway. "It's a good place to start," he said. "Let's see what you can find out."

"I've been thinking about it," Sam said. "The patterns of solar flares are statistically similar to events like avalanches or earthquakes. That is, energy builds up until it reaches a point of criticality, when the event occurs. Now if I can model that, obviously taking into account the fluid dynamics of the sun's plasma, I can—"

"Carter?"

Sam nodded. "Yes sir. It's just— If I can work with an Asgard computer, this could come together a lot sooner than we'd been expecting."

"You're talking about creating a statistical model?" Jack said.

"Yes sir."

"And I'm guessing that not just any old solar flare will send us where we want to go?"

"That's right. I'd need to accurately predict a flare of the correct magnitude and vector. We can keep a wormhole open for thirty-eight minutes so that's our window in terms of the exact timing of an event." She made a face. "But the harder part will be determining the point in time to which we return. A couple years too late and it's all over, a couple years too early and we'd be looking at entropic cascade failure because we'd effectively have entered our own timeline."

"And right now we're in an alternate timeline?"

"That's correct, sir. Right now we're in an alternate future. There are no other versions of us here because, in this time line, SG-1 disappeared a hundred years ago."

"Okay." Jack took another mouthful of oatmeal.

"But I'm optimistic, sir," she said. "I think this is a good first step."

"Sure." Jack glanced at her over his spoon. "A first step on a long road."

"Sir—"

"Let's keep our expectations realistic, Carter. That's all I'm saying."

"Yes sir." Sam frowned at the table and said no more.

A difficult silence fell, punctuated by the sounds of the mess hall — people eating, talking, and whispering. There were eyes on them, curious but not unfriendly. Daniel glanced over at Jefferson, his tattoo hidden beneath his shirtsleeve.

"Did you talk to the guy serving?" he asked Sam. "Lieutenant Jefferson?"

She nodded. "I get the feeling we have a fan club."

"Jefferson said they still had faith," he said. "Faith in us?"

Jack shot him a sideways look. "They think we're here to save them, Daniel."

"Maybe they're just looking for hope? A kind of talisman, perhaps." He turned so he could look at Jack properly — he was toying with his spoon, tapping it against the edge of his empty bowl. "Right now they're doing nothing to help the people on Earth," Daniel said. "Maybe we can change that?"

Jack cocked an eyebrow. "And how do you—?"

"No." Teal'c brought his hand down on the table so hard the crockery jumped. In a low, fierce voice he said, "We cannot be what these people wish us to be, Daniel Jackson. That is not our purpose here."

"Teal'c's right," Sam said. "I understand why you want to help, Daniel, but we can't let ourselves get distracted from the mission." Her attention switched to Jack. "Right, sir? Your orders still stand: you have to get home and save the Protected Planet Treaty."

Jack frowned. "Thing is, Carter, what if—"

"Colonel O'Neill?"

A soldier appeared at the head of their table and snapped off a salute. "Sir, when you're ready, General Bailey has asked me to escort you and your team to the datacenter."

Jack pushed his bowl away; he didn't look sorry to be interrupted. "We're ready," he said. "Carter?"

"Yes sir." She was already on her feet. "Let's get to work."

But her expression was tense and Daniel was very aware of Jack's unfinished sentence, his 'what if' left hanging in the air between them.

What if they couldn't find a way home? What if they shouldn't?

CHAPTER TEN

The datacenter was a large building that wouldn't have looked out of place in the Wild West. It didn't quite have saloon doors, but it possessed a certain rustic charm that reminded Jack of old movies. There was a CMF guard on the door and he gave SG-1 a serious nod as they entered, his wary gaze roving past them to the quiet street beyond.

The latent unease that hummed in the air felt different from the day before, when they'd strolled into town behind General Bailey. Jack could only assume that word of their arrival had spread and, since Bailey had wanted to keep it quiet, he guessed the leak had come from President Jones' people. That was no surprise; in Jack's experience of politics, both on- and off-world, there was nothing like a little internal dissent among the populace to keep them from examining the motives of their leaders.

Carter and Daniel, eager to get started, led the way inside, but Jack hung back as they entered the building. "Expecting trouble?" he asked the guard.

The kid shot him a look of surprise; he was clearly green as grass. "Just some intel officers down last night, sir," he said, "stirring things up."

"Stirring things up, how?"

The guard looked uncomfortable, shifting beneath his wide brimmed hat. It cast shadows over his face, the sun high and hot behind dusty yellow clouds. "You know," he said, "the usual."

"Let's pretend I don't know." Jack was glad of his sunglasses, but pulled them off to get a better look at the guy.

"They're saying you'll bring the enemy here," the guard said, "now you've opened the Stargate."

It wasn't the first time he'd heard that argument; Kinsey had said more or less the same thing. "The enemy doesn't usually wait for an invitation," Jack said, but softened the words with a nod of approval. "It's good to know you're out here, son."

The kid puffed up a little. "Thanks, Colonel O'Neill. It's my honor."

Inside the datacenter, it was cooler and dimmer. Jack had to blink a little to adjust. Carter and Daniel were already heading up a wooden flight of stairs to his left, Teal'c following, but Jack was stopped by another guard who stepped in front of him. "Colonel O'Neill?" the young woman said. "General Bailey would like to talk with you."

Teal'c turned around, stopping halfway up the stairs. Carter slowed too, throwing an anxious glance over her shoulder. No one liked splitting up off-world, but Jack figured Bailey had already had plenty of opportunities to do them harm. He waved the others on. "I'll catch up with you," he said. "Carter, Daniel — geek out. Teal'c, keep an eye on them."

Teal'c acknowledged the order with a nod and followed as Daniel and Carter disappeared through a door at the top of the stairs.

"This way, sir," said the guard, and showed him into a room on the first floor. It was small and cluttered, full of what Jack might call junk and Carter might call fascinating.

Bailey stood by the window, gazing out over the empty street beyond. She turned as they entered, and dismissed the soldier. "I trust you slept well?" she said once they were alone. "You look rested."

"Yes ma'am."

She gave a tired smile and said, "I think we can dispense with the formality, Jack, if that's okay with you?"

"Sure," he said. "Umm...?"

"Roz. You can call me Roz."

"Okay." Then, noticing the shadows under her eyes, he said, "I hear there was trouble last night."

She made a face. "Unfortunately, yes."

"Jones' men?"

"I should have expected it, I suppose. Needless to say, your arrival has stirred up some old feelings."

He moved a little further into the room, picked up something from the table — a circuit board? — and turned it over in his hands. "I'm guessing they're not warm and fuzzy feelings."

Bailey laughed, opening up her tight expression. "Definitely not, I'm afraid." She sighed and smoothed a hand over her unruly hair. "There's always been conflict here," she said, "from the very start. People who wanted to go back and fight, others who wanted to hunker down and protect the colony."

"Sounds familiar." He looked up at her. "There was no one called Kinsey here, was there?"

"I don't recognize the name, no."

"But you know the name Maybourne." It was a guess, but not exactly a longshot.

"Maybourne was a traitor."

"A traitor?" He held up a hand before she could answer his rhetorical question. "I'm just surprised that you know; I thought he'd have had more influence here."

Bailey crossed the room and leaned back on the table next to him. Arms folded across her chest, she let out a sigh. "Maybourne was Air Force, Jack."

He let a beat fall, waiting for the rest. When she didn't carry on, he said, "And that's a bad thing because...?"

"Because a lot of influential people blamed the Air Force for what happened: for opening the Stargate in the first place, for keeping its existence a secret, for not preparing for an invasion. For...well, everything, really."

"And what about the NID?" Jack said angrily. "What did they blame them for?"

"Nothing. Jack, the NID founded Arbella. Without it, there'd have been no safe haven. No escape." She looked at him for a long moment and then said, "Unless you know different?"

"I know that Maybourne *was* NID," he said. "And I think it's a good bet that Arbella was the base of operations for his shadow team — the shadow team that screwed up the alliances that kept us safe."

"*Maybourne* founded Arbella?" Bailey looked incredulous; clearly some wires had gotten crossed over the years. "Everyone says it was Simmons."

"Never heard of Simmons," Jack said. "The point is that Maybourne was crooked. The NID was crooked. But Stargate Command wasn't. We were fighting for Earth — we still are."

Bailey lifted her hands. "You're preaching to the choir, Jack. The CMF always held faith with Stargate Command."

"But the people in power didn't."

"Right. And they'll see you all hang if they think you're stirring up dissent."

That got his attention. "Hang?"

"Sedition is a capital crime."

He raised an eyebrow, but only said "Noted." Dropping whatever it was he'd been fiddling with, he strolled around to the other side of the table, thinking. "How many of you want to help the people on Earth?"

"Opinion has always been divided on that," Bailey said. She was watching him but didn't move to join him. "At times the idea of returning to Earth gains popularity. At other times..." She spread her hands. "This is one of those other times."

"Because...?"

Her expression turned neutral; she wasn't going to tell him. "The point is, Jack, you and your people need to be careful. You can't do anything that gives Jones an excuse to accuse you of stirring up trouble."

"I get the feeling that just being here is stirring up trouble."

"These are deep waters, Jack," she said. "Who knows what you might stir up?"

For a moment, they shared a silent look and he got the impression that she was searching for something, for some clue in his face. Then a noise in the street outside drew her attention and she looked away. When she turned back her expression had closed down.

"Tell your people to be careful," she said. "The CMF is solid and on your side, but the others…?"

"Understood," he said. "We're not looking for trouble."

Bailey gave him a dry smile. "Problem is, it might come looking for you."

CHAPTER ELEVEN

Evacuation Site — 2000: When the final chevron locked, Janet's anxiety heightened — a strange mix of trepidation at what lay on the other side of the wormhole and a fierce longing to just go home. This place in which they'd found themselves was so alien, and not just in a literal sense. The machinations of creating a new society were fraught with pitfalls at every turn and she feared that she'd fall into a hole so deep she'd never find her way out. But she wasn't so foolish as to believe that a happy alternative awaited her back on Earth. Fragmented as it was, Arbella was probably the least dangerous option.

"Colonel Reynolds, you have a go."

It pained her to hear anyone but General Hammond call the mission go, and Janet glanced around to see the colonel grimace in reaction to Major Newman's words, but all he said was, "Ok, Doc, let's move out."

With a sharp intake of breath, Janet stepped through the shimmering blue of the event horizon — and into a world of shadows and orange light. She blinked, fighting the wave of nausea that she'd yet to master as a by-product of gate travel. The orange haze resolved itself into the glow of sodium arc lights, which highlighted the shapes of people moving around in a low ceilinged room. The concrete above them was barely higher than the gate itself, though the hangar-like room stretched back at least 150 meters, and banks of computer consoles lined the walls. There was a DHD too, wires trailing from its insides to what was obviously a naquadah generator. It had to be the one they'd retrieved from Antarctica a couple years back, but it looked makeshift and beat up — like this whole place.

"Colonel Reynolds, Doctor Fraiser," called a female voice from the darkness, her tone one of desperate relief. Janet hoped it wasn't misplaced. "Thank you. Thank you for coming."

A blond woman approached them, emerging from the gloom into the blue light of the active gate. From her bedraggled appearance, Janet surmised that personal hygiene was even more of a luxury here than back on Arbella. The woman snapped off a salute, though her grimy T-shirt and cargo pants gave no indication of her rank.

Janet returned the salute, as did Colonel Reynolds who said, "At ease….?"

"Captain, sir. Captain Sarah Marston out of Groom Lake. Colonel Dixon wanted to be here for your arrival, but he's out on recon. He asked that I meet you."

"Recon?" said Reynolds. "Isn't he the commander of this base?"

The captain's brow furrowed, a pained expression. "Our numbers don't allow for the privilege of rank, sir. Not… not all military personnel made it."

Reynolds nodded in understanding and what looked like sympathy.

"You came here with Colonel Dixon, Captain?" asked Janet.

"Yes, ma'am."

"All of you?" asked Reynolds dubiously, looking around at the people in the gate room who were watching them curiously. On their faces, Janet took in a variety of expressions, from hope to wariness to a terrible deadened resignation. Even at first glance, though, she could tell that not everyone present was military.

"No, sir. They… uh… some of them are local civilians."

Reynolds raised his eyebrows. "You let civilians into a top secret Air Force base? And you let them in *here*?" He gestured to the gate behind them.

Marston looked chagrined, but her jaw was set and she locked eyes with Reynolds. "It's a naval base, sir, and, like I said, we needed the numbers. And they—"

"And they were dying." The voice echoed from the other end of the chamber and Janet looked past Captain Marston to see

Colonel Dave Dixon striding towards them. He looked even more beat up than Marston, his face dirty and a fresh cut oozing blood from his eyebrow.

He handed his weapon off to the captain with a nod and smiled at Reynolds and Janet. The expression struck her as weary, yet determined, just like Marston's. "They were dying, Colonel," he repeated, "so we opened our doors. And I'd love to stand here and debate ethics versus protocol with you, but we brought wounded with us just now and I could very much use your help. Doctor, with me?"

Without another word, he strode back out of the hangar, leaving them with no choice but to follow.

Arbella — 2098: Time was a strange thing, Sam reflected as she made her way along the dark streets of Laketown. On the one hand, she felt an urgent pressure to get home. On the other, she knew it wouldn't matter if it took her fifty years to find the solution so long as she found it in the end. In the moment of her success, all this would be wiped out and the world would never know how close it had come to disaster.

So she had unlimited time at her disposal and yet every wasted second felt precious. Every day that passed here was another day that her friends were dead and that Earth suffered. The paradox was tying her in knots, niggling at her concentration. She needed to relax, to take a breath, but how could she when she was the only person who could save the world?

She scrubbed a hand through her hair and stifled a yawn as she walked. It had been a long day already but she was too wound up to sleep, so after eating dinner in the mess hall she'd figured she might as well keep working. Luckily, the route from the CMF headquarters to the datacenter had become so familiar over the past couple of weeks that she could find her way in the dark. There was no street lighting here and neither of the planet's moons was visible through the clouds tonight, but enough light spilled from the buildings to at least make the streets navigable. She was beginning to recognize some faces too, as well as the buildings, and to get used to the stares that followed her — some friendly, some not. Word of SG-1's return had spread, and Sam had learned to walk fast and keep her head down. The colonel had made it clear that not everyone was pleased to see them back.

There was a bakery on the corner, across from the datacenter, and the aroma of tomorrow's bread was familiar and reminiscent of home. According to Daniel, the colony had brought crop seed and breeding animals through the gate during the forty years between Apophis's attack and the Wraith invasion. It seemed that communication between Earth and Arbella had been regular, if difficult, during those years. A number of refugees had made it through too, although the records didn't say why their numbers were so few. Sam could guess though; there simply wouldn't have been enough resources here to support the thousands of people who must have been desperate to flee the Goa'uld.

She pushed the thought away, tried not to imagine what it must have been like on Earth during that time, and walked on past the bakery.

"Traitor!"

Startled by the shout, she stopped and looked around. A couple of figures lurked in the shadows, but they were also looking around as if searching for the troublemaker and Sam couldn't see who'd shouted at her. She felt a twist of resentful anger, but she was alone and without backup and she didn't like her odds in a fight, so she lengthened her stride and walked on.

Suddenly she was aware of someone coming up on her right and she spun to face them, hands raised to block a blow.

"Easy, Carter." The colonel lifted his own hands in mock surrender. "Just us."

Daniel and Teal'c stood behind him, shadows in the dark street.

"Sorry, sir," she said and glanced back over her shoulder.

"There was someone…"

"Yeah." The colonel followed her gaze. "We heard him."

After a silent moment, Sam said, "What are you guys doing here anyway?"

"One might ask you the same question, Major."

"I was…" She gestured toward the datacenter. "I wanted to check on one of the programs I left running."

"Not tonight," the colonel said in a tone that made it an order.

"Sir—"

"We're going out," he said. "You're coming with us."

"Out?" She glanced at Daniel for confirmation. "Where?"

"To a bar, apparently."

"They have a bar here?"

"Carter," the colonel said, "Laketown was built by the Air Force. Of course they have a bar."

She smiled, but took a step toward the datacenter. "Actually, I should probably go check—"

"Ah!" The colonel held up his hand. "One night won't make a difference, Carter."

She hesitated, glanced at Teal'c. He stood a step behind Daniel, almost hidden in the dark. Only the gold of Apophis's brand caught the scant light from the datacenter's upstairs window. "I believe Colonel O'Neill is correct," he said. "You appear weary, Major Carter."

"See?" the colonel said. "Even Teal'c agrees you need a night off."

And maybe he was right. She'd lost count of the days since they'd left Earth and she hadn't stopped for a moment since then. She was exhausted. And now that she was actively working on a plan to get them home, Teal'c had relaxed too, which made her feel less pressurized. She wondered how he'd take it if, or when, she reached an impasse in her work, but figured she'd cross that bridge when she reached it. For now, at least, perhaps she could afford one night of R&R?

"Okay," she said, surprised by how relieved she felt. "A break sounds good."

The colonel gave a brief smile and waved her back the way she'd come, toward the center of town and the lakeshore. "According to Roz," he said, "this place is a CMF hangout. So it should be pretty friendly."

She exchanged a glance with Teal'c as they walked; neither of them was keen on the colonel's growing friendship with General Bailey. As they'd feared, he was getting drawn into the concerns of Arbella and its people.

"I thought 'Roz' wanted us to keep a low profile," she said, aware that her tone wasn't entirely appropriate.

The colonel gave her a sideways look. "You think we can't keep a low profile in a bar?"

"I think alcohol rarely defuses tense situations, sir."

"Oh sometimes it does, Carter," he said. "Sometimes a stiff drink is exactly what you need after a long day's apocalypse."

That provoked a reluctant smile. "Yes sir," she said, and then yawned and pressed a hand over her mouth. "Sorry. Teal'c's right, I'm tired." And she wasn't sure if she was apologizing for the yawn or the attitude.

"We're all tired," the colonel said. "So let's just go hang for a while, huh?"

"As in 'out'," Daniel clarified as they walked on. "Hang-out, not *hang* hang."

Teal'c raised an eyebrow. "I am grateful for your linguistic acuity, Daniel Jackson."

And that made Daniel smile, which made them all smile, and for a moment, there on the cooling street in the middle of Earth's only surviving colony, Sam felt at home. It was somehow both a welcome and dangerous sensation.

"Apparently they have beer," Daniel said.

The colonel nodded. "I hope it's cold."

It wasn't a long walk to the bar — the town wasn't all that big — but Sam realized that Daniel and the colonel knew their way around much better than she did. They'd been out and about much more, winning hearts and minds. But as they rounded the corner and she saw the bar her previous unease was overtaken by amusement. The sign, white paint on polished wood, read: 'The FU-Bar.'

The colonel huffed a laugh. "Oh yeah," he said, "definitely Air Force."

For once, Teal'c looked genuinely perplexed.

"It's a joke," Daniel explained. "F.U.B.A.R is a military acronym for, um, 'Fouled' Up Beyond All Repair." He glanced at Sam. "Right?"

"Something like that," she agreed. "But The FU-Bar's pretty funny."

"Pretty accurate," the colonel said. "Considering."

"Gallows humor," Daniel nodded. "I like it."

Inside it kind of looked like a bar and kind of didn't. There *was* an actual bar, and behind it Sam could see actual kegs — wooden ones — some labeled 'Steiner's Original'. There were tables and chairs, mostly makeshift, and the bar was pretty full. The air was filled with chatter, but there was no music, no TV, and no cigarette smoke. It was oddly old-fashioned and she half expected to find someone in the corner playing a fiddle.

"Well this is quaint," Daniel said, almost at the exact moment everyone in the bar noticed their arrival. His voice echoed in the surprised silence rather louder than he'd probably intended. "Um," he added, lifting a hand, "hi?"

For a moment, Sam had visions of being driven out with pitchforks and torches, but then she saw Jefferson with his gap-toothed grin standing up. "Colonel O'Neill!" he called, waving them over. "Come sit with us."

And then everyone was talking again. Most were smiling and Sam just ignored the ones who weren't. "Come on," the colonel said, leading the way toward Jefferson's table, "let's get a drink."

The beer, as it turned out, was good. Really good.

"Now this," Daniel said, peering into his earthenware mug, "is much better than that cheap stuff you buy, Jack."

The colonel didn't argue. "Strong too," he said, with a pointed look that made Sam smile. Daniel was a notorious lightweight and despite the colonel's talk about a night off, they all knew that they had to keep their wits about them.

"It certainly has more flavor," Teal'c agreed.

His presence was getting the most attention, but Teal'c seemed unfazed by the looks darted in his direction. It was something he'd gotten used to on Earth, she supposed, and this was no different.

"So." Jefferson returned from the bar with a new pitcher of beer that he set in the center of the table. "The thing we want to know is, what's next?"

"Next?" the colonel said, feigning non-comprehension. It was his favorite way to avoid answering awkward questions.

"For your team, sir," Jefferson said. "You must be working on a plan."

He glanced at the man next to him, one of the CMF guards Sam knew from the datacenter. His name was Kiowa and, like Jefferson, he had the Earth glyph inked onto his arm. "There's a bunch of us who can't wait to take the fight to Earth, ma'am," Kiowa said. "We'll be right behind you when you go back."

"We're working on it," Sam said, swallowing the lump of lie in her throat. "It's going slowly, but… we'll get there."

"We know you will, Major." Jefferson tapped his arm where the glyph was hidden beneath his shirt. "We have faith."

Faith. Sam took a mouthful of beer and told herself she wasn't really lying. She *was* planning to save Earth, just not in the way Jefferson or his friend believed.

Kiowa shifted closer, dropping his voice. "So what's it like there, Colonel?" he said. "On Earth, I mean. What's it like there, now?"

No one answered. The image of the brown, ashy world they'd seen from orbit hung in silence between them.

"We've only been to a couple places," Sam said at last, unsure how to answer the question. "But it looks—"

"Like it's recovering," the colonel said. "There are trees, birds. People." He shared an inscrutable look with Daniel. "Lots of people."

Jefferson rubbed his hand across his mouth. "Are they sick?"

"Sick?" Daniel said. "Not especially. I mean, people get sick, but we didn't see a lot sickness. Why?"

"People say they're sick," Jefferson said, swallowing a mouthful of beer. "They say, if we go back, we'll get sick too. They say there are diseases there."

"And there aren't here?" Daniel said, then softened his tone and added, "I mean, really, you don't have any sickness here?"

"We have medicines."

And stolen alien technologies, Sam thought.

A moment of silence fell amid the chatter of the bar and then the colonel said, "They're ready to fight, you know." He blurted it as if the words had slipped out past his better judgement. "They're already fighting."

Jefferson and Kiowa shared a look. "How?" Jefferson said.

"Any way they can. Dix could tell you more."

They both stared, as if waiting for more, and then Kiowa said, "Who's Dix?"

"Um, Jack?" Daniel's eyebrows were up into his hairline; so much for not stirring up trouble.

The colonel glanced away, past Teal'c. "I'm just saying."

"Who's Dix?" Kiowa repeated.

"He's someone on Earth," Sam said, before the colonel could dig himself in any deeper. "He's the leader of the resistance against the Wraith."

Jefferson frowned into his beer. "Don't much like the idea of folk on Earth fighting and us not covering their backs."

"But we're going to help them, right?" Kiowa said. "That's the plan?"

"Yeah," the colonel said in that way he had of shutting things down. "We're gonna help them."

Teal'c shifted, put his beer on the table. Sam watched him,

afraid he was going to start an argument they couldn't have in public, but instead he said, "There are several men at a table to our right who have been watching us intently."

The colonel nodded. "Yeah, I've seen them."

"Jones' men?" Sam said.

Jefferson glanced over his shoulder. "Damn it," he said, getting to his feet. "Tyler."

In response, four men rose from a table close to the bar, spreading out into a practiced formation. One of them, the leader, looked like he was carrying a weapon under his rough jacket. They'd come for a fight.

"Hey," the colonel said, catching Jefferson's sleeve. "We don't want trouble."

"Looks like we already got it," Jefferson said and there was a glint of anticipation in his eyes that spoke volumes. "Hey, Tyler," he called, "thought you were banned?"

Broad-shouldered and narrow-eyed, Tyler didn't look like the brightest star in the cosmos. "Is that them?" he said. "The so called 'SG-1'?"

"What's it to you?" Kiowa said, moving to stand next to Jefferson.

"What's it to me?" Tyler's focus shifted to Sam, then drifted over the rest of her team. "They got blood on their hands, and you know it. Everybody knows it."

"Sir?" Sam glanced around in search of a way out. None of them were armed and this guy Tyler could be hiding anything under his coat.

"Let me talk to him," Daniel said, starting to rise.

"No." The colonel put a hand on his arm. "Sit down. This is a setup."

"A setup?"

The colonel darted a glance to his left, toward the back of the room. Sam looked and realized there was another table hidden in the shadows. A man and a woman sat there, watching the whole encounter. One of them she recognized; it was

Agent Yuma, from the President's office, and she had a small camcorder on the table in front of her.

"They want us to get into a fight," the colonel said. "They want us to cause trouble."

"You think Jones set this up?" Daniel said.

The colonel shook his head. "I don't think Jones is the boss."

"Then who is?"

"Who the hell knows? This is the NID's mutant grandchild, Daniel. It could have any number of heads."

"The colonel's right," Sam said. "We have to get out of here before we're implicated in anything."

Jefferson and Kiowa had moved apart, giving each other room to fight and putting themselves between Tyler's men and SG-1. "Go back to your sheep, farm boy," Jefferson said as several other people in CMF uniform stood up. "Feed *them* your crap, we don't want it here."

"That one's a snake-carrier," Tyler said, pointing at Teal'c. "Keeps it in his belly."

"Yeah?" Kiowa said. "Like how you keep your brains in your ass?" That earned a snigger from the crowd, but Tyler's eyes narrowed to a squint and from under his coat he pulled the club he'd been hiding. At least it wasn't a gun.

"Those bastards killed my grandma."

"Oh come on," Jefferson said, shaking out his arms, flexing his hands, ready for the fight. "Everybody knows your grandma was a sheep, Tyler."

The club came down with a crash on a table, sending it splintering, and then all hell broke loose.

"Ah, crap," the colonel hissed, scrambling up from the table and taking a step back as all the CMF personnel in the bar barreled into the brawl.

Behind SG-1 the two intelligence officers were also on their feet, the camera rolling. The colonel saw it, kept his back to them, and darted a look at Daniel and Sam. She knew what he wanted. "Everyone out of here," the colonel barked and headed past the intel officers.

Daniel lurched after him in apparent clumsy panic, knocking his shoulder into Yuma and sending the camera flying. "Oh, I'm sorry!" he said, just as Sam stamped the heel of her boot down hard on the camera. It gave a satisfying crunch.

"Daniel, Carter," the colonel snapped. "Move it!"

Sam hunkered down, snatched up the broken camera and snagged what she hoped was the memory card. She held the rest out to Yuma. "Sorry," she said with an awkward grimace.

Yuma regarded her through emotionless eyes and made no move to take the camera.

"I'd get out of here if I were you," Sam said, pressing the pieces of camera into her hands, "before anything else gets broken."

Perhaps threatening her wasn't wise, but it certainly felt good.

"Advice we should follow ourselves," Teal'c said, crowding in behind Sam and hustling her away from Yuma, around the brawling men, and out the door.

She almost felt like whooping when she hit the cool night air.

"Sonofabitch," the colonel said, as they backed away from the bar. "So much for a quiet night out."

Daniel barked a grim laugh. "Welcome to the new world."

CHAPTER TWELVE

Earth — 2000: "Doctor Fraiser, with me!" Colonel Dixon didn't wait to see if Janet was following as he raced up the corridor pushing the gurney. She caught up with him, checking the kid's vitals as they moved. The boy's pulse was weak and thready, his body temperature soaring, and he was unresponsive to stimulus. It wasn't hard to spot the signs of severe dehydration.

She looked up at the other civilians who had been brought down by Dixon and his team. "Which one of you is this boy's parent?" None of them answered, their beleaguered expressions barely registering her question as they staggered along behind, nursing their own wounds.

"If this kid's parents are still nearby, they're probably dead," said Dixon, a barely perceptible flinch giving lie to his matter-of-fact tone.

Ignoring what his words meant, Janet turned back to the boy. "We've got to get him on an IV," she said, just as Dixon pushed open a set of double doors ahead of them to reveal a room in chaos.

There were ten beds lining the walls, all of them occupied with patients whose most obvious injuries were burns, some of them severe. A young man was changing the dressings of one of them. At the end of the room was what looked like triage, where a bespectacled woman in her mid-fifties was conducting a respiratory exam on a man seated on the floor. She pulled the stethoscope from her ears and looked up as they entered.

"Saline IV, Stephen!" she called, needing no consultation with Janet to establish what was wrong with the boy. Only once did she pause in dealing with the newcomers, to exchange a questioning glance with Colonel Dixon. Apparently his nod was enough to re-assure her and she gave Janet a grateful smile.

"Doc? You'll be okay here?" asked Reynolds.

"Go," Janet said. "I'll come find you in an hour and we'll check in with Arbella." She grabbed another stethoscope from a nearby tray. Only peripherally was she aware of Reynolds and Dixon leaving the makeshift infirmary, as she busied herself with the comforting and familiar routine of treating those who needed help.

Arbella — 2098: Bailey's office was at the top of the CMF building and looked out across the lake. In the yellow morning light everything had a jaundiced appearance, the water turning drab beneath the mustard colored clouds. It wasn't very appealing.

"Nice view," Jack said as Bailey closed the door behind them. "Makes a change from all the trees." He considered the rocky landscape, arid and barren except for the strip of civilization along the lakeshore. "You have trees here?"

"Not here," Bailey said after a moment. "But further north there are forests. We harvest wood in the summer, before the ice-storms make it impossible."

He turned away from the window and found her leaning against the door, watching him with serious eyes. Over the past couple of weeks, he'd talked with Roz Bailey a great deal. She was a shrewd woman, practical and smart, and he was pretty sure she hadn't invited him here to talk about the Arbellan logging industry.

"I can't pretend that I really know you, Jack," she said. "But I've known *of* you all my life. They say you were — are — an honest man. A good man." She paused. "I need to know if I can trust you."

Good question. He was, after all, planning to end not only her life but the lives of everyone she knew, most of their ancestors and all of their descendants. He swallowed the queasy thought and said, "With what?"

She considered him. "With my life."

"I'm gonna need a little more than that."

Pushing herself away from the door, she turned and threw the bolt, locking them in. "I'm going to show you something," she said, her back to him. "If you tell the President or his intel officers what you've seen here, they will hang me."

Jack backed up a step. He had no idea what was about to happen and that made him nervous. So did the locked door. "How about we dispense with the Mystery Theatre and you just tell me what's going on?"

"I like that about you," Bailey said, facing him with a smile. "You're always straight to the point. A man after my own heart."

She crossed the room to a chest of drawers, opened the bottom one and lifted out a pile of papers. Setting them on the floor, she pulled out the drawer's false base and retrieved a cloth bag from inside. It looked like it contained a tennis ball; Jack suspected it was something infinitely more dangerous.

"No one knows I have a personal one of these," she said, setting the bag on her desk and opening it. As Jack had guessed, inside was one of the smaller Goa'uld communication devices.

He flexed his fingers, dispersing the anxiety tightening his muscles. "And who do you chat with on that thing?"

"Dix, of course. It's a back channel."

Jack let his surprise show. "I take it you and President Jones don't see eye-to-eye on 'Dix'?"

Bailey gestured for Jack to take a seat and sat down next to him so that they could both see the Goa'uld device. "Dix gave this to me two years ago," she said, "after Jones was elected. Before that..." She sat back in her chair, her gaze wandering out over the lake. "Dix and I had persuaded the previous President to approve a series of off-world missions. The idea was to look for new supplies, technologies..."

"Allies?"

She threw him a sharp look. "No. Our so-called allies let Earth die, Colonel. They could have saved us, but they let us die. We won't make that mistake twice. 'Never forget. Never forgive' — that's our credo now."

He tried to imagine what it must have been like to witness the end of the world and to know that allies you trusted — the Asgard, the Tollan, the Nox — had let it happen. Even Thor? Had he done nothing to intervene? He couldn't imagine it, probably because he still couldn't accept that it had really happened, all evidence to the contrary. "What about Dix?" he said eventually. "Isn't he an ally?"

"That's different." Bailey turned back to the communication device. "We need Hecate's Jaffa if we're going to drive the Wraith from Earth."

"Ah." That made him sit up a little straighter. "So that *is* the plan."

"It's my plan," Bailey said. "But it's not Jones' plan. Yet."

"Yet?"

From her pocket, she produced a photograph and handed it to Jack. It showed the smiling face of a young woman, pretty with short dark hair. "That's Lana Ewart, Jones' wife. She was a botanist on one of the teams we sent off-world. We were looking for ways to diversify our food supply and increase its nutritional density." Bailey shook her head. "Unfortunately, Lana's team never returned. They were taken by the Wraith."

Jack winced, struck by a memory of the creature trying to suck the life out of Carter. He could still remember the expression on its face as it pinned her to the wall. He shifted uncomfortably; the unexpected stab of fear and anger put him on edge. "And that's why opening the gate's not top of Jones' to-do list?"

"People like Gunnison Jones have always believed we're safer staying secret, staying hidden."

"But that's not what you think."

"I think we have a responsibility to do more," she said. "I think we have to reclaim our world from its enemies, not hide from them."

"I think you're right."

Bailey gave a thin smile. "Good," she said, reaching out to touch the communication device. "That's what I hoped you'd say."

"Hey, I didn't mean—"

Before Jack could protest any further, Rya'c's face appeared on the misty surface of the globe. He gave a serious bow, so much like his father. "Colonel O'Neill," he said. "I am glad General Bailey has persuaded you to join our cause."

Jack fixed the general with a glare. "Yes," he said. "She's a smooth operator."

Bailey ignored him, her attention fixed on Rya'c. "You have news?" she said.

"I do." He glanced to one side, obviously looking at something or someone else in the room. "With the aid of the Lady Hecate's healing," he said with a bow, "your man has woken from his delirium. "

Bailey sat forward. "And?"

"He has given his name as 'Jamie' and speaks as if the rest of his team still lives."

Bailey's shoulders sagged in relief. "Jamie Fraiser. Thank God…" She stopped, took a moment to compose herself, and then looked at Jack. "Jamie's one of our most gifted biochemists. I think you knew his grandmother."

Jack's heart cramped. "Janet?"

"Cassie."

He opened his mouth and then closed it again. He had no words for the way that made him feel.

Perhaps sensing that, Bailey didn't wait for a response. "Dix's men found Jamie some time ago," she said. "He was on Earth, wandering naked and incoherent. He didn't even know his own name." She nodded at the communication device. "The Lady Hecate has been caring for him; her healing technologies are more advanced than ours."

Jack didn't like the respect in Baily's voice when she talked about Hecate and he wondered how much she really knew about the Goa'uld as a species. Perhaps he should fill her in? But in the back of his mind he could hear Teal'c's stern voice:

we cannot be what these people wish us to be. That is not our purpose here.

Problem was, it was difficult not to give a damn when they were right there, fighting for their people. He huffed out a breath and, ignoring Teal'c's warning, said "You think this Jamie can lead you to the rest of your team?"

It was Rya'c who answered. "It is possible," he said. "But his grip on reality is fragile at best. Even when lucid, we cannot be sure that what he says is truth. And we must assume that he has been compromised."

After two years that was a certainty. Jack glanced down at the photo of the young woman — if she was still alive, she'd look very different now.

"The point is," Bailey said, "that there's a chance we can find Lana."

"And finding Jones' wife will convince him to start fighting back?" Jack was doubtful. "He seemed like a frightened man to me." Not to mention the fact that he was surrounded by NID creeps.

"Small steps, Jack," Bailey said. "If there's any chance of rescuing Lana, Jones will authorize an off-world mission. He loves his wife, and if we find her he'll have to start trusting Dix. Maybe then he'll listen to the Lady Hecate's plan to rid the world of the Wraith."

"I'm hearing lots of 'ifs'…"

Bailey spread her hands, acknowledging his point. "I'm not saying it'll be easy, but perhaps that's why fate brought you here, Colonel. If anyone can rescue Lana and rally support for intervention, surely it's the legendary SG-1?"

There it was again, that stupid hero-worship. He rubbed a hand over the back of his neck. "You really think Jones will let my team anywhere near the Stargate?"

"He will if he thinks there's a chance to find Lana."

"He'll want to send his own people," Jack said. "People he trusts."

Bailey shook her head, her smile turning wry. "Who will he send? CMF? His intel officers? Jack, with the passing of the First Generation we lost all combat experience. That's why our off-world team was taken so easily. Even Gunnison Jones understands that."

"I've seen Earth," Jack reminded her. "I've fought the Wraith. Even if your people are still alive, what you're asking us to do might not be possible."

"But isn't that what SG-1 did?" she said. "The impossible?"

Jack gave her a flat look. "Don't believe everything they say about us," he warned. "We're not superheroes."

"Maybe not." She leaned forward, elbows resting on her knees. "But if you want to leave Arbella, if you want to fight for Earth — and I think you do, Jack — then this is your best shot. It's the only way you're getting within a half mile of the Stargate."

Jack leaned back in his chair, studying her. She'd maneuvered him into a corner and they both knew it. He admired that. She had to be a tactician and she had to be hardnosed about it, but his gut told him she was honest too, that she wasn't spinning him a line. "I'll ask my team," he said in the end. "It's their call."

Bailey looked surprised. "Isn't it your call, Colonel?"

"I don't think so," he said. "Everything's different now."

Her bright eyes narrowed. "Be careful," she said. "Old lines matter here, Jack. That's what the First Gens taught us. Just because you've found yourself someplace new, don't forget where you came from. Don't lose who you are."

Jack glanced at Rya'c, First Prime to Hecate, and then at Bailey, leader of a fearful little colony on the edge of nowhere, and wondered if either of them realized how much they'd forgotten — or how much they'd lost.

He wondered whether it was his job to show them.

CHAPTER THIRTEEN

Earth — 2000: Though the parties from both sides of the gate had plenty to talk about, Janet found herself glad of the distraction in the infirmary. Dixon was bound to have questions that she wasn't sure she could answer. Questions like 'Can you help us?' Colonel Reynolds had been given explicit instructions that, at all costs, they were to prevent the survivors from travelling to Arbella — with the use of deadly force if necessary. Janet hoped fervently that it wouldn't come to that.

As it turned out, one hour became two. Once the patients in the infirmary had been dealt with, she was directed to other rooms that had been appropriated for wards. In there, she found patients with less severe injuries awaiting treatment. It was only when Reynolds tapped her on the shoulder that Janet realized how long she'd been away. "What time is it?" she asked, panicked that she'd missed the scheduled contact with Arbella.

"It's cool, Doc," said Reynolds. "I checked in and explained the situation. They expect contact at 1800. We've another hour by my watch. Dixon would like to see you now if you're done here."

She would never be done here while there were patients who needed her, but now was as good a time as any to talk to Dixon, so she pulled off her gloves and followed Reynolds out and down the corridor, to a small room at the other end.

Colonel Dixon sat at a small table and gestured for them to sit when they walked in. "Good work, Dr. Fraiser. Our medical officer has more on her hands than she can possibly handle," he said, pouring them each a foul smelling cup of coffee. "We have a civilian nurse working with her, but both of them are surviving on about two hours sleep per day. They appreciated the assistance."

"How many people you got here, Dixon?" Reynolds asked,

grimacing as he took a sip of the hot brew.

Dixon let out a breath and shook his head, as if calculating. "We started out with sixty-two personnel, made up of Air Force, RAF and Royal Navy. Lost fifteen, gained forty-three civilians. Forty-nine now, I guess." After a pause he said, "How's the kid?"

"He'll be okay. As long as he gets food, water and shelter."

"We can give him that. But the question is for how long."

A silence stretched, all three of them knowing what was not being said: the question that Janet had dreaded. None of them were willing to broach the subject. The tension was broken by the door opening. Dixon's CMO made her way to the table, apparently oblivious to the atmosphere, and slouched into the only empty seat without a word. She propped her elbows on the table and pushed up her glasses to rub her eyes. She widened them as if to ward off sleep, and then looked between Janet and Reynolds, as if just noticing them. "Oh," she said, "hello again."

"I take it you two have already introduced yourselves," said Dixon, pouring another cup of coffee and pushing it towards her.

Janet let go a short laugh. "Actually, no. We exchanged patient notes but not names. A professional failing, I think."

"In that case," said Dixon, "Surgeon Lieutenant Aitchison, this is Captain Dr. Janet Fraiser of the SGC. Janet, this is Beth Aitchison, Medical Officer of the Clyde Naval base."

Janet extended her hand to shake Dr. Aitchison's. "Clyde?" she asked, searching her memory. "You mean we're—?"

"You're in Scotland, Doctor," said Aitchison with a smile and a firm grip. "Best place to be at the end of the world. And considering the work you've just done here, I'll tell you I'm very pleased to meet you."

Janet looked to Dixon. "Scotland?" That explained the RAF and Royal Navy presence, not to mention Aitchison's accent.

Dixon shrugged. "General Hammond said find somewhere remote."

He glanced at Aitchison with a sheepish smile, and she

rolled her eyes. "Apparently Colonel Dixon was very surprised to find out we actually have television here." She blinked and gave a rueful smile. "*Had* television here. I'll never get used to saying that. So many 'hads' now."

Dixon laughed, not acknowledging her last comment. "First of all, that's a lie. Second of all, was I wrong? Stargate's still standing, isn't it?"

Aitchison rubbed her fingertips across her forehead, her eyes wide. "The Stargate. It still beggars belief that you can talk about it as if it's all so normal." She looked at Janet. "And you. I take it you're quite familiar with the whole thing? Because apparently we have two of the bloody things, in case you didn't know."

Janet smiled. "Yes, I've been CMO for Stargate Command for some time now." She gestured to the door. "You've certainly got your hands full here, Dr. Aitchison."

"And those are just the ones fortunate enough to get beds. It's mainly burns and trauma from the blasts and the fires. We're doing what we can."

"I can see that, Doctor," said Janet. "I'm not sure I could have coped so well." It was true. For all the harsh conditions back on Arbella, Janet realized they had it easy compared to what the survivors on Earth were dealing with. It was an impossible situation and Janet didn't know how she could make it better, though she desperately wanted to.

"We've lost a few to internal bleeding," continued Dr. Aitchison. "Most of our supplies from the base were exhausted in the first week. We just don't have the equipment or the resources, Doctor." Aitchison fixed Dixon with a pointed stare, as if this was a familiar but unresolved subject. "We need morphine and antibiotics. If I could just get across the water and into the naval base, there's a whole store—"

Dixon shook his head. "You know the answer to this, Doc. It's a Jaffa frat party over there. We can't risk it."

"So the sick die here," she said, with some rancor.

"Doc…" Dixon scrubbed a weary hand over his face, smoothing down the thick beard that had grown since Janet had last seen him at the SGC.

Aitchison took a breath. "Colonel, I'm afraid we have different priorities and I'm sorry to tell you I'll never let this go."

Janet understood Colonel Dixon's position, but in Aitchison's shoes, she knew she'd be making the same argument. "One thing that struck me," she said, keen to gain a more thorough perspective on the situation, "is that I didn't see any patients presenting with nausea or vomiting." Aside from the burns, it was the first thing she'd expected coming through the gate. "I assume there was a nuclear counterstrike?"

Aitchison shook her head. "We've been spared that at least. For now."

"And that means...?" asked Reynolds.

"It means the Goa'uld concentrated their offensive on major population centers — London, New York, Moscow," Dixon said. "But they only sent gliders and al'kesh into the Earth's atmosphere." His gaze moved to the ceiling. "With the exception of Cheyenne Mountain, the motherships stayed in orbit. So that's where we hit them back."

"With nukes," said Reynolds.

Dixon leaned forward, his elbows on his knees. "We hit them with everything, Al. For as long as we could. It wasn't enough. They're still up there."

"So what now? What are you going to do next?" Though Reynolds' determination was admirable, Janet cringed at his inability to understand the reality that was being lived here on Earth.

Dixon barked off a sardonic laugh. "You're not getting it, Reynolds. We're living day to day here. Without help from you guys, there is no next for us."

"Couldn't you go someplace else off-world?" Janet suggested, although it was hard to imagine where. They were barely surviving on Arbella, and that had been a fully supplied base before they arrived.

"The SGC is gone, Doc," Dixon snapped. "We've got no address list of friendly planets. And even if we did, we've got a MacGyvered DHD that only works half the time, no provisions, no meds…" He turned back to Reynolds. "General Hammond ordered me to keep the gate open to the evacuation site for as long as I could, Al, and I intend to obey that order. So, like it or not, it's on you to help us."

"Dave, I'm sorry," said Reynolds, his voice pained. "But I have orders. Even if I disobeyed them, as soon as we start letting people through the gate they'll shut that shield. Then you really will be on your own."

Dixon turned his hands palm up. "From what you've said, Al, we're already on our own."

Janet could say nothing to deny the accusation.

Arbella — 2098: It was a strange place to be, this human colony at the end of the world. The anthropologist in Daniel couldn't help but be fascinated each time he set foot outside the datacenter and walked alone through the streets.

Teal'c and Sam might see no future here, but Daniel saw it all around them. He saw it in the architecture, in the developing social order, in the mythology surrounding the colony's creation — but mostly he saw it in the faces of children whose cultural and ethnic heritage was so mixed that they were creating their own civilization, a civilization that was more Arbellan than anything else.

Arbella. Even the name was telling — the flagship of the Winthrop Fleet whose Pilgrim passengers had landed in Massachusetts and started a new world of their own. A very American choice, but of course those first evacuees through the gate had been almost entirely American. There were other influences evident in the colony now, though, that spoke of different nationalities. Daniel wondered how long the beta gate had remained open, how many people 'Dix' had helped flee to this new world. According to Elspeth's stories, the gate had stayed open for years — maybe even decades. He wondered where all those evacuees had come from and how warmly they'd been welcomed by the original colonists; it must have been more of a crucible than a melting pot.

It was fascinating to be here only a hundred years after the apocalypse, to see this reinvention of humanity, and yet it was devastating too. General Bailey had been right about the evacuation records, they were accurate, detailed, and incredibly painful. After three weeks immersed in the tragedy that had befallen Earth, in the First Generation's desperate struggle to survive, Daniel felt exhausted.

Familiar names leaped out from lists of the dead and the wounded. He felt a stab of pain for each one, a knot tightening in his chest. It didn't even ease at night, his fertile imagination taking flight in the darkness, breathing life into the dry statistics that told the colony's history.

Occasionally, though, there were moments of relief. He'd smiled when he saw the name Cassandra Fraiser handwritten at the bottom of the evacuation list, but in those penciled words he also saw Janet's desperate fight to get her daughter on the list. And he saw the faces of all those who couldn't get their children through, who'd stayed behind to die with them.

Harriman had gotten through, so had Colonel Reynolds. But not George Hammond. He wasn't surprised, of course; they'd set the self-destruct and Hammond would have stayed to see it done. But he couldn't help wondering whether this fractured colony would have been more united with a man like Hammond in command.

President Turner had made it through, of course, along with the Chiefs of Staff and a number of names Daniel didn't recognize but whose job titles spoke of congressional committees and White House lackeys. He wondered what use any of them had been in building this colony from the dust and dirt of a new world.

Pulling off his glasses, Daniel pushed the papers aside and

pressed his face into his hands. After three weeks, he couldn't read any more.

"Daniel?" It was Sam, looking uncertain in the doorway that led from the room where she'd been working on her computer model.

He looked up. "Hey."

"What's wrong?" she said, stepping into the small room that served as both archive and museum. She grimaced. "I mean, you know, aside from everything."

He dragged a smile onto his face. "Sorry," he said. "It's just…" He gestured around at the few artifacts that were on display: the SGC logo from the briefing room wall, the faded photographs of General Hammond and others, the heroes who'd died fighting for Earth.

Janet's face was among those photos, faded but painfully familiar. He'd seen her, what, less than two weeks ago? Two weeks before her world had come to an end. And now she'd been dead for a hundred years. In the records it simply said, 'Died in combat, 1999,' and although he already knew she was dead, that everyone he'd known was dead, it felt like bereavement to see her death recorded in black and white.

Sam glanced at the pictures on the wall, but her eyes shied away immediately. "Don't dwell on all this, Daniel. We're going to stop it from happening."

And right there, right then, he wanted to believe her. He wanted to believe that they could — that they should — prevent this future from unfolding. He wanted to keep his friends from having to live that nightmare. Yet he couldn't shake the feeling that the dice had already been rolled and that there was no going back. This was no mirror universe after all, this was their future.

With a sniff, he put his glasses back on. "How are you getting on?" he said, standing up to stretch his back. He felt stiff from sitting too long.

Sam made a face. "I've been thinking about it and I'm pretty sure I've gotten as far as I can go here."

"Meaning?"

"I need observational data to populate the model and at this point I have no idea how to get it."

"Observational data of the sun?" Daniel clarified.

"Of *a* sun, yeah — a sun near a Stargate we can actually access."

"Which isn't Arbella on either count."

"Doesn't look like it." She sank into thought for a moment, then, suddenly remembering why she'd come to find him, she said, "Colonel O'Neill's here. He wants to talk to us."

"About what?"

She gave an unhappy shrug and stepped a little further into the room. In a low voice she said, "I think the colonel's getting too involved with these people. I think he's lost focus on the mission."

Daniel glanced through the open door that led from the archive to the room where Sam had been working. Jack was leaning against the doorjamb, talking to Teal'c. Neither of them looked like they were enjoying the conversation.

"You don't feel for the people here?" Daniel said.

"Of course I do. But that's not the point, is it?"

And maybe it wasn't. He didn't know. He was too churned up to make sense of any of it anymore. But there was something niggling at the back of his mind, something he couldn't square. "It's just," he said, "when Apophis took Sha're, when she died, no one looked for a way to go back and stop it from happening."

"Daniel," Sam protested, "this is different."

"Is it?" It was a genuine question. "Why?"

"Because... Because something went wrong. We're only here because something went wrong."

"Sha're only died because something went wrong," Daniel countered. "Jack's son only died because something went wrong."

"No," she insisted. "This is different. It's... This future only happened because we weren't there to stop it."

"How do you know that?"

Sam chewed on it, but didn't find a reply. Through the doorway Daniel could see Jack watching him. He and Teal'c had probably heard the whole thing.

"Hey," Jack said, pushing himself away from the door. "You done? We need to talk about something."

Daniel glanced around the archive and wondered what 'done' could ever mean. He decided to answer the question he thought Jack was really asking. "I've got a pretty good idea of what happened immediately before and after the evacuation — which, by the way, occurred less than a week after we were due back from P5X-104. The records tail off after a couple months, though. I guess they had more important things to do than keep notes."

"Like survive?" Jack suggested.

"Right." Daniel glanced at Sam, at her closed-up face. "But there's something else," he said, "something we all need to hear."

Jack raised his eyebrows, but didn't object. Neither did Teal'c and a moment later they were all crowded into the small room that was somewhere between an archive and a museum dedicated to the First Generation.

Daniel indicated a gray control panel on the wall, a little below the battered SGC sign. Above the panel was written: *'Never forget, never forgive' — Major General George S. Hammond.* He'd been ignoring it for three weeks. "It's a recording," he said. "I thought we should hear it together."

"A recording of what?" said Sam.

"Of General Hammond's last message, broadcast through the Stargate before…" He swallowed. "Before the end."

Jack sucked in a sharp breath.

"I don't think I want to hear that," Sam said, retreating. "I mean, what's the point?"

"The point," said Jack, "is to honor him."

"But—"

"He died, Carter. They all did. We can't ignore that just because we might — I repeat, *might* — be able to change it someday."

Sam clamped her jaw shut. "Yes sir." But she looked upset, rigid as stone. She didn't want to face any of this, Daniel realized. Sam simply wanted to make it go away. He understood the sentiment, but it was a dangerous route to travel. Ignoring reality was never wise.

"Play it," Jack said, shoulders back, bracing himself.

Taking a deep breath, Daniel started the recording. There was a long hiss of static and then a familiar voice began to speak.

"This is a distress call from planet Earth. We are under attack and in need of assistance. If you have ever called yourselves our friends, we ask that you help us now. But if we must stand alone, we will stand strong. Though we may fall, we *will* fight. Though we may be outnumbered, we *will* endure. And for those who have abandoned us, know this: we will never forget. And we will never forgive. This is Major General George S Hammond, signing off."

The static continued for a couple more beats, and then all was silent.

Jack closed his eyes, so did Sam. Her mouth was a hard line of anger and Daniel wondered who she hated most right then — Apophis for attacking Earth, or their former allies for abandoning it.

Into the silence, Teal'c said, "Tell me now that you believe we can allow this reality to endure." He swept them all with his fierce gaze, letting it come to rest on Jack. "General Hammond pleads for the assistance of his friends," he said. "Are we not his friends, O'Neill? Are we not bound to assist him in Earth's darkest hour?"

Jack was still, impassive, but the tension in his shoulders gave him away. "What makes you think that's not what we're doing?"

Teal'c's eyes slid over to Sam.

Jack's gaze followed. "Carter?"

She looked uncomfortable, but nonetheless said, "Sir, we can't stay here any longer; we can't get involved with these people. If I'm going to make the predictive model work, I need to be able to study a star's surface up close. I need to return to Rya'c's ship."

"And you think you can get there without the cooperation of these people?" Jack said. "You think you can leave here and set up a lab on a Goa'uld mothership without getting involved? Is that it?"

Sam gave a small shake of her head, but didn't back down. "No, sir, but our interests and theirs are diametrically opposed. With all due respect, they're not going to help us."

"Can you blame them?" Daniel said.

"No, of course not, but if we stay here we'll get too drawn in. We'll never get home."

"Major Carter is correct," Teal'c said. "We must leave this place, O'Neill. To stay would be a mistake."

And that, Daniel thought, was a direct challenge.

Jack held Teal'c's glare for a long silent moment. It felt like everyone was holding their breath. "Well," Jack said eventually, his expression entirely neutral save the angry burn in his eyes, "it turns out that we might have a solution to that problem. General Bailey has a proposal."

CHAPTER FOURTEEN

Earth — 2098: The Lantean was gone, disappeared beyond the range of the Ancestors' device.

It was a bitter blow, especially to Stormfire. Sting had left him some days ago now, raving in his laboratory, tearing at his hair in frustration. There was nothing to be done with him in such wild moods and Sting's patience was thin; his own disappointment was no less keen.

A chance had slipped through their fingers and now it was lost.

How it had happened, they did not know. One moment the Lantean had been in orbit, presumably aboard Shadow's cruiser, the next the blinking light had gone dark. Dead, Stormfire said. It was not an improbable answer; if Shadow's clevermen had failed to understand what the Lantean was, he could have been fed upon and discarded.

Perhaps they should be grateful for that? Better that the Lantean die at her hand than that Shadow understand the power he offered her.

If they knew him to be dead, Sting would at least rest more easily. But they did not know. It was equally possible that Shadow had discovered the Lantean's potential and had already taken him to the Ancestors' city. Sting was sure it could hide him, if he commanded it.

But whatever the truth was, Sting needed to discover it.

There were no answers to be found in the ailing hive of Brightstar, however, nor in the sprawling human encampment beyond. And if the Lantean was lost, then it was more urgent than ever that they find an alternative place for Stormfire to continue his search; once the hive was dead it would putrefy and Stormfire with it if he remained behind.

So it was that Sting found himself in the woods on the

outskirts of a vast, ruined city. Destroyed by the murderous weapons of the parasite-gods, there was little left to see but the stubs of old buildings, grown through with trees and scrub in the years since the war.

In this place of devastation, Shadow had created her facility.

The central building was grown, some element of her hive seeded here. That in itself repelled him; the Wraith were a nomadic race, born for the stars, not to grub in the dirt like humans. A long history of persecution had taught them the risks of permanence, and yet, in this place, Shadow had overturned all the old ways. Though it revolted him, it did not surprise him to see the sheen of hive-flesh rooted in the ground.

He snarled and bared teeth. Had it not seemed fanciful, he would have said he could taste Shadow's corruption on the chill breeze that blew across the facility and stirred the trees around him. He looked up through their black bones to the sky. Far above, too high to be seen, a dart circled — Hearten was piloting, awaiting his order.

Sting had seen enough. It was time to act.

He found Hearten's mind, as sanguine as always, and said, *Now.*

The whine of the dart came as swift as Hearten's reply; he must have been closer than Sting had ordered. *Good fortune, brother,* Hearten said as the culling beam whipped through the trees. *Though you will not need luck.*

Sting's reply was cut off as the beam swept him up into the dart.

A moment later he was inside Shadow's facility.

The seedling hive was ahead of him, other buildings of baser human construction to his back. He looked around quickly, but saw no one. Hearten was already gone. One of their best pilots, he could coax a dart into the steepest of climbs and was lost in the planet's low cloud by now. So much the better.

The encampment was quiet and the out-buildings appeared unused. Sting moved past them toward the Wraith-grown structure, but the sudden sound of running feet behind him made him stop. He turned, hand dropping to his stunner and mind reaching for Hearten and rescue. A group of Wraith rounded the corner, a blade and four drones. They were moving fast, but not toward him. He let out a breath, relaxed his shoulders. They were armed with stunners, but Sting's attention was drawn to the heavy black cosh each man wore at his side; he had not seen such a weapon before.

Then the blade saw him and slowed his pace. His mind was young and full of bravado. Sting knew the type well and immediately assumed the bearing of command that had served him well in the zenana of Brightstar. He stepped into the path of the young blade, off-hand raised to halt him. *Where are you going?* Better to ask the question than to be asked himself.

The blade drew to a halt, his mind the keen edge of a knife. *To the preserving room,* he said. *There is a disturbance — again.* He cocked his head, teeth bared in suspicion. *I do not know you.*

No, Sting said. *And you should pray that you do not get to know me.*

Keenedge flexed his feeding hand. *And why so?*

Why indeed. Sting took a gamble. *Because I am sent by our queen to report on these 'disturbances'. She is displeased by their frequency.*

It is not our fault! Keenedge protested. *The revival pods damage the minds of the humans. It turns them into wild creatures. We have warned the clevermen but they—*

Sting gestured for silence. "Show me," he said aloud.

Keenedge gave a grudging nod and ran on. Sting fell in at his side, slowing as they approached the hive-building and watching Keenedge touch the panel to open the door. He wondered whether this fragment of hive had awareness enough to respond to the mind of a queen and navigate the infinity of space, or whether its consciousness was dull, fit only for the opening and closing of doors. He wondered, if he touched its flesh, whether it would know him as an enemy to Shadow. His fingers flexed but he dared not test the idea unless he had no other choice.

Inside, Keenedge led him along a corridor toward the sound of a fight, the drones following. He could hear a human shouting, the discharge of a Wraith stunner. A shrill scream — a female?

Keenedge began to sprint.

Further ahead, an archway opened onto a long room containing a number of large, strange-looking pods. Perhaps they had once belonged to the Ancestors? If Stormfire were here he would know; they were certainly not of Wraith origin.

Most of the pods were closed, but the three at the back of the room were open. A human female and two human males crouched on the floor next to them. They had subdued a Wraith — a cleverman, by his dress — who lay sprawled facedown and unconscious on the floor. He may even have been dead. One of the men crouched over him, bent double and banging his head against the floor until red blood flowed. The other sat behind him, his back to the wall and his legs drawn up beneath his chin, staring at nothing. The woman, feral looking, rocked on her heels between the men and Keenedge, as if on guard. Although, from the look in her eye, Sting thought she was more likely to run than fight.

He felt a stirring of hunger; it had been some time since he had fed, longer still since he had hunted. But this woman... He did not like the look of her. There was something about her skin, stretched too thin, that felt distasteful.

Then the man crouching over the fallen Wraith looked up and Sting recoiled in horror. The man's mouth and stubby teeth were covered in blood — Wraith blood. "Not so tasty," he said. "But we can feed too, see? We can feed on you bastards too."

The human had sunk his teeth into the cleverman's feeding hand. Sting could see the wound gaping and black with blood.

Keenedge snarled and Sting shared his disgust. "Animals,"

the blade hissed. He raised the cosh he carried, but at the sight of it the human woman screeched and leaped forward, knocking Keenedge off-balance. He staggered sideways until a drone grabbed the woman and threw her, snapping and snarling, back to the floor.

"Come closer and I'll kill him!" the human male warned. He had no weapon, but he bared blooded teeth. "I'll rip his throat out, I swear."

The woman, her ragged clothing torn, resumed her rocking. One arm appeared wounded; she held it at a strange angle. She was a pitiful specimen; they both were. Sting wondered why Keenedge didn't just kill them.

That is Adroit, Keenedge answered, mind-to-mind. *Do you not see?* His surprise was evident. *We cannot risk harm befalling him.*

Sting knew Adroit, Master of Sciences Biological. He had once served Brightstar and Sting had called him friend. To camouflage his unease, he said, *How is it that he was not better protected?*

I do not know. Keenedge's attention moved to Adroit. *He should not be in the preserving rooms alone. He has been warned how the humans behave when revived.*

Revived?

Sting turned his attention back to the humans. The second man hadn't moved from his position by the wall. If he was possessed of the same madness that drove the others, it did not show. Even so he bore little resemblance to the free humans Sting had hunted in the feeding grounds of home. Nor did he look like the humans in the encampments of this planet. Somehow, this one, like the other two, appeared hollow, as if his skin were stretched over something decaying. Repulsive, Sting thought, in every way repulsive.

We must retrieve Adroit, Keenedge said.

Sting nodded and lifted his stunner. The woman growled at him, her red-rimmed eyes full of hatred and hunger. He fired and she writhed beneath the energy discharge. But she did not fall, she did not stop.

"They don't work!" Keenedge growled as the woman launched herself at Sting, her jaws snapping as if she might bite him. He flung her back in disgust, but she was tenacious, her bony fingers strong.

Keenedge grabbed her and she screamed, but not so loud as the male crouching over Adroit. He threw back his head and howled like a beast. Then he bared his gory teeth and fell on the throat of Adroit.

At that moment, the other male acted. From behind his back, he produced a weapon — some piece of metal or a rock — and brought it down hard on the human's head. The man collapsed atop Adroit, bleeding scarlet from the wound opened in his skull.

The woman began to wail, but Keenedge turned her around and plunged his feeding hand into her chest, silencing her. Sting turned away; the thought of feeding on such a creature revolted him.

Her body fell to the floor and Keenedge growled his satisfaction. "Put the husk into a pod," he ordered one of the drones. "I will see to Adroit."

Sting watched in bemusement as the drone lifted the woman's husk and laid it inside one of the pods, closing the device. He could not imagine its purpose.

Pulling the unconscious human from Adroit's body, Keenedge crouched and turned the cleverman over. "He lives," he said, examining Adroit's throat and then lifting his hand to inspect the wound. "The human did not damage him greatly."

"Yes, yes," the remaining human, the one holding the bloody piece of metal, shuffled closer. "I saved him. I'm loyal. Everyone says I'm loyal, yes? I won't betray you."

Keenedge peered up at the human. "As is right, Steadfast."

The human nodded so hard his head looked like it might snap from his scrawny neck. There were few Wraith worshipers on this planet, yet it appeared that this 'Steadfast' was one such.

Silently, Keenedge ordered the drones to take Adroit to be treated for his wounds. *Do you wish to go with him?* he asked Sting.

He did not; when Adroit regained consciousness he would recognize Sting. Also, he wished to know more about this room, these devices. *What of *him*?* he said, nudging the fallen human with the toe of his boot. Adroit's blood still rimmed his slack mouth.

Feed, if you are hungry, Keenedge said.

I prefer to hunt my food, Sting said, which earned him a curious look. He spread his hands, to show no offence. *I am old-fashioned.*

You would not be so fastidious in deep space, Keenedge grunted. *And light years from a feeding ground.*

It was a strange comment.

"I would not," Sting said out loud so that he could keep his mind closed. He did not want to reveal his ignorance, nor his growing suspicion about the use of these pods. Was it possible that they somehow bestowed the gift of life on the humans?

Put this one in a pod, Keenedge said to a drone. Then, to Steadfast, "You, come here."

Steadfast did as he was bid, head ducked in submission. Keenedge grabbed his face, squeezing his chin between the fingers of his off-hand and forcing him to look up. "You served us well today."

Steadfast nodded. "Yes, always. I am loyal."

"Then you deserve a reward." Keenedge settled his feeding hand against the human's bare chest. Steadfast gasped, eyes rolling back as Keenedge began to feed. But he stopped while Steadfast was still conscious, his body marked by the feeding but not dead. Keenedge released him, letting the human stagger away.

"Thank you," Steadfast said, pressing a hand over the wound on his chest. "Thank you…"

"Now get into your pod."

Sting watched without comment as the human stumbled over to the remaining open pod and clambered inside, lying down with a great effort. Keenedge touched a control and the pod's lid closed. His eyes lifted to meet Sting's. *The humans enjoy the pods,* he said. *They crave it. This is his reward.*

He wanted to ask more, to confirm his theory, but dared not. He had long ago learned that silence was a most effective form of interrogation; someone will always attempt to fill it.

It will be glorious, Keenedge said eventually, *when Shadow's hive is equipped with sufficient pods to feed us all.*

Sting held his silence.

Then, we will not need the Ancestor's city to traverse between galaxies. We will not need the help of any Lantean to pilot it. He curled his hand on top of the pod, caressing it with well-shaped talons. *Our reach will be infinite and all will fall beneath Shadow's power. We will be unstoppable. Masters of the galaxy.*

Sting barely nodded, too busy processing the revelation to respond. He was right, then; the pods gave the humans the gift of life. Somehow, in a way he did not fully understand, they returned even the dead to health. The implications were enormous, for a limitless food supply would break all the chains which bound the Wraith to their feeding grounds, to the cycles of culling and sleeping that had shaped them as a race.

But such food as this? Depraved and corrupted humans, restored to life repeatedly by alien technology, un-hunted and un-culled: what would feeding on such fouled creatures do to his kind?

It might make them masters of the galaxy, but would they still be Wraith?

CHAPTER FIFTEEN

Arbella — 2098: "Thoughts?" Jack said, once he'd finished outlining the plan.

There was a general pause, a couple of weighted glances thrown about, and then Daniel said, "One question: how do we recognize Jones' wife even if we find her?"

"Photo." Jack fished out the picture Bailey had given him. "Lana's got a mole, right there on her cheek. It should be pretty distinctive even if…" He let that thought trail off and Daniel gave a grim nod.

"At least this gets us back to Rya'c's ha'tak," Carter said, "which gives me a better shot at the observational data I need." She was looking at Jack, but he got the feeling her words were aimed at Teal'c. "Not to mention the fact that Rya'c has an operational Stargate, when the time comes."

If, Jack added silently. *If the time comes.* He just nodded, though, and turned to Teal'c. "I know what you're gonna say."

Teal'c raised an eyebrow, hands clasped behind his back. "Rescuing this woman from the Wraith does not further our mission."

"Yep," Jack nodded. "That was it."

"However," Teal'c continued, "I agree with Major Carter. Returning to Hecate's ha'tak would be of more use than remaining here. Once aboard, we could travel elsewhere in search of assistance — perhaps there are those among the Tok'ra still able to assist us?"

"Or," Daniel said, peering over the tops of his glasses, "we could actually do what we've been asked to do and rescue Jones' wife from the Wraith."

Silence. Carter looked awkward, Teal'c stiffened. "To endanger our lives on a mission of no value would be unwise."

"So…" Daniel glanced at Jack, and then carried on anyway.

"What you're suggesting is that we tell Bailey we're going to find this woman and then we just… don't?"

"We must do whatever is necessary to protect the future, Daniel Jackson."

"It just seems a little… dishonorable."

Teal'c's eyes narrowed. "Is it not less honorable to ignore General Hammond's plea for aid, and turn our backs on our friends in their hour of direst need?"

Daniel grimaced but didn't answer. Jack wasn't sure there was an answer, at least not one they could all agree on, and he was reminded of Bailey's caution about old lines and not forgetting who you were in this strange new world. In his case, it meant he was in command and got to make the tough calls — at least for now.

"We're taking the mission," he said, in a tone that brooked no argument. "Bailey's right, it's our only chance to leave Arbella without fighting our way to the gate. And, frankly, I don't like our odds in that fight."

"O'Neill—"

"Ah!" He held up a hand for silence. "I don't care how screwed up this future is, Teal'c, we don't lie to our friends. If I tell Bailey we're taking the mission, then we're taking the mission. Once it's done…" He let that hang for a moment. "Well, then we can look at our options. At least we won't be stuck here."

Teal'c said nothing, but Carter gave a short nod; she understood where he was coming from. Daniel just dug his hands into his pockets and avoided looking at Teal'c, as if it might be construed as gloating over his victory.

If you could call this a victory.

When they arrived in the gate room later that day, the atmosphere was strained. Bailey and Jones stood together in an unconvincing show of unity, their respective forces in position on either side of the gate room. The President's intelligence officers watched SG-1 with blatant distrust, while the

CMF forces looked like they might follow them through the Stargate given half a chance. Jack saw Jefferson and Kiowa among ranks and threw them a wave as the gate began to spin. They grinned like kids.

"Colonel O'Neill."

Turning around, he was surprised to see President Jones step past his honor guard and walk toward him. "Mr. President?" Jack said.

Jones hesitated, glanced back at the woman, Agent Yuma, who was watching him closely, then fixed Jack with an intense look. "Find my wife," he said in a low voice. "Bring Lana home to me and I'll be in your debt, Colonel."

"We'll do everything we can, sir," Jack said, and meant it. Whatever else Jones was, he knew grief and loss and that was something Jack understood.

Saying no more, Jones just nodded and then stepped back hurriedly as the wormhole exploded out into the room.

Fear was ripe; even General Bailey watched the event horizon with unease as she came to attention and offered a sharp salute. "Good luck, Colonel," she said. "Our prayers go with you."

Jack returned the salute and then turned to face the open wormhole, taking a moment to settle the weight of his weapon in his hands. He took a breath and started walking. "SG-1," he said, "we have a go."

With Daniel at his side, Carter and Teal'c behind, he strode into the wormhole and left Earth's last outpost.

A moment later they stood face-to-face with the Jaffa reception committee. "Hi," Jack said, eyeing the staff weapons pointed at them. "Hope you guys didn't wait up."

"Colonel O'Neill." Rya'c stepped forward and offered a courteous bow as his men lowered their weapons. "I am glad you were able to return."

Which translated as: I'm glad they let you go. "Me too," Jack said.

"Major Carter, Daniel Jackson," he said. "Father."

Teal'c inclined his head in a slight bow, but didn't speak. Jack felt a spike of irritation; however screwed up things were, the man was still Teal'c's son. Why the hell couldn't he treat him like it?

After a beat Rya'c said, "Follow me. I will take you to the man we found. Perhaps you can understand his words better than us."

"We'll do our best," Daniel said.

The patient, if that was the right word, was being held in a room that did, in fact, look more like a hospital than a cell. He lay on a narrow cot, pushed hard against a blank white wall, his eyes closed. He was thin to the point of emaciation, but not sucked dry like victims of the Wraith.

"This is Jamie Fraiser," Rya'c said.

Daniel glanced up. "Fraiser as in...?"

"Cassie," Jack said and tried to trace her features in the man's — Jamie's — face. But it was no good, he was too skeletal. He just looked sick.

"He spends much time asking for sleep," Rya'c said. "And light."

"Sleep deprivation?" Carter guessed, with a quick look at Jack. They both knew he was familiar with that, and worse. He just shrugged — it was possible — and she took a step closer to get a better look at the guy. "How long was he a prisoner?" Carter hadn't let go of her MP5, holding it defensively in front of her. Jack guessed that, like Teal'c, she was trying hard not to get involved with these people. Unlike Teal'c, Carter looked like it was a struggle.

"For over two years," Rya'c said. "They were taken by Wraith on another world, but we found him on Earth. They must have brought him there."

"Brought him to Earth?" Daniel reached out and touched his fingers to Jamie's head. "I wonder why."

At his touch, the man's eyes flew open and Daniel pulled back his hand. "Sorry," he said. "I didn't mean to wake you."

But Jamie was looking with unseeing eyes, his waxy skin sunken and yellow. "The bright sleep," he said in a scratchy voice and grabbed Daniel's wrist. "Where is it?"

Jack made a move forward, but Daniel waved him back. "It's okay," he said. Then, to Jamie, "It's okay. What is it you need?"

"The light," he whispered. "I need the light."

Daniel closed his free hand over Jamie's fingers. "There's light here," he said. "No one's turning it off." Squeezing his hand he said, "Can you tell me where you were held?"

"On the farm," Jamie said, clutching Daniel's arm, "they're breeding. They're breeding monsters."

Daniel's eyebrows rose. "Okay. What exactly do—?"

Jamie bolted upright, staring around as if seeing them for the first time. "Don't take me back!" he said, huddling against the wall.

"We won't," Daniel said. "You're not going back. But we need your help to free your friends."

Jamie shook his head, pressed his forehead into his knees. "No, no," he muttered, his voice muffled. "No friends. No friends anymore, just monsters in the water and cattle in the pens. All dead until the light comes. All dead."

"When he becomes agitated," Rya'c said, nodding to one of his men, "he must be sedated."

"Wait." Jack put himself between Jamie and the approaching Jaffa. "Just wait. Daniel…?"

With a nod, Daniel rested his hand lightly on Jamie's shoulder. "Are your friends alive, Jamie? Are they still in the farm?"

Jamie shook his head, started knocking it against the wall. "In the pens," he said. "Like cattle in pens, waiting for the monsters. Waiting for the light. Where's the light?" He looked around, eyes narrowing in sudden anger, and grabbed Daniel's shirt, knotting his fingers into the fabric. "Give it to me," he hissed. "I earned it. I died for it!"

"Colonel?" Rya'c said and Jack stood back, letting the Jaffa press something into Jamie's neck. A moment later he slumped.

Daniel caught him and helped lay him down, folding his hands on top of his chest.

"Are we any the wiser?" Jack said, catching Carter's eye.

She shook her head. "I don't know, sir." She looked at Rya'c. "Where did you find him? Was it in the Shacks?"

"No," he said. "But close. We think he escaped the Wraith when you attacked their ship above the camp."

Carter smiled at that, a fierce little expression. "At least some of them got out," she said.

Some of the many trapped like insects waiting to be eaten. Jack could still remember the faces of those they'd had to leave behind. "This 'farm'," he said, pushing the memory aside. "Is it there, in Colorado?"

"My people have looked, but we have found no such thing," Rya'c said. "But that is not a surprise; the snatcher beams transport their prey great distances across the planet."

"Just like we were," Carter reminded them. "We ended up a couple time zones away from where we started."

Jack gave a frustrated sigh. "So it could be anywhere."

"Maybe not." Daniel pulled off his glasses and pinched the bridge of his nose, thinking. "Like cattle in pens," he said. Then he looked at Jack. "We've heard that description before."

They had, back in a fire-lit cave on Earth.

"Aedan Trask," Carter said, catching on. "He talked about seeing a camp where humans were penned like animals and fed on by the Wraith."

"What are the odds of it being the same place?" Jack said. "Earth's a big planet."

Daniel scratched a hand through his hair, thinking. "I don't know," he said. "The whole thing seems a little strange. I mean, if they're keeping humans to feed on, how come he's still alive after two years?" He looked at Jamie, whose his face was now slack and unresponsive. "I feel like there's something I'm missing."

Jack paused for a beat to see if Daniel had anything else

to add, but he was lost in thought, so Jack said, "Either way, I guess Aedan Trask is the only lead we've got. And at least we know where to find him."

"I will speak with the Lady Hecate about your return to Earth," Rya'c said. "We risk discovery by the Wraith ship if we leave our current orbit, but I will seek permission for you to travel to Earth's beta gate. Since that is how you first arrived it will be close to the people you seek, and I believe the Lady Hecate will be amenable to the idea."

"We'll be stuck there," Carter pointed out. "The gate has no power and no DHD."

"The Lady Hecate can provide you with a naquadah reactor and a portable dialing device," Rya'c said. "It will allow you to use the Stargate, but it will not protect you from the Wraith should they be close when you arrive."

"We know the risk," Jack said.

Bowing in acknowledgement, Rya'c made to leave.

"Hey, how about we come with you to see your boss?" Jack said, deciding to push it a little. "We haven't been introduced."

"That is impossible. The Lady Hecate sees only me."

"A little reclusive, isn't she, for a Goa'uld?"

Rya'c's gaze slipped sideways, over Jack's shoulder. "It has always been so," he said, and beckoned to one of his men. "Take our guests to the gate room and ensure they are provisioned. I will join you there shortly."

Jack watched him leave, watched Teal'c continue to ignore his son, and felt another stab of anger; he'd give anything to have Charlie back, even fully grown and in charge of a Jaffa army. He'd give his life to see his boy again and here was Teal'c pissing away his relationship with his son. "For crying out loud, Teal'c—"

"Sir?" Carter's tone was light but cautionary. She gave a little shake of her head: *Not now.*

He took a breath, pushed his anger and loss back into the dark where he kept it, and fell in next to Daniel as they were shepherded out of the room. Teal'c strode ahead, putting as much distance between himself and Rya'c as possible, Carter a step behind him.

"You know," Daniel murmured, as they brought up the rear, "I'm getting a funny feeling about Hecate."

Jack grunted. "I'm gonna start calling her the Great and Powerful Oz."

CHAPTER SIXTEEN

Earth — 2000: They made for a solemn group as they stood at the silent gate, Janet and Reynolds already past due for their scheduled return to Arbella. Janet supposed they were going home now, back to a planet of red dust, cloying heat and a sky that looked wrong. She'd only been here for a few hours, but despite the darkness and distant sound of bombing, despite the fact that technically she was on the other side of the world from Colorado, she'd known that *this* was home as soon as she'd set foot on the concrete floor, connected through her boots to the very bones of Earth. This was home, this was where she belonged, and yet here she was, about to say goodbye to it once more. This time, perhaps forever.

The low light cut the edges of their faces out from the dark of the bunker in stark orange lines. She wondered if she looked as weary as Dixon. She certainly felt it.

"Dave." Colonel Reynolds extended a hand to Colonel Dixon, a gesture of comradeship that went beyond their military rank. "I'm sorry. Truly."

Dixon grasped the hand and shook it. "I know, Al. So am I, buddy."

"You know that we have authority to take one person back with us. You were on that evac list. You have a place on the other side."

Dixon's smile was tired and sad, but his expression was determined. He shook his head. "My place is here, Colonel."

Reynolds nodded slowly. "Figured you'd say that."

After their earlier conversation, Janet had realized too that honor would keep Dixon on Earth. The offer of refuge on Arbella was real, from the mouth of the President himself, but it meant nothing to Dixon, not while others would be left behind.

He turned and nodded to the airman who stood at the

DHD, waiting for the order to dial out. A few seconds later, the gate began to spin.

Dixon let go a sudden, frustrated sigh and looked up at the gate as the chevrons locked. "God! If they could just see what we're living through here, surely they'd understand. Surely they wouldn't let these people die here."

Behind them, the gate whooshed into life, fusing its liquid blue with the orange sodium glow. Reynolds moved toward the makeshift ramp, but on impulse Janet reached out and halted him.

"Colonel, what would happen if I didn't go back right now?"

Reynolds narrowed his eyes. "We have orders, Doc."

"I'm ranking medical officer. My decision overrules any orders."

"Yeah, on medical matters."

"I'd say this is one big medical matter." She glanced back at Dixon who was watching the exchange intently. "Dr. Aitchison said there was a supply of meds in the naval base. Are there antivirals?"

He shrugged. "I guess so. From what she says, there's a pretty extensive supply."

"Then show me. Whatever's in that base could be a bargaining chip we can use." She looked back at Reynolds.

He said nothing for a moment, then took a breath and straightened. "Seems to me there are a few medical emergencies that need your expertise here, Doctor. Your orders are to remain here until you're done."

"Thank you, sir."

He gave a grim nod. "Make it worth it." He walked up the ramp, before halting once more. "Oh, Doc, do you have a camera?"

She shook her head, confused.

He pulled the pack from his shoulder and crouched down on the floor, searching through its contents. When he rose, he held a small camcorder. He tossed it to Janet and she turned it over in her hands, thinking suddenly of Daniel and the hours of footage he'd bring back from a mission. To everyone else, it looked like endless shots of walls and stone, but Daniel could pore over those shots and extract all kinds of meaning from them.

She flipped open the tiny screen and glanced at Reynolds. "Sir?"

"Make a record. Let them see. Who knows what good it might do?" He paused then, and put his hand on her shoulder. "You understand what you're taking on here, Janet?"

She looked down at the tiny gadget and considered the course ahead. To leave this bunker was to face whatever dangers lay on the surface, and by Dixon's account it was a formidable environment — less a warzone and more a decimated wasteland now. The risks would be high, and there was no guarantee that anyone on Arbella would even listen to her.

The hum of voices and movement in the vast gate room seemed louder in that moment, the sounds of lives being lived, military and civilian alike thrown together by circumstance and doing the only thing they could think to do: survive. She thought of Dr. Aitchison and her hopeless task of saving a people for whom extinction seemed inevitable, yet not once did she waver. And nor should she. Theirs was an oath to maintain the utmost respect for human life and it made no provision for the end of the world.

"I understand, sir," she said, "but I have to do what I can."

Reynolds nodded and turned to Dixon. "You want them to see what it's like here? Then show them. I don't know if it'll make any sort of difference, but I can't go back there without trying something."

In the flickering light, it was hard to discern Dixon's expression, but when he spoke his tone was sober and grateful. He knew this was a last ditch hope. "Thank you."

"There's about four hours battery on that camera. Make it count," said Reynolds, and checked his watch. "Contact in

T-minus twelve hours, Doctor. And I don't have to tell you, if you're not here, I can't guarantee we'll call back. If you can, be here. If you can't…"

He didn't need to finish that sentence. There would be many reasons for her not being able to make it back — and most of them were permanent. But if this was her only chance to help these people, *her* people, then she'd take it. The consequences, she'd think about another day.

Earth — 2098: "The phrase 'Back to square one' springs to mind," the colonel said as he picked himself up off the cold, ashy ground.

Daniel was already on his feet, dusting himself down. "On the plus side," he said, "I don't have a giant hole in my side this time."

"There's that," the colonel conceded, squinting back at the cockeyed gate. "Rough landing," he said. "Someone needs to straighten that thing up."

Sam spared him a slight smile, but kept her finger on the trigger as she did a slow three-sixty. "I'll add it to my to-do list, sir," she said, scanning the horizon. No sign of any Wraith.

A moment later the generator fell through the gate and onto the ground, puffing up a cloud of ash — radioactive ash. Teal'c emerged last, the only one of them not to fall on their ass as he dropped into a low crouch and caught his balance.

"Show off," the colonel said, and reached into his pocket for his sunglasses. Although the sun was hidden behind cloud, the sky was white and glared against the ashy ground.

At least it wasn't snowing this time, Sam thought. Lowering her weapon, letting the others take over the watch, she reached into her vest and pulled out the dialing device Rya'c had given them. "Sir," she said, "I'm going to connect the generator and test the portable DHD."

He nodded. "Make it quick, Carter. We're sitting ducks here."

"Yes sir." Crouching down next to the generator, she connected it to the gate and then powered up the portable dialing device. It was clever and she wondered where Rya'c had got it. The design wasn't Goa'uld. It looked like it might be Tollan, or— "Oh!"

"Oh?" the colonel said.

"Um, one moment, sir." She looked at the data output again, scrolled down the display and felt something bright pop in her chest. "Colonel!" She looked over her shoulder, didn't bother to swallow her grin. "This device can interface directly with the Stargate and it just downloaded the last seven — scratch that, eleven — gate addresses the gate connected to, as well as the telemetry for each wormhole."

The colonel didn't try to play dumb. "Including the trip that brought us here in the first place?"

"Yes sir," she said. "Just retrieving the data now. It's…" She frowned. "Wait, that can't be right, that…" But it was right; it was just definitely not what she was expecting. "Holy Hannah."

"Carter?" The colonel took a step toward her, his boots crunching in the dirt. "A little more detail?"

"Sorry sir," she shook her head, refocused on the data. "It's, um… I don't think it was a solar flare that brought us here, sir. I think it was something else."

"Like what?"

"I don't know, but according to the telemetry we were actually in transit, in real time, for 861,480 hours." She looked up at him, his face a shadow against the white sky. "That's a little under ninety-eight years, sir."

"What?" Daniel said, coming to join them. "We were in transit that whole time? How's that possible?"

She shook her head. "I don't know. I didn't think it *was* possible."

"Maybe Rya'c's device is hinky?" the colonel said.

"Maybe." But she was doubtful.

"Does it change anything?"

"I guess not." Standing up, she disconnected the dialing device.

"Okay," he said. "Then file it under 'interesting, but not urgent' and let's get the hell out of here."

"Yes sir."

As the colonel and Daniel moved away, scanning the surrounding hills, Sam's attention was caught by something else: a little pile of stones, ten paces from the Stargate. She felt a pang of loss as she trotted over. A few of the stones had fallen away in the days since she'd set the marker, but her SG-1 patch was still visible — waiting for the rescue that would never come. She crouched down and looked at it, rain-sodden and contaminated with radiation by now. She didn't touch it. A month had passed since she'd left it there, convinced that General Hammond would send people after them and confident that all they needed to do was make camp and wait. But their friends had been dead the whole time and the colonel had been right all along; no one was coming to find them.

"Carter! We're moving out."

"Yes sir," she said and hurried to join the others.

"Teal'c, take point," the colonel ordered. "Head up into the tree line as soon as possible, then strike east."

"As you wish," Teal'c said, making no attempt to hide his disapproval of the mission. The colonel's jaw was set but he didn't comment, just waved Daniel and Carter ahead of him.

The gray hills and scrappy trees were unchanged, and she could see a thin dusting of snow in the distance. But it felt different. The knowledge that this blasted landscape was home sat like a stone in the pit of her stomach. She couldn't help but wonder how many people had died here, people like her, like Mark and the kids. Innocent civilians destroyed by alien invaders they knew nothing about.

It was dangerous, negative thinking. And she knew she didn't have time for that kind of distraction, not if she was going to fix this whole mess. So, instead, she started trying to figure out where exactly on Earth they were. Nothing looked familiar. It could be anywhere, really, north or south of the planet. But it must be close to one of the poles, to have such long nights.

As before, there was no life to be seen and no sound but the distant wash of the sea. She remembered that last time the colonel had seen a light on the horizon, across a body of water, and she wondered what it had been: Wraith or human? Back then, they hadn't known what they were looking at.

"Hey, you doing ok?" She glanced up to find the colonel walking along next to her, watching her the way he sometimes did, with a little more Jack than colonel in his eyes.

"I keep thinking about when we first got here," she admitted. "I was so sure they'd find us, but if we'd waited for rescue, Daniel might have—" She broke off and glanced at Daniel walking ahead of them, his long strides eating up the ground. He was strong again, and healthy. No thanks to her.

"No point dwelling on might-haves, Carter," the colonel said. "Waiting for rescue would have been the right call, in normal circumstances."

"Normal circumstances," she said with a slight smile. "Right."

"You couldn't have known, Carter."

That was true. There had been no real clues, nothing to indicate that this desolate place was home. "I could have trusted you more, sir," she said. "Not doubted you so much."

"Carter…" He kept his gaze roving, watchful as they walked. "I was trying to *make* you doubt me."

"Really?" She frowned. "Why?"

"Part of the mission," he said. "You needed to believe that I was nuts enough to steal some Tollan gadget just because I was pissed off with them for not sharing."

Despite herself, Sam laughed. "I'd never have believed that, sir."

"Then I guess the mission would have been a bust." He threw her a quick glance, a curious look in his eyes. "They were going to retire me," he said, "and hope Maybourne recruited me into his shadow team."

"Wow." She tried to imagine what it would have felt like to

see the colonel dismissed from the Air Force, what it would have felt like to think he'd betrayed what they were fighting for. Not good, she decided. Not good at all. "I guess I'm glad we didn't have to go through that, sir."

The colonel huffed something like a laugh. "Yeah, because this is so much better."

"Silver linings," she said.

"Right, silver linings." He gave a ghost of a smile. "You know we—"

"O'Neill!" Teal'c lifted his arm, signaling a halt, and raised his weapon. "There is movement in the trees."

"Crap." The colonel reached for his gun, stepping up next to Teal'c while Sam and Daniel dropped back and took positions either side.

She scanned the trees where Teal'c was looking, but his eyes were sharper than hers and it took a few moments before she saw them: figures flitting through the trees, running down the hillside.

"They're Aedan's people," Daniel said, relieved. He took half a step forward.

"Hold your position," the colonel growled.

"But Jack—"

"Hold your position!"

With a sigh, Daniel subsided and waited with the rest of them as they were swiftly surrounded by a group of young men. They certainly looked like Aedan's people, dressed in the same rough fabric and animal skins he'd worn, and armed with what, Sam now knew, were Wraith stun weapons.

But it was disturbing, meeting these people now that she knew who they were — *where* they were. Instead of seeing them as descendants of an ancient society taken from Earth by the Goa'uld, she saw in their gaunt faces and medieval clothing the decline and fall of her own civilization.

"Hey," the colonel said. He kept his hands on his weapon but left it at port arms. "We're looking for Aedan Trask."

There were a few sharp looks thrown around the group, and then one of the men swaggered forward. He lacked the charm she remembered Aedan possessing, but then again the kid was young. He was nineteen if he was a day and he looked like he had something to prove. "Maybe Aedan Trask doesn't want to be found."

"Well that's a shame," the colonel said, "because we need his help."

"And why should he help you?"

The colonel gave a flat smile. "Because we're—"

"Daniel Jackson!" The excited cry came from further up the slope and a moment later a familiar figure came bursting out of the woodland, hurtling down the hill. "Daniel!"

"Elspeth," Sam said with a smile of relief. At least there was one friendly face.

"Someone's pleased to see you," the colonel said, watching in amusement as the girl crashed through the men surrounding them and flung her arms around Daniel.

"Elspeth!" The kid in charge looked mortified. "Get out of there."

"I knew you'd come back!" Elspeth said, ignoring him. "I told them you would!"

Laughing, Daniel grabbed her shoulders and set her on her feet. "It's good to see you too," he said.

Her eyes widened. "And you've recovered." She touched his side where his wound had been. "So fast? Meagan said you'd not last two days."

"Oh, I—" He stopped. "Really? Two days?"

"She said the infection was in your blood and there's no cure for that anymore."

"Well," he adjusted his glasses. "I, uh, I guess I got some good medicine."

Yeah, it was probably best, Sam figured, not to mention that a Wraith had healed him.

"Elspeth, get over here," the kid snapped. "I'm—"

"Ah, stop flapping your lips, Geraint Arden," Elspeth said. "No-one's impressed."

That seemed to be true; Sam caught a couple of smirks among their would-be captors and Geraint flushed an angry pink.

"You'll come back with us?" Elspeth said. "Aedan was sure you'd be husked by the Devourers by now, but I knew he was wrong. I knew you'd come back." She seized Daniel's arm, her wide eyes earnest. "But did you find him?" she said. "Is that who cured you?"

Daniel blinked. "Um, did I find who?"

"Dix!" Elspeth said. "Did you find the resistance? Did you find a way to leave?"

"Ah. Well," he cast a quick look at the colonel, "as it happens, yes. Yes we did."

For a moment, Elspeth just stared at him, then her hands went to her mouth and Sam realized the girl was crying with shock. "The gods save us... I knew it. I *knew* it!"

The colonel looked decidedly uncomfortable and the humor that had flitted through the little group fled, replaced with disbelief and a shifting unease. "That's bollocks," Geraint said with a nervous laugh. "Dix is a myth and everyone knows it."

"Actually, Geraint, you're right," Daniel said. Then, to Elspeth, he added, "You're both right, in fact. Dix *is* a myth. I don't know who he was originally, but the name has been passed on to another — to the man now leading the resistance."

Geraint looked ruffled by that. Perhaps his pride was hurt, perhaps he felt foolish. He certainly looked edgy and Sam felt the threat level spike; jumpy people were unpredictable and therefore dangerous.

Apparently the colonel agreed. "Hey, Geraint," he said, lacing his voice with the laidback tone of command he used to put nervous young officers at ease, "how about we go see Aedan?" He glanced at the empty sky. "We don't want to attract the wrong kind of attention and we can let these kids talk someplace warmer." He made a play of looking cold. "A nice fire sounds pretty good right about now."

"Yes, yes," Elspeth said, impatient. "Of course we're going back. Geraint—"

"Ah!" The colonel held up a hand, cutting her off. He kept his attention on the kid. "It's your call, Geraint."

And there was nothing more likely to relax a kid like Geraint than letting him feel like he was in control of a situation — even when he wasn't.

After a moment, Geraint nodded. "Aye," he said. "Aedan will want to hear this for himself, right enough. Even if it's fever-talk." He levelled his weapon at the colonel. "No messing about," he said. "You do as you're told."

The colonel lifted his hands away from his gun. "No problem," he said. "You're the boss."

Sam glanced at him. Sometimes, he really was quite good.

CHAPTER SEVENTEEN

Sting heard the footsteps before daybreak and sat up, reaching for his weapon.

Beside him, the queen reached out to touch his arm. *It is Hearten and Flint,* she said. *They have news.*

He looked at her. *What news?*

I cannot tell, she said.

Leaving the queen to her rest, Sting met the blades at the cave's hidden entrance, watching their approach from the hive through the trees, shades amid shades. He had only recently returned from Shadow's encampment and was eager to rest and feed. *Can this not wait?* he said when they were close.

Flint bared teeth. *If it could,* he said, *would we be here in the dark of the night?*

Stormfire sent us, Hearten explained, gleeful at the news. *He is back.*

For a moment, Sting did not understand. *Who is back?*

The Lantean.

He felt a bolt of excitement. This was unlooked for good news among so much bad. *Come in,* he said, and led them deeper into the cave. The queen must be consulted, of course, but it would have suited Sting better to keep the news from her until he had the Lantean in his hands; Earthborn had a propensity to become involved and it was getting harder to keep her hidden and safe.

As they entered the central chamber of the cave, the queen rose from her resting place, uncurling with a grace that still mesmerized. Hearten and Flint bowed, though slightly. There was little ceremony in the zenana of Earthborn; her mother would have been shocked to see it. But her mother was long dead and Earthborn did as she chose. "Where is he?" she said aloud, to them all. "With Shadow, still?"

Hearten looked to Flint, then back to the queen. "Unclear. But Stormfire believes he returned to the planet through the Astria Porta."

That was a surprise indeed. "Is he certain?"

"That is his location," Flint said. "For what certainty that gives."

Earthborn touched Sting's hand, a casual intimacy that made him awkward before the others. *That is close to where you found him,* she said. *This is significant, yes?*

Perhaps, he conceded. It was the queen's belief that the Lantean was not native to this world. Having met him, and the humans with whom he travelled, Sting could not deny the possibility that they originated off-world. They were most certainly different.

You will find him, Earthborn said.

Sting bowed in agreement. *I shall pilot the dart myself.*

She turned her head away, addressed the next comment to them all and out loud. "I will travel with my consort to the place where the Lantean has been found. I wish to meet him for myself."

Sting drew air through his teeth but could not contradict her, not before Hearten and Flint, which was, no doubt, why she had chosen to speak so publically. "Ready a dart," he told them. "I will return to the hive shortly."

Hearten and Flint exchanged a glance.

"Now," he snapped and they left in some hurry, chased out by his anger.

The queen could certainly feel it and he saw it in the stiffening of her spine. Once they were alone he seized her arm, an impudence Brightstar would not have tolerated from her consort. But, as Earthborn often pointed out, she was not her mother and she did not follow her rules. It was a freedom that sharpened both edges of the blade. Into the intimate space of her mind, he said, *This is foolish.*

Her chin lifted. *I have made my decision.*

It is too dangerous. I will bring the Lantean here, if you wish to speak with him.

I wish, she said, *to leave this cave. I wish to do more for my people than sit and wait.*

He tightened his grip on her arm. *You are a queen,* he said. *That is what you must do.*

My mother did more, she said. *My mother fought in battle.*

Your mother died! In anger he let go and turned away, but not far. After a moment he said, *My queen, you are too precious to us to take this risk.*

There was silence. He could hear her breathing, felt the shimmer of her anger and frustration in his mind. After some time it settled and she ghosted a touch against his shoulder. *The Lantean returned through the Astria Porta,* she said, *which has been closed to us since the parasite-gods destroyed the dialing device.*

He did not leave through it, Sting pointed out.

We do not know how he left, Earthborn countered. *And we do not know from whence he came, but we do know that he has the power to fly the city of the Ancestors, to take us home and to destroy the corruption of Shadow.*

All this we know, Sting agreed.

After a pause, Earthborn said, *We cannot treat the Lantean as we would a human, bending him to our will by force.*

I do not intend to do so.

You intend to snatch him from among his friends and transport him here against his will. She moved so that she stood before him again, beautiful in the shadow-light. *This will not help us gain his trust.*

He may share the blood of the Ancestors, Sting said, *but do not make the mistake of thinking he is one of them. He is human and humans will not trust us. It is not in their nature.*

Perhaps he could not trust a blade such as you. Earthborn reached out and touched his hand, the caress of feeding-hand to feeding-hand. *That is why I must travel with you and meet him myself.*

The danger—

"The world is full of danger." She spoke aloud, filling the space with her voice. "I was born in danger, took my first breath amid war and catastrophe. I do not fear danger."

He closed his fingers around her hand. *But I do,* he said. *I fear for you, going alone into this ravaged world, my queen.*

I will not be alone, she said, pressing her hand against his. *You will be with me, and Hearten and Flint.*

Three blades to protect a queen? Your mother would have had an army.

I am not my mother.

No, he said, studying her, *you are not.* Her eyes were as bright as her mother's and intense as the stars. He thought, with pain, that Earthborn had never seen the stars. No one on this world had seen them since war had entombed the planet in dust and ash.

We must make an ally of the Lantean, she said. *Not a conscript.*

And if he does not wish to ally himself with us? We do not know why he has come here. Perhaps he is already allied with Shadow.

She tossed her head, shrugging away the idea. *Until we speak with him, how can we know?*

Stormfire has spoken with him, he reminded her. *Stormfire imprisoned him too…*

Her expression soured. *Yes. Only another reason that I must speak with him myself, as a supplicant—*

"Supplicant!" Sting spat the word aloud. "You are no supplicant, you are a queen!"

"A queen of what?" She spread her hands. "Of a dying hive and ever fewer blades. Soon, I will be a queen of nothing but memories." She touched his wrist again, calming herself. *We need the Lantean. Do you not see? I must do this. It is the only way.*

It was not the only way, but it was probably the best way. In silence, he wrestled with her arguments, wishing he could find more fault with them. But in truth he could not. *We must take every precaution,* he said at last, striving to be gracious in defeat. *I will find the Lantean first and speak with him. You will be… elsewhere, guarded by Hearten and Flint. When I am satisfied that it is safe, I will bring him before you.*

Earthborn nodded in compliance, although he could see triumph brighten her eyes. *You are my consort and my protector. I will be guided by your experience.*

Be sure that you are, he said, refusing to soften his tone. *For everything we do, everything we have worked for, depends upon your survival.*

CHAPTER EIGHTEEN

Earth — 2000: Once Colonel Reynolds had disappeared through the event horizon, there was no reason to delay the ascent to the surface. They geared up as they went, Captain Marston handing the colonel extra ammo and Janet a fully loaded Glock with an extra clip. Dixon took a quilted jacket from Marston and threw it to Janet. She held it up, trying to count the weeks since she'd been in Colorado. "It's… June, isn't it?"

He grinned. "It's Scotland."

She conceded the point, having felt the chill of the bunker, and shrugged on the jacket. It was big enough to cover her tac vest, but not warm enough to ward off the gooseflesh that wasn't just a symptom of the low temperature. She hadn't seen the true extent of the destruction and wasn't sure she was prepared.

When they reached a flight of stairs, Marston turned back without a word, a military coping mechanism that was familiar to Janet. To wish them luck, to tell them to be careful, would be acknowledging the threat that lay ahead. And to acknowledge it was to fear it.

They emerged through the door at the top of the stairs into a long low corridor, broad enough to accommodate the armored trucks and military support vehicles that lined its walls. At the other end a huge metal door began to open, sending a chill blast down the length of the corridor.

"We'll take the Jackal out," said Dixon, heading up the corridor and climbing into a smaller, roofless vehicle with what looked like a Mark 19 mounted on its rear. "If we fall under fire, it'll get us out of there fast."

"And if we're hit?" asked Janet as she climbed into the passenger side.

Dixon smiled at her as he revved the engine and swung the

Jackal round. "Welcome to Earth, Doctor."

She was flung back in her seat as the car accelerated up the ramp, and suddenly she was outside, feeling the needles of wind on her skin and the dusting of moisture from a light rain. An involuntarily laugh burst from her mouth and she closed her eyes. She hadn't realized how much she'd missed the sensation of wind and rain until that moment. It was almost exhilarating. But the feeling died when she noticed the smell that carried on the wind. Burning, mixed with an underlying rot. She kept her eyes closed as they drove until, after an indeterminate length of time, the Jackal came to a stop. The chassis bounced as Dixon climbed out and she opened her eyes to see him head up a small embankment by the side of the highway, cutting through sparse fir trees. He turned back and gestured for her to follow him, but she hesitated.

"Janet," he said, "you have to look." Reluctantly, she left the car and climbed the slope, flipping open the viewfinder on the camera.

In truth, it wasn't the sight she'd expected. Not nearly so bad in fact. Ahead of them stretched a body of water, gray and stark under somber skies, mirroring the clouds that glowered there. In the distance, it opened up into what might have been the sea, or maybe just a broader stretch of the same lake. There, the sky seemed brighter, as if the setting sun was trying in earnest to break through; Janet, though, knew the true source of the light. For across it all, hung a pall of smoke, tossed about by the wind, but refusing to dissipate. The illusion of sunset was nothing more than the world on fire.

As she scanned the opposite coast, she saw a sight that chilled her. "Is that...?"

"Take a look for yourself," replied Dixon, handing her his binoculars.

Magnified through the viewfinder, the sight was even more awful.

The ha'tak loomed on the horizon, it's dark pyramidal outline dwarfing everything that surrounded it.

"Our Lord and Master surveys his kingdom," said Dixon.

"I thought you said the ha'tak's were in orbit,".

"It came down not long after we arrived, after the fighting was over. It makes it hard to launch any offensive on the base." From his crouched position, Dixon pointed to a cluster of low buildings on the far shore that might have been white once, but were now blackened and half in ruins. "Across there, that's the naval base. There's no one left though. Crawling with Jaffa now."

A thought struck her. "What about the Vanguards?"

"The subs went out three weeks ago, heading south after the first wave. They never came back. Who knows if they're still operational? Either way, there's nothing left here but what we have in the bunker. We've avoided discovery so far. If we're careful, we could maybe hold out for a while yet. It's running recon that heightens the risk of being found."

"But it's necessary."

He nodded. "It's necessary. We need supplies, but our location..." His gesture took in the rolling hills behind them and the miles of coast, shrouded in woodland. "We're on a peninsula here, safe enough from any ground troops with a choke point to the north, but there aren't any real resources. Food, medical supplies — it's all over there on the other side of the water. I understand Dr. Aitcheson's frustration, but with that thing watching, those supplies may as well be on the moon."

"There has to be a way we can infiltrate the base," Janet said. Aitcheson's need aside, those antivirals might be the only way to convince Turner that Arbella needed Earth as much as Earth needed Arbella.

Dixon's jaw tensed and he sucked in a breath. "They cut us down like bugs, Janet. I've been under enemy fire before — my unit's faced a dozen Jaffa squadrons — but I've never seen anything like this. There's no position where we can hold the line, no safe place. Everywhere's hostile ground."

His words were disheartened, but not defeated. It was perhaps that underlying steel that strengthened Janet's own determination. Whatever the cost, she would help these people one way or another. The world was burning and they couldn't save it, but maybe they could save this small part. "What if we—"

At first, the tremor was almost imperceptible, but then a deafening roar sounded from across the water, and the ground shook as if it might crack apart. Janet didn't need the binoculars to see what was happening. The ha'tak was lifting.

"It's leaving!" she cried.

"Oh my God, I've never seen anything like that."

But there was no time to admire the sight. This was the chance they'd been waiting for, the window of opportunity. If ever there was a time for them to make their move, this was it. *Disheartened, but not defeated.* "Colonel, I have to get back to Arbella. Now."

Earth — 2098: Daniel's memories of Aedan Trask were hazy with fever. But he remembered the large cave that served as a general living area for these people; he remembered the fire and the men and women sitting around watching him from thin, underfed faces. And he remembered the healer, Meagan, and smiled when he caught her eye across the fire.

He understood better, now, why they lived below ground. Safe from Wraith eyes, yes, but perhaps their ancestors had retreated underground even before the Wraith had arrived, to escape the worst ravages of the war that had raged on the surface.

"Well," Meagan said, picking her way through the crowd to stand before Daniel. "You're more alive than I'd expected."

"So I hear."

She cocked her head, eyes narrowed. "I'd like to think it was my skill that healed you, but I doubt I can take the credit."

Daniel was about to obfuscate when Meagan, much as Janet Fraiser might have done, reached out and pressed her hand against his side where the wound had been. When he didn't wince, her eyes widened. "Impossible," she said.

"Let's just say we have a story to tell."

Meagan grunted and looked over at Elspeth who was hovering nearby. "You'll like that, girl," Meagan said. "More stories."

"True ones," Elspeth said. "They've found Dix, and a way to escape this place."

Meagan looked at Daniel for the truth.

"It's not quite that simple," he said, to both of them. "But it's true, we have found Dix."

Further into the room, Jack was talking with Aedan Trask — tall and lithe like the rest of his people, Trask had a face full of suspicion and very little hope. He was a cynic. Jack would have his work cut out if he wanted Aedan Trask's help.

Perhaps Jack could feel Daniel's eyes on his back, because at that moment he turned around and beckoned him over.

"Come on," Daniel said to Elspeth, including Meagan in the invitation, "let's go sit down and we'll tell you what we know."

They sat close to the fire on matting that covered the floor. Something was cooking; he could smell a meaty aroma of stew and tried not to let his stomach growl. Aedan kept his distance, Elspeth putting herself somewhere between Daniel and Trask, sitting on her heels and all but bouncing with excitement. In the firelight, her eyes gleamed and for a moment he was reminded of Sha're, of her enthusiasm and beauty. He looked away with a frown and told himself it was only the light.

Jack gave a swift recount of their capture by the Wraith, their escape and their discovery of Dix and the buried Stargate.

"Then it's close!" Elspeth looked ready to pack right there and then.

"No, I'm sorry, but it's not," Sam said. "When we were taken by the Wraith we were transported a great distance. Probably across an ocean."

"Ah," Aedan said with a skeptical twist of his lips. "Convenient."

"Truth," Jack said, matching him look for look.

"You just don't want to believe," Elspeth snapped. "You don't want anything to change, to get better. I think you're afraid of—"

"Enough!" Aedan snapped and Elspeth subsided, although without much grace. After a moment he turned his attention back to Jack, "If this 'Stargate' is buried," he said, "how can you pass through it?"

"We can't," Jack said. "But Dix has another way off the planet." He gestured to the ceiling. "He has a… an aircraft, in orbit."

"*He* does not," Teal'c said. He'd refused to sit and stood as if on guard at the entrance to one of the many tunnels that ran out from this central space. "The man you call Dix is a Jaffa and he is enslaved by a Goa'uld — one of the race who destroyed your world. *She* has a ship in orbit. But she is your enemy, not your friend."

"Teal'c…" Jack glared but Teal'c didn't back down.

"Why would you hide the truth from them, O'Neill?"

Elspeth looked between them in confusion. "It's no secret that Dix serves the old gods."

"False gods."

"No secret?" Aedan said with a bitter laugh. "It's nonsense, Elspeth. They're just telling you what you want to hear." He rose to his feet, tall in the cramped space, and looked down at them with obvious hostility. "What I don't understand is, why? What is it you want from us, O'Neill?"

"Your help," Jack said, not getting up.

"If you're friends with the gods, why do you need our help?"

"Because they're not gods," Jack said. "Teal'c's right. They're aliens and they're no one's friend. But right now, they're the only people putting up a fight against the Devourers."

Aedan barked a laugh. "Fight the Devourers? That's what you want us to do?" He turned in appeal to the rest of the people, their murmurs rising in a soft bubble of discord. "You come here with fairy tales and then ask us to help you fight creatures that can suck out a man's life with the touch of their hand?" He shook his head. "You're fools. Dangerous fools. We want nothing to do with you."

He made to leave, but Jack was on his feet, blocking his way. "The camp," he said. "We need to find the camp you saw — the one where the Devourers hold people in pens, waiting to feed on them. That's what you saw, right?"

Aedan froze.

In a softer, but no less forceful tone, Jack said, "We think some friends of ours are being held there. We need your help to find them."

Aedan stared. "I will never go back to that place," he said. "And neither will you, if you value your sanity. Your friends are dead — or longing for death. Forget them." With that, he pushed past Jack and headed out.

"Aedan Trask!"

Daniel was surprised to see Meagan on her feet, her voice cracking with authority. Even Aedan couldn't ignore her. He slowed, stopped, but didn't turn around.

"There is one thing they have not explained," Meagan said.

"Which is what?"

"How this one," she indicated Daniel, "still lives."

Carefully, as if expecting a trap, Aedan turned. "Why does it matter?"

Meagan didn't answer his question, instead she said to Daniel, "Stand up, show me where you were wounded."

"Um…" He glanced at Jack. He didn't know where Meagan was going with this, but his gut told him that she was on their side.

Jack must have thought the same because after a moment he gave a curt nod, permission to go ahead.

Pulling off his tac vest, Daniel stood up, unzipped his jacket and lifted his shirt. It still had a burn hole where the staff blast had hit him but underneath his skin was smooth and healed.

Meagan looked at him with eyes full of questions, but she didn't ask a single one. Instead, she turned back to Trask. "Who but the old gods could do this?"

Aedan looked at Daniel, at Meagan, but didn't answer.

"If they have this kind of power," she pressed, "perhaps they *can* fight the Devourers."

Aedan's jaw clenched and in silence he turned and stalked away into the tunnel.

"Crap," Jack murmured under his breath.

Daniel let his shirt fall. "I understand why he's suspicious," he said to Meagan. "But we're telling the truth."

"I'll go after him," Elspeth said, getting to her feet.

But Meagan touched her arm, stopping her. "No. Let him think on it and come to you." She offered Daniel a thin smile. "We will eat while we wait. I'd like to hear about the medicines the gods wield."

"They're not gods," Daniel said but decided to play along with the rest; telling them that a 'Devourer' had cured him might be pushing credulity. "They're a parasitic alien life form that uses humans as hosts."

"Fascinating," Meagan said with a lift of an eyebrow that implied 'you'll have to convince me'. "Come," she said, inviting them all with a gesture to join her. "I suspect there's more of your story to tell."

Daniel caught Jack's eye — there *was* more to tell and even more to conceal, especially the parts about time travel and alternate timelines. Somehow he got the feeling that *that* wouldn't go down too well with these no-nonsense people.

CHAPTER NINETEEN

Elspeth Reed had spent her life chasing ghosts; this was a dead world after all and there were plenty of them. Aedan and the others thought that she was a fool to spend so much time with her head wrapped up in stories, but they didn't understand. She had thought no one would ever understand — until she met Daniel Jackson. And it was his return that had set her on her current mission.

She hurried down the tunnels, heading for one of the oldest parts of the caves where the community kept their least essential supplies: detritus left behind by previous generations or scavenged from the outlying areas, items deemed worthless and abandoned by those travelers who had sometimes passed through and taken shelter with them. Daniel was one of those travelers and she wondered what he would make of her collection. Something told her he would not dismiss it as worthless.

Her feet found the small cave almost without her thinking, so often had she retreated here. Unlike the newer parts of the cave system, its walls were daubed with old words and symbols whose meaning had long been forgotten but whose presence linked her to the lost world of her past: 'Scrap Trident', 'Bairns not Bombs', 'No WMD'. She traced her fingers over the fading paint as she made her way inside, picking through the various crates and boxes until she found the one she was looking for. The hinge creaked despite frequent use. Elspeth reached in and withdrew the first item her hand touched. The leather cover was cracked and damaged, but the pages still turned and the words were still clear.

"Trying to hide again?"

Elspeth whirled, dropping the book. She winced as it hit the ground and landed splayed face down on its pages. "How can I be hiding when you know fine and well where to find me, Aedan?"

"I wasn't talking about this room," he said, glancing at the book whose pages she was now smoothing under careful hands. There didn't seem to be any damage, beyond that which had already been inflicted years ago. He flicked his chin towards it. "You hide in these books."

"I *learn* from these books."

"And what is it you learn, Elspeth? What is there to be found in words that are old as the dust that clings to them?" He wrinkled his nose, then turned and spat to the side, as if the dust was clogging his mouth.

"Don't you ever wonder, Aedan, what came before? Don't you ever wonder about the old gods and where they went?"

"I know what came before, Elspeth. War. One that killed everyone and everything." He swept a hand over a crate and turned his palm up to show the dust that coated it. "There is your past, Elspeth. The crumbled bones of the dead. What use were your gods to them?"

She shook her head and gave a huff of frustration. Aedan didn't understand about the old gods. But, for that matter, neither did she. There was so much she didn't know, so much she still had to learn. Daniel and his people could teach her, but for now she knew one thing for certain. "We're still here."

He laughed at that, bitter and heartsick. "For how long?"

"Long enough to escape, like Dix. "

"Escape?" Aedan raised his eyebrows, looking at her as if he thought she might be joking. "Elspeth, these people didn't even know about the Devourers two weeks ago." He flung a hand out in the direction of the tunnel. "And yet now they claim to have travelled across the world, escaped the Devourers, discovered 'Dix' and met the old gods? How can you believe them?"

Whirling back towards the box, one of many in this room, which held so many books, she began picking through the titles. "They came through the Eye in the valley. They say there are other worlds, places where the Devourers have not yet reached.

Places where we can live free."

"Fairy tales."

"But what if it's true?" She found the book she was looking for and pulled it out.

"You only want it to be true," he said, sounding weary.

She took a step closer, feeling her irritation subside, and touched his arm. "But, Aedan, isn't it worth the risk?"

He looked down at her hand on his sleeve and said, "You trust this Daniel Jackson?"

"I do," she said. "Don't you?"

After a moment he said, "He seems honest. They all do, but what they say is still unbelievable."

"If you'd read these books," she said, "you wouldn't think so." Opening the precious volume she flipped through the pages, searching for the picture she remembered. "This book was made in the time before the Devourers came," she said. "It was— yes, look." She showed him the image; men dressed in short armor, carrying a weapons like the one held by the stranger, Teal'c, and on their heads the same symbol. "Do you see? These were the servants of the gods." She touched her forehead. "He bears the same mark."

Aedan studied the picture, his breath leaving him in a slow sigh. "This proves nothing."

"But isn't it enough to take a risk, Aedan? If there's a chance of leaving this place, of finding a new home far from the Devourers, isn't it worth risking everything?"

He lifted his eyes to hers, dark and haunted as they had been ever since he'd returned from the Devourer's camp. "I swore I'd never go back there."

Elspeth closed the book, put it down, and took his hands in hers. "You only have to lead them to it. You don't have to go inside."

He shook his head and when he spoke the sharpness was gone from his voice. "And in return for my help, they'll help us escape?"

"I think they'd help us anyway, if they could," she said. "But Colonel O'Neill says it will be difficult to return without freeing their friends first. He said the people on the other world are distrustful of strangers and that we must help him win their trust so that they will take us in."

Aedan's fingers tightened around hers, then let go. "If I refuse," he said, "you'll help him anyway?"

Elspeth lifted her chin. She wouldn't deny it. "My help will be less valuable than yours, but yes. I can at least lead them across the water."

"Then I suppose I have no choice."

"You'll help them?"

He cut her a brief look, then turned away and headed for the door. "I wouldn't see you die, Elspeth," he said over his shoulder. "I'd miss our fights."

The comment made her grin in a way that took her by surprise and she stood there for a long moment watching the empty doorway.

Evacuation Site — 2000: At night, Arbella was a different landscape, the red rocks painted in deepening shades of blue and the lake turned crystalline in the glow of the planet's two moons. It was almost beautiful, thought Bill Turner, as he stood at the open tent flap of his family's living quarters. Behind him, his wife and two sons slept on low pallets. Too young to fully understand what was happening, the chaos of the evacuation had scared his boys in the same way a noisy rodeo show had scared them during a campaign trip to Texas. Both of them slept soundly now. It was Miranda who still had nightmares.

They'd been given a plot high on a bluff overlooking the camp, a location that could be considered prime real estate in their little community. After only four months in office, he supposed the canvas over his head was as much home as the White House ever was. It didn't stop him missing the scent of the Rose Garden. Here, the air smelled strange, hung with the iron tang of rust, or blood.

Just beyond the bluff, the Arbellan camp stretched out, silent now, dotted here and there with the light of a few lanterns. There were plans in place to bring power to the camp, providing electricity to essential work areas. Work had already begun in upgrading the solar array that had already been installed on the planet by whatever rogue element had set up the base. The irony that their survival now relied on those responsible for them being here in the first place did not escape him. It galled him that they would go without punishment, but crimes against humanity were unimportant when compared to the continuation of humanity itself.

From here on in, though, lawlessness could not be tolerated; measures must be put in place to prevent anarchy. How to do that was a matter still under discussion.

Behind him, Miranda muttered in her sleep and Bill froze, hoping it wouldn't turn into a whimper. Her nightmares could be sudden and crashing, and he was helpless to stop them. The coward in him took over, and he stepped away from the tent, walking to the very edge of the bluff.

Home played on his mind more than ever these days. In the lead up to his inauguration, he'd been invited, as was the tradition, to make his own mark on the Oval Office, choosing from the rich archives of the nation, the artwork and furnishings that best represented the love he bore for his country, and his dedication to preserving its heritage and history. His first choice had, of course, been from his home town; The Fog Warning by Winslow Homer, on loan from the Boston MFA. A fisherman at sea in a tiny boat, adrift from the mother ship and confronted by the ominous cloud on the horizon, having to decide on a new course to row if he has any hope of staying alive. That painting would be ash now, of course.

He sucked in a breath of metallic air, held it, waited for his heart to slow.

"If you're thinking about jumping, Mr. President, at this

height, the best you could hope for is a broken leg." The voice was loud in the still night, and Turner spun to find Frank Simmons climbing the bluff. His feet barely made a sound on the uneven ground.

"For God's sakes, Simmons, it's the middle of the night. What are you doing here?"

"Good evening, sir," said the colonel, ignoring the challenge.

Turner glanced towards the open tent, worried that Miranda might hear them, worried that Simmons might hear her. "This is my private residence. You're out of line coming here."

Simmons glanced around. "Perhaps if you hadn't dispensed with your Secret Service detail you would be better guarded, sir."

Turner tensed his jaw. He'd claimed that the reason for doing away with his detail was because the men were needed more elsewhere. In truth, it was guilt that had made him send them away; how could he ask for special protection, when he'd been unable to protect his own people?

"Besides," said Simmons, "there are matters to be discussed."

"Then I recommend discussing them in the morning. In front of the Joint Chiefs."

Simmons looked down and Turner saw that he held a folder in his hands. "I somehow doubt that you'd want the Joint Chiefs to hear about this matter. Although, there's a possibility that they already know."

There was a note of conceit about the man's words that Turner wanted to ignore, but couldn't. He grabbed the LED lantern from its hook and jerked his head in the direction of the slope. Only when they had walked a sufficient distance further up the incline and stood in the shadow of the cliff did he turn back to Simmons.

"This better be good."

"I don't know if 'good' is the word I'd use, Mr. President, but it's certainly important." He held out the folder and, after a beat, Turner snatched it from his hands.

"What is it?" he said, opening it up and holding it to the light.

Inside were pages and pages of handwritten notes.

"A report."

"I didn't order any report."

"No, sir," said Simmons. "I took the liberty of having my men gather some intel from the camp. Weather watching, if you will." His words were deferential, but his entire demeanor stank of guile. "In the interests of the administration, of course. Anyway, there's a place they call the Fu-Bar…" He paused, as if waiting for Turner to react to some joke, but merely raised his eyebrows and carried on when Turner's expression remained blank. "Not only has this place become something of a local haunt for bad hooch, it's also the perfect spot to pick up the latest scuttlebutt, to steal a term from our navy colleagues."

This time, Turner did get it. He slapped the folder closed and thrust it out to Simmons. "I'm not standing here reading gossip."

"No, I wouldn't expect you to, so I'll give you the Cliff Notes. There's growing dissent among the population, Mr. President — especially from those loyal to Stargate Command."

A small beat of panic lurched through his stomach. The machinery of government was being eroded here and this was what he'd feared; a motion of no confidence from the people themselves. He cursed and looked away. "I won't step down, Simmons."

"I'm not suggesting you should. But you have to play smart here, Bill."

If his situation had been less precarious, Turner might have laughed at the man's audacity in using his given name. Now it was just another slap across his already stinging face. "Remember your position, Colonel."

"And if you want to keep *yours*, you'd do well to listen to me. You're under threat here. There are others who could beat you down without even trying — I'm talking about a coup, Bill. A military coup. And before you say it, the threat doesn't come from me. I'm on your side."

Turner let out a mirthless laugh and scrubbed his hands

over his face. He felt so much older than his forty-seven years. Old, and dry as dirt. "You've got to be kidding me."

"SG-1."

"What about them? They're dead."

"Not in the way that counts," said Simmons with a shake of his head. "The idea of SG-1 is still very much alive to those SGC personnel who idolize them. And there's one person among our number who's a living reminder of that idea."

It didn't take much to figure out who Simmons was referring to; Janet Fraiser was a well-known and well respected figure among their small Arbellan community, just as she'd been respected on Earth. Turner could understand why. She'd been an asset to this operation, a sounding board for him on many occasions, and someone he trusted implicitly.

Dead, but not in the way that counts.

He didn't like where this was going. "I'm not quite sure what you're suggesting, Simmons."

"How can you lead when the people are clinging to an illusion of dead heroes? You might not realize it, but Janet Fraiser stands in opposition to stability, to order—to everything you're trying to achieve here. She defies the rules at every turn. Look at how she's gotten her way on everything so far." Simmons pointed at him with the folder. "Don't think people haven't noticed the power she has here."

Turner snorted and began to walk back to his tent. "Get out of here, Frank."

"She'll humiliate you."

The words halted him, his feet stuttering to a stop and sending pebbles rolling down the hill. It was as if Frank Simmons had found a loose edge to his skin and peeled it back, to reveal the very wound that Turner had tried to deny all this time. Because beneath the anger at what had befallen Earth, beneath the desire to save his people and avenge the massacre by the Goa'uld, lay the raw and shameful burn of humiliation.

He'd fought for this presidency, done things he'd never

thought he could even have contemplated in the past, but it was all done for a reason. He'd wanted to conquer kingdoms and raise empires. He'd wanted his name to be remembered alongside the Founding Fathers, the builders of history, and as a leader of the free world, it had all lain ahead of him. But his plans had never accounted for a race of malevolent aliens. Now the only legacy he could hope to leave was a world built on rubble and sand. Yes, he was humiliated.

And Simmons knew it.

Fury took control then. He covered the ground between himself and Simmons in three strides. Only when his hands were fisted in the man's jacket did he consider his actions, but the satisfaction he took from the look of alarm on Simmons' face outweighed any misgiving. "Don't presume to manipulate me, Frank," he snarled, "not when I know exactly what part you played in bringing us here. You think I don't know about User 4574? You think I'm unaware of the dangerous games you've played? I will not order the death of an innocent woman just because it suits your agenda."

Simmons' expression became passive once more. "Oh this isn't my agenda, Bill. And besides, I never suggested the good doctor has to die. There are other, more effective ways of bringing about someone's downfall. It's your good fortune that I've already taken the appropriate steps." He pressed the folder against Turner's chest, forcing him to let go of his jacket to catch the pages before they spilled on the ground. "Be prudent, Bill. We're standing in the dust of a dying civilization. It's the stuff of myths, and this is how gods are born." He nodded at the folder, before walking away down the cliff. "You should get back to your wife, Mr. President," he called over his shoulder. "I think I hear her having another nightmare."

CHAPTER TWENTY

Earth — 2098: SG-1 had been walking for half a day, heading south over rolling hills, always keeping to the trees.

"Sometimes," Trask had warned at the outset, "the Devourers make you see things that aren't there. You need to keep your wits about you."

"Some kind of telepathy?" Carter had suggested.

It fitted in with the silent communication Jack had seen in Crazy's lab. "And here I am without my tinfoil hat," he'd said, earning a smile from Carter and a blank look from Trask.

They'd fallen into a natural formation after that — Jack taking point with Trask, Daniel and Elspeth behind, Carter and Teal'c on their six. He could hear the bass rumble of Teal'c's voice, but it was too low to make out the words and he wondered what they were talking about. One way or another, though, he figured he and Teal'c had a reckoning to come. He'd rather not do it in the field — at home, over a beer, would be ideal — but since it needed to happen before the proverbial hit the fan that meant ASAP.

Trask didn't talk much as they walked, which suited Jack fine, but he couldn't help noticing how the man's attention was turned inward. He recognized the look in his eyes, that harsh tamping down of fear and memory. He figured he might be wearing the same expression if he ever found himself walking back into Iraq.

It wasn't a comforting thought; the last thing he needed was their guide going bat-shit at the first sign of trouble. But what choice did he have? Aedan was the only guide they had.

"Down!" Trask hissed suddenly, crouching low, his head tipped up as he scanned the sky. There wasn't much to see between the rattling branches of the trees, but something swift and black darted across the patch of sky Jack was watching.

Too fast to be a bird, it had to be a fighter.

"Wraith?" Jack whispered, tracking it until it was out of sight. "Devourer, I mean."

"What else?" Trask was still watching the sky.

"We saw a Goa'uld fighter last time," he said. "In a dog fight with the Wraith."

Trask lowered his gaze. "I've seen them. Didn't know what they were, though. They belong to these 'Goa'uld'?"

"To Hecate, I'm guessing," Jack said. He shifted, easing the pressure on his bum knee. "She's the one who seems to be up for the fight."

Trask rubbed his hand over his mouth, thinking. "Why?" he said at last. "Why would she fight for us?"

"I doubt she's fighting *for* us," Jack said because, no matter what Rya'c might say, there was no point in sugar-coating it. "One thing I can tell you about Goa'ulds is that they're only out for themselves. But sometimes..." He shrugged. "Occasionally our interests coincide with theirs. Maybe this is one of those times?"

Trask gave a thoughtful nod and rose to his feet, walking on.

Jack glanced over his shoulder as he followed and saw the rest of his team getting to their feet, still watching the sky.

"Your friend," Trask said, "believes the Goa'ulds destroyed our world. Is he right?"

"Yup," Jack said. "That's what it looks like."

Trask threw him a sharp look. "And how do you know that?"

"Old records, on Arbella." He indicated Daniel. "Our resident historian did some digging. It looks like the Goa'uld invaded about a hundred years ago, and the Wraith — the Devourers — came along forty years later."

"That was the war that my grandparents remembered?"

"I guess."

Trask thought for a while longer, taking them east, down a steeper incline. Every so often, over the last few hours, Jack had glimpsed a flat body of gray water off to his left. It was closer now and in the distance he could hear the soft wash of water against the shore. Not a sea, he thought, or at least, not quite. Some kind of estuary, perhaps?

"I wonder," Trask said then, "what it was like here, before the Devourers came — before the Goa'uld. My grandfather described cities where hundreds and thousands of people lived together. Elspeth has images of them in one of her books."

Jack was struck by a moment of unfocused guilt. It was safer to hide the truth about where they'd come from, because how could they explain it when they barely understood it themselves? Yet he didn't like misleading people he considered to be allies — friends, even. Carter and Teal'c would say it didn't matter, that nothing they did in this dead-end branch of history mattered, but it didn't feel like that to Jack. Lying was lying.

"You can see them still," said Trask, mistaking Jack's silence for doubt. "Well, you can see the ruins anyway. The cities were destroyed by the killer bombs in the war with the Devourers, but you can still see the roots of the buildings. The ruins go on for miles."

"Were there—?" Jack cleared his throat, a kind of dread making it difficult to speak. "Were there any cities near here?"

He wasn't sure he wanted to hear the answer. It was easier to not know exactly where they were, to imagine this place as alien and not somewhere he might recognize. But not knowing something didn't make it any less real and good intel could save your life.

"There was," Trask said, drawing in on himself for a moment. "That's where they built the farm — in the bones of the old city."

Jack nodded and made himself ask the next question. "What's it called? The city?"

But Trask only shrugged. "We just call it the old city." He nodded toward the far shore. "It's over there, across the loch."

"Um?" Daniel said from behind them. "Did you say 'loch'? As in Loch Lomond or...?"

Trask gave him a searching look. "It's called Gare Loch," he said, gesturing back in the direction of the gate.

Jack raised an eyebrow; he knew that name. "Faslane," he said, figuring it out. "The naval base." He'd been part of NATO exercises out of Faslane a couple times, back in the Cold War. "We're in Scotland."

"There was some kind of military base north of here," Trask said. "Nothing much left now. Good hunting, though, in that area."

Jack thought back to that devastated valley, to the Stargate knocked sideways by the nuke that had failed to destroy it. "Is that where the gate is now?" he said. "Was that the base?"

"No," Trask said. "The remains of the base are on the other side of the loch, the Eye is on a peninsula."

"Safer," Carter said from behind them. "Easier to defend."

That made sense of course, although Jack still had no idea why the beta gate had wound up anywhere near a British submarine base. He glanced over his shoulder at Daniel, but Daniel just shrugged.

"There was no mention of the gate's location in the Arbella archives, beyond 'Earth'."

"You sound as if you know this place," Trask said, slowing down as the trees began to thin out. He looked suspicious. "You know names of old places, yet you act as though you've never been here before. How is that?"

"Maps," Jack said, striding ahead of him and down to the water's edge. "Lots of maps."

They'd arrived at the tip of the peninsula now, and behind them the loch stretched flat and bleak beneath the overcast sky. Before them the water flowed faster.

"This is the mouth of the river," Trask said, joining him. "And over there is where we're going."

Jack squinted at the far shore. "That's a lot of water to cross," he said.

"Don't worry." Trask almost cracked a smile. "You won't have to swim."

They made camp close to the shore, beneath the scant shelter of the winter trees, waiting for the cover of dark before they crossed the estuary. Trask didn't want to light a fire in such an exposed position, but Jack was freezing his ass off so showed him how to build a fire pit to hide the light from enemy eyes. Easier to do it here, he thought as he dug, than in the Iraqi desert. More fuel, for one thing, and fewer fractured skulls.

"That's clever," Trask conceded when he peered into the hole and watched the flames burn hot beneath the ground.

"Never eat cold food when you can eat something hot," Jack said. "First rule of survival."

"Really?" Carter said as she dug a couple of purification tablets out of her pack. "I thought the first rule was 'Assess the immediate situation'."

"No one likes a smart-ass, Carter," he said, dropping down next to her. "Especially before they've eaten."

Not that they had a lot in the way of food, but at least there was hot water for coffee. The MREs were long gone, but Rya'c had supplied them with a few packs of the Jaffa equivalent.

"I'd have bagged us a rabbit," Trask said, sniffing at the strange spicy biscuit, "if I'd known about the fire pit."

Once their meager meal was done, Jack wiped his fingers on his pants and said, "So, Trask, once we get across the estuary, how far until we reach the 'farm'?"

"Another day," Trask said. "It's in the skirts of the city." He chewed on the last of his food. "We'll rest for a few hours now and row across the water before dawn."

Jack approved of the plan. Trask may not be a soldier but he'd lived his whole life behind enemy lines; he knew what he was doing. "How long until sun-up?" Jack said, checking his watch.

"About nine hours."

"Long night," Daniel said.

"We're a long way north," Jack reminded him. To Trask he said, "How long will it take us to get across?"

Trask glanced at Teal'c's arms, cocked his head. "A couple

of hours if we go with the tide."

"Okay," Jack said. "Set three two-hour watches: Carter and Elspeth, Daniel and Trask. Teal'c, you're with me."

Across the fire pit Teal'c lifted an inscrutable eyebrow, but didn't object.

Carter shifted, jostling him as she leaned forward. He moved a little closer, stealing some of her heat. "Aedan," she said, "how close did you get to the farm last time? Did you go inside? Did you see what kind of technology they were using?"

Trask glanced at Elspeth. She hugged her legs up to her chest, watched him with her chin resting on her knees. Jack couldn't exactly figure out what was going on between the two of them — half the time the girl seemed besotted with Daniel, the other half she was looking at Trask like she either wanted to slap him or hug him.

"We got through the perimeter fence," Aedan said, his gaze missing Carter's and winding up some place on the ground near her boots. "Enough to see what was going on, but I didn't go into the bunker."

"Bunker," Jack said, catching Carter's eye. "What's happening in the bunker?"

Trask shook his head. "I don't know. I didn't want to find out. The place is crawling with Devourers."

"Why'd you go in at all?"

His gaze was still fixed on the ground. "We thought... We wanted to understand them better."

"We?" Jack said, because there was something in Trask's voice that sounded familiar.

"I went with a friend," he said shortly. "He died there."

Jack let out a breath. "I'm sorry."

Trask just nodded but didn't answer.

"They wanted to find out more about them, so we could fight them," Elspeth said, her voice quiet and her gaze still fixed on Trask. "That was Aedan's plan."

"And now I know better," he said. "Now I know it's not possible." He looked at Jack. "You'll see for yourself, when you get there. We can't fight monsters like the Devourers."

Jack offered him a smile. "We can try."

"Have you ever seen them feed?" he said, lifting his hand claw-like before him.

Jack slid a look at Carter and wished he could scrub the memory out of his head. He imagined Trask was haunted by something similar. "Yeah," he said. "I've seen it."

Carter held his gaze for a moment and when she turned back to Trask Jack knew what she was going to say. "One of them tried to feed on me."

Trask's head jerked up, so did Elspeth's. "How did you stop it?" the girl said.

"I don't know." They were probably Carter's least favorite words and she gave a frustrated little shake of her head as she said them. "It just let me go. But Hunter, one of the resistance fighters, said it was something to do with the Goa'uld." She looked at Daniel. "Right?"

He nodded. "Sam was once, briefly, a host to one of the... um..." He made a vague gesture toward his head.

"To the gods?" Elspeth supplied, her eyes wide.

"No," Carter said firmly. "No, it was different. But — the point is, it left something in my blood. And I wondered if you'd ever heard anything about the Devourers being unable to feed on 'the gods'."

"No," Trask said shortly. "There's nothing that—"

"Yes, there is." Elspeth cut Trask a triumphant look, sitting up a little straighter. Jack hid a smile; there was a lot of Daniel in the girl's eagerness. "I read it in one of my books," she said, her smile moving to Daniel. "My library — you still haven't seen it."

"My loss," he said, and sounded like he meant it.

Trask grumbled something beneath his breath, his irritation obvious.

"So what did it say?" Carter prompted.

"It said that the gods were impervious to assault by the

Amam," Elspeth said, frowning as if trying to recall the exact words. "It said that any Amam who touched them would 'recoil as if burned by a thousand suns'."

"Sounds like your typical Goa'uld understatement," Daniel said.

Jack glanced at Teal'c. "What about their Jaffa? Did it mention them?"

"No," Elspeth said. "But their warriors must have died aplenty or else they wouldn't have been defeated, would they?"

Carter grinned. "She makes a good point, sir."

He spread his hands. "You're right, stupid question."

"But the point is," Carter said, serious again, "I might be immune to their feeding."

"Not to their weapons."

"They only have stunners, sir."

And he didn't like that gleam in her eye. "Your point is what, Wonder Woman? You think you can go in alone?"

"It's a tactical advantage," she said. "That's my point, sir."

She was right, of course, but he wasn't comfortable with Carter getting all gung-ho about this. "There are lots of ways to die, Major."

"Yes sir, but it looks like my risk level could be considerably lower than everyone else's."

Jack tried to ignore exactly how much that didn't make him feel any better and distracted himself by grabbing a stick and giving the fire a poke. But he could feel someone watching him and when he looked up he saw Trask eyeing him with a speculative expression on his clever face. That kid was too smart for his own good.

"Time to turn in," Jack said, to head off any awkward questions. He got to his feet. "Trask, Daniel — wake me and Teal'c in two hours. Carter, Elspeth, you've got the last watch, so get some shuteye. We've got a long day tomorrow."

Teal'c woke with ease when Daniel Jackson placed a hand on his arm and murmured, "Your watch."

O'Neill was already awake, pouring himself coffee. He glanced up when Teal'c stood, gave a nod of greeting. Teal'c had no doubt of the reason why O'Neill had chosen him as his watch partner and he was not afraid of the dispute to come. It saddened him, though, that he and O'Neill — his brother — were at odds over such a grave issue.

As Daniel Jackson bedded down, pulling the sleeping bag up over his head against the freezing night air, Teal'c moved to sit next to O'Neill. Major Carter slept close by, little but her hat visible, while Trask lay down close to the girl, Elspeth, on the opposite side of the fire pit. They looked more comfortable than SG-1, for all their experience of such conditions, and Teal'c recognized in Aedan Trask and Elspeth Reid the hardihood of people born only for struggle. It was difficult not to admire their resilience — the resilience of all those left to scavenge an existence by the Tau'ri who had fled to Arbella.

Teal'c turned his gaze away from them, out toward the few lights on the distant shore. He did not want to admire these people; he wanted to save them from ever having to endure this life at all.

He and O'Neill sat in silence for some time, until both Daniel Jackson and Aedan Trask slept. O'Neill sipped his coffee, fingers wrapped around the mug, his attention drifting from his team to the horizon and back again.

"So," he said at length, his voice little more than a murmur. "Tomorrow, maybe the next day, we're gonna see some action. And I need to know you've still got my back, Teal'c."

"Do you doubt it?"

"I know you think this mission is a waste of time," O'Neill said. "I know you think nothing that happens here matters."

"That is correct," Teal'c agreed.

"And yet...?"

Teal'c turned to look at his friend, to study the shadows of his face. "The Goa'uld call me shol'va," he said, "but you know I am no traitor."

"No," O'Neill said with a curt shake of his head. He appeared ashamed to have doubted him. "No, you're not."

More time passed, measured only by the beat of his heart for there was no moon to mark its passage and no hint of dawn to lighten the sky.

"What if we can't get back?" O'Neill said later. "You ever think of that?"

"I will not accept that possibility." It was a half-truth, however, and he suspected O'Neill knew as much.

"Come on," his friend said. "You're a tactician, Teal'c. You have to accept the possibility."

His reply was a compromise. "I will do everything in my power to prevent it from occurring."

Another silence passed, shorter this time, before O'Neill said, "If we *are* stuck here, then everything is different. Between us, I mean — the team."

"In what way?"

"I can't keep giving you orders, Teal'c. You or Carter."

"You are our commanding officer."

"Not if we're stuck here forever." He let out a breath, a frustrated sigh. Teal'c shared the sentiment. "Look, if you and Carter want to spend your whole lives looking for a way back then I'm not gonna stop you, but…" O'Neill frowned down into the dregs of his coffee. "We'll have to go our separate ways, buddy, because I'm not spending years chasing down the impossible and ignoring what's happening here."

Teal'c waited until he had mastered his feelings before he said, "Then it is as Major Carter feared. You are giving up."

O'Neill's expression changed but he did not look up from his mug. "She said that?"

Teal'c considered his answer. He did not want to misrepresent Major Carter, yet it frustrated him that O'Neill was so eager to embrace this dark future. They had barely been absent for three weeks. It was much too soon to consider remaining here forever. And he knew that O'Neill valued the major's opinion, perhaps more highly than he realized. "Major Carter feels that you were quick to abandon hope of returning home while you were stranded on Edora," he said, choosing his words with care. "She fears that you will be quick to do so again."

O'Neill nodded, brow drawn down into a frown. "On Edora," he said, "I saw people who needed my help to survive — and I needed their help too. I wasn't giving up, I was adapting. I was surviving." He glanced up. "I know you understand that."

He did and found himself unable to meet O'Neill's frank gaze.

"Here," O'Neill continued, "it's the same. I see people who need our help, and we sure as hell need theirs. We're not getting out of this alone. So, no, I'm not giving up. But I am adapting. I'm surviving, Teal'c, and if you and Carter can't—" He took a last swallow of coffee, wiped his mouth on the back of his glove. "We finish this mission," he said. "We get back to Rya'c's ship and then we reassess."

"Reassess?"

"Look around you, Teal'c. This planet is my home." He gestured across the water and up to the ashy clouds. "You think I'm gonna sit on my ass for years waiting for Carter to maybe — *maybe* — figure out how to get us back where we belong?" He got to his feet, shook out his mug. "We finish this mission," he repeated. "We take stock, and then…" He took a breath. "Then maybe I don't give the orders anymore."

Teal'c stood up too, held his friend's gaze. "That would be a sad day."

"Yeah," O'Neill said. "But there are a lot of sad days here, Teal'c, and I can't pretend there's nothing I can do to help."

CHAPTER TWENTY-ONE

Evacuation Site — 2000: Whatever Janet had expected on her return to Arbella, it wasn't half a dozen semi-automatics in her face the moment she stepped from the Stargate.

"Stand down," she said. "I'm alone."

The airmen's weapons didn't move. She looked around for Colonel Reynolds, wanting to ask what the hell was going on, but instead it was Frank Simmons who walked forward to meet her. "Colonel, I haven't brought anyone through with me," she said, struggling to remain calm despite the alarm bells ringing in her head.

"I can see that, Doctor. Nevertheless, you are under arrest."

She glanced around, but there was no one present that she could call an ally. From what she could see, everyone in the room was under the NID chain of command. "On what charge?"

Simmons gave a short laugh as if it should be obvious. "On the charge of Failure to Go. You were granted a pass to return to Earth under your own recognizance, Captain — and, might I remind you, after significant negotiation by you — on the understanding that you would return here at 1800 hours. By my watch, you're over seven hours past that time."

"Didn't Colonel Reynolds explain? I was tending to the sick," she said, aware that her voice was rising. She fought to get it under control, not wanting to add insubordination to this ridiculous charge.

"I shouldn't have to remind you that we have sick here."

"I'm aware of that, Colonel, and I've been doing what I can to help them."

"Oh yes, the meds. Colonel Reynolds told us all about them." Simmons made a show of looking her up and down. "And where might you be concealing these meds?"

"It's not as simple as that."

"Oh I think it is," said Simmons. "I think it's quite simple. You, Doctor, believe you are above the chain of command." He gestured to the airmen nearest her, who took her pack and handed it to the colonel, before securing her hands behind her back with a plastic tie. Janet could see that there was no point in fighting this. To struggle or to run would just give them more ammunition. And besides, where would she run to? Her best bet was to play along and hope that President Turner would sort out the mess.

"Take me to the President, Simmons. This is important. We're running out of time!"

"I don't think you're in any position make demands of the President, Doctor," said Simmons. "After this stunt, I think you'll find granting you favors is very low on his list of priorities. Get her out of here."

Flanked by two airmen, she was marched from the gate room and out of the ruins. The descent down the cliff was precarious, and she kept an eye on her feet, hoping that at least one of her guards would have the decency to catch her if she went flying. She didn't relish the idea of her face breaking her fall.

By the time they reached the camp, Janet was sweat-stained and limping, and it was only when she caught the stares of the people she passed that she realized the extent of Simmons' game. He wasn't just teaching her a lesson; he wanted to teach everyone else a lesson too, and she was the example. He could easily have detained her back at the base, but instead she was being put on parade in front of the entire camp. The bindings on her wrists were as much a symbolic gesture of power as a means to prevent her escape.

It was a surprise then, when she found herself being led to her own tent. One of the airmen cut loose her hands once they were inside and went to join his colleague on guard outside the door.

"Mom!" Cassie leapt up from her bed and into Janet's arms, squeezing her in a fierce hug that Janet returned. "Where have you been? Colonel Reynolds came to see me and said you'd stayed behind on Earth. I thought you weren't coming back."

"Oh honey, I'll always come back to you."

Cassie pulled away and looked up into Janet's face. "He said you were helping the survivors."

Janet nodded. "I was. Or at least, I thought I was. I think I've done more harm than good." She brushed Cassie's hair back from her face. It was always so unruly and, when she'd been younger, many mornings had ended in a tantrum when Janet insisted on brushing it properly before letting her leave for school. Only recently had Cassie started to tame it with straightening irons, but here, in this heat, it was a losing battle.

Janet cursed herself for letting herself forget what should be more important than anything else to her right now. "I'm sorry, sweetheart. I'm sorry I worried you."

Holding Janet's hand, Cassie touched her finger to the red mark left on her wrist by the plastic tie. "It's ok, but… Those men at the door. Mom, are you in trouble?"

Janet sat back and considered her daughter for a moment, realizing for the first time that, emerging from her childish features was the face of the young woman she was becoming. It had never been Janet's way to couch the facts with vague assurances that all would be ok; Cassie had always been smarter than that. "Maybe. I should have come home when I said I would."

"But you didn't."

"No, I didn't."

"You must've had a reason. The people on Earth needed help."

Janet nodded.

Cassie's brow furrowed as if she was working through some of her own ideas. "When… when I first came through the Stargate, I was in danger, and Sam stayed with me even though she wasn't supposed to. Everyone thought that what she was doing was wrong, but she still did it."

The memory of that time stung the back of Janet's throat, but she swallowed back the threat of tears. "She did it because she loved you. And because she wanted to protect you."

"I remember her saying I was brave, but I think she was the one who was brave."

"She was, honey," said Janet. "She was very brave."

Cassie looked up at her then. "I think you are too, Mom. And if they're going to get you into trouble for it, well to hell with them."

"Cassie!" Janet stifled a laugh.

Cassie wasn't deterred in her outrage though. "No, Mom! It isn't right for them to try and stop you from helping people. You're a doctor. That's what you're supposed to do. That's what we're all supposed to do."

There was nothing Janet could say to that. There were still so many times that this kid caught her off guard. "You are the smartest person I know," she said, pressing a kiss to Cassie's forehead and pulling her close. "But I'm here now. I'm not going anywhere."

Raised voices at the door drew her attention then and she looked up to see Colonel Reynolds push his way into the tent, casting a sour look at the guard who followed him. "I don't know what the hell they think I'm gonna do," he muttered to Janet.

"Well, maybe getting me out of here would be a good start."

"No can do, Doc," he replied, chagrined. "This one goes further up the chain of command. I'm so sorry. I told them it was on my orders that you stayed behind, and at first it seemed like they were okay with that. But then this morning… it was like all hell broke loose. I don't know what happened."

"Colonel, you have to help me. Go to the President and let him know what's going on. There's no love lost between him and Simmons, and when he finds out what he's done –" The expression on Reynolds' face stopped her dead. "What?"

"Janet, don't you know? This isn't Simmons' doing. Your arrest? That order came direct from Turner himself."

Earth — 2098: By the time Sam stepped out of the wooden rowboat, it was already astronomical twilight and the sky was fading from black to inky blue. She helped haul the boat up onto the beach and cover it with branches while Teal'c rolled his shoulders after the exertion of the crossing; he'd done most of the rowing, for obvious reasons.

"We should get under cover," Trask said, his eyes on the sky. "This way."

He led them up a shallow bank and into tree cover once more. He looked nervous, pallid in the creeping dawn light as he turned and drew them closer with a gesture. "Many more Wraith on this side of the water," he said in a low voice, his eyes mostly on Elspeth. "Stay close. But if you see the snatching beams, split up and run. Give them more than one target to chase."

Sam nodded, so did the colonel, but he didn't say anything himself and let Trask to take the lead.

He'd been quiet all morning and seemed even more tightly wound than the night before. It was only when they started walking, in the same formation as the previous day, that she understood why.

She stared at Teal'c as he told her about his conversation with the colonel, his voice pitched low as they walked.

"Disbanding SG-1?" she hissed once she'd found her voice again. Her worst fear was taking shape before her. "Colonel O'Neill said that?"

"He said he would no longer issue orders," Teal'c confirmed. "That he wishes to help the people of this world while he waits for us to find a way home."

And, of course, they both knew that might take years — but she was sure she could find a solution much sooner, given a little luck. Not that there was much of that hanging around these days. She shook her head, trying to shake some sense into the situation. "I can't believe he'd disband the unit."

"He implied that we should each walk a separate path."

She felt a hot flare of anger at the idea. "What gives *him* the right to make that choice? He's not—"

Something rattled in the trees to their left.

Aedan flinched at the sound, dropping into a half crouch, weapon raised. The colonel lifted his gun and clicked off the safety.

"Sorry!" Daniel winced, holding up a hand. "Sorry, that was me. I accidently kicked a stone."

The colonel lowered his weapon. "Watch where you're putting your feet, will you?"

Before he started walking again, he darted a glance at Sam and Teal'c; he could probably guess what they were talking about. Sam looked away, angry and hurt in a way she didn't dare examine too closely. But in truth she was afraid too — afraid the colonel might have a point. "What if it does take years…?"

"It will take longer without O'Neill and Daniel Jackson assisting us." That was also true. "We cannot let this happen, Major Carter," Teal'c said. "The future of your world may depend on it."

She kept her eye on the colonel's back as they walked on, trying to play through what he was thinking. He was right about one thing; if they were stuck here then there was a limit to how long they'd all defer to him as their CO. A short limit, she imagined, especially for Teal'c and Daniel. For her…? It was more complicated. But, still, there was a limit.

"On the other hand," she said, "if the colonel isn't in command then we can do whatever we think is necessary to fix this. We don't have to wait for his orders."

"Nor follow them." Teal'c gave her a long look. "In a world without consequences, any risk is worth taking to achieve our objective."

"Any risk," she agreed and glanced again at the colonel. Her stomach felt tight, twisted into a knot, but she knew that she was right: everything they did here would be erased when they succeeded in changing this future. All that mattered was getting home.

"Major Carter," Teal'c said quietly, "perhaps we should—"

"Daniel, watch out!" the colonel yelled.

Startled, Sam reacted too late. The Wraith landed a step

behind Daniel, one arm snaking around his throat and its feeding hand pressed against his chest, before Sam could lift her weapon. It bared its teeth in a snarl, claws flexing when Sam made a move for her gun.

She lifted her hands away. "Easy," she said.

The Wraith backed up a step. Its eyes fixed on the colonel and it jerked its head in the direction of the trees.

Trask was ghost-white, weapon shaking as he tried to aim it at the Wraith. Gently, the colonel put a hand on Trask's arm and pushed his weapon down. There was no point in letting a panicky trigger-finger ignite the situation.

"Um," Daniel said, "I think he wants us to go this way."

"Yup," the colonel said. "I got that."

The Wraith took another step back and then gestured for the others to precede him into the woods. He didn't take his hand away from Daniel's chest the whole time. Sam looked to the colonel, waiting for orders, and when he nodded she moved out.

"Come on," she said, taking Elspeth by the arm and pulling her along. She could feel the girl trembling. "Just stick with me. We'll be okay."

But she didn't know that. None of them did. So much for a world without consequences.

CHAPTER TWENTY-TWO

Evacuation Site — 2000: It was the quiet that kept her awake at night. In Colorado Springs, no matter what time Janet arrived home from her shift on the base, there was always the white noise of traffic on I-25 to lull her to sleep. Here there was nothing but the *shush* of the lake lapping at the shore and the infrequent bark of some animal they had yet to spot but that sounded something like a coyote. From the other side of the tent came the sound of Cassie's gentle snores. Even the guard outside her tent kept a silent watch, his utter stillness a trait of someone who was not unfamiliar with covert ops.

Nothing but the best for me, thought Janet.

If it hadn't been so quiet, perhaps she would've missed the two distinct thuds that came from just outside the tent opening, the second one sounding like a body hitting the dirt.

They'd taken her firearm as soon as she'd stepped through the gate and Janet scanned the inside of the tent, searching for anything that might serve as a weapon. They'd been thorough, but her eyes alighted on the bar of soap that lay on her wash cloth by the bed. She grabbed it and then rolled off her sock, dropping the soap inside. She gave the makeshift club a few practice swings, satisfied that its weight would at least stun the intruder if aimed right. Enough time to grab Cassie and run. She slid on her boots.

"Mom?" Cassie was sitting up in bed, rubbing her eyes. Janet put a finger to her lips and gestured to the doorway. Her daughter, shrewd enough to understand the situation, swung her legs around and pulled on her own sneakers. She moved silently to join Janet at the entrance to the tent, just as the zipper on the door began to open. A head appeared between the flaps of canvas.

Janet swung her club and brought it down on the back of

the intruders head. He staggered and went down with grunt.

"Run, Cassie!" She grabbed the girl's arm and pulled her through the door, out into the night, barely registering that her guard was gone.

The camp was silent apart from their feet pounding the earth and the sound of their quick breaths as they ran. She expected to hear a shout behind her, the alarm raised, but no voices called out. She knew, though, with a gut-twisting certainty that they *were* being pursued.

They dodged through the camp, darting between the tents, trying to shake off whatever threat tailed them. She hadn't considered what direction to head in, and soon her legs ached from the sprint across uneven ground. Just up ahead lay the camp's outskirts, with the open valley beyond. She was about to yell to Cassie, whose younger limbs would carry her further and faster, to head on without her, when she heard the running footsteps behind them. They were gaining fast, but still no cry for them to halt. Whoever was giving chase, whatever their intentions, they didn't want to be heard. Not a good sign.

"Cassie, go –"

A body barreled into her from behind, knocking her full force into the ground. The wind left her and her forehead struck dirt.

"Mom!" Through the multicolored stars that danced across her vision, she saw Cassie skid to a halt and start to run back.

Cassie, get out of here!

She opened her mouth to call out, but a rough hand was clamped across her mouth. "For God's sake, Doc, I'm not gonna hurt you. Either of you."

The hushed voice was one she knew well, but in her dazed state it took a few moments to place it. It was Cassie who recognized him first.

"Colonel Reynolds?"

The weight left her and Janet rolled over to find Reynolds standing over her, dusting himself down. She pushed herself to her feet, and touched her fingers to her forehead. They came away wet, but by the feel of it, it was just a graze. "What the hell are you doing, Colonel?"

"Getting my skull cracked open I think," he replied, rubbing the back of his own head.

She crossed her arms and stared at him.

He shrugged. "The plan *was* to break you out," he said, and then looked around him. "So I guess that part went well."

She closed her eyes and rubbed the bridge of her nose. "Colonel, I'm under house arrest for failure to go, ordered by the President himself. This isn't just me facing court martial, this is bigger than me. If Simmons or Maybourne find out what you're doing... With all due respect, are you crazy?"

In the darkness, his expression was hard to make out, but she heard him sigh. "Doctor, I just might be."

It was then that she saw the figure that approached from the direction of the camp. She didn't need any lantern light to see who it was.

"Good work, Colonel," said Maybourne, and clapped Reynolds on the shoulder. "Dr. Fraiser, I think you and I need to have a little talk."

Earth — 2098: Daniel had assumed they were on their way to the 'farm', so he was surprised when the Wraith herded them deeper into the underbrush and away from any discernible path. The creature's massive clawed hand bit into his arm but at least it wasn't hovering over his chest any longer. Nonetheless, the threat was implied and the Wraith's strength was intimidating in itself. There was no way Daniel was breaking free anytime soon.

He cast a surreptitious glance at his captor and wondered whether he'd seen the creature before. It was difficult to tell with such alien features, but he thought he recognized the tattoo on the side of the Wraith's face. Could it be one of the Wraith who'd held them captive in the pods?

"Now where?" Jack said from up front. He'd stopped in a slight clearing, the undergrowth thinning out but with no obvious path ahead.

Without releasing Daniel's arm, the Wraith stalked past Jack and started clearing away branches and leaves to reveal the foundations of a brick wall and a flight of stone stairs that led to an underground doorway. He gestured for the others to precede him down the steps.

"I don't think so," Jack said. It was subtle, but Daniel noticed the way his weight moved forward onto the balls of his feet, how his grip on his weapon shifted. He was getting ready for a fight and Daniel did the same; they all knew that he'd be the first victim if things got ugly and he didn't plan to make it easy.

Teal'c's staff sprung into life and Sam thumbed off the safety on her MP5.

Daniel braced himself, waiting in hope for the mistake that would let him free himself and run.

But it didn't happen. Instead, the Wraith spoke. "Trust me or you will die," he said, baring teeth in a way that didn't exactly encourage trust.

"Don't you mean 'Trust me *and* you will die?'" Jack said.

"This area will be swept by darts within moments. If you are above ground, you will be culled."

Jack lifted his eyebrows. "And you're helping us because…?"

"Because you are of use, Lantean."

It was rare that Jack ever showed genuine surprise, but for a second he looked stunned. And then the moment was gone and he was all hard edges and reflection once more. "And how do you know who I am?"

A sound, like the faint whine of a mosquito, made the Wraith look up.

Aedan dropped like a stone, so did Elspeth. "They're coming," she said in panic.

The Wraith growled, hauling Daniel around and shoving him down the stairs. "Inside."

A heartbeat of hesitation, then Jack said, "Go. Everyone, inside."

Daniel went first, pushing open the door and stumbling into darkness. He heard the others' boots on the stone steps behind him and then a dim light flickered on inside, revealing a large underground room that faded into shadows outside the circle of lamplight. It must have been a basement once; he could see windows running along the top of one wall, but they were underground now and looked out onto nothing but dirt.

The Wraith was the last to enter, closing the door behind him and cutting off the daylight. Elspeth backed up closer to Daniel and he took her arm in reassurance. "If he wanted us dead," he said, "he'd have left us out there."

"Perhaps he just wants to feed on us himself?" Aedan growled.

"I don't think that's what's going on."

From beyond the door came the sound of aircraft overhead, the mosquito whine amplified to a sonic boom. Darts, the Wraith had called them, and Daniel remembered the needle-nosed ship that had crashed close to Aedan's camp, whose pilot they'd saved from—

"It's you," he said out loud, as the Wraith stepped further into the light. "You're the pilot we rescued." The one who had saved his life and then summoned the darts that had snatched them.

The Wraith was massive in the closed space, taller than Teal'c, his presence larger still. "I am."

"Sonofa—" Jack bit off the curse. "You sold us out," he said, leveling an angry finger at the creature. "We saved your ass and you sold us out."

The Wraith looked unmoved. "I gave the gift of life to that one," he said, pointing to Daniel.

"Oh," Jack said, "well that's okay, then."

The Wraith ignored him, cocking his head as if listening to something—perhaps the fading sound of the darts leaving, perhaps some telepathic communication. After a moment, his attention returned to the room and he said, "Sit, if you wish."

"And if we don't wish?" said Jack.

"Then stand." The Wraith moved past them to a wooden bench that ran along the wall. He sat down, setting his stunner on the bench next to him. "It is not safe outside during daylight hours. You must stay here until nightfall."

Daniel rubbed at his arm where the Wraith's claws had dug into him. Jack seemed to be at an impasse — torn between wanting to leave and being afraid that the Wraith was right about their chances topside. Sam hovered anxiously next to Teal'c, her attention moving from Jack to the Wraith and back again. Teal'c just looked on with his usual cool appraisal, while Aedan and Elspeth cowered near the door and looked very much like they were coming face-to-face with their worst nightmare. Which, of course, they were.

Clearing his throat, Daniel stepped forward. "My name is Daniel Jackson," he said; it was always a good place to start. "Thank you, for saving my life."

"A life for a life," the creature said. "A debt paid."

"Yes, but… thank you." The creature just stared at him, so he said, "Um, do you have a name? Is there something we can call you?" He touched his chest. "I'm Daniel. This is Jack, Sam, Teal'c, Aedan and Elspeth."

The Wraith considered that for a moment, as if the idea were novel. "They are just sounds," he said. "Your names are not of you, they have no meaning."

"Um, well, okay. Ah, actually they do have a meaning. Daniel, for example, means 'God is my judge'."

"And which god judges you, *Daniel*?" the Wraith said. "The parasite-gods?"

"If you mean the Goa'uld, then no. It's a… actually it refers to the Abrahamic god, but let's not get into that." He ran his hands through his hair. "What about you, what can we call you?"

The Wraith bared his teeth again and Daniel was beginning to understand that it wasn't necessarily an aggressive expression. It could, perhaps, also indicate pride. "My name," the

Wraith said, "is the sharp bite of a blade as it slices your skin; the bitter moment you understand your defeat."

"That's quite a mouthful," said Jack.

The Wraith turned his eyes on him. "You may call me 'Sting.'"

"Sting," Jack repeated, and threw a glance at Daniel that he just knew meant trouble. "Okay, Sting, just remember this: don't stand so close to me."

Daniel shook his head. "Really?"

"I'm just saying — every breath you take, every move you make, I'll be watching you."

Sam looked like she was torn between amusement and exasperation. Amusement seemed to be winning and she pressed her lips together to keep from smiling.

"Stormfire has been tracking you, Lantean," continued the Wraith. "Your escape from our hive was impressive. And damaging."

And with that all humor fled Jack's face. "And Stormfire is...?"

"Our Master of Sciences Physical."

"Ah," Jack said, "my old friend Crazy."

An expression flitted through the Wraith's eyes that might have been humor, although Daniel couldn't be sure. "He is named aptly," Sting said. "His mind rages and burns. But do not underestimate him."

"I don't," Jack said. "But I do want to know how he tracked me."

Sting didn't answer, but he moved to lean forward. Everyone took a step back. The Wraith bared its teeth again; Daniel wondered if it was a smile. "I will not harm you," Sting said. "I believe we can make common cause."

"I doubt it," Jack said. "Unless you're planning on driving your own people back to wherever the hell you came from?"

"That is exactly what we seek to achieve," said a new voice, "but we will need your help to do so."

Daniel turned, astonished to see another Wraith — this one young and obviously female — emerge from the shadows in the depths of the cellar. Jet-black hair, elaborately braided, hung to her waist, a stark contrast to her bone-white skin. She was dressed humbly and for the cold in a fur-lined tunic and cloak, a weapon at her side. Yet the tilt of her head, the confidence of her bearing, gave her the look of one born to rule. Daniel knew an aristocrat when he saw one.

Sting rose. "You were to wait with Flint," he said.

"I did not choose to wait." She touched Sting's hand in a gesture that was at once reassurance and command, and there was a moment's pause as if the rest of the conversation was carrying on in silence. Which it probably was, Daniel reflected.

Her attention left Sting and found Sam, though her hand remained on his arm. "I am Earthborn," she said, and then she turned to Jack. "You are welcome, Lantean. In you, we place great hope."

Evacuation Site — 2000: They sat on the ruins at the summit of the cliff path, a fallen column serving as a bench for Janet and Cassie, while Maybourne sat on the broken stump of a pillar base. Colonel Reynolds had returned to the camp, mentioning something about tying up loose ends to make sure no alarm was raised, and Janet thought of the guard who'd suddenly disappeared from outside her tent. She hoped he hadn't been hurt for just doing his job. Reynolds had offered to escort Cassie back to the camp, but Cassie had been adamant she wasn't leaving her mom. For once, Janet was happy to go along with her daughter's stubborn streak; she wasn't ready to let her out of her sight.

She still wasn't sure whether Reynolds' colluding with Maybourne constituted betrayal. The very reason they still sat outside the base, despite the biting wind that blew through the ruins and cut them to the bone, was because she didn't trust Maybourne enough to go inside. There was no knowing what might be waiting for her in there. Here, amid this rubble, was just enough of a safe ground; she could run again if she had to. The only concession she'd made was to let them bring a blanket for Cassie, who'd been shivering in the t-shirt and sweats she wore to bed.

"Do you want to tell me what this is all about, Colonel?" Janet made sure her tone was even, biting back the resentment she felt; the chain of command here was a taut thing, and she'd already spun the rope to the very end of its frayed strands. Besides, she didn't want to alarm Cassie with any confrontation.

"Some things can't be discussed in the light of day, Doctor."

"So you staged a jail break just to talk to me?"

"No, not just that. You need my help."

"I need your help?" The idea was just too bizarre to even laugh at. "I think I've managed to screw myself over well enough without your help, Colonel."

"Reynolds told me about the ha'tak and your plan."

She hesitated, not sure whether she wanted Maybourne knowing about that particular plan, though she couldn't think what influence he'd have on it one way or the other. It made no difference to her now anyway. "Why would you want to help me? Last time I checked we weren't on the same side."

"You're very focused on sides, Doctor. Have you considered that maybe this is bigger than the good guys versus the bad guys? Right now, it's not about sides."

She brought up her arm in front of her chest, indicating red marks where the cuffs had cut into her skin. "Isn't it?"

Maybourne paused and then nodded. "That wasn't my doing. That was Simmons."

She raised an eyebrow.

"Okay, I'll admit there's a power struggle here, but don't tell me that you're happy to buy into it. I'm offering you an alternative."

"And what alternative would that be?"

"You want to help the people of Arbella, and those back on Earth? Then I'll help you. Come with me now and I'll send you through the Stargate. Those are my people in there, no matter what Frank Simmons might think. They'll help you if I say so."

Janet squinted at him in the darkness, trying to read his features to make some sense of what game he might be playing. He gave nothing away. "So you want to help me now? Suddenly Simmons isn't your ally?"

"He was never my ally, Janet. A man would have to be a fool to think Frank Simmons was on his side. So yes, I want to help you. I want to help us all."

She shook her head, still not buying it. "Why?"

There was a beat, and she thought she heard him swallow, thought she saw his jaw tense and his eyes flick away. "I... because I... " He sucked in a breath through his nose and looked up at her. "You're a doctor, Janet. You've no doubt had to make difficult choices. Have you ever made one that you regretted so bitterly that you'd give up everything to change it?"

"Truthfully? No." She wouldn't let him play the pity card. "Not like this. Don't tell me you didn't know what you were doing."

"I thought I was serving the interests of Earth."

She almost balked at that; as far as she was concerned, Maybourne had never served any interests but his own. "How could stealing from our allies help Earth? How could you not see this coming? Someone must've told you what you were doing, what would happen."

He flinched, as if she'd hit a nerve, but it was a fleeting expression. "I never wanted this," he said. "I wanted to *save* Earth, not destroy it. But it's not too late."

She exchanged a glance with Cassie. Her daughter, huddled in her blanket, looked just as apprehensive as she felt. "Not too late for what?"

"To save it. To save Earth. Isn't that what you've been asking us to do all along?"

Save Earth. The words were exquisite, the idea dangled like fruit on a tree that was ever out of reach. But the notion that Earth could be saved after the Goa'uld had all but destroyed it, or that she could play a part in such a plan, was ridiculous.

This conversation was pointless and she should go. After what she had decided today, she should stand up and walk away. "How?" she said.

"We need to prove that Earth is still viable. That it still has resources we need. According to Colonel Reynolds, there are drugs there that we could use against this flu. Is that right?"

"Dr. Aitchison told me that there are antivirals at the naval base. Possibly equipment too."

"Then we go get them."

"What does the President say to that?"

"Once you've come back with the means of eradicating this flu, the President won't have much choice but to listen to you. Hell, most of the people here would be ready to vote you into power if given the chance."

"I don't want power, Maybourne."

"Well, you have it. Like it or not. Now it's down to you how you use it."

There was nothing she could say to that. She was a doctor, not a leader. It was Jack and Sam and Daniel and Teal'c who should be here, not her. But it seemed that she'd fallen into this role by default.

"It won't be immediate, Janet, but we have to start somewhere. We plant the idea and give people hope again. The only thing we didn't have during the evac was time. But there are people back on Earth. Governments, armed forces, people willing to fight, people like Dixon. And resources too, if we only move now, before everything falls under Goa'uld control."

She wondered if this was how he'd recruited those servicemen and women who'd become part of his rogue division; by selling them a goal that sounded not only noble, but achievable too. She had to admit he was good at it. "We're on permanent lock down. Turner won't allow anyone to return to Earth. I'm proof of that."

Maybourne shook his head. "That's just posturing. He's

scared and Frank Simmons has him in the palm of his hand. All he needs is a gesture, something to show him that this is the right thing to do. If the people make themselves heard, he'll have to listen. But our people need a symbol, someone to show them that this isn't the end."

The reality of what he was saying slowly dawned. She stood and walked to the edge of the cliff. The red rock fell away before her and she felt she was falling with it.

"You're the one who could do that, Janet! I have a team standing by in the gate room, ready to head back through with you. You help Dixon and let me do the rest. But we have to move fast."

His look was expectant and Janet wondered if she'd landed on the other side of the looking glass when she'd stepped back through the gate, a place where Harry Maybourne was on her side when no one else seemed to be. She didn't trust him, but the offer he was making was everything she'd been arguing for since they'd first heard Dave Dixon's transmission.

It didn't matter now though; she'd already made her decision. Janet walked over to sit on the pillar again. "I'm sorry, Colonel. I'm not the person you're looking for."

"What do you mean?"

"I mean, I can't help you… or Colonel Dixon, or anyone else. This isn't my fight anymore."

"You're not making sense, Doctor. Isn't this what you've been pleading for? Isn't this why they had you under lock and key?"

"Yes, Colonel. Yes, that's exactly why. I tried to do what I thought was right and that's what it got me. I tried to do what–" She bit off and pressed her lips together, eyes closed. *I tried to do what they would've done* was what she'd been about to say. But she refused to give him that much, to let him see how much she missed them and how much she wished she wasn't so damned alone in all of this. "I guess I forgot myself," was all she said. She glanced at Cassie who was watching the exchange intently. "My loyalties need to lie here."

"On Arbella." Maybourne's tone was flat and cynical.

"Yes." In the distance, a coyote creature howled, its cry taken up by others in its pack. The strange-scented wind blew through the ruins, stirring up the planet's red dust. Janet leaned forward on her knees and pressed her forehead against the balls of her palms. She was so tired.

Maybourne held up his hands as if to try and appease her. "If you're worried about repercussions, I'd make sure you could come back, no court martial."

She eyed him, gauging his credibility, but then shook her head. "I'm done taking risks."

"Why?"

Janet started; the question hadn't come from Maybourne. It had come from Cassie.

Her daughter shrugged off her blanket and came to kneel in front of her. "Why are you done taking risks, Mom?"

Janet smoothed her hand across Cassie's cheek. "Honey, you know why."

"Because of me?"

"Of course, because of you. You're the only person I should be taking care of now."

"But what if I don't want you to?"

"Cassie, don't –"

"Mom, I'm fourteen — Let me finish," she said, when Janet began to object. "I'm fourteen. I'm old enough to take care of myself. And I don't mean like the time I wanted to stay over at Piper's house when her parents weren't home. I mean, I'm fourteen, and I already know all about the bad things that can happen in the world… in *any* world." She took Janet's hand from her face and squeezed it between both of hers. "You can't make decisions because of me anymore."

Janet lifted her chin, feeling more like the stubborn teenager. "And what if I just don't want to leave you? What if I just love you that much?"

Cassie shrugged. "Then what's the point of anything you've ever tried to teach me? You taught me that it matters when we stand up for others. That we should always try to do the right thing. If we don't do that, if living in this world means that we always just do what *we* want to do, and don't look out for each other... Well, I don't think I want to live in a place like that. And I know you think you're not brave, but you are. I don't know anyone braver! That's why General Hammond trusted you."

The mention of the general's name made her throat tighten and she pressed her eyes closed. She'd been ready to stand beside him at the end, until he'd told her what he'd done, that he'd saved Cassie and she was waiting on the other side of the gate.

If there's a chance... If any of us survive this, will you come back? Will you come back and fight for us?

In that moment, she'd pressed her hand against her heart and vowed that she would, though she knew he couldn't hear. And she'd meant it.

Will you come back and fight for us?

Did that vow still matter, even when the fight was probably futile? She opened her eyes and looked at Cassie's earnest face. This wise little girl who'd grown up when she wasn't looking. Yes. Yes, of course it mattered.

"You," she said, as the tears finally spilled over onto her cheeks, "are the smartest person I know." She pulled her daughter into a fierce hug.

"Just make sure you come back, okay?" said Cassie, her voice thick with her own tears.

"I will, honey," replied Janet, and glared at Maybourne over Cassie's shoulder, letting him know that he better come through on his assurances. "I promise I will."

They had to move quickly then, their time window hinging on how long Reynolds could cover their tracks. On Janet's request, an escort was arranged for Cassie back down the cliff; she couldn't bear any more goodbyes, and stepping through the wormhole would be difficult enough.

Waiting in the gate room were two airmen, one of them

being Major Dean Newman.

"Two?" She directed the question at Maybourne as she donned the kit she'd been given.

"For now," he said. "Any more and there would have been questions. Reynolds will head through with another unit once we have more weight behind us."

"And when will that happen?"

"Patience, Doctor. Rome wasn't built in a day."

She checked her clip. "Rome was ruled by a morally bankrupt class of despots for whom political corruption was as routine as breakfast. Not the best strategic model, Colonel."

His smile was withering.

"Doc!" The call came from Colonel Reynolds, who had come running into the base, sweating and breathing hard.

"Colonel?" said Maybourne. "Is there a problem?"

Reynolds shook his head. "No, coast's still clear for now." He looked at Janet. "I just wanted to say good luck. Make this one count."

"I will, sir."

"Oh, and I brought you your pack." He handed Janet the rucksack he'd been carrying. "You might want to check it's got everything you need."

"I'm sure it'll be fine, sir."

"I've never been good at packing. You should check." He fixed her with a look. "Just in case."

Trying to hide her puzzlement, she unzipped the pack and looked inside. Moving aside some MREs she saw, hidden in the folds of a Gore-Tex poncho, the camera he'd given her on their first mission to Earth.

"Just in case," he murmured again, casting a glance at Maybourne who'd turned to speak with Newman.

"Understood, sir. Thank you."

He took a breath and nodded, then after a beat said, "You sure you want to do this, Doctor?"

"No. But I don't see that there's any other choice." She joined

Newman and the other young airman as they waited in front of the gate.

"It's funny," said Newman, without taking his eyes from the wormhole as it whooshed into life, "when we came here, we were told it was a one way trip. I never thought I'd be making a return journey."

"Then let's hope they make it an open ticket, Major," said Janet, and stepped through without waiting for a reply.

CHAPTER TWENTY-THREE

Earth — 2098: "My mother," Earthborn said, "brought us to this galaxy."

Daniel rested his back against the cellar wall. Jack sat opposite, perched on an upturned crate with his weapon cradled in his lap. It was interesting that the Wraith had made no attempt to disarm them. Either they didn't fear their weapons or they were confident that they wouldn't use them. Daniel wasn't sure which option he preferred.

Teal'c hovered close to the door and Sam sat with Elspeth and Aedan, as far from the Wraith as they could get. Daniel guessed Sam was trying to reassure them with her presence, although her attention was tightly focused on what Earthborn was saying.

"My mother was allied with her sister, Shadow," the Wraith said, "who set her clevermen to unlocking the secrets of the Ancestors."

A matriarchal society, Daniel noted, itching to ask more. He wanted to chase every rabbit down its hole, but he knew Jack wouldn't appreciate the distraction and so swallowed his surmises about Wraith social structure, along with his theories about who the Ancestors might be, and kept listening.

"Some years before my birth," Earthborn said, "the hive of my mother's sister stumbled upon a great discovery: the city of the Ancestors, known as Atlantis."

"I'm sorry?" Okay, so there were some rabbits he couldn't let go. "Did you say *Atlantis*?"

Earthborn turned imperious eyes on him. "You know of it."

"Um, I've heard of it. Legends, really. But..." He glanced at Jack who was all-but rolling his eyes. "Well, we all know how legends start," Daniel said, for Jack's benefit. "In our culture," he said to Earthborn, "we call it the Lost City of Atlantis. It was said to have sunk beneath the sea."

"And so it did," Earthborn said. "As they fled our galaxy at the end of the great war, the Ancestors hid their city beneath an ocean and left it there in the hope, perhaps, of one day returning. That day never came and after many thousands of years the city's power failed and it floated free of its resting place to breathe the air once more. There, abandoned, the hive of Queen Shadow found it." Her expression changed to something that Daniel interpreted as disdain. "It is a pity that a treasure so great should fall into such hands."

Daniel looked over at Sam. "And pretty astonishing that we should know about it here, in another galaxy."

"There must have been some contact," she said and he knew she'd reached the same conclusion he had. "The Ancients?"

"I'd take that bet."

"It is certain fact," Earthborn said, "that the Ancestors fled to your world — and you, like us, are their children."

Sam shook her head. "No, that's not possible. We understand the evolution of our species and it doesn't involve aliens."

Earthborn looked at her. "Are you certain? Your blade, here," she indicated Jack, "carries the mark of the Ancestors in his blood."

Sam's eyes widened as she looked at Jack. "He has Ancient DNA?"

"Hey, who are you calling—?"

Daniel cut off the inevitable joke. "Are you certain?" he said.

Sting bristled. "Do you doubt the word of a queen?"

"Um, no," Daniel said, hands lifted. "It's just surprising. You know, Jack's not very—" He cleared his throat. "Anyway, you were telling us about Atlantis."

Jack gave him a narrow look, but didn't interrupt.

"Atlantis," Earthborn repeated. "I have not seen it with my own eyes, but Sting can tell you more. He was a blade in my mother's zenana when she brought us here."

Sting looked as though he didn't really enjoy telling stories, but there was enough command in Earthborn's voice to make him comply. "It is a vast city," he explained, "with great power. It is because of Atlantis that we were able to travel so far. The hive of Brightstar was carried within the shields of Atlantis as it crossed the vastness between galaxies. But it—"

"Wait." Jack held up a hand. "Are you saying it flies? It's a flying underwater city?"

Sting looked at him. Daniel had seen General Hammond give Jack similar looks. "It is no longer beneath the water."

Jack waved that away. "Where is it?" he said, and there was nothing humorous about the question.

"It lies in the southern ocean of your world."

"Atlantis is *here*?" Daniel was astounded.

"And that," Earthborn said, "is why we need you."

Jack looked skeptical, folded his arms on top of his gun. "Uh-huh."

"The Ancestors were chary with their gifts," Earthborn said. "The most powerful were kept only for their own use in case they fell into the hands of the enemy." She spread her own hands, giving Daniel a disconcerting view of her clawed fingers and the strange feeding mouth on the palm of one hand. "Once her clevermen had discovered the location of this world, my mother's sister found a pilot able to fly the city and, on the promise of food unlimited, my mother brought us here. But the pilot is dead now and Atlantis is once more tethered."

"Because she can't find another pilot?" Daniel guessed.

"That can't be right," Sam said. Then, to Earthborn, "If what you say is true about the Ancestors coming here, then Colonel O'Neill can't be the only person on Earth with their DNA marker."

"He is not," Sting said. "Stormfire has tested many humans, but their blood is weak. In this one, it is strong."

Jack looked a little pleased with himself, or pretended to be. It was always hard to tell, which was probably his intention. "So this queen of yours wants me to fly you guys home?"

Jack said. "I should tell you, I charge double this time of night."

"Queen Shadow," Earthborn said, "does not seek a pilot. She does not seek to leave this feeding ground."

And that was a nice term for Earth. "But you do?" Daniel said.

Earthborn looked at Sting and another silent communication passed between them. After a moment, she said, "Shadow has become corrupted and in turn she corrupts our people. We are born to hunt, to sleep, to hunt again. But in these fields of plenty our people need do nothing but feed. They are losing their souls to this world."

"So what is it you want me to do?"

Again, another silent look and then Sting spoke. "Our hive is dying," he said. "After the battle that brought it down, Queen Brightstar did all she could to heal it but she herself was mortally wounded and heavy with child." He looked briefly at Earthborn. "After giving life to her daughter, our queen's own life failed. Many of her blades and clevermen now serve Shadow. Some have stayed loyal to the young queen, but without a viable hive we are marooned upon this world."

"Again," Jack said. "What is it you want me to do? And, more importantly, why should I do it?"

"You wish us to leave your world and your galaxy," Earthborn said. "I wish to lead my people home."

"Okay," Jack said, non-committal.

"To do so I must seize Atlantis from Queen Shadow. I must end her corruption of our people. And you, Lantean, must make Atlantis fly once more."

Earth — 2000: During the weeks they'd been on Arbella, Janet had often wished for rain. Not for any practical purposes; the lake provided an ample water supply. Rather, she'd missed the ambience of a rain shower — the scent, the sound and the feel of raindrops on her face.

As she squatted on a muddy hillside just north of the Dixon's bunker, concealed by sodden scrub and soaked to the skin, she decided that there was some truth to the adage 'be careful what you wish for'. Scotland was doing its level best to live up to its reputation for inclement weather by pelting them with an unrelenting rain. There was no storm to go with it, no wind to drive the downpour in sheets, no thunder or lightening for added drama. It was simply a constant curtain of gray water falling from the low hung sky.

"How long do we have to wait?" muttered the junior airman whose name had turned out to be Todd Levine. The boy looked barely old enough to be out of the Academy, yet here he was on a mission to save the Earth.

"You wait until Colonel Dixon comes back, Levine. And longer, if I tell you to," said Newman, scanning the area through the foliage with mini binoculars.

Airman Levine huddled further into his poncho, looking chagrined. "Yes sir."

Janet herself had been about to comment on how long Dixon had been gone, but instead kept silent. Her boots slid on the mulch that covered the ground and she adjusted her position to stop from skidding down the slope and out into the open.

On Colonel Dixon's orders, they'd left the base on foot. The Goa'uld were regular in their air patrols, and this was the time window in which Death Glider fly-pasts could be expected. It was too risky to take a vehicle out on the open road, and so, for concealment, they were forced into the undergrowth, pushing forward inch by inch. It was slow going and uncomfortable, but then Janet knew they'd all endured worse conditions. Except for Airman Levine perhaps.

As they'd rounded the coast and moved off of the peninsula, Dixon had gone ahead to carry out a recon of the area, but by her watch it had been almost thirty minutes since he'd left them. She was growing concerned and could tell that Newman was too.

A rustling in the undergrowth to their left had them reaching for their weapons, and then sighing in relief when Dixon's blackened face appeared.

"We're good," he said. "Air patrols are done. Time to move out."

The open road made the going much better, the six of them falling into a steady pace rather than the uneven stumble and crawl they'd endured for the past few miles. The rain still fell, but it was less miserable now that they were moving. Janet fell into step beside Dixon, who had taken point, while Newman covered the rear.

"You doing ok, Doc?" he asked after a while.

"I could do with some dry socks, but I'll live."

"I didn't mean that. I meant about your kid. Cassie isn't it? Couldn't have been easy leaving her behind."

Janet kept her eyes fixed on the tarmac ahead of her. "At least I know she's safe. A lot of people don't have that comfort."

Dixon said nothing, but turned away from her, looking out across the water. It was only then that Janet remembered his family and what had happened to them. She cursed inwardly. "I'm sorry, Dave, I —"

He shook his head. "No, it's… It's OK. I brought it up. It's just sometimes I forget, y'know? I can pretend that this is just another tour, and Lainie's waiting for me back home. Besides, I'm not the only one who's lost." They walked in silence for a few minutes before he added, "I guess what I'm saying is that I wouldn't have blamed you if you hadn't come back. If I was in your position, I'd have been tempted to be selfish."

Janet gave a wry chuckle, "It's hard to be selfish with a kid like mine. She's my compass. She reminded me that I'd made a promise."

"To General Hammond?"

She nodded.

He grinned. "Yeah, I hear you. It was hard to say no to him, huh?"

"You've got that right. He inspired that. I'd have followed him to the ends of the Earth, I think."

"In a way, you did," said Dixon, with a short laugh.

Not quite, Janet wanted to say. *Not quite to the end.*

"Anyway," he said, "what I'm saying is I'm glad you came back. It's good to have you on the team."

"For whatever use I'll be."

"Are you kidding me? Dr. Janet Fraiser? The world's foremost expert on the Goa'uld? You'd be an asset to any team."

Janet wasn't sure how much of his praise was to make her feel better, but it was good to hear anyway and she returned his grin.

Dixon looked over his shoulder to where Major Newman had their six about ten yards behind them. "What about him?" he murmured.

Janet didn't have to ask what he meant. Dixon was aware that Newman had been Maybourne's man, and she could tell that he didn't entirely trust him. She was inclined to share the sentiment. "I'm not sure," she replied in low tones. "I guess he's here to keep an eye on us."

"Then maybe we should return the favor."

The rain had eased to a drizzle by the time the group reached what looked like the start of a village; a collection of pretty houses, some old, some new, which lined either side of the road. Beyond, tiny boats bobbed disconsolately in the bay. The homes looked deserted, but were still remarkably intact.

"We searched this place after we got here with the gate. It was deserted then. We think the people fled before the Jaffa came for them," said Dixon. "I doubt they made it far though. If they'd stayed put…" He shrugged. "Maybe they'd have been safe, maybe not."

It was strange in this picturesque little ghost town. A dead place, yet perfectly preserved. Janet retrieved the camera from her pack and began filming. The only sign that anyone had ever been here were the newspapers strewn across the sidewalk in front of a convenience store. The sodden sheets bore headlines from a time before everything had gone to hell; the attack had been so swift that there hadn't been time to get new editions out afterwards.

Across the street from the store was a small church. "We should check it out, sir," said Newman to the colonel. "If people were taking refuge, they may still be inside."

The hope proved futile. As they rounded the side of the building, they saw that the tall arched windows were smashed, the wooden door hanging from its hinges and blast marks scorching the white stone of the walls. The village, it seemed, had not gone unscathed after all, and if anyone had been inside, they would not have escaped what had clearly been a Goa'uld assault.

It had been a small hope, but Janet could see that the others shared her despondency. Only Dixon remained stoic, and she guessed that he was used to the fact that survivors would be scarce. He gestured towards the door of the church. "Well, I guess this'll be as good a place as any to regroup. I doubt any Jaffa will be coming back here."

They made their way inside, weaving between the broken pews and glass that littered the floor. On the camera's small screen Janet saw the blankets and sleeping bags strewn across the space near the altar, giving credence to Newman's suggestion that the church would have been used as a refuge. She tried not to think about what might have happened to those who had slept here. They cleared a space and hunkered down, as Dixon pulled a plastic covered map from the pocket of his BDUs.

"Alright, this is our current position." He indicated a point on the map and then dragged his finger down the white line that followed the curve of the coast. "We need to take the road about three klicks south, and this is where we split. Newman, you and Levine head further on, to where the propane tanks are. Plant the C4, set it off at the right time. Fraiser and I go through the water." He looked at Janet ruefully. "Sorry Doc, but it looks like we'll be getting a little wet."

"I think the rain's already taken care of that, Colonel."

"If your explosion is big enough, hopefully it'll clear out most of the Jaffa from the base itself and get them topside. Levine, that's where you come in, kid. I hear you're quite the deadeye."

Levine shrugged, abashed. "I can hit a mark, sir."

Dixon clapped him on the shoulder. "You get yourself into position and take them out one by one. If there's one thing Jaffa don't understand it's subtlety. They won't make you until it's too late. Which gives us a shot at making it inside without too much opposition. Dr. Aitchison's described the layout of the base, so we should be able to make it to the infirmary without too many problems. Once we've got what we came for, we set our own charges and then hightail out of there. We might not be able to take this base by force, but we can do some pest control. You all ready?"

Expressions grim but determined, they all nodded their consensus. It was time to move out. They gathered their packs and Janet flipped open the camera once more, ready to film their progress; this area was valuable territory and if they hoped to return here in numbers, they'd need intel on the terrain. The tiny screen blurred and then focused on a pile of sleeping bags heaped beneath a pew that had been upended against the wall.

It moved.

"Heads up!" she cried, reaching for her MP5. But she wasn't fast enough. A figure burst from the hiding place with a scream. In her hand, there was a flash of silver and she lunged for Colonel Dixon who had turned in surprise. The colonel grabbed for her weapon, but the blade caught him across the palm of his hand and he let go with a yell. It was enough of an opening for the woman to thrust her knife towards his middle. The blade found its mark and Janet saw the bloom of red through the torn fabric of his jacket. Before he'd even hit the ground, their weapons were turned as one on his attacker.

Earth — 2098: "With all due respect, sir," Sam hissed, "that's insane."

Jack lifted an eyebrow. "Due respect noted, Major."

SG-1 was in a huddle in one corner of the cellar, trying to keep their voices low enough that neither the Wraith nor Aedan and Elspeth could overhear their conversation. Daniel wasn't sure they were succeeding.

"You can't possibly agree to fly this city — whatever it is — to another galaxy," Sam persisted. "There'd be no way home. It would be suicide."

"Carter, everything about this situation is insane. Why should this be any different?"

"Because," she said, with the exaggerated patience you might use on a child, "it's deflecting us from the mission in hand, which is to get *us* home and –" She dropped her voice to a whisper "—and to stop this future from ever happening."

"I knew you were going to say that."

"Because it's true!"

Daniel couldn't help noticing a distinct lack of 'sir' in Sam's conversation, something he was pretty sure Jack was noticing too.

"Major Carter is correct," Teal'c said. "There is only way to prevent this situation from unfolding."

Jack tugged off his cap, scrubbed a hand through his hair. "I'm getting tired of this argument."

"Then cease arguing," Teal'c said.

Jack glared at him, Teal'c glared right back and Daniel said "Um, one thing?"

"What?" Jack snapped.

"We don't actually know that there's anything we can do to stop the Wraith from invading," he said. "I mean," he glanced around, lowered his voice again, "their timeline is totally independent of ours, right? So even if we could change things to stop Apophis invading Earth, it would only buy us another forty years."

"That's—" Sam looked at Teal'c, then back at Daniel. "He's got a point," she said with obvious frustration.

"In which case," Daniel pressed on, "perhaps we're meant

to be here. Perhaps we're meant to use *this* opportunity, right here, right now, to free Earth from the Wraith. Maybe it's fate."

Sam made a face. It was her 'I'm a scientist, don't give me any of that crap' face. "I don't believe in fate."

"Neither do I," Jack said. "But Daniel's right. Even if we went back and saved the Protected Planet Treaty, that doesn't stop these guys from showing up forty years later."

"If you preserve the Protected Planet Treaty," Teal'c said, "the Asgard and the Tollan would stand with Earth against the Wraith."

"Or maybe," Sam said, "something else happens that we simply can't predict. Who knows how far we'd get in forty years?"

"Doesn't matter," Jack said. "We can only deal with what's happening on the ground right now." He glanced over at Aedan, who was watching them through troubled eyes. "I for one," Jack said, "don't plan on turning my back on these people." He looked at Teal'c and, with more reluctance, at Sam. "We finish this mission," he said. "We infiltrate the farm, exfil Jones' wife and get back to Rya'c's ship. After that…" Sam's mouth tightened into a pursed, unhappy expression. "Then we make some decisions."

Daniel felt his eyebrows climb up into his hairline. "Decisions?"

"About our next move." By which, Daniel guessed, he meant how far to pursue a means of getting home and how far to help the people on the ground.

Teal'c gave a nod of agreement, but Sam just looked away without responding.

"Major?" Jack said, putting a little bark into it.

"Understood," she said, but Daniel didn't hear much respect in it. From Jack's expression, neither did he, but he didn't call her on it either.

Daniel glanced over at the Wraith. Earthborn sat on the wooden bench, as still as a sculpture save the restless movement of her eyes. Sting paced before her, his claws flexing. Daniel hoped he was nervous, not hungry. "So are you really considering Earthborn's offer?" he said to Jack. "Although maybe demand is a better word for it, given the situation…"

Jack's gaze rested on Earthborn and her eyes stopped their impatient motion, fixing on him instead. "She might act like the prom queen," he said, "but if her army consists of Sting and Crazy then she's in no position to make demands."

"So you're going to turn her down?" Daniel wasn't surprised, but he couldn't hide the wistful edge to his voice; the Lost City of Atlantis would be the archeological find of a lifetime. Well, second to the Stargate and, possibly, to Heliopolis. Then there was the Cartouche Room on Abydos…

Jack patted his arm. "I'm not going to turn her down," he said. "I'm going to make a deal."

"For what?"

Jack gave a slight smile. "For help getting Bailey's people out of the farm."

CHAPTER TWENTY-FOUR

Earth — 2000: The woman stood hunched and panting, haphazardly swinging the bloodstained knife through the air. She looked half-crazed, her hair matted, her face gaunt and skeletal.

"Don't shoot," grunted Dixon, still lying on the floor. "Don't hurt her."

Janet, Newman and Levine still trained their weapons on the woman, while Dixon pushed himself to his feet and moved in front of them. Blood poured through his fingers where he clutched the wound in his side, and Janet was torn between dealing with the danger at hand and taking a look at the extent of his injury. He looked steady on his feet though, so she guessed any treatment could wait until the immediate danger had been dealt with.

Dixon walked toward the woman, one hand held out in front of him. "Hey, we're not here to hurt you. We can help. How long have you been here?"

The woman said nothing, but her hand with the knife shook. It looked like a steak knife, a weapon scavenged for self-protection rather than with the intention of doing any real damage. Behind her, among the sleeping bags from which she'd sprung, lay a few tins of food and other meager supplies. They'd obviously stumbled on her hiding place and her actions had been born of fear; in this new world, how could anyone know who were really the good guys?

"Sir?" Levine's firearm was steady, but his tone betrayed his borderline panic, and Janet guessed that, end of the world notwithstanding, this was the first time he'd come face to face with a potentially life-threatening situation. No amount of training could prepare cadets for the first time they had to read a situation in an instant and make a judgment call on instinct. Too often it could end badly.

Fortunately, Dave Dixon had enough instinct for everyone.

"Levine, you take your finger off that trigger and stand down. We're all fine here," he said without taking his eyes off the woman. He gestured to Janet and Newman and they too lowered their weapons, although Janet suspected that Newman would be ready to move in a second. She wished her own battle senses hadn't been dulled from so long spent in the SGC.

The woman's arm dropped almost imperceptibly and Dixon inched forward.

"Alice?" The voice came from the church doorway and all but Dixon spun towards it, firearms at the ready. The woman screamed and raised her knife once more. Dixon moved, grabbing her wrist and twisting it, until the blade clattered to the flagstone floor. With his other arm, he encircled her upper body, pinning her arms to her sides.

"Easy," he said, trying to stop her from struggling, then, "Hands where I can see them!"

This last was to the man who stood just inside the church. He ignored the colonel's shouted warning and the weapons that were trained directly on him. "Alice, it's okay, love. It's okay."

"He said hands where we can see 'em!" shouted Major Newman. "Get on the ground!"

"Easy there, brother," said the man, kneeling down with his hands raised. "You're in no danger from me. Or from her. Just let her go." The man's hair was long and woven into dreadlocks, and he had a thick beard that almost reached his chest. His woolen sweater was full of holes, and fell down to the torn knees of his faded denims.

The woman had begun to cry, her fear evident now that her weapon was lost.

"Levine," said Dixon, "search him."

Levine let his rifle fall to his side and approached the man gingerly. "He's clean, sir," he said, after patting him down.

"Alright, now take it easy," said Dixon to Alice, though Janet suspected this was more for the woman's benefit than theirs. Still holding her arms, he escorted her over to the man kneeling on the floor, before letting go.

"Go on," said the stranger to Alice, with a flick of his head toward the door. "I'll see you back there. Don't worry."

Alice wasted no time in making her escape, leaving her friend kneeling on the floor, looking up the barrel of three guns.

"You're from across the water, eh?" he said, in what was almost a conversational tone.

Dixon exchanged a glance with Janet. "How would you know where we're from?"

"We've been here a while, brother. We know the comings and goings, and we know there's been more happening here than just those clowns with the tattoos on their heads."

"We?" asked Janet.

"Oh aye, there's a few of us, love."

"You live around here?"

He gestured with his thumb. "Just back there. Alice is one of us. I'm sorry she had a go at one of you? I hope she didn't hurt you."

"We're just fine," said Dixon, his MP5 steady, his eyes not shifting from the kneeling man.

"You'll have to forgive her. We've never had what you could call trust in the military. But that's in the past. We're all on the same side now, eh? The name's Scott Simpson, by the way. Simmy's what most folk call me." There was a beat of silence, the air strung taut. Simmy looked at each of them, and then said to Dixon, "Look, man, you can lower those things. I swear down you'll get no bother from me."

"Alright, Simmy," said Dixon, lowering his weapon. "We're done here. Why don't you get going back to your people?"

Simmy laughed. "Mate, I didn't come out here just to say hello. In fact, I didn't even know our Alice was in here 'til I walked through the door. You look like you're heading somewhere, and my guess is the base."

Janet looked around at the other three, but no one offered an answer.

"Look, you lot can wave your guns about all you want, but the fact is you're not even from these shores, and you don't know your way around. You want to get inside that place, it seems to me you'll need someone who knows the lay of the land."

"And that's you is it?" said Dixon.

"Colonel Dixon, we have to get out of here, sir," said Newman.

"Dixon, is it?" said Simmy. "Well, Dix, why don't you follow old Simmy here and see how the experts do it?"

The colonel looked at Janet. She pursed her lips and shrugged. She didn't see what they had to lose.

"Alright," he said, and gestured with his chin to Simmy. "Let's go. And Simmy? Don't call me Dix."

Earth — 2098: "This is stupid," Aedan hissed, crouching in the dark behind Jack as he lifted his monocular to scope out the Wraith farm below. "Trusting Devourers is madness."

"I'm not disagreeing," Jack said. "I'm just out of options."

It looked nothing like any kind of farm he'd ever seen and a lot more like a prison camp, complete with wire fences and cell blocks. In the center crouched a large building. It was only a single story, but given the history of this place, Jack suspected it delved deeper underground. There weren't many lights on in the camp either, which made it difficult to see the shadowy figures guarding the gate. On the plus side, it would also make his team harder to spot too. So he hoped.

Next to him, the Wraith — Sting — was watching the farm closely. "A blade and two drones guard the entrance," he said. "They will have to be dispatched."

"Can't you just pretend we're your prisoners?" Jack said. It was the oldest trick in the book, but not ineffective.

Sting gave him a long look. "Wraith do not take human prisoners."

"That place doesn't look summer camp to me." At Sting's

blank stare he elaborated. "The people we're looking for are prisoners here."

"Not prisoners, test subjects. Selected by Shadow's clevermen."

"Right," Jack said. "So long as we've got that clear."

Sting's gaze lifted to the sky, distracted, as if listening to something only he could hear. "Hearten is close. With the culling beam he can—"

"No," Jack said. They'd already had this discussion. "We'll get in the old-fashioned way, thanks."

Sting gave a shrug, or something that looked very like one. "As you wish." Again, that distracted look. "I have told him to stay close, in case we require… assistance."

"Told as in…?" He made a vague gesture toward his head.

"We've never met a telepathic race before," Daniel explained. "The implications for social structures are quite—"

"Daniel?"

"Yeah?"

"Can we just concentrate on getting past those guys on the gate?" Which gave Jack an idea. He cast a speculative look at Sting. "I don't suppose you can…" He wiggled his fingers. "You know."

Sting looked nonplussed and glanced at Daniel for a translation.

"He wants to know if you can use your telepathic ability to help us get past the guards." When Sting still looked perplexed, Daniel said, "He's asking if you can affect what they think or see."

The Wraith made a sound that could, perhaps, be interpreted as a laugh. "I could command the drones, if their blade was not so close, but I could not bend another blade's mind to my will. Only a queen has that gift." His face set like stone. "And I will not bring Earthborn so close to this place. Do not ask it."

Jack raised his hands. "Okay. No one's asking."

"I'm curious." Daniel scratched his head, repositioning his hat. "Can you communicate with us telepathically too?"

"Daniel?"

"What? It could be useful."

"Useful as a hole in the head." Jack did *not* want these things poking about inside his mind.

Sting bared his teeth. "Do not concern yourself, Lantean. Your brain is too primitive to allow us to do more than suggest shadows in your mind."

A flicker of something caught at the corner of Jack's eye and he turned his head, reaching for his weapon.

"Such as that." Sting didn't exactly smile but Jack heard a sardonic humor in his voice. Odd, that these creatures could find anything funny.

"Nice trick," Jack said. "Does it work on your friends?"

Sting shook his head, setting his hair swaying. "The Wraith mind is too sensitive to be deceived."

"Yeah," Jack said, turning back to the camp. "You're a real sensitive bunch."

"O'Neill." Teal'c came up behind him, moving silently through the trees, Carter on his heels. Her hair looked a little wild. "There is no obvious point of entrance," Teal'c reported. "And it appears that the fence carries a charge."

Carter winced, flexing her left hand, and Jack lifted an eyebrow. "Okay?"

"Yes sir."

"It's a good look," he said, with a nod at her spiky hair. "Perky."

"Thanks."

Sting said, "We must dispatch the guards on the gate before we enter."

"That will raise an alarm," Teal'c said.

"Not if we are fast." It had the sound of a challenge. "Are you fast, Jaffa?"

Jack looked between the two of them. The last thing he wanted was a Jaffa/Wraith pissing contest, but if it got the job done… "Do it," he said. "Quietly. We'll be right behind you."

With nothing more said, Teal'c and Sting moved off into the

trees and, despite Sting's pallid hair and skin, he disappeared into the dark almost immediately. Jack didn't want to know how, exactly, he did that. Putting Wraith tricks out of his mind, he shifted so he could see Aedan and Elspeth.

"I'm not going in there," Aedan said before Jack could speak. "Told you I'd bring you here, but that's all. I'm not going inside."

And that was fine by Jack; there was no way in hell he wanted to walk into that camp with Aedan flashing back to whatever it was he'd seen inside. "Just wait here," he said, his gaze landing on Elspeth. She was more likely to be trouble. "I mean it. Stay put."

He'd zat the girl if he had to, but before Elspeth could open her mouth Aedan put a firm hand on her arm and said, "We'll wait."

She looked at him as if she might argue, but whatever she saw in Aedan's face changed her mind and she backed down. "We'll wait together."

"Good," Jack said. "But if we don't come back, you need to get the hell out of here. Understand? Go home to your people."

"But you'll come back," Elspeth said and didn't quite make it a question. "You'll come back and take us to Dix."

Jack gave her a smile. "Sure," he said. "Piece of cake." Except for the part about 'Dix', but he'd cross that bridge if they ever got that far.

"Um, Jack?" Daniel was squinting into the dark, toward the camp. "We might want to get down there."

Jack glanced up and saw the flash of weapons fire — it looked like Wraith stunners. "So much for quiet," he said. "Carter, Daniel– let's go."

It was a short scramble down the rest of the slope. There were a few trees here, but lots of rocks too. Actually, he realized with a sick kind of horror, they weren't rocks — they were lumps of concrete and brick. Buildings. This had been a city once, or the edge of one. These had been houses, schools, offices, and shops. All gone now, destroyed in the catastrophe that had overtaken the world.

He held up a hand to signal a halt, crouching behind the stubby remains of a wall and the tree that had grown right through it.

"Who do you think's winning?" Daniel whispered.

It was hard to tell in the dark.

"I think the Wraith have better night vision than us, sir," Carter said, hunkering down beside him. "I noticed it on their ship. The low light levels?"

He nodded. "Makes sense."

"And puts us at a disadvantage."

"Shame we can't switch the lights on," he said. He'd like to floodlight the whole damn camp and blind the bastards.

At the gate, the skirmish appeared to be over. No one spoke, waiting to see if the alarm was raised. Of course, as far as he knew, the Wraith had some kind of telepathic alarm that was already blaring and any moment now one of the snatcher beams would sweep over and scoop them all up. He cast a quick look at the sky, but it was too dark to see anything.

"O'Neill." Teal'c's voice emerged from the night a moment before his friend appeared. "The guards have been suppressed."

"Sweet," Jack said, pushing to his feet. His damn knee was not appreciating all this abuse. "Where's Sting?"

"He remains at the gate. We must hurry."

With a nod to Daniel and Carter, they moved out. There was a stretch of open land to cross — a road, nature pushing up through its fractured tarmac but scraps of white lane markings still visible — and then more scrub and the fence. He slowed as they approached the gate; there were three Wraith on the ground. One looked similar to Sting, all long hair and teeth, but the other two were the odd faceless things he'd seen on Crazy's ship.

Daniel crouched to get a closer look. "What are they?"

"They are drones," Sting said, appearing out of the dark, or perhaps just making himself visible. "We must not linger here.

If your friends are still alive, they will be held in the preserving rooms."

Jack didn't like the sound of that. "I'm guessing we're not talking about the fruit kind?"

"More like Soylent Green," Daniel suggested.

Jack lifted an eyebrow. "Nice."

"We must move quickly." Sting gestured to the fallen Wraith. "Their absence will soon be detected."

Stepping over the legs of a drone and into the camp, Jack said, "Lead the way."

CHAPTER TWENTY-FIVE

Earth — 2000: "You're injured, Colonel," said Janet. "Let me take a look at it."

"It's fine, Doc."

"Colonel." Janet's tone brooked no argument and Dixon rolled his eyes with a sigh, but let her lift his shirt. The wound across his side was long, but shallow, the blood soaking into his shirt making it look worse than it was. The initial bleeding had already eased.

They sat sheltered from the rain, which had returned in force, inside what seemed to be the hide-out of Simmy's people. He'd led them away from the main road, and into the deep woods that ran alongside it. Newman had voiced his apprehension at following the man, eyeing Simmy with distrust, and Janet couldn't deny that his reasoning was sound. They'd just been attacked and Simmy seemed to be a friend of the very woman who'd knifed the colonel.

But she also couldn't help agreeing with Dixon's gut instinct. "He could prove useful, Major", he'd said. "He's had eyes-on experience of the Jaffa presence around here, while we've been too scared to put our heads above the parapet. We either trust him or we stumble in blind."

"For what it's worth, Major," Janet had said. "I think the colonel's right. We might know the Goa'uld, but we don't know this place. We need all the help we can get."

Newman had conceded the point, but with clear reluctance. And so they'd circled around, walking for what felt like miles through deep undergrowth, until they'd reached a rocky opening in the ground. It was well disguised behind branches and foliage, and they would have missed it if Simmy hadn't led them right to the entrance. The hidden opening led into what turned out to be a series of shallow caves that smelled of something that was definitely not incense.

He'd disappeared into the depths of the cave as soon as they'd arrived, leaving them under the scrutiny and suspicious stares of the other cave residents. Newman and Levine had propped themselves on the opposite wall, while Janet had snapped a few images with the camera, wanting to save the battery to film the base later. She took the opportunity to tend to Dixon's wound, something he'd refused to let her do until they were out of the open.

"It just needs to be dressed," she said. "No stitches."

"That was a stupid mistake back there," said Dixon. "I should've been more vigilant."

"We all thought the place was deserted, Colonel." Janet used an antiseptic swab to wipe the wound, and Dixon hissed, jerking away involuntarily from her touch. She raised her eyebrows at him and he looked away sheepishly.

"I guess we're just so busy watching our backs against the Goa'uld, it's easy to forget that Earth has its own share of threats."

"She wasn't a threat, she was just scared."

"Yeah, I know. And I know that scared people can do stupid things. I'm just glad this is the worst that happened." He looked down at his side. "Are we done?"

She taped a dressing over the wound and pulled his bloodied shirt down to cover it. "We're done."

"You know, I remember you having a much more pleasant bedside manner, Janet."

She glanced pointedly around at the dank cave. "And I remember having a much more pleasant bedside."

Dixon laughed. "Can't argue with that." He sat, wincing a little at the pain. "Thank you, Janet."

She shrugged. "It's just a dressing. Any field medic could do the same."

"No, I mean... thank you. For backing me up, for coming back, for making me feel like maybe I'm not crazy for trying to make a difference." He leaned forward and touched her arm. "It means a lot that you believe in this too."

She sighed and gave a smile that felt tired on her face. "We have to believe in something, Dave."

"You guys hungry?" Simmy appeared from the rear of the cave, his voice loud in the small cavern. "We've not got much, but we— Whoa, sorry, brother. Didn't mean to interrupt here."

Dixon shook his head and stood. "Simmy, the only reason we're here is to find out how you can help us. And we're kinda short on time."

"Right, aye, of course. Let's see that map, eh?"

Newman and Levine gathered around, as Dixon spread the map on the cave floor. Simmy scrutinized it.

"Well, this is where we are roughly," he said pointing to a vast expanse of empty space on the map.

"Where exactly is here anyway?" asked Levine.

"We dug this place out a few years back. It's where we went when the police decided it was time for a wee raid on the camp. They tried to bust us for anything, so they did. And some of us… well we tried to stay off the radar, y'know? Fingerprint records didn't really sit well with how we liked to do things. So we've got this home from home. It's been here for God knows how long. People keep digging more tunnels. It's how we've managed to avoid those cake guys. What did you call them?"

"Jaffa," said Dixon.

"Aye, them. Well, they're the ones who've got the base under their control, but they're… I don't know. They're obviously dedicated to what they're doing, but there's no rhyme or reason to it. They're all brute strength and no finesse. I mean, I wouldn't want to mess with them, but at the same time I think, with a bit of thought, you could get one over on them easily."

"And how come you're an expert?" said Newman, with more than a little rancor.

"Look, mate," said Simmy with a grimace. "I don't want to put a dampener on this relationship we're building here, but I've spent my full adult life trying to get one over on folk like you: the police, the government, the military. It's why we we're here in the first place. And after a while you get to know your sort. But these guys…" He shrugged and shook his head. "They're not just soldiers. It's like they're a cult or something. And then there's that weird tattoo on their heads."

"The snake," said Dixon.

Simmy pursed his lips and shook his head. "Looks nothing like a snake, brother. More like…" He reached out and drew a few lines in the dirt of the cave floor. The sight of it made Janet cold to the bone: a horned circle with a strange looking cross underneath.

"A new System Lord on the scene?" said Dixon to the others. "I've never seen this symbol before."

"I have," replied Janet, her tone leaden. "Hecate. Her Jaffa were found on the planet where SG-1 were last seen."

"You know what these things are?" said Simmy. Then he shook his head and sounded almost disgusted. "Of course you do. Secrets and lies from the powers that be. Nothing new there. You've known these guys were up there for a lot longer than just a few weeks."

No one replied. Standing in the ash of an apocalypse, it was difficult to defend decisions made five years ago, when all of this had seemed an impossibility. None of them had been part of that decision making, of course, but Janet wasn't sure she could disagree with the choices made; what else could they have done?

"So Hecate's the new player in town," said Newman. "Where do you think she stands in Apophis' pecking order?"

"That's a question for another time, Major," said Dixon. "Let's focus on the facts that matter. What are the numbers like around the base?"

Simmy frowned. "It's hard to say. We never see them arriving or leaving, but sometimes there seem to be more one day and less the next. And then there're the people."

"What people?" asked Janet, though she was afraid she knew the answer.

"The ones who didn't hide... They took them. Herded a whole load of folk into that ship and they never came out. Must be at least a thousand people, from what we've seen."

Janet and Dixon exchanged a look. If people were going in and not coming out, then they were likely being sent off-world.

"You think she has a gate on the ha'tak?" said Dixon.

With a tight nod, Janet looked back at the map. There was never any doubt that the Goa'uld would be taking people from Earth — it was their standard MO after all. But to hear it from someone who had witnessed it first hand and had seen the people being led off to become either slaves, or worse, hosts, galled her.

"Alright, Simmy," continued Dixon. "How do we get inside?"

"We normally go in by water."

"Normally?" asked Janet, her eyebrows raised.

The man grinned and winked. "As you Yanks like to say, sister, this isn't our first rodeo."

Earth — 2098: Sting moved as fast and quiet as Teal'c, leading them straight toward the central building. The rest of the structures, the pens, were empty — perhaps they'd used up all their test subjects? It wasn't looking good for finding Jones' wife alive.

"You know," Daniel said — he still hadn't mastered the art of the patrol whisper — "there's a chance he's leading us into a trap."

Naturally, Jack had considered that possibility. "Why bother when they could just beam us up like last time?"

Daniel shrugged an acknowledgment. "You think we'll be able to recognize Lana if we find her?"

They had the photo, but Jack had only spent three months in an Iraqi cell and Sara had barely known him when he got out. Jones' wife had been missing two years. "I guess it depends on how well she's been 'preserved.'"

Daniel didn't answer that; what was there to say?

The central building looked new — that is, it didn't look like something that had withstood a nuclear blast. It was made of some kind of dark material and when Jack ran his fingers across its surface it felt smooth, slightly organic, similar to the Wraith ship in Colorado.

"This way," Sting said. There was a door ahead and a panel next to it. Sting hesitated, his claws hovering over the panel but not touching it. "There is a chance," he said, "that when I command it to open the door, the hive-flesh will recognize me as a blade of Earthborn, not Shadow."

"Hive-flesh?"

Sting indicated the building. "This was seeded from Shadow's hive; it may know me as an enemy."

"Can you open it or not?"

"I can." Sting looked at him without expression. "But there is a risk of discovery. And now you have been warned." He placed his hand on the panel and the door slid open. Sting paused again for a moment, as if listening, but seemed satisfied and slipped in through the door. "I do not believe there is mind enough here to present a danger," he said, lip curling in disgust. "This is almost a dead thing."

"Better it than us," Jack said, and followed him into the building. It wasn't a whole lot lighter inside than outside, a diffuse sickly glow that reminded Jack of his time in Crazy's lab.

"The preserving rooms are this way," Sting said and headed left along the corridor. "I warn you, they are unpleasant."

"No need to tell us that." The memory of those leathery cocoons they'd found themselves trapped inside still made him shiver. "Been there, done that, and still wearing the t-shirt."

Sting didn't reply and a short distance later he stopped in front of an archway. "There are a number of pods," he said. "Your friends could be in any of them." He made no move to enter, which was odd, Jack thought, until he turned and looked into the room himself.

It was nothing like the place they'd been held on Crazy's ship. "Crap." He backed up a step, bumping into Carter.

She peered around him. "Oh my God."

"Sarcophaguses," Jack said. Rows of them — there had to be at least twenty of the things in there.

"Sarcophagi," Daniel corrected, pushing past him and into the room. Then, to Sting, "This is the 'preserving' room? There are humans inside?"

Sting nodded. "It is a perversion of nature."

Carter slipped past Jack to get a closer look. "What do they need them for?"

"With such devices," Sting said, "Wraith hives will be able to travel great distances without the need to cull or sleep."

"You mean they feed on people and then use the sarcophagus to revive them?" Carter sounded revolted.

"A permanent food supply." As much as it disgusted him, Jack understood the tactical advantage; the old adage about armies marching on their stomachs wasn't a cliché for nothing.

"The man on the ha'tak," Daniel said in a flat voice. "Jamie. That's why he was so…"

Daniel didn't say 'nuts' but he didn't have to; Jack's mind had reached the same conclusion. They'd all seen the effect repeated use of a sarcophagus had had on Daniel, and that was without being sucked dry by a Wraith before each use. He felt sick to his stomach. This was the most sadistic kind of abuse he could imagine. "Bastards," he said, striding into the room. "Open them up. We're getting these people out of here. All of them."

"Sir, wait!" Carter was a step behind him.

He turned. "For what?"

"Sir, if the people inside these sarcophagi are anything like Jamie we'll be lucky to get *one* of them out of here alive, let alone twenty. If we release them all…?"

"She's right," Daniel said. In the low light, he looked ghostly. "As much as I hate to say it, she's right."

Jack swallowed a bitter taste.

"We have to look for Jones' wife," Carter said. "She's the one we need."

She *was* right, of course, and Jack rubbed a hand over his face until he'd got his outrage under control. This place, this reality, was starting to get to him. He felt adrift from himself, from the non-existent chain of command, from orders a century old and long obsolete. "Okay," he said, pulling it together. "We look for Jones' wife first." He let his hand drop back to his weapon. "But we're not letting this place stand, Carter."

"No sir," she said. "We won't."

He knew what she meant by that and it wasn't what he meant; from the expression in her eyes she knew it too. But they'd deal with that later, once they were out of this and back on Rya'c's ship. "Check the ones on the left," he said. "Teal'c, help her. Daniel, with me. Sting — watch the door."

They started at either end of the row, opening each sarcophagus, taking a look at the haggard face inside and closing the lid when it wasn't the woman they were looking for. Jack toyed briefly with the idea of double-zatting them all, but cold-blooded killing wasn't his style — not even mercy killing. He was on his fourth sarcophagus when he heard Carter gasp.

"Sir!"

He turned. "You got her?"

She was staring into one of the sarcophagi in shock, head shaking. "You'd better see this, Colonel."

In two strides he was with her and then he stopped dead. "Oh for—" He quite literally couldn't believe what he was seeing. "*Maybourne?*"

"He must have been here since the invasion…"

"I guess it's true then," Jack said. "Roaches *are* the only things to survive the apocalypse."

Carter huffed a bitter laugh.

"Leave him." Teal'c loomed over the sarcophagus. "Colonel Maybourne's treachery brought this upon us. His punishment does not seem unfitting."

"On the other hand," Daniel said, "he probably knows a lot more about what's going on here than we do."

"If he's still sane enough to tell us," Carter warned.

Jack gave a sigh. Just when you thought the situation couldn't get any screwier. "As much as I couldn't give a rat's ass about Maybourne," he said, "Daniel's right. He could have intel we can use." He shifted his hold on his weapon. "Besides, if we pull him out, I might get the chance to shoot the bastard myself."

He gave Carter a nod and she set the sarcophagus to complete its reviving cycle. Outside, near the door, Sting crouched lower. Jack felt the skin prickle across the back of his neck. "Trouble?"

"A patrol is close."

"Three more minutes," Carter said, watching the controls on the sarcophagus.

Damn it. "Teal'c, go cover the door. Daniel, keep checking the rest of the sarcophaguses."

"Sarcophagi."

"Daniel!"

He held up his hands. "I'm going."

Inside Maybourne's sarcophagus, the man's eyelids began to flutter. He looked older than he had last time Jack saw him, grayer and thinner. And there were lines around his mouth and nose that made him appear frail, but even so he wasn't looking bad for a guy pushing a hundred and fifty.

From the corridor outside came the sound of movement, the tread of footsteps. "Carter, how long?"

"Thirty seconds, sir."

"O'Neill, we must leave now," Teal'c hissed, stepping back from the doorway. "It will serve no purpose to die here."

"Just hold on—"

Maybourne's eyes flashed open and he sat up with a jolt, like he was late for work. A bolt of abject despair crossed his miserable face and then his gaze fixed on Jack and he started back like he'd seen a monster. "You!" he hissed.

Jack, keeping it casual, lifted his weapon. "Long time no see, Harry."

"I'm dreaming," Maybourne said, looking about him. "But why you? Why dream *you*?"

"Get up," Jack said. "As crazy as it sounds, we're rescuing you."

"Rescuing?" he looked bemused for a moment, but then seemed to understand. "Ah," he said. "Yes, I see. They always said SG-1 would come back." With some effort — he was weak — he climbed out of the sarcophagus. Carter offered him a hand, but he hesitated to touch her. Perhaps he thought she might really be an illusion?

Sting slipped back into the room. He studied Maybourne with as much disgust as Jack might feel for a maggot-infested steak. "We must leave," the Wraith said. "Now."

Jack glanced at Daniel, still searching the sarcophagi. "We haven't finished."

"If you do not leave now you will die."

"Sir," Carter said, "Teal'c's right; we can't risk dying here. The consequences would be…" She tried to communicate the rest with a look, but he understood well enough: if they died here, there would be no one to go back and stop this disaster from unfolding. On the other hand, if they left without finding Jones' wife they'd lose their best chance of bringing Arbella on board with Rya'c's attempt to free Earth from the Wraith.

"Sir?" Carter prompted.

"We'll circle around, come back when the patrol's moved on." He gestured to Sting. "Take the lead."

Sting shook his head. "I do not know this place any better than you."

Heavy footsteps drew closer. Teal'c backed away from the door. "We are trapped."

"Trapped? No, no," Maybourne said, making his way around the sarcophagus. He was dressed in a shapeless tunic and pants of some rough fabric and leaned on the side of the sarcophagus as if he needed it to keep himself upright. "I know the way." His eyes darted to Sting and away. "A secret way, Jack. I'll show you."

"We cannot trust him," Teal'c warned, fixing Maybourne with a look full of bile. He blamed him for all of this, and for what had happened to Rya'c.

"Believe me," Jack said, stepping between the two men. "I *don't* trust him. But right now he's got as much to lose as we do if we don't get outa here in one piece."

Maybourne gave a smile; some of his teeth were missing and his smile stretched the skin too thin over the bones of his face. "Hurry," he said with another glance at Sting. "The Wraith are fast and clever. They'll catch us if we don't run."

There was a back door at the other end of the room, invisible until Maybourne pressed his hand to the wall and part of it slid aside. "See?" he said over his shoulder. "I know all Shadow's secrets." He slipped through and Jack followed him into a narrow corridor that led to a flight of stairs. Maybourne scurried down them, but Jack backed up. "What's down there?"

Maybourne's face, raw in the dim light, peered up at him. "I know you don't want to trust me, Jack, but you don't have any other choice."

The rest of his team crowded behind him, Sting's looming presence only adding to the tension. "That one's mind is despoiled," he said. "He is corrupted."

"Yeah," Jack said. "And that was before your friends got ahold of him."

Sting looked like he had more to say, but instead he whirled around as if he'd heard something. "They have discovered the guards at the gate," he growled. "Blades have been sent out in search of us."

Jack didn't like the sound of that. "Okay," he said to Maybourne. "Move it. And, so help me, if you're playing us I'll let Sting here have you for breakfast."

Maybourne glanced at Sting with an odd expression and said, "I know what I'm doing."

Earth — 2000: Dawn was a threat on the horizon by the time they left the tunnels, a suggestion of gray light picking out the jagged tree branches whose buds were only starting to open. Time was against them and they had to move fast, if they were to beat the light. They walked further south led by Simmy, who kept a steady, silent pace. The man's hippy stoner façade was obviously a front for a sharp tactical mind. Dixon didn't doubt that he must've caused Her Majesty's Navy no end of trouble in his attempts to stall their activities here.

Dixon kept an eye out on either side as they walked; despite Simmy's accurate assertion that the Jaffa were lacking in stealth, he didn't want an enemy squadron stumbling across their position before they'd even had a chance to get this plan off the ground.

Up ahead, Simmy stopped suddenly, a finger to his lips, and Dixon signaled for the others to halt. They froze, breath held, listening, but all Dixon could hear was the odd chirp of a bird. Apparently satisfied that there was no danger near, Simmy began moving again, pushing his way through a thick cluster of branches. Dixon and his team followed, and found themselves in the center of a cluster of small trailers, all of them trashed. Debris was strewn up and down the long narrow clearing, some of it evidence of some sort of domesticity; blankets, shoes, cooking pans. The hush of the water was much louder here, and through the trees Dixon saw the tarmac of the road that skirted the coast.

Following Simmy, he found himself picking his way between less commonplace items, rainbow flags and aluminum sidings painted in bright colors. As he drew to a stop beside their guide, he saw that he was standing on a sheet of plywood with a peace sign clumsily daubed across it in white paint.

"Give me a hand here, would you, brother?"

Dixon and Newman bent to help Simmy, who had pressed himself flat below one of the trailers until only the bottom of his legs were sticking out. After a few moments of grunting, the tip of something made of red plastic appeared. Dixon grabbed it and dragged it out. Soon after another one appeared, this one orange.

"Kayaks?" said Dixon, marveling a little at the ingenuity.

Simmy slid himself back out from under the trailer and stood wiping the dirt from his beard and clothes. "Always useful when we want to throw a bit of sugar in the petrol tank. Give us that map again, mate."

He took the plastic wrapped map from Dixon and studied it. "OK, here's where we're going. This stretch of fence is down completely. We'd been quite proud of ourselves, managing to cut a gap in the wire a few months ago, and then those Jaffa guys came along and blasted the whole lot down. Kinda killed our buzz a wee bit."

"Simmy!" Dixon was starting to lose patience with the man's tangents, but from the corner of his eye he was sure he saw Janet's mouth twist in a failed attempt to hide a grin.

"Sorry, man, sorry! Anyway, what was I saying?" Simmy stared down at the map for a second, his brow creased. "Oh aye, the fence. So we're heading about a hundred yards south, boats in the water, row ourselves up to the base. Now here's where it gets tricky, because we've never made it that far before."

"We know a way in," said Dixon, but said no more about the maintenance door that Dr. Aitchison had described to him. Simmy's eco-warrior days might be behind him, but Dixon guessed the man wasn't one to shy away from a challenge, especially if he thought there was an injustice to right — and God knew, this entire situation was one huge injustice. It was probably best not to give him ideas.

Simmy clapped his hands and rubbed them together. "Superb! Then let's go."

"Sorry, man," said Dixon. "This is where we leave you." He

unzipped his pack and began emptying the contents on the ground, and Janet began doing the same; this was a one-time only trip and they needed to carry as many meds out as possible.

"Now, hold on–"

"Trust us, this one's ours. You wait here for us. Once those charges go, we'll need an easy escape. Newman, Levine? We rendezvous back here."

"Yes sir."

"Good luck," he said. Newman nodded, and with a final glance at Janet, he and Levine moved out.

Simmy looked from Dixon to Janet and back again with misgivings. "Well, it's not often I'll say this to anyone that salutes the Man for a living, but look after each other, eh?"

Dixon nodded and shook Simmy's outstretched hand, as Janet hoisted a kayak onto her shoulder with a grunt. "Thank you."

"Don't worry, Simmy," said Janet, sounding more confident than Dixon suspected she felt. She reached into her bag again, this time pulling out the camera she'd been using since they left the base. Her footage of the base would have to take a backseat; it was more important to make room for the meds. After a moment, she handed it to Simmy. "Why don't you keep a hold of this for me? Maybe say a few words into it? Get your people to do the same. I think it'll make a big difference to a lot of people to know that you're out here."

Simmy nodded, and said, "Just make sure you come back to collect it, eh?"

Dixon was determined to make it so.

Earth — 2098: At the bottom of the stairs, Maybourne turned left, along another dim corridor at the end of which were a set of heavy steel doors. They had an ominous feel. Jack slowed down. "What's through there?"

Maybourne bared his gappy teeth. "The way out."

"It doesn't look like a way out."

In answer, Maybourne pressed his hand against a glowing plate at the side of the door and Jack heard a locking mechanism disengage. Behind him, Carter un-safetied her weapon. Jack pulled his zat.

"But it is," Maybourne said as the doors swung open. "This is the way out for all of us."

The massive doors revealed some kind of laboratory. It took a moment for Jack to take it in. Hospital beds ran along one side of the room, weird cocoons covered the walls of the other, backlit to show figures — people? — moving inside, and at the center of it all sat a horribly familiar tank of water that writhed with Goa'uld symbiotes.

Daniel stopped dead. "I've got a very bad feeling about this."

"Yeah," Jack said. "We're out of here." He turned around, but the corridor behind them was blocked by at least a dozen of the faceless drones. The trap had been sprung. "Maybourne," he growled, "you sonofabitch."

Teal'c and Sting turned, braced for the fight, Carter leveled her weapon. But anyone could see it was no good; they were trapped and outnumbered. "Stand down," Jack ordered. "No point in dying here."

Maybourne barked out a laugh. "Die here, Jack? Oh, no one dies here. No one ever dies here. That's the point." Then he frowned, cocked his head as if thinking. "Except SG-1, of course, but you're already dead, aren't you?"

"Don't count on it," Jack said, although he was starting to suspect that Maybourne was a couple of beers short of a crate.

"What is this place?" Daniel said, looking around as the drones herded them further into the lab.

"It's a test, of course," Maybourne said. "A test of loyalty. But I'll pass. I'll pass any test, because I'm loyal. I've always been loyal, everyone says so. Even Simmons knows I'm loyal."

Simmons?

"Colonel," Carter said. She'd turned to her left, her weapon aimed at someone emerging from the shadows behind the symbiote tank.

A Wraith. Ashy gray hair in elaborate braids swung as he moved, his clothes more ostentatious than Jack had seen on any of the other Wraith. Some kind of leader, then?

Maybourne dropped to his belly, face pressed into the floor. Jack just tightened his grip on his weapon, for all the good a couple of clips would do against this thing. "Nice creepy lab you got here," he said. "Any chance of a tour?"

The Wraith fixed him with a long look. "I am Sobek-Boneshard," he said, teeth bared.

Daniel said "Oh crap" a moment before the Wraith's eyes flared gold.

CHAPTER TWENTY-SIX

Earth — 2000: The rain returned in force as Janet and Dixon trekked through the woods once more, this time battling their way with their arms hooked through the kayak's cockpit. Though the fiberglass body had felt light when Janet had first lifted it, a half mile hike made it feel like she was carrying a racing yacht. The rain mixed with the sweat on her face, leaving her cold and clammy. But there was no time to rest. The gray sky was lightening and it would be dawn soon.

Neither she nor Dixon spoke, both conserving their energy for the walk, though she suspected that Dixon, like her, was mulling over his own doubts and uncertainties about this mission. She wouldn't voice her fear however. Dixon was relying on her, not just for the additional manpower, but for the promise she represented. If she failed, then there would be no help from Arbella, no haven to be found anywhere.

"Hold up a minute," whispered Dixon. He slid the kayak from his shoulder with a hiss, swinging his arm around with a grimace.

"You alright?" said Janet, not wanting to drop her own boat for fear she wouldn't have the strength to lift it up again.

"Yeah, I've got to check our location. I think our entry point's just up ahead." He rubbed the water from his face and pulled the map from his pocket. Janet realized she could see the road through the trees up ahead. They edged forward, Dixon peering through the sparse branches with his binoculars. "Yep, we're just a few –"

The sound of boots was barely perceptible at first, but both of them heard it at the same time, their heads pivoting in unison to where the squad of Jaffa had appeared further up the road. Janet dropped the kayak just as Dixon grabbed the waistband of her pants, yanking her backward down the slope. They threw themselves along the length the bright red kayak, trying to disguise it as best they could with their bodies. Dixon's arm was across her face, pressing it into the dirt alongside his own. Pain flared as her shoulder cramped up and she bit back a yell; she would only have ended up with a mouthful of dead leaves anyway.

The *tramp-tramp* of the boots got louder and Janet squeezed her eyes shut, heart pounding and mouth like metal. They were practically on top of them now, and she could feel the vibration of their march against her cheek. It went on and on, until she was sure that all Goa'uld forces had converged on the West of Scotland.

Eventually, she felt a hand on her shoulder and opened her eyes, but it was only Colonel Dixon who looked back, and not a Jaffa soldier. He puffed his mud-covered cheeks out and let go a breath that was half laugh. She let her eyes close again briefly, this time in sheer relief, and dropped her forehead on to the dirt.

Dixon looked upward, towards the road and she followed his gaze, to find it clear, the sound of boots now fading as the Jaffa marched on.

"Where do you think they're going?" she asked.

He shook his head, pushing himself cautiously to his feet. "Not sure, maybe just a patrol. But I think we better get gone before they come back."

With speed, they hoisted the kayaks back onto their shoulders, Janet biting her lip against the pain. A quick glance up and down the road told them they were alone for now and they sprinted across. Simmy's intel proved reliable and they found the downed track of fence that left the entire stretch of shore open to them. There was no jetty here from which they could slide into their kayaks, but Dix knew how to launch from shore. They anchored the kayak with their paddle, keeping it from wobbling in the shallow water. Janet slid in easily, but Dixon's size and weight proved a hindrance and it looked like he was swallowing a few curses in his failed attempts, until at last he made it inside.

They pushed off, dipping their paddles into the water as silently as possible, though the noise of the rain made for an adequate cover. This stage of the plan was finely tuned, a matter of precise timing; they needed darkness to disguise their progress, while Levine, waiting further up the road, needed daylight to maximize his chances of scoring a hit on the Jaffa using as little of their precious ammo as possible. It was the sunrise that governed when they would make their move, with Newman ready to blow the tanks at 0445.

By her watch, their little encounter with the Jaffa had set them back seven minutes. It was 0437 and they still had to find the access door and get it open. The wind was blowing against them, dragging the water and their boats with it. The concrete hulk of the naval base loomed ahead and Janet scanned its walls for any sign of a door.

After a moment, Dixon stowed his paddle and signaled toward a ladder set into the side of a concrete quay, then drew a three-sided square in the air with his finger. The door was up ahead.

Dixon went first, grabbing a metal rung and pulling himself from the cockpit of his boat. Once he had both feet on the ladder, he reached down and offered an arm to Janet. The ladder's rungs were wet and slippery, and she watched her footing as she climbed.

At the top, Dixon stuck his head over the edge and signaled for her to halt. Jaffa ahead. Two of them. Another wait and then the signal to go. They clambered onto the quay and ran for the cover of the building's northern wall, skirting its length until they reached the narrow cul-de-sac that matched Dr. Aitchison's description.

It was locked, of course, but they'd known that and come prepared. Janet kept a watch at the corner as Dixon pulled the little lock picking kit from a pocket on his vest, crouched at the door… and cursed. "There's no lock."

"What?"

"There's no damn lock!" He made as if to pound the door with fist and caught himself at the last second. Janet crouched next to him and saw that, sure enough, the handle was just that — a handle with nothing but smooth metal around it. Perhaps Aitchison had forgotten, perhaps she'd never seen the door from this side, but either way, one thing was certain: the door was locked from the other side, with no way to break in.

A quick glance at her watch showed Janet it was 0444. One minute before the tanks blew and they had no way inside. They had to —

The explosion seemed to rock the very air itself, sending tremors through the bedrock.

"Goddammit, Newman! I told you to check your goddamn watch!" Above them, shouts in Goa'uld could be heard over the echoes of the explosion as the Jaffa poured out into the open. Without wasting a second, Dixon pulled his handgun and sent three bullets into the handle of the door, leaving it mangled and useless. The door swung open. "Well," he said, "I guess they know we're here by now. C'mon!"

They pressed onward, up into the darkness of the corridor, following the directions that the base's doctor had made them memorize: left, left, second right. And there it was: the double door to the infirmary. Janet could only hope that the drugs they needed were still inside.

Earth — 2098: "You have *got* to be kidding," the colonel said.

Sam only wished it was a joke.

The Wraith raised clawed fingers, a Goa'uld hand-device obscene against its grey flesh. Its gaze fixed on the colonel and it said, "I know you, O'Neill."

"Yeah?" He sounded casual, but his stance was tense, ready to act. "Can't say I've heard of you."

Sam risked a glance over her shoulder, but the drones had

formed an arc behind them, cutting off any chance of escape. Teal'c had his staff weapon leveled at them — she doubted he'd let them disarm him, whatever the cost.

The hand device clicked as the Wraith moved its fingers, flexing its claws. "Humans do not live so long without assistance. How is it you are still alive Colonel O'Neill of SG-1?"

"Bran," the colonel said. He glanced around the lab. "You wanna tell us what's going on here?"

"You will answer my question," said the Wraith. Goa'uld. Whatever is was. "How is it that you are still alive?"

The hand device activated with a malevolent hum and the colonel tensed, waiting for the impact, for the pain to begin. He was as defiant as always, but Sam's stomach turned and she looked away; she didn't want to watch, she didn't want to hear him scream.

"You know these creatures by name?" the Wraith said, this time without the sepulchral bass of the Goa'uld. It bared its teeth. "For what purpose? They are only fit for food or servitude."

Sam was confused for a moment: who was he talking to? But then the creature tossed back its head and the Goa'uld voice answered, "There is more here than you understand, Boneshard."

"Oh boy," said Daniel.

"Is that the *host*?" Sam whispered. "Is he talking to the host?"

"Looks like it."

"Maybe he's Tok'ra?" But a Tok'ra using a hand device? Not likely. Then again, who knew what might have happened in this twisted version of their future?

"I know the name Sobek," Daniel said beneath his breath. "He was a minor system lord, a servant of Ra. There's some indication that he was allied with Bastet but—"

"You are Daniel Jackson," the Goa'uld said, watching him through Wraith eyes. "Slaughterer of Ra."

"Hey, don't give him all the credit," the colonel said. "He had some help with that."

The Goa'uld ignored him as his gaze came to rest on Teal'c. "And you are the shol'va, the betrayer of Apophis." He took a step forward. "Your god is dead, Teal'c. What say you to that?"

"I say that you will soon follow him."

A strange cackle filled the room and it took Sam a moment to realize it came from Maybourne, still prostrate on the floor. "No one dies here," he said. "No one dies here, not even the gods."

Casually, the Wraith kicked out with its booted foot and caught Maybourne hard in the ribs. He curled up, but made no sound as the Wraith hissed. That was Boneshard, Sam realized, not Sobek. The host seemed able to take control of his body whenever he chose. She'd never seen a Goa'uld permit anything like it before.

Boneshard stalked past Maybourne, barely sparing him another glance as he moved toward Sting. Stopping in front of the Wraith, Boneshard cocked his head as if he could taste the air. "Earthborn has grown bold," he said, "to send her consort here."

"My queen has always been bold."

The Wraith spread its fingers wide. "And foolish. Now she will mourn you."

Sting drew back. Not afraid, Sam thought, but revolted. "I knew you once, Boneshard, you and Adroit. You were valued in Brightstar's zenana. But I do not know what you have become." His lips curled. "You are no longer Wraith."

Boneshard hissed breath through his teeth. "I am more than Wraith," he said. "I am a god!" He spun away from Sting and walked over to the symbiote tank, trailing a clawed hand across the surface of the water. "The knowledge of an entire race is now mine," he said. "Shadow knows every feeding ground in this galaxy, every hidden outpost of humanity. She commands technology that will free us from the hunger, from the long sleeps and endless hunts." His head lifted, his gaze meeting Sting's. "And she understands the truth about the Ancestors."

"She has betrayed everything that she is," Sting spat. "She is corruption and death."

"She is strength!" Boneshard plunged his hand into the tank and pulled out a squealing symbiote. "Shadow will lead us as we take what we are owed from the descendants of the Ancestors — from the children of those who created us and then called us abomination, who sought the extermination of their own kin."

"Your queen will destroy us all."

The Wraith's eyes flared angry gold. "My queen is a goddess! And she will command an army that none can stand against. All those who oppose her will be swept aside — including the child you call queen."

An army? Sam looked at the tank of symbiotes, then at the wall to her right, covered by the weird back-lit cocoons. Inside them, something was moving. Wraith?

"I am the first." Sobek placed the symbiote back into the tank. "But I shall not be the last."

The tension in the room spiked. Sting's claws flexed and clenched, the colonel backed up a step, bracing himself. "You're taking Wraith as hosts?"

"They are infinitely superior to humans," Sobek said. "Stronger, faster, more enduring. More ruthless."

But it didn't make sense to Sam. "I thought you were poison to them," she said. "Wraith can't even feed on human hosts."

Sobek didn't answer and Sam made a mental note to think about it later; it felt significant. But then she remembered that it wasn't, that none of this was significant, because the only thing that mattered was getting out alive and finding a way to undo it all.

It was difficult to believe that, though, standing there watching as Sobek's eyes, all Goa'uld malevolence, fixed on the colonel. "But you," he said, "require explanation."

"Don't ask me," the colonel said. "I have no idea what's going on here."

Sobek, moving with the arrogant stride of the Goa'uld, drew closer. "Which god do you serve, Colonel O'Neill, that you have been permitted to survive so long?"

"I don't serve anyone."

"You lie." Sobek drew closer. "Tell me who you serve."

"Bite me."

On Sobek's silent signal, two drones stepped forward. One seized the colonel's arms, pinning them behind his back, while the other disarmed him.

Sobek narrowed his eyes and lifted his hand, the Goa'uld device glinting in the low light.

Sam raised her weapon, took aim. "Sir?"

"Don't. There's too many."

"You are a fool," Sobek said and unleashed the hand-device, driving the colonel to his knees as it bore into his head.

Sam clenched her jaw against the sound of the colonel trying not to scream. From the corner of her eye she saw movement, a drone approaching her, clawed hand reaching for her weapon. She glanced sideways then back to the colonel. He let out a half-swallowed scream and she thought: *this is a world without consequences.*

Nothing I do here will matter once I've changed the past and saved the future.

She didn't have to stand there and let him take this, and she didn't have to wait for the colonel's orders to fight back. All that mattered was getting out of there alive, by any means necessary.

Next to her, she sensed Teal'c shift. A quick shared glance was all it took and her decision was made. She switched to single shot, stepped forward and took aim at the hand device. Giving no warning, she fired and watched the bullet tear through the device and into the creature's hand.

The Wraith screamed.

The colonel sank forward, onto hands and knees, breathing hard.

Behind her, came the sizzle of a staff blast — Teal'c, opening up on the drones.

Sobek's scream became a furious hiss as Boneshard took control of his body and whirled toward Sam. His other hand — the feeding hand — lifted. *He can kill me*, Sam realized. If he could carry a symbiote, surely he could feed on her? She backed up, fired another shot, but it didn't slow him. Damn it. She fired again. She was down to her last clip.

Then she heard zat fire — Daniel — and something burned her left shoulder, racing fire through half her body, and she dropped. Wraith stunner blast, but only a glancing blow. She was still conscious as Boneshard stalked closer, one hand dripping black blood and the other ready to feed, his teeth bared in fury.

Sam tried to scrabble away, but her left leg was numb and not cooperating. "Daniel!" she yelled, but another shape barreled past her and into Boneshard. They both fell, stumbling in a tangle of limbs. It was Sting.

A hand grabbed her under her good arm, hauling her to her feet. "What the *hell* were you thinking?" The colonel yanked her behind the symbiote tank and she half fell, half dropped to the floor. "I did *not* order you to start a damn firefight, Major!"

His anger didn't matter, nothing that happened here mattered except escaping. "We have to get out of this alive."

"And this is *helping*?"

"I couldn't—" She flexed her left arm. The pins and needles had started, which was a good sign, but it hurt like hell. "We were always going to have to fight our way out, sir. I didn't see the point of letting him torture you first."

"Not your decision to make," he growled, peering up and firing over the top of the tank. He was using single-shot too, conserving ammunition.

"That's not what you told us yesterday."

"Hell of a time for this, Carter." He ducked back down behind the tank. Teal'c and Daniel were hunkered behind a couple of overturned beds on the other side of the room and Sting was still slugging it out with Sobek. Or Boneshard. Or both. Maybourne was nowhere in sight. "There'll be reinforcements on the way," he said. "And there's no way out." He glared at her. "Nice thinking."

"We should rig the tank, sir," she said. "I have enough C4 left."

"And take us all with it? The idea is to get out of this in one piece."

She nodded. "Bargaining chip, sir. They're building an army. You don't think the Goa'uld larvae are their most precious asset?"

He considered the idea for a moment. She could see a dozen possibilities flicker across his face and then he gave a curt nod. "Do it and make it fast."

She did, pulling out the last of her explosives and fixing them to the side of the tank. The colonel took the remote detonator from her without comment. "Over there," he said, pointing off toward Daniel and Teal'c. "I'll cover you."

"But what about—?"

"Follow your damn orders, Carter!"

She swallowed her objection. "Yes sir."

Under a burst of gunfire, Sam sprinted across the space and dived in behind the makeshift cover Teal'c and Daniel were sharing.

"What's going on?" Daniel said, making room for her. He was bleeding from a gash to his forehead, but otherwise looked okay.

"Hostages," Sam said, catching her breath. She peered up over the bed. Drones lay sprawled in front of the door, but she could see others in the corridor beyond and behind them a flicker of movement further back down corridor. In the distance, something rumbled. It sounded like an explosion.

Sobek had Sting, who was bleeding and limp in his grasp, pushed up against the wall and held by the throat. Sam wondered if Wraith ever fed on each other; was it even possible? "Yet your queen will weep for you before the end," Boneshard said aloud. "Before she begs." It sounded like a snatch of conversation, part of something larger.

Sting spat black blood into Boneshard's face. "Earthborn will never beg."

"We shall see." Boneshard's finger's tightened around Sting's throat. His fingers scrabbled weakly at Boneshard's hand, but the Wraith-Goa'uld hybrid was too strong.

"Hey!" It was the colonel, standing up behind the symbiote tank. "Hey, Bonehead, over here!"

"What's he doing?" Daniel hissed.

Sam smiled. "Just wait."

Boneshard turned around, but it was Sobek who spoke. "I will deal with you later, Tau'ri."

"How about you deal with me now?" The colonel held up the detonator.

Sobek stilled.

"That's right." The colonel tapped the tank, making the symbiotes squirm. "Boom! And it's goodbye to all your little snakes."

Daniel dabbed at the cut on his head, swiping the blood away from his eyes. The wound didn't look bad. "That got his attention," he said. Sam grinned.

"You would not dare detonate it here." Sobek released Sting, letting him slump to the floor, and turned toward the colonel. "The explosion would kill you all."

"You're gonna do that anyway." The colonel moved his thumb on the detonator. "So let my people out of here now or I blow this whole joint."

"Um?" Daniel said. "What's he doing?"

Sam sighed in irritation. "Playing the hero, as usual."

The colonel lifted the detonator higher. "I'm gonna count to five. One — Mississippi. Two — Mississippi…"

Behind Boneshard, Sting stirred. He looked woozy, his head tipped up toward the ceiling, eyes closed.

"… Three — Mississippi…"

"We must attempt to reach the door," Teal'c said. "Before

O'Neill detonates the explosive."

"We can't leave Jack behind," Daniel said.

"He has made his choice and it is better that Major Carter lives."

Sam stared at him. "Teal'c!"

"It is unlikely that O'Neill will be able to find a way to return us to our true time," he said. "Only you can do that, Major Carter. Colonel O'Neill knows that."

She felt her stomach drop. Is that what this was? The colonel was going to sacrifice himself to give her a chance to end this future?

"There are no consequences in this reality," Teal'c reminded her, a hand on her arm. "All that matters is to end it."

Even if that meant leaving the colonel to die here?

Daniel shook his head. "No. I don't accept that."

"Then you may stay," Teal'c said. He tugged on Sam's arm. "But I must take Major Carter to safety."

She was half on her feet when, across the room, she caught the colonel's eye. He could see what was happening, what they were doing, and she couldn't bear for him to think she was leaving him behind. "I can't," she said, pulling free of Teal'c.

"You must."

"No—"

A detonation right on top of the room rocked the ground beneath their feet, sending a spray of warm liquid into the air. She wiped a hand across her face, rubbing her fingers together.

"It's like the building's bleeding," Daniel said in a voice somewhere between awe and disgust.

Another explosion and the whole structure seemed to move. Sam dropped into a crouch, bracing one hand against the floor to keep her balance. The colonel caught hold of the symbiote tank, glancing warily at the ceiling. She knew what he was thinking; she was thinking the same. Who the hell was out there and whose side were they on?

Boneshard spun toward the door as a half dozen Wraith

stormed into the room. Backup. Damn it.

Sam reached for her weapon.

"Tell them to back off!" the colonel shouted as another explosion sounded. This time it was further away, but Sam could still feel the pressure wave of the blast in her ears.

"He cannot," said another voice. "They are not his to command."

As the Wraith spread out into the room, Sam saw the slighter figure of Earthborn follow them, well-armed and dressed for battle. She glanced quickly about the room, going still when she saw Sting's prone body. "Secure the room and the corridor," she ordered and hurried over to crouch at Sting's side. She pressed her hand against his, palm to palm.

Earthborn's soldiers surrounded Boneshard, his head flicking from side to side as if searching for something. He looked angry, but not desperate. "This is an act of war," he hissed.

"This place," Earthborn spat, "is an act of war against our whole species."

Warily, Sam rose to her feet. Daniel did the same and they exchanged a cautious glance. Teal'c, already standing, didn't lower his staff weapon. "Be vigilant," he warned.

"No sudden moves, Bonehead," the colonel said as he came out from behind the tank. The detonator was still in his hand and he held it up. "I mean it."

Boneshard didn't try to resist, but neither did he look cowed. Sam tensed, kept her weapon fixed on Boneshard and made her way around the hospital bed. Earthborn had bought them time and a chance, but there was a lot of dark corridor between themselves and escape. She felt another detonation through the soles of her boots. "Aerial bombardment," she realized, glancing at Earthborn where she crouched next to Sting. That really was an act of war. Or of love, perhaps?

"You are no queen," Boneshard said then. "You are a child. And as a child you will be punished."

Earthborn's head snapped around and she rose to her feet,

a graceful unfolding of her body. In two steps she was before Boneshard, defiantly within arm's reach. "You dare to speak so to the daughter of Brightstar, your queen?"

Boneshard bared his teeth. "Shadow is my queen now."

"She has misled you."

"No," he said. "It is you who are misled if you believe you can resist her." Then his eyes flashed gold and he grabbed Earthborn's arm. "Steadfast!" Sobek shouted. "Now!"

From the shadows sprang Maybourne, darting over to the wall and slamming his hand down onto a panel.

Sam understood what was happening the moment the colonel started running. As the Goa'uld ring-platform appeared, rising up out of the floor, he dived for Earthborn. His weight knocked her sideways and out of Boneshard's grip half a second before the rings slammed down around the Wraith. "No!" Sobek yelled as light flared and the rings whipped up into the ceiling again. He was gone.

Another ring platform appeared around the symbiote tank and Maybourne flung himself inside it. On the floor, outside the rings, Sam saw the detonator the colonel had dropped.

"Maybourne, wait!" Daniel yelled as Sam dived for the detonator, fumbling it in her haste.

The rings stacked around Maybourne. "I'm loyal!" he laughed into the flaring light. "I've always been loyal!"

Sam hit the detonator, but it was too late. Maybourne and the symbiotes were already gone. "Damn it!" she yelled, and hurled the detonator against the wall. The noise of it rattling to the floor echoed in the sudden, dazed silence.

The colonel lay on his back, breathing hard as Earthborn clambered to her feet. Half a dozen Wraith stunners were aimed at him and he lifted his hands. "I saved her," he pointed out.

Earthborn looked back at the empty space where the tank and Boneshard had been. "Shadow would not have treated me kindly," she said, and Sam could hear a tremor in her voice. "Lower your weapons. See to my consort."

The colonel sat up, wincing a little. He rolled his left shoulder, like he'd landed on it badly. Sam offered him a hand up and after a slight hesitation, he let her haul him to his feet. "Okay, sir?"

"The ground's getting harder, Carter."

She almost smiled. "Yes sir."

Sting was on his feet too, though he looked weak and was supported by one of the other Wraith. Above them, the bombardment continued. Whatever of Shadow's people were left up there, none of them were coming down into the lab. Earthborn clearly had more firepower at her disposal than Sam had realized.

"Boneshard was right," Sting said as he drew closer. "This was an act of war. And it was foolish."

Earthborn's chin lifted in defiance. "You would rather I let you die here?"

"Yes."

The silent exchange that followed charged the air until Sam thought her hair might stand on end. She glanced at the colonel who lifted his eyebrows in something like amusement. It made Sam smile.

"O'Neill," Teal'c said, breaking into the moment. "We must leave this place while we are able."

"Yeah." The colonel tugged off his cap, running his fingers through his hair; he looked tired. "You and Carter get out of here," he said. "Find Aedan and Elspeth and we'll rendezvous at Sting's hideout."

"What about you and Daniel?" Sam said. "What are you doing?"

There was a pause, then a curt nod of understanding between the two men. "There's something here we need to take care of," the colonel said.

He meant the people in the preserving rooms, of course. "You can't save them all, sir."

"I know!" he snapped. Then, gathering his temper, he said, "Look, Carter, I understand that you think none of this matters, but I won't leave those people behind. I can't."

And he was right; the Colonel O'Neill she knew and respected would never leave those people behind. No more than he would leave her behind, or Daniel or Teal'c.

She felt a squirm of guilt, remembering that she'd almost left him to die here — to die so that she could escape and save the future.

"I'll help you, sir," she said and ignored the growl of frustration from Teal'c.

CHAPTER TWENTY-SEVEN

Far from being over, the battle on the surface above Sobek's lab seemed to be intensifying. The lights went out as they ran up the steps from the lab and acrid smoke filled the corridor. It smelled like burned flesh. Daniel almost gagged on it.

Crouching, his back to the wall, he pulled out a bandana and wrapped it around his mouth and nose. He didn't want to think about what was burning.

There were Wraith ahead of them — Earthborn's — although the queen herself hung back, helping Sting. He was in a bad way, bleeding heavily from a wound in his arm. Daniel couldn't hear the silent communications between Earthborn and her consort, but he could imagine it. He wasn't sure which of them was angrier. It fascinated him that these alien creatures could act so human and it made him long to dig down into their origins. If only he had more time — any time — to talk to them about more than battle plans. But then, there were a hundred different peoples he'd have loved to study in more depth and there was never time to talk about anything but war. He sighed, drawing an enquiring look from Jack who crouched next to him, waiting for Teal'c's signal.

"You know, the odds of us finding her alive are pretty slim," Daniel said. He meant Lana, Jones' wife.

Jack grunted agreement. "It might be easier on her if we don't."

"But not on us. Not if we want Jones' help."

Up ahead, Teal'c glanced over his shoulder, beckoned, and began to move out. Jack pushed to his feet. "True. But maybe there's another option," he said, following Teal'c. "Sounds like these guys have some firepower after all."

Sam was behind them, covering their six, and Daniel heard her huff a sigh. He glanced back at her.

"Sir, you can't seriously be thinking of…" Apparently remembering where they were she lowered her voice. "… of acting as a cab driver for our new friends."

Jack didn't turn around, his attention fixed on Teal'c's back as he disappeared around the next corner. "Can't I? It sounds like a win-win to me."

They crept around the corner, and then Jack stopped and held up a fist. The smoke was denser here, sticky and bitter, stinging Daniel's eyes and making it difficult to see. Sam coughed and wiped her mouth on the sleeve of her jacket.

"The preserving room," Teal'c said, his face hazy through the smoke. "There is no power inside."

"No kidding," Jack said. Even the twilight glow the Wraith preferred had dimmed to shadows, although the Wraith didn't seem to have any trouble seeing. Their excellent night vision, Daniel supposed, must have given them an advantage over the humans they hunted. When your prey was equally intelligent, a number of evolutionary advantages would be required to survive. Such as telepathic communication, enhanced strength and speed… He could see why the Goa'uld would want to take Wraith as hosts.

Ahead, over the more distant sound of bombardment, came another noise. It was human and desperate, a keening that ran sharp fingers down the length of Daniel's spine. In the gloom, he saw Jack tense until the sound had stopped.

"That doesn't sound good," Sam said. "Sir…"

"I know. We'll do the best we can, Carter."

The truth was, there might not be much left of these people to save.

Teal'c stopped at the entrance to the preserving room. It was full of moving darkness, but somewhere daylight must have been finding a way into the building because a thin gray light seeped through the archway at the far end of the room. By its light, Daniel could see that all the sarcophagi were standing open.

"They must have opened when the power cut off," Sam guessed. "A failsafe."

Daniel shuddered at the thought of waking up trapped inside one of those things, but he didn't have long to contemplate the idea because the wailing started up again. It was coming from inside the preserving room.

For a moment, they all hesitated on the threshold. Despite the terrors they'd faced, he felt an atavistic fear of these dehumanized people that he couldn't rationally explain. He suspected that they all felt it.

In the end it was Jack who stepped forward first. "We're here to help you," he announced as he strode into the room. "Don't be afraid."

Then all hell broke loose.

Evacuation Site — 2000: The body was found at dawn. Cassie heard the clamor through the fitful dozing that had passed for sleep since her mother had left. She hadn't been scared, watching her go, not for herself; on her home planet, it had been custom for girls her age to leave home and travel. She wasn't scared at being left alone. Her fear was for her mother, stepping into danger, both known and unknown. She wasn't so naive that she couldn't see what games were being played here. She was scared for her mom, and she missed her.

It was a scream that first alerted her that something was wrong, followed by shouts. The sound of people in distress was nothing new; there had been more than enough sadness to go round since they got here. Screams were not an unusual sound in the camp at night, when the terrors took hold, but this didn't sound like the product of a nightmare.

Cassie lifted the flap of her tent to see people darting past towards the lake, and decided to follow. The crowd had huddled on the shore, with soldiers holding them off from whatever spectacle was unfolding. Cassie pushed her way through. Bile rose in her throat at the sight in front of her, and she clamped her hand over her mouth.

Colonel Reynolds lay on his back, flesh grey and bloated, eyes staring sightless at the sky.

"He's been shot. Looks as if he's been in the water a few hours," said the officer crouched over the body.

One of the other airmen scratched the back of his head. "We should get Doc Fraiser down here. Find out what happened."

"Dr. Fraiser is missing!" The voice echoed loudly from the back of the crowd, and everyone turned as Colonel Maybourne pushed his way through. He took one look at the body and closed his eyes with a frown. Cassie's gut began to churn. "I knew she was desperate," Maybourne said, "but I never thought she would resort to something like this."

"What?"

Maybourne's gaze darted around at Cassie's challenge, and his eyes widened a little, as if he hadn't expected to see her here.

"What are you talking about, Colonel?"

He took a moment before replying. "Cassie, I think you should go back to your quarters. Someone will come and speak to you once we've dealt with this situation. This isn't the place for a child."

"I'm not a child, Colonel Maybourne, and I want to know what you meant? My mom isn't missing—"

"Cassie!" he barked, and then glanced around at the assembled crowd. "Alright then, seeing as you asked. Your mother escaped custody last night while she was being escorted by Colonel Reynolds to see the President, like she'd been demanding. Everyone heard her." A few people nodded and she heard murmurs of assent. "She made it up to the base and took Major Newman hostage to get through the Stargate to Earth." He looked back down at the body. "It looks like that wasn't all she did."

"You're lying! You're a goddamn liar!" She could hear her own voice, shrill and almost hysterical, but she couldn't believe the low-down, bare-faced effrontery of this man, to stand here and spew lies while her mother was out there fighting for Earth. While poor Colonel Reynolds lay dead at their feet.

"That's enough, Cassie!" said Maybourne, unrelenting in his distortion of the truth. "I know you're upset, but let me get someone to take you –"

She felt a hand on her arm and forcefully pulled it away. "No!" Looking around at the gathered crowd, she saw a few familiar faces. SGC faces. Surely they wouldn't buy this? "You can't believe him," she pleaded with them, tears streaking down her face. "You know my mom! She saved the lives of half of you here! None of what he's saying is true. I was there. He told her he wanted to help her, that it was to help all of us. He sent her through the Stargate!"

A few people looked doubtful, as if finding it difficult to believe that Dr. Janet Fraiser would do such a thing, but then Maybourne said, "C'mon now, Cassie. That's not true. I know you want to protect your mother, but everyone here knows how desperate she was to help Earth. It wouldn't be the first time she's defied authority. It looks like the end of the world just pushed her that little bit too far." He turned back to the soldiers by Colonel Reynolds' body and began giving orders to have him removed, and Cassie realized she was being shut down. The other soldiers began to usher the crowd from the scene. She could do nothing but stand in tears and watch them go. It was only when the crowd had almost cleared that she felt a hand on her arm once more, and turned to find Dr. Rothman standing next to her.

He cleared his throat and, with a glance at Maybourne, said in a low voice, "For what it's worth, I don't believe your mom could do something like this. She was a good woman, a good doctor. I believe you." He shrugged. "For what it's worth."

In that moment, to Cassie, it was worth the world, and she decided that this most certainly wasn't over.

Earth — 2098: They attacked from all sides, wild creatures, leaping out from behind the sarcophagi. Men and women, thin and wild-haired, with nothing left to lose. Not even their minds.

They lunged at Jack, one man getting close enough to rake his hand across Jack's face before Daniel zatted him.

"Sir, watch out!" Sam yelled as a woman hurled herself at him from the top of a sarcophagus. Sam's shot found her mid-air and the woman fell twitching to the floor.

The rest of them backed off then, snarling and whimpering.

"Settle down!" Jack barked, dabbing at the scratch on his cheek with the back of one hand. "Damn it."

"O'Neill, we should leave," Teal'c said. "These people are beyond help."

Jack ignored him. More out of principle than pragmatism, Daniel suspected; Jack wasn't always logical when it came to leaving people behind — unless he was the one being left, naturally.

"We can get you out of here," Jack said, turning in a slow circle, watching the people cowering in the darkness. "We're not Wraith. We're not Devourers, or Snatchers, or whatever the hell you call them. We're human, like you. You can trust us."

Another explosion made the building shudder; the battle outside was drawing closer. But the strange fleshy walls of the Wraith-built structure shivered rather than shook. It seemed extremely robust, stronger than an ordinary building. Another advantage the Wraith had developed.

"He's right," Sam said, stepping forward to join Jack. "Come with us and we'll take you somewhere safe."

Daniel had no idea where that might be — he doubted Arbella would be in a hurry to take these people. Not that it mattered. Anywhere was better than here. He was about to add his voice to the others when someone touched his arm. It was Earthborn.

She looked at him with inscrutable alien eyes and said, "Sting is dying. He must feed, now."

Feed. On people.

Daniel pulled the bandana away from his mouth and said,

"Oh." He hoped he didn't sound horrified.

"I understand it will be... disconcerting for you," she said. "But it is necessary." Her gaze shifted to the preserving room, to the humans hunkering in the shadows. "It does not matter which of them."

Daniel stared at her. Did she actually expect him to *choose* someone? He found himself shaking his head, backing off. "I can't," he said. "I can't make that choice."

Earthborn bared her teeth in apparent frustration. "Then do not get in my way," she said and pushed past him into the room.

Daniel expected the people inside to react and they did, but not in the way he'd imagined. A half dozen of them surged forward, men and women throwing themselves at Earthborn's feet and begging to be chosen. The others kept to the shadows as if uncertain, their gaze twitching between Jack and Earthborn. The Wraith queen looked as discomfited by the display of devotion as the rest of them.

"What's going on?" Jack said. He held his zat ready, but didn't raise it.

Daniel felt trapped in the moment, wavering between letting this happen and stopping her. It was an impossible call to make. Sting had helped them, they needed him, and he was dying. But to live, he must take the life of one of these pathetic creatures who'd been driven to the edge of humanity by the torture they'd endured at the hands of the Wraith.

The impossibility of the choice froze Daniel and all he could do was stare at Jack over the heads of the people scrabbling about on the floor at Earthborn's feet.

Jack must have understood, seen the truth in his eyes, because he raised his zat and said, "No way."

"Sting will die," Earthborn told him. Her voice was strong, but sharpened by fear. "I will not allow that to happen."

Her obvious anxiety loosened Daniel's tongue. "They can't help being what they are, Jack. This is how they live."

The expression on Jack's face didn't change, the zat didn't

waver, but after a long beat he gave a nod that was barely more than a twitch. It was enough, though.

With an expression of distaste, Earthborn reached down and touched the head of an emaciated man who fawned at her feet. He looked up at her touch, lips stretched into something that might have been a smile. "Then the sleep?" he said. "Then the bright sleep?"

Earthborn looked confused and glanced at Daniel, as if he might know the answer. Unfortunately he did.

"Yes," he told the man. "Then the bright sleep."

It was a lie. The sarcophagi weren't working; there would be no euphoric return to life this time. But better that it end here, Daniel thought, than that this man be revived to die again and again — or to suffer the torment of withdrawal from addiction to the sarcophagus.

"Come," Earthborn said and the man, pathetically grateful to be led to his death, scrambled to follow her.

Daniel turned away, unable to watch.

But then a woman bolted out of the shadows, screeching protest. "No!" She shoved the man aside. "The bright sleep, I need it…"

She was thin, like the rest of them, with unkempt hair. But her face… Sam must have seen it too, the mole on her cheekbone, because she barreled into the woman and tackled her to the ground. "Daniel," she yelled. "Sedative!"

He fumbled for the med kit in his vest, administering the sedative with shaky fingers. His bedside manner might be lacking, but the drug took hold pretty fast. A moment later the woman's arms stopped flailing, the fight draining from her.

Earthborn looked at the woman, at Sam, and then at the man she had chosen to feed Sting. "Quickly," she told him. "There is not much time."

A moaning lament rolled around the room as Earthborn left, a sickening accompaniment to the rattling scream that soon came from the corridor beyond. To distract himself from what was happening, Daniel focused on the woman now laying limp in Sam's arms. He brushed lank hair away from the woman's face and touched the mole on the crest of her cheekbone. She'd been young and beautiful in the picture Jones had given them and Daniel could almost trace that beauty in her ravaged features. He looked up as Jack stepped closer. His face was drawn very tight, everything locked down. None of them wanted to think about what they'd just let happen.

"Is that her?"

Daniel nodded.

"So now what?" Sam said.

"We take her home."

"Like this?"

He looked down at her, this lost wife of a desperate husband. "Trust me," he said, his voice thick. "Jones won't care. He'll just want her home."

Over his head, he could sense Jack share a look with Sam. He wasn't sure if it was pity for him or something else, something between themselves. "Yeah," Jack said after a moment. "He will."

Lana was light, nothing but skin and bone, even limp as she was from the sedative. She wouldn't stay that way, though, not when she woke up, so Sam bound her hands and feet.

"She'll struggle," she said as she helped Daniel heft her over his shoulder.

"I know," he said. "I'll be okay."

"Listen up!" Jack had backed up to the archway at the far end of the room, closer to the daylight. Some of the people just sat and rocked back and forward in the dark, lost, but others were listening. Those ones they could save, Daniel thought. "Follow me," Jack said. "Do what I say and we'll get you outa here. I swear it."

Just as he turned, preparing to lead them out, Earthborn and Sting appeared in the doorway at the back of the room. A frisson of confused emotion skittered through the people, as if they were torn between Jack and the Wraith.

Sting looked less deathly than before, but his expression was grim as he studied the people cowering around him. "Go," he told those who stared up at him. "Follow him. He speaks the truth."

"We must hurry," Earthborn added, addressing her words to Jack. She looked frightened. "Shadow's cruiser is close and now we are at war. She will not be merciful."

"Great." Jack swung his weapon into his hands. "Okay people, stay close, stay low, and don't look back." He glanced over their heads at the rest of SG-1. "Teal'c, stick with Daniel. We are *not* losing this woman. Carter, you've got our six."

"Yes sir."

With a final nod he turned back to the door, bracing himself. "Okay," he said. "Let's do it."

CHAPTER TWENTY-EIGHT

Earth — 2000: "What is it I'm looking for here, Doc?" Dixon's question was taut, the ticking clock stretching both their nerves tight.

Janet grabbed the stacks of white boxes from one of the cabinets they'd broken open, scanning the labels and stuffing as many as she could into her emptied backpack; amoxycillin, fentanyl, diamorphine. It was a well-stocked larder they'd kept here in the base, and it maddened Janet that she couldn't stay. There was equipment too; old and slightly well worn, but state of the art compared to what they had back on Arbella. But all they had time to do was grab what they could and make sure the antivirals were among their plunder.

"Tamiflu," she said, "or Relenza."

"I'm not seeing it!" He swiped boxes of what looked like ibuprofen from the cabinet he was searching, scattering them across the room. "Wait, I got… oste… osel —"

"Oseltamivir! That's it. Grab as much as you can."

He hooked his arm around the stacks of boxes on the cabinet shelf, pulling the whole lot into his pack. It looked like more than enough to treat the patients she'd left back on Arbella, and Janet prayed it was the bargaining chip they needed.

"Alright," said Dixon, zipping the bag tight. "Let's set these charges and get out of here. I don't wanna guess how much longer Levine and Newman can engage the Jaffa topside."

Together, they planted the blocks of C4 along the corridor leading from the infirmary, enough to take out the three floors that made up the base, and any Jaffa remaining inside. The timer left them fifteen minutes to get clear. More than enough time to get to the kayaks and back up the shore, especially if the wind favored them.

They sprinted towards the door that now swung freely on

its hinges, and out into the open. But as they rounded the corner of the building, Janet's stomach lurched. At the top of the ladder stood three Jaffa, staring over the quay into the water, obviously perplexed by the sight of the kayaks bobbing below. Dixon gestured backward. There was no other way to make their escape, apart from heading back into the building — the same building they'd just rigged to blow sky high.

"*Kree!*"

Their options narrowed even further, as one of the Jaffa looked over his shoulder and spotted them. Without a word, Dixon grabbed Janet's hand and hauled her in the opposite direction, toward the far side of the quay. There was nothing there but a sheer drop into water whose depth they could only guess at.

But Dixon didn't even slow, and he didn't let go of her hand. If he was going over, she was going with him. As a staff blast pounded into the concrete inches from their feet, they leapt, arcing through the air towards the gray water below.

The cold hit Janet like a slab of steel. She sank down and down, kicking furiously, but unable to gain any upward momentum. Dixon had let go of her hand and she pushed her aching arms through water that felt like tar. Her lungs were burning, yearning to inhale, and just when she thought she had no choice but to give in to their demand, her head broke the surface and she sucked in an exquisite lungful of air, choking it back out immediately.

"I'm here," she croaked to Dixon, who was treading water, frantically scanning the surface of the loch. But there was no time for them to check if the other was okay. The Jaffa were already at the edge of the quay, searching for their quarry.

Janet and Dixon struck out for the nearby foreshore, and were dragging themselves up the shingly beach when the blasts started anew. Janet summoned her last reserve of energy and sprinted after Dixon, struggling to keep up with his long strides. The Jaffa, however, seemed reluctant to follow their escape route and soon they were out of range.

And faced with another problem. Unlike their point of entry, the wire fence on this side of the base was very much intact. Dixon hooked his fingers through the links and gave it a hard, but ineffectual shake. It stayed put. Janet squinted down the length of it, as far as she could see, but there was no visible gap. The links were small and climbing might be possible, but would take forever. They only had eight minutes.

"We gotta start running. There might be a gap further down."

"Sir, as long as we're on this side of the fence, we're sitting ducks."

"Janet, I know that, but what else –?"

"Pssst!"

Dixon broke off at the sound, and looked around, puzzled.

"Hey!" A face accompanied the hissed shout this time, peering out through the trees across the road.

"Simmy! What the hell –?"

"Thought you might need these if things went pear-shaped."

A smile broke across Dixon's face at the sight of what their new ally waved at them.

"And you just happened to have a pair of bolt cutters lying around your camp?"

"Dix, mate," said Simmy, scampering low across the road, "you say that as if you hardly know me at all!"

Earth — 2098: Despite the risk of discovery, they'd had to stop and top-up Lana's sedation twice before they reached Earthborn's hideout. Daniel had carried her the whole way with great gentleness, and there was something heart-breaking about that, Sam thought as she watched the colonel help him lay the woman down on the scrubby grass outside the underground shelter.

It had been a long night and, through the bones of the trees, Sam could see the sky fading from black to steely gray. Not that she needed anything beyond the ache in her own bones to tell her how long they'd been on their feet. She felt exhausted and longed to shrug off her pack and rest, but they weren't safe yet.

The skies buzzed with the mosquito whine of the Wraith ships. "We must leave this place," Sting said, watching the sky. "It is not safe to remain." He still looked unwell — not that it was easy to tell, given his alien appearance, but he was moving with less force and less speed. Sam hoped he wasn't looking for another meal.

"We won't be safe underground?" Daniel said. He was still catching his breath, sweating despite the chill air. Lana might be skin and bone, but she was still a weight and often a struggling weight.

In the trees around them, those who had survived the flight from the preserving room hunkered down. There weren't many, yet still more than they could reasonably accommodate in Earthborn's shelter.

"They will send blades to search on foot. Shadow will seek vengeance for the damage done to her facility." Sting looked at Earthborn and she lifted her chin, all defiance. He turned away in anger. "We are at war now."

"He's right," the colonel said, standing up from where he'd been crouching next to Lana. "We have to go."

Daniel shook his head. "I don't think I can carry her much further right now…"

He glanced at Teal'c who, after a moment, said, "I will carry her, if you wish." His reluctance was clear, but he didn't elaborate. By now, they all knew he thought this whole escapade was a dangerous waste of time. For herself, Sam was too tired to think about that anymore. She was hungry too, and the burn on her hand where she'd touched the electric fence — stupid! — stung where the skin was red raw. She just wanted to rest.

"If you attempt to return to the Astria Porta by foot, you will be captured," Sting said. "There is only one way we can leave."

His gaze landed on the colonel who grimaced.

At the far edge of the clearing, Aedan and Elspeth stood

with their backs to a tree. Aedan's face was tight, Elspeth's more curious but both looked so far out of their depth that they were close to drowning in all this. "I know what he means," Aedan said. "He's talking about the snatcher beams."

"Yeah," the colonel said. He was never one for soft-peddling the truth.

Aedan took a step backward, his hand gripping Elspeth's. "They'll kill us."

"Shadow's blades will kill you," Sting said. He looked Aedan up and down as if he'd not really seen him before. Perhaps he hadn't, perhaps he wasn't used to looking at humans any closer than people might look at chickens.

"You're all the same to me," Aedan said, returning the favor. "All killers."

Above — not too far above — came the whine of an approaching dart. Aedan and Elspeth crouched, watching the sky with controlled fear. It looked like something they'd done a thousand times. Sting cocked his head and said, "It is Hearten. He will take us now, back to the Astria Porta."

"O'Neill..." Teal'c warned.

The colonel nodded, glanced down at Daniel who still sat with one hand on Lana's shoulder. She was starting to stir, twitching and edgy. Soon, she'd try to fight again; if they hadn't tied her hands and feet she'd have run already.

Then he looked at Sam, a question in his eyes. She held his gaze and said, "I think we have to trust him, sir."

A brief nod and she knew she'd supported the decision he'd already made. "Back to the gate," he confirmed with Sting. "Not... that other place you guys took us."

"Our hive? No. That is no longer safe." Another pointed look at Earthborn. "We must find a new place of refuge on this world."

Good luck with that, Sam thought.

"And what about them?" the colonel said, gesturing to the refugees from the farm. They crouched in small groups, watching Sting with hungry eyes. "We can't leave them here, they need medical attention."

Sting's gaze swept over the refugees before fixing on the colonel. "Do you wish to take them through the Astria Porta?"

"They won't be welcome on Arbella," Daniel said, from where he sat with Lana. "But maybe Hecate would take them in?"

"I don't like handing them over to a Goa'uld," the colonel said. "However friendly her Jaffa."

Which didn't leave many options.

"Wait a second!" Daniel scrambled to his feet. "Sting, can't you heal them the way you healed me?"

The Wraith shared a look with Earthborn. "That is not— The Gift of Life is not bestowed on such creatures. There are strict protocols..."

"But it's possible," Daniel persisted. He looked at Sam. "Remember? Hunter told us about 'Feeders', people who work for the Wraith and are given 'life' in return."

She did remember, although she wasn't sure dooming these people to a lifetime of servitude to the Wraith was such a great idea.

"Worshipers," Earthborn said, distaste clear on her face. "That is not something my mother or I have ever sanctioned."

"They don't have to worship you. You just have to heal them."

"My queen," Sting said, "does not *have* to do anything."

"No, she doesn't," the colonel agreed. "Unless, of course, she wants our help with something..."

Earthborn's attention snapped to the colonel and for a moment they just stared at each other in silent contest. Above them, the whine of the Wraith ships grew louder. Time was running out. "Very well," Earthborn said at last, setting a hand on Sting's arm as if to forestall argument. "They are few. We will aid them, if you wish it, Colonel O'Neill."

If Wraith could grind their teeth, Sam imagined Sting was doing just that. His face was a rigid mask of disapproval.

"But we must leave this place quickly," Earthborn continued. "And there is only one way to do so."

The colonel nodded. "Then we have a deal," he said. "So how does this snatching—" A kerfuffle broke out to their right. "Damn it!"

Aedan and Elspeth were running, into the trees and the brightening dawn, him dragging her behind like a child he'd not let go.

"Carter!" The colonel dropped his pack and was after Aedan and Elspeth, Sam a heartbeat behind.

The woodland was sparse, the remains of the city as much part of it as the woods. She found herself vaulting over stubs of wall and around stripling trees. Aedan was fast, better rested, and he knew the terrain. He was getting away from them.

"Dammit," the colonel hissed, coming up short ahead of her. In one move he pulled his zat and didn't even shout a warning before he fired. The first shot went wide, sizzled against a tree, but the second caught Elspeth in the back and she jerked back with a cry.

Some of the shock must have passed hand-to-hand to Aedan, because he yelped as he stumbled, Elspeth's weight pulling him down. "Elspeth?"

"She's just stunned," the colonel shouted, his zat trained on Aedan. "You're both gonna be okay. Just trust me."

"*Trust* you? You're giving these people to the Devourers!" Aedan jumped to his feet, but his gaze darted back to Elspeth. "You're a fool."

"I'm trying to keep you alive."

"We'll take our chances, thanks."

"Then you'll die here."

"I'd rather die than let them take us."

After a pause, the colonel nodded. "Okay," he said. "It's

your funeral." For a moment even Sam was convinced as he lowered the zat to his side. Aedan relaxed, ducked down to Elspeth, touching his hand to her face, as in one fluid motion the colonel lifted his weapon and fired. Aedan fell, twitching, on top of Elspeth and then lay still.

The colonel looked at Sam, face impassive, waiting for her response.

She just shrugged. "Let's hope we're right, sir."

CHAPTER TWENTY-NINE

Earth — 2000: A few snips and there was a gap wide enough for them to crawl through. Simmy greeted them on the other side with a smile and a crushing hug. Janet saw that he still had the camera, its red recording light blinking. A strange thing to document, she thought, but it wouldn't hurt to show President Turner what sort of dangers were facing the people of Earth. Their reunion was cut short by a shout from further up the road.

"Shak'na kree!"

Simmy winced. "Ah sh—"

"C'mon!" Dixon's yell spurred them on once more, this time Simmy running at their side. All the while, Janet was aware of the pursuing Jaffa. They moved too fast for the staff blasts to find their mark, but all it took was one. So focused was she on getting one foot in front of the other and not stumbling, that she almost missed the two figures standing on the road up ahead.

"Down! Get down!"

On instinct, she dropped, as what sounded like rifle shots fired over her head. The staff blasts stopped.

Gingerly, Janet looked up. Standing in the road were Newman and Levine, the major with his handgun drawn. But it was the young Levine who had the rifle to his shoulder, hand steady and expression steely. "I call that an even twenty, Major," he said, "and you owe me ten bucks."

Janet rolled over and looked down the road. Three Jaffa lay there, apparently dead.

"You weren't lying when you said you can hit a mark, kid," said Newman, "I'm glad you're on our side." Something in his tone made Janet look back, and she saw that he hadn't taken his eyes off her. And he hadn't lowered his weapon.

"Stand down, Major," said Colonel Dixon, though his tone

was wary. He slowly got to his feet.

"Not so fast, Colonel," said Newman, his weapon still trained on Janet. "Let me see your hands. Where are the anti-virals?"

"They're in the bag," said Janet, pointing her thumb to the pack still slung over her shoulders. "What are you doing, Newman?"

"Nothing personal, Doctor. Just following orders. Toss me the bag. Easy now."

"Newman, have you lost your mind? There's no reason for this. We've got what we came for and it's going where it's needed. Now lower your damn weapon!"

"Sorry, sir, but these orders come from higher up. And it's not just about the meds."

The realization was almost amusing, though Janet knew the joke was most definitely on her. She'd known, of course, that there was some agenda behind Maybourne's participation in this plan, but she'd been foolish enough to think that she could play along and get what she wanted. Little did she know that she was, in fact, a pawn in a wider game.

"It's about me," she said, her tone neutral, all hurt and anger used up long ago. She thought of the glances, the judgements being cast as she'd been led to her tent in cuffs. God, that seemed so long ago now. "I'm a symbol, he said. And I was too stupid to figure out what I was a symbol for. I'm the sacrificial lamb, am I, Newman? Is that how Simmons is going to secure his power? By offering me up on a plate as a traitor."

Newman watched her down the sight of his pistol. "No one's going to be sacrificed here, Doctor. You just give me the meds, I use you to get back through the gate, and you stay here with the good colonel. That's what you wanted wasn't it? To stay and save the world? What does it matter what people back on Arbella think? Now just give me the antivirals and Levine and I'll escort you both back to the bunker."

"She doesn't have them. I do," said Dixon. With a heavy sigh, he unhooked the straps of his pack from his shoulders and

Newman extended his hand to catch it. But as Dixon made to toss it over, the air was rent by the second explosion of the day and the ground shook once more. Newman was caught off-guard, unaware of the timing of the C4, and he staggered as the ground shook, his weapon hand lowering.

Dixon, however, had clearly counted on the blast. He swung the rucksack, aiming for Newman's head, but the major had recovered his footing and ducked the blow. Dixon dropped the bag, going for his weapon, just as Janet turned to run.

Shots rang out, cracking through the cold of dawn.

Janet looked to Dixon, but the colonel had frozen in the act of reaching for his handgun. Neither shot had come from him. When she looked behind her, though, blood spatter marred the tarmac of the road. Her eyes rose to meet Newman's, but his gaze was blank below the angry hole in the center of his forehead. He crashed to the ground, revealing the stricken face of Airman Levine, the rifle still clutched in his steady hand.

"I didn't know," he said, his eyes darting from Dixon to Janet. "I swear I didn't know." But his words died in his mouth suddenly, and his gaze dropped as he looked at Janet. "I only needed one shot," he said, sounding almost puzzled as he stared at her.

"Doc?" It was Dixon's voice, but she couldn't understand why it sounded so far off when he was standing right next to her, couldn't understand where the icy fog that encased her body had come from, couldn't quite fathom why the ground was so hard at her back.

With effort, she rolled her head, which felt heavy and dull, to the side. Next to her, lay Major Dean Newman, eyes staring, bullet hole leaking gore onto the wet road.

I only needed one shot.

But there had been two of course. Two shots. One from Levine for Newman, and one from Newman — for her.

"Doctor Fraiser! Goddammit, Captain, you look at me! That's an order!"

Her hand, she realized, had been pressed to her middle,

and Colonel Dixon pulled it away. He'd taken his jacket off and was pressing it onto the wound. There was pain, but not a lot, and Janet knew she was going into shock. She raised her hand almost absently and stared at the blood that dripped from it. A gut shot then.

Her head was heavy and fell to the side, her loosened hair sticking to the wet tarmac of the road. Next to her face, a red light blinked, and she found herself staring into the cracked black eye of the camera. She knew it was watching her die.

Through the yells of Dixon and the sobs of Simmy who knelt alongside her, Janet became aware of another sound. She didn't hear it as much as felt the tremors through her back, reverberating up through the ground. A steady, rhythmic *tramp-tramp*.

In a moment of clarity amidst the fog that was descending, she realized that the Jaffa unit they had hidden from earlier was returning, perhaps drawn by the sounds of the explosion. It was too late now, anyway. She guessed that the bleeding from her stomach was bad, though she couldn't lift her head to look. With a bloodied hand, she pawed at Dixon's arm, leaving red streaks along his skin.

But he didn't move and she pushed harder. "Go..."

"Not a damn chance," he said through gritted teeth.

"Sir?" The alarm in Levine's voice confirmed everything she needed to know.

"They're... they're coming. I can hear them." She could barely hear her own voice, though she could feel the rattle in the back of her throat.

"Aw, man, she's right." Simmy's voice came from further down the road. "They're coming, brother! We need to get out of here."

"Grab the bags and I'll carry her," shouted Dixon, but Janet gripped the sleeve of his shirt and made him look at her.

"No." It was the only word she could summon and yet it carried all the weight of the only choice open to them. She was bleeding out rapidly. Even if he could carry her and still escape the oncoming Jaffa, she'd be dead by the time they got halfway down the road. It wasn't a risk worth taking. Better they get away with no hindrance.

Dixon's hand brushed the wet hair back from her forehead. "Janet... I'll come back. I promise, I'll come back. Just hold on for me."

She nodded weakly. "You better," she whispered, though it was a promise that both of them knew would be pointless to keep.

"Dix, mate, please!" Simmy came into view, his reddened eyes catching Janet's for just a moment, before both he and Dixon were gone from sight.

She let her eyes close then, and thought of home. Then she thought of Cassie. And then she thought of nothing at all.

CHAPTER THIRTY

Earth — 2098: A snatching beam, Hunter had called it, the white light that swept through the trees. Sam clenched her jaw, resisting the instinct to run as she saw it take the fleeing refugees. Teal'c looked up, staff primed and ready as it took him, Daniel's hand tightened on Lana's shoulder. Aedan and Elspeth were still out when they disappeared, and the colonel's eyes were on her as she felt a white shiver of nothing and was gone.

It wasn't like gate travel — there was no sense of movement — and it wasn't like Goa'uld transport rings, where reality seemed to change around you. It was more like turning the lights out and then waking up elsewhere.

She found herself on her back staring up at an empty gray sky, which was a vast improvement on last time she'd been 'snatched' when she'd woken up inside a dark, slimy cocoon. Beneath her hands she felt ashy soil and she sat up, remembering the radiation contamination.

The rest of them were nearby, Teal'c already on his feet, Daniel crouching in front of Lana, trying to talk to her. She was awake, whimpering and making weak attempts to fight against her bonds. Sam heard the words 'bright sleep' over and over and Daniel reached out to touch her, but she pushed his hand away with her bound wrists and snarled. He pulled back, settled on his heels to watch her.

Further away, Sting stood apart. There was no sign of Earthborn or the refugees.

Elspeth was close by, though, staring around in wonder while Aedan climbed to his feet and glared at Colonel O'Neill. The colonel was watching them both from a careful distance and Sam felt a pulse of relief at the sight of him. Part of her had been afraid that Sting would take the colonel straight back to his headquarters.

"So much for trusting you," Aedan growled.

The colonel lifted his hands in mock surrender. "You're home, aren't you? And you're both alive."

"But what about the people from the farm? Where are they?"

"They're being helped." The colonel glanced at Sting. "Right?"

The Wraith inclined his head. "As my queen commanded."

"It was the best we could do," the colonel said, turning back to Aedan. "You know it was."

He didn't have an answer to that, just kicked up an angry cloud of dirt instead.

"What will you do now?" Elspeth said. She spoke to the colonel, but her gaze drifted to Daniel. If Aedan noticed, or cared, he didn't react, and Daniel was too absorbed in calming Lana to pay attention.

The colonel followed her gaze. "We have to take Lana back to her people," he said. "After that…?"

It was a good question, Sam thought. After that, the colonel wanted to disband SG-1 and persuade the people of Arbella to help Hecate fight the Wraith. Or maybe he'd decide to adopt Earthborn's insane plan of stealing an Ancient city and flying to another galaxy. Either way, it looked like his path would diverge from hers and Teal'c's. Somehow that felt like betrayal and it hurt in a way she hadn't expected.

"You'll come back," Elspeth said, throwing half a glance at Sting. He stood some distance away, silent and still, watching but not interfering. "You'll come back for us and you'll take us to Dix," she pressed. "Daniel said so."

The colonel frowned; he was uncomfortable with making promises he didn't know he could keep. "We'll come back," he said. "And I'll talk to Dix…"

At that, Teal'c made a gruff noise deep in his throat. The colonel spared him a look, snatched off his cap and ran his fingers through his hair. Sam could feel his frustration, his weariness, and felt a flash of irritation with Teal'c. The situation was more complicated than he saw it. Perhaps it was more complicated than she'd thought too.

"When?" Elspeth pressed. "When will you come back?"

"I don't know," the colonel said, and that was the truth. He glanced at Sting. "I've got a few details to work out first."

Aedan grunted his disbelief. "Right, like how many Devourers to bring here?"

"I swear to you," the colonel said, "I'll do everything I can to help your people. I know you don't trust me, but that's all I've got."

Aedan didn't answer and for a long moment the two men just looked at each other.

"Go home," the colonel said at last. "Go home and stay safe." To Elspeth he added, "Keep an eye on the gate."

"Go fast," Sting said from his place on the edge of the group. "When the Astria Porta is opened, it is likely that Shadow will know. Her blades will come to investigate."

Aedan's jaw clenched and he gripped Elspeth's wrist. "I don't know if you've brought help or trouble, O'Neill," he said. "But if you hurt my people, if they're hurt because of you, I'll count you as an enemy."

The colonel settled his cap back on his head, hands coming to rest on his MP5. "Likewise."

With no more said, Aedan turned and started off toward the hills and home, less than half a day's walk. Elspeth looked over her shoulder once, but Aedan's grip on her arm was firm and she didn't look like she really wanted him to let go. They both looked exhausted.

"I'm putting a lot of faith in you," the colonel said to Sting as they watched Aedan and Elspeth leave.

Sting's answering look gave little away, but what he said was, "Stormfire asked that I deliver you directly to him." He paused. "I did not."

"You gonna tell me why?"

Another pause, this one less assured. "It is difficult to explain," Sting said. "You are... different." His alien eyes swept around the group. "All of you. Earthborn believes you will serve her better if you choose to and are not coerced."

"I'm not serving anyone," the colonel pointed out.

Sting's expression changed. "But you will assist us."

"I'm thinking about it." His gaze came to rest on Sam and to Sting he said, "You want to give us a moment?"

Sting looked between them and inclined his head, but before moving away he said, "Hearten will return me to Earthborn now. But do not forget, we can track you, Lantean. We will know where you are when you return."

The colonel gave a flat smile. "Comforting."

With a nod, Sting touched something on his wrist and a moment later a dart slipped out of the clouds and swept past, scooping him up in its snatcher beam. In the distance, Sam saw Aedan and Elspeth crouching, tracking the ship as it disappeared back into the clouds. Then they were moving again, jogging across the valley toward the hills and the scrappy tree line. Heading home.

She sighed. If only the rest of them could.

"Hey," the colonel said as he approached. He nodded at something behind her and when she turned she saw the Stargate, cockeyed and staring up into the sky. "Think you can get that working?"

The portable DHD was stowed in her vest, and she flexed her fingers against the burn on her palm as she reached for the pocket. But the colonel stopped her before she could touch the zipper.

"Let me see that," he said, turning her hand over.

"It's nothing," she said, although in the morning light it looked worse than she'd hoped. There was blistering at the center of the wound that needed to be cleaned before it got infected.

"Next time you're breaking into a secret alien facility," the colonel said, touching the raw skin with his pad of his thumb, "don't just grab the high voltage electric fence."

"Yes sir," she said. "I lost my balance, actually."

"Ah. So that's what happened."

She started to tug her fingers away, but he didn't let go. "So I guess this is it," he said.

"What do you mean?"

He nodded toward the gate. "Once we get back to Rya'c's ship, it's mission over."

And by mission over, he meant SG-1 was over. He meant he really was going to let it all fall apart. "Sir," she said, but then stopped because she realized she had nothing left to say. They'd argued this to a standstill already.

"You saw what they're doing here, right, Carter? Implanting Goa'uld into Wraith hosts?"

"All the more reason to stop it from happening in the first place."

His fingers tightened around her hand for a moment, then he let go. "And maybe you'll do it," he said. "Eventually. But I can't just sit back and do nothing while you try. I have to help these people."

"Sir, our mission is—"

"Our mission is to defend Earth." He gestured at the bleak world they stood on. "This is Earth, Carter. These are the people I have to defend."

"You mean 'we', sir. These are the people 'we' have to defend — as SG-1."

He shook his head. "Sam, I can't tell you guys how to spend the rest of your lives."

"The rest of our *lives*?"

He cocked his head, looking at her with more honesty than was comfortable. "You think it'll be a quick fix?"

She didn't reply; they both knew the answer. It could take years, a lifetime. "But we're still SG-1," she said. "That hasn't changed."

"There's no SGC, Carter. There's no Air Force. There's no United States. Are we really going to keep up the whole 'yes sir, no sir' thing until we're drawing our non-existent Air

Force pensions?"

Despite it feeling more like the end of the world than pretty much anything else that had happened, Sam couldn't keep her lips from twitching. "Probably worth a lot by now," she said.

"And that doesn't even include the hundred years of Combat Pay we've racked up."

She gave a sad smile. "It feels like we're giving up."

"It's about making the best of things, Sam," he said, with a look that was a little less Colonel O'Neill than usual. "It's about finding that silver lining."

Awkward beneath that steady gaze, she looked up at the Stargate instead. It had always been the way home, their salvation — maybe, one day, it would be again. "I don't think I'm ready to look for silver linings yet, sir."

"I know," he said and his boots crunched in the ashy dirt as he turned away. "But let me know when you are."

Evacuation Site — 2000

There was a whisper in the Arbellan camp, a hiss of words he couldn't quite hear, but that he knew spoke against him. Maybourne would have called it paranoia, except that in this line of work, nine times out of ten they most certainly *were* out to get you. Besides, he wasn't imagining the huddled groups of grave-faced people talking among themselves, who fell silent when they saw him coming. Most of them, he'd noticed, were from Stargate Command.

It was the girl's fault of course. When Reynolds had been discovered, Maybourne hadn't expected her to be there in the crowd so quickly and certainly hadn't expected her to be so… vocal. People had been listening to him and the seeds he was planting were growing quite satisfactorily before she'd spoken up.

They had been idiots to discount her, but when Simmons had suggested that Cassie was another loose end to be tied up, Turner had baulked.

"She's a child, Frank. We're not so desperate that we need to resort to those measures."

Not yet, were the unspoken words that Maybourne heard, but in truth he was glad of Turner's refusal; no matter his past crimes, he wasn't sure if he could stomach such an act.

And so Cassie had been left alone, on the assumption that she was just a kid and no matter what she said after the fact, no one would take her seriously. After all, what daughter wouldn't lie to save her mother?

How wrong they'd been.

But there was one ace still up his sleeve, one last move to save all of their skins. For all Simmons' scheming and politicking, it would be Harold Maybourne who'd lift their necks from the chopping board.

He climbed the last few steps up to the base and crossed the narrow bridge. Newman was due back soon and he would bring with him, not only the drugs which would cure the flu and let Turner play the part of savior, but a first-hand account of the reckless acts to which Janet Fraiser had been driven, and the extent to which she'd put Arbella in danger.

He walked into the embarkation room just as the gate was spinning. Maybourne checked his watch. Newman was early. Things must have gone even better than they'd planned. On protocol, the technician on duty activated the shield.

"It's Major Newman's IDC, sir."

"Open the shield," said Maybourne. He felt on edge, antsy. This was a delicate play and the least deviation from the plan could knock it off course.

It was Airman Levine who walked through the wormhole first, but from his red eyes and tight expression, Maybourne knew something was wrong, even before the next man walked through the gate. That man was not Major Newman.

"Colonel Dixon." Maybourne cursed the tremor in his voice.

Dixon walked slowly down the steps, the sound of his boots echoing in the suddenly silent chamber. He stalked forward and for a second Maybourne thought he might hit him. He fought the urge to flinch. "Where is Major Newman?" he asked.

"Major Newman is lying on a road in Scotland with a bullet through his head, Colonel."

"I don't understand." Maybourne's eyes flitted from Dixon to Levine, but the young airman just stood staring at the floor with empty eyes.

"Why don't you ask where Dr. Fraser is?" said Dixon.

But Maybourne could hardly speak. All he could think of were the whispers and the huddled groups and the rock solid plan that was gradually turning to sand.

Dixon grabbed a fistful of Maybourne's jacket and pulled him up to his face. "Why don't you ask where she is?" he yelled.

"Why would I...? Where is...?"

"She's dead." The voice was small and choked, and came not from Dixon, but from Levine, whose gaze was still fixed on the floor. "She died. Major Newman... he shot her. I don't know why. So I shot him."

Dixon shoved Maybourne back. His jaw had tightened and he looked away as if the very sight of Maybourne sickened him.

This wasn't the plan. This was as far from the plan as they could possibly have strayed. And Maybourne knew then that the loose ends had just become a frayed mess.

CHAPTER THIRTY-ONE

Earth — 2098: The final chevron locked and the wormhole erupted into the sky, the angle sending it fountaining up into the air before it settled into its usual shimmer of blue. Lana was too far gone to know what was happening, but at least Daniel had managed to calm her enough that they hadn't needed to sedate her again. There seemed to be enough of her mind left to understand the consequences of struggling too hard.

Teal'c offered to help carry her, but Daniel waved him away. "She trusts me," he said as he scooped the frail woman into his arms rather than over his shoulder. It was only a few steps to the gate, although the angle would make arriving a little tricky.

But Jack was up ahead and he'd catch them on the other side if necessary.

He'd stopped in the blue wash of the gate, turning to face them all. Jack wasn't one for speeches, but they all knew that things were about to change between them. "Whatever happens next," he said at last, "I've got your backs, and I always will. Remember that."

Teal'c gave a slight nod. If a Jaffa could look sheepish he might, Daniel thought, look something like Teal'c in that moment.

Sam just murmured "Back at you, sir" to which Jack gave a slight smile.

And Daniel said, "Not that I don't appreciate this moment of *esprit de corps*, but Lana's holding on by her fingernails here… And so are my shoulders, if you'll pardon the mixed metaphor."

"Consider it pardoned," Jack said, and turned to face the gate. He took a moment to brace himself, like he always did, hands on his weapon — which had to be more use as a club than a gun at this point, since they were all out of ammo — and then he stepped up and over the lip of the awkwardly cockeyed

Stargate and dropped down into the wormhole.

He was gone.

Sam stepped up next to Daniel, Teal'c waited behind. "Need a hand?" she said.

"I got it." He glanced down at the suffering face of the woman. "You'll see your husband again soon," he said.

She blinked at him. "Gunnison."

"That's right." He shifted her weight in his arms. "Hold on, this might feel strange."

Then, with Sam at his side he stepped into the wormhole and let it take him apart.

An instant later he was in the warm, still air of the ha'tak, the floor rushing up to meet him faster than usual and at an odd angle. He stumbled, but Jack grabbed his arm and kept him and Lana upright. Sam dropped to one knee next to him, but was back on her feet an instant later as Teal'c stepped out of the gate behind them with no apparent problem.

Decades of practice, Daniel reminded himself.

But Teal'c's eyes were fixed straight ahead, a tight expression on his face, and Daniel followed his gaze to Rya'c who stood with his men at a safe distance from the Stargate.

"Welcome," Rya'c said as the wormhole collapsed behind them, leaving the room bereft. "I am pleased to see you all return unharmed." He took a step closer, a gesture keeping his men at bay, and glanced at Lana. "And you have been successful?"

"It's her," Jack confirmed. "Kinda."

Rya'c's mouth tightened. "She is damaged, like Jamie Fraiser?"

"Yeah," Jack said. "And now we know why."

Rya'c's gaze lifted and in that moment Daniel realized something. "You already knew," he said.

"Suspected." Rya'c spread his hands in apology. "That is, the Lady Hecate suspected the Wraith were using a sarcophagus to revive humans who had been fed upon. We had no confirmation, but she was familiar with the effects of addiction to the sarcophagus. Besides, the tactical advantage it would give them was clear."

Daniel shifted Lana in his arms; she was starting to squirm. He hushed her as best he could and risked a glance at Jack. How much, he wondered, was he going to tell Rya'c about what they'd discovered?

Everything, apparently.

"It's worse than that," Jack said. "They're taking Wraith as hosts."

Rya'c stared. "Impossible. The naquadah in the blood of a host prevents the Wraith from feeding on them. They could not take a Wraith as a host."

"Well, we saw it," Jack said, pulling off his hat. His hair stuck up in all directions and he looked as exhausted as Daniel felt.

"It seemed to be more of an… equal… relationship," Sam said. "The host and the Goa'uld were both present."

Rya'c looked genuinely shocked and behind him his men shared uneasy glances, but he was in command of himself and them. "See to the woman," he said, beckoning a couple of Jaffa forward. "Take her to the medical bay."

"I'd rather take her myself," Daniel said, holding her close. He didn't know what, if anything, Lana had seen of the Goa'uld, but he wanted to minimize her distress.

"Very well," Rya'c said. "I will contact Arbella and tell President Jones the news."

He didn't call it 'good news'. Daniel knew it wasn't, but at the same time it was better than the worst news. "Tell Jones she's alive," he said. "Tell him there's hope she'll find herself again, but that it'll take time."

"As you wish," Rya'c said. Then, to Jack, he added, "I will tell the Lady Hecate what you have told me and seek her advice." One of his eyebrows lifted in a gesture that was the image of his father's. "Meanwhile there are quarters here are at your disposal, if you wish to rest and… bathe."

"God, yes," said Sam. "Uh," she added when she realized all

eyes were on her, "you know, if there's time."

"There's time," Jack said as the Jaffa led them way from the gate room. He glanced at Daniel. "You too, as soon as she's settled."

Daniel nodded. The truth was, he wasn't certain how long he'd be able to stay on his feet anyway. The last time they'd slept had been on the shores of Gare Loch and that was, what, two days ago?

But it took another couple of hours before he could leave Lana, and of course Jack wouldn't leave either until Daniel was ready to go. By the time Lana had been sedated and was as comfortable as possible, both he and Jack were dead on their feet.

In the quarters Rya'c had provided, Daniel bathed, changed, and fell onto one of the hard Jaffa beds. His sleep was dark and absolute and lasted all of thirty seconds before Sam was shaking him awake.

"Get dressed," she said, pushing a miraculously clean uniform at him. "Rya'c's here, he has news."

Daniel blinked at her, disoriented, grasping with sleepy fingers at what was going on and coming up empty.

"You've been asleep for almost six hours," Sam said, tousling his hair. She picked up his glasses from the bed and handed them to him. "Get dressed. Rya'c looks spooked."

Evacuation Site — 2000: Maybourne was sweating and breathless by the time he reached the President's official tent. Getting here had been like running the gauntlet, the Arbellan residents having lost their propensity to huddle and becoming more vocal. In the distance, he could hear calls of 'Justice for Janet' and the echoing cries of support. They had to put a lid on this now or the mess would never be cleaned up.

He burst past the Secret Service agent at the door and the man grabbed him just as he pushed his way inside.

"It's alright, John." Turner waved a calming hand at his guard. "Let him in."

The President stood leaning both fists on his desk, looking haggard and worn. On the other side of the desk stood Frank Simmons.

"This is getting out of control," said Maybourne. "You have to do something, before we end up with a full scale revolt on our hands."

Simmons shot a look at Turner. "Don't you mean *we* have to do something, Colonel?"

"Don't get picky with semantics on me now, Simmons," he growled. "Of course that's what I mean."

"Good, I'm glad you realize that we're all in this together. We *all* have to play our part in the grand plan."

"Janet Fraiser is dead! Was that part of the grand plan?"

The shock on both Turner and Simmons' face would have given Maybourne great pleasure if he wasn't so fearful of crucifixion by an angry mob.

There were a few moments of taut silence before Turner asked, "What happened?"

"Well you know that stuff that normally hits the fan? It's the same stuff we're all about to land in if we don't get a handle on this." His heart was hammering in his chest and his sweat-soaked clothes clung to him. "I don't know what happened, but something went wrong. Shots were fired and both Fraiser and Dean Newman went down and didn't get back up. I'm holding Colonel Dixon and Todd Levine up in the base ready to tell the whole sordid story to anyone who'll listen."

"What?" barked Simmons. "Dave Dixon is here? Why the hell did you let him through the gate?"

"He had Newman's IDC. What the hell was I supposed to do?"

"This is out of control, Frank," said Turner gravely. "Janet Fraiser was never supposed to die." He took a breath as if making a decision. "We have to go to contingency."

Frank Simmons frowned and then nodded.

"There's a contingency?" asked Maybourne. "Why wasn't I told?"

Both men ignored him.

"John," called the President to his guard.

"What you have to understand, Maybourne," said Simmons, as the agent entered the tent, "is that we had to prepare for every eventuality. We had to account for the weak link in the chain. There was always a chance that this would happen. And so Janet Fraiser wasn't our only fall guy."

"I don't follow."

President Turner straightened. "John, have Colonel Maybourne escorted under guard to the holding cells in the base. He's been charged with treason against the people of Earth and of Arbella."

"No! What is this?" cried Maybourne, as John secured his wrists behind his back.

"We have evidence to suggest that you were complicit in the events that led to the invasion of Earth by the Goa'uld, Maybourne," said Simmons, and Maybourne had to admire the man, for his game face was text book. "Not only that, but your actions caused the death of two members of our community. Your fate will be decided at court martial." Simmons nodded to the guard, who began leading Maybourne to the door of the tent.

"At court martial?" he shouted back. "Is that another lie? Like the ones you got me to feed Fraiser? I did everything you told me to, Simmons! Everything! I was loyal!"

But as he was pushed from the tent he realized that, no matter Janet Fraiser's fate, no matter his loyalty, this had been the outcome they'd intended for him all along.

CHAPTER THIRTY-TWO

The notion of justice had always been a fixed quantity to Dave Dixon. All his life he'd believed in letting the punishment equal the crime, and his experiences in the military had only served to solidify that belief. But as he stood in the Arbellan gate room, waiting on them leading out Harold Maybourne to begin his sentence for crimes against humanity, he felt sick to his stomach. The court martial had been kangaroo from start to finish, with no counsel offered to the defendant. The whole set-up reeked.

Not that he believed in Maybourne's innocence — he'd long been aware of the man's reputation, and General Hammond had filled in the blanks for him on the details of Maybourne's part in the fate of Earth. But, sure as he knew that down followed up, he was in no doubt that Maybourne wasn't the puppet-master in this whole catastrophe. His money was on the man called Frank Simmons, a tin-pot dictator wannabe if ever he'd seen one.

President Turner stood at the far end of the room, close to the gate, looking a lot less groomed than the man who'd stood smiling at his inauguration just a few months ago. Dixon had always thought that Turner didn't quite have the stones required to be President of the United States, and he sure as hell didn't vote for the guy, but he'd always looked very in control, very capable. He guessed that maybe an apocalypse was a true test of a man's fortitude, and by the look of it, Turner had failed badly. Perhaps the blame here lay at more than one doorstep.

Regardless, Dixon felt no satisfaction at the fate that was about to befall Harold Maybourne. Justice in any form was an empty concept now. Janet was gone, left to die alone in enemy territory. No matter what retribution was meted out now, there was no changing that. No bringing back the woman who'd been willing to risk everything for just the idea of hope. No bringing back Cassie's mom.

The girl's grief had been a hard thing to witness. She'd wept, of course, her tears coming with raw, gut-wrenching sobs, and he'd sat with her all the while. But then her tears had subsided, and in their place came a quiet anger.

"It won't be for nothing, Colonel," she'd said with a clenched jaw. "I won't let them do this to her and have it be for nothing. I swear to God I won't."

He'd nodded, unsettled by this fierceness, but admiring it also, and had made an unspoken pledge to do whatever it took to help her.

A hush suddenly fell over the assembled crowd and Dixon looked up to see Maybourne being led out by two guards. He wasn't cuffed, but he showed no sign of resistance. Instead, he looked a cowed shadow of the smug blowhard with whom Dixon was familiar.

The spectators watched his progress up to the gate like rubberneckers at a car crash. It was macabre, this gathering. He'd never been a believer in having an audience at an execution, and even though Maybourne's sentence was to be exile rather than death, Dixon still felt uncomfortable even with his own presence here.

At the bottom of the steps, the guards stopped him as the wormhole whooshed into existence, an address picked from a list of inhabited planets. He was being sent through with supplies enough for survival, but he would have to adapt and find the closest town or settlement if he was to last. If he didn't... Who knew what his fate might be?

An Air Force officer stepped forward, the same one who had presided over the court martial, and read the list of charges of which Maybourne had been found guilty. "Do you have anything to say before sentence is carried out?" he asked.

For a second, Maybourne wavered and opened his mouth as if to speak. But then his gaze darted to the side and he closed it again with a shake of his head. Dixon followed his line of sight and saw Frank Simmons staring, unblinking back at Maybourne. It looked more and more like Dixon's guess was on the money, and he wondered what manner of threats he'd thrown at his lackey to make sure his mouth stayed shut.

The formalities done with, the officer nodded to the guards, and Maybourne was turned and led to the event horizon, with no choice left to him but to step through. Two large packs were thrown through unceremoniously and the wormhole vanished a second later. The crowd, with nothing left to anticipate, almost seemed disappointed that proceedings had gone without drama, and they began to mill around, most of them heading for the exit. The bitter taste in Dixon's mouth soured further when he saw both Turner and Simmons heading in his direction.

"Colonel Dixon," said Turner, extending a hand that Dixon had no choice but to shake, "we appreciate your coming here today."

"I could hardly turn down an invite from my hosts now, could I?"

"Oh you mustn't think of yourself as a guest here. You're one of us. This is your home."

Dixon choked back a retort. Less than a week ago, he was anathema to these people, an unwanted reminder of the people they had left behind. He most certainly was not one of them. "That's a nice sentiment, Mr. President," was all he said.

"I'm just sorry that these are the circumstances that bring you to Arbella." There wasn't a trace of artifice in Simmons' tone.

"No sorrier than I am, Colonel."

"Janet Fraiser was a good woman."

"I'm glad you know that," said Dixon with a tight smile. "Believe me, it's not the Goa'uld I blame for her death."

Simmons regarded him with narrowed eyes. "But the punishment has been dealt now. Although I daresay Maybourne remains unapologetic for his crimes."

Dixon didn't waver as he held Simmons' eyes with his own. "I imagine that three more deaths don't add up to much, when you've already got five billion under your belt."

The two men stared at one another, until Turner gave an uneasy cough. "There will be a full apology, of course, for any defamation of Dr. Fraiser's character. A public ceremony would be fitting I think. We'll have Cassie there and –"

"No, you will not." Dixon's tone had a hardened edge as his gaze flicked to Turner. Over his dead body would he let the girl be used as some political tool to gain favor with the Arbellan people.

Turner cleared his throat again and part of Dixon disdained the man's weak will. "No, of course, you're right. She's been through enough."

"What you will do, however, is to honor Janet Fraiser's memory and allow free travel between Earth and Arbella for all refugees. If I'm welcome here, then so is everyone else who called Earth home."

"But there's no way... " The words withered in the man's mouth, and Dixon knew that he'd won this round, and all he'd had to do was smile at the man. And the smile was far from friendly. It was a smile that spoke of the trouble Dixon could create for him, and it echoed Cassie's fervent vow that there was nothing they wouldn't do to make sure Janet's death wasn't in vain.

He would do whatever was necessary to protect her memory, and protect Earth.

He'd make a deal with the devil if he had to.

Hecate's ha'tak — 2098: By the time Daniel had dressed and combed his fingers through his hair — it was getting long, also he needed a shave — his brain had almost caught up with him. He'd have killed for a coffee, but even without the caffeine hit he was getting up to speed.

Outside his room, Rya'c was pacing the living quarters. "Dr.

Jackson," he said and, in the same moment, Jack appeared from one of the other rooms looking as rumpled as Daniel felt. He wedged his cap over hair that looked like he'd slept on it wet.

"What's going on?" he said, and propped one foot up on a chair to finish tying his boot.

Rya'c stopped pacing, looked at them all, hands clenched behind his back. "The Lady Hecate is concerned about the news you bring." His chin lifted but he swallowed hard, at once defiant and nervous. "She wishes to speak with you."

All of a sudden, Daniel was wide awake. From the sharp look Jack threw him, the news had been as effective as a double espresso for him too. "I didn't think she ever came out from behind her curtain."

Rya'c blinked, nonplussed.

"He's never seen the movie," Daniel pointed out.

Jack shot him an eloquent look and said, to Rya'c, "So let's go see the wizard."

Rya'c led them himself through the corridors of the ha'tak. Daniel was familiar with the layout of the ships, but even if he hadn't been the increasingly ornate décor made it clear they were heading toward the seat of power.

"What do you think this is about?" Sam asked in a low voice.

"What's it always about?" Jack said. "A power play of some kind."

Sam made a face; she wasn't convinced. Neither was Daniel. Not that he didn't expect this to be a power play, but there was something about the way Rya'c was behaving that was strange. "He looks nervous," he realized. "Don't you think?"

"It is shame," Teal'c said, not quietly. "He does not want us to see him serving this false god. Why else would he keep us from her presence for so long?"

It could be that, Daniel supposed. Maybe.

Ahead of them was a set of double doors, the entrance to a throne room. Rya'c drew to a halt, turning to face them. His expression was unreadable, but the muscles in his lean shoulders were taut with tension. "I would have you know," he said in a voice that was more the boy than the man, "that I was asked by Dix himself to take on not only his name, but his role as first prime when he fell. It has been my honor to do so."

"Okay," Jack said. He kept his uncertainty in check but Daniel knew him well enough to hear it beneath the surface. Something weird was going on here, and Jack hated surprises. "Let's just get this over with, shall we?"

Rya'c nodded, but instead of opening the vast doors behind him he gestured to a smaller door to one side. It opened by some silent command. "Follow," he said.

Daniel felt a buzz of unease and swallowed hard. He exchanged a look with the others; they had no choice but to follow.

"We are unarmed," Teal'c pointed out.

"Yeah," Jack said. "I noticed that."

But there were Jaffa behind them and there was nowhere to go but straight ahead. "Out of the frying pan?" Daniel said.

Jack just grunted. "Stay sharp," he said and led the way into the room.

It was ornate, but less so than your typical Goa'uld throne room and smaller too. Daniel immediately recognized the iconography in the room's friezes as Hellenistic — appropriate for Hecate, the Greek goddess of gateways — and slender Ionic pillars rose from a low dais at the far end of the room. It was shadowy and at first Daniel didn't realize that Hecate was there, on a chair that wasn't quite a throne.

Rya'c stopped and bowed, not letting them past him. "Lady Hecate," he said in a strained voice. "SG-1 is here."

Hecate rose to her feet. "As I see," she said, her voice resonant yet still feminine. She stepped down from the dais as Rya'c moved aside and then she was walking toward them, into the light.

Sam made a choking sound that cut off savagely. Jack rasped harsh words, but Daniel couldn't hear what they were. All he could hear was the rush of blood through his ears as the Goa'uld before him resolved into a sickeningly familiar face.

A hand grabbed his arm, fingers biting into his flesh — Jack, full of rage and in desperate search for control. "No," he growled, staring at Hecate. "Sonofabitch, no. This can't happen."

And right then Daniel knew that everything had changed, because now none of them could let this reality stand. Not with Hecate watching them through this woman's eyes. Because this was their colleague. This was their friend.

This was Janet Fraiser.

EPILOGUE

Hecate's ha'tak — 2000: The searing heat surged through her, again and again, pulling her towards a pain-racked consciousness she didn't want to face. The hard surface at her back wasn't the uneven surface of the road, but something smooth and clean. The cold too had gone, replaced by this hideous burning. The pain stopped suddenly and Janet sobbed in relief.

"She returns." The voice was cracked and knotted, but held that reverberating tone that sent dread into the very depths of her gut.

Janet opened her eyes, almost scared to see what lay beyond. It was dark, her vision blurred, and she blinked until shapes became clear. Above her stood the owner of the voice, and Janet recoiled as her face came into focus.

The woman was wizened beyond anything Janet had seen in her life, professional or otherwise. Wrinkles lined every inch of her skin, sinking deep into each other on a face that sagged as if the flesh inside had given up any pretense of holding onto the skull beneath.

"You are known to me," said the woman — the Goa'uld, for it was clear what she was. Now that her eyes were more accustomed to the low light, Janet saw that she lay on a table in the middle of what seemed to be the bridge of a hat'ak. She tried to move, but pain dragged at her middle, and she remembered: gunshot wound. She should be dead. "Am I known to you?" asked the woman.

Janet tried to speak, but her throat was dry and brittle and nothing but a rasp came out. Yes, she knew who this was.

Hecate.

"You are a trophy," said the Goa'uld. "Not the best trophy, of course. I tried to catch them, but they slipped through my fingers." She opened and closed her hand like a snatching claw.

Did she mean SG-1? Did that mean they were still out there?

"But Janet Fraiser, hmm?" Hecate purred in pleasure. "Healer of the Tau'ri, the scourge of Hathor, bane of my lord Apophis. Mother, indeed, to Nirrti's little toy. Tell me, has the experiment on the girl come to fruition?"

She felt a surge of panic — was Cassie in danger?

Hecate looked to the side, as if working something out and murmured, "No. No, not yet. But soon." Her eyes slid back to Janet. "Yes, quite the trophy I've stumbled across."

Janet sucked in a labored breath and tried to move her arms, but every extremity felt heavy as if it were chained to the surface of the table on which she lay.

"*Tch-tch-tch,*" Hecate scolded, waving a long, knotted finger. "No need to move. No hope of moving," she added with a chuckle. "I am a healer too, you see, and I know of potions to hold one between life and death." She circled the table and tipped up Janet's chin with a gnarled finger. "Now which will it be for you?"

"You…" Janet choked with the effort of speaking. "You can kill me if you want. I won't give you information."

At that the crone threw back her head and laughed, a cackling hiss, broken up by an ugly hacking. "And what 'information' would I want from you?" She threw back her arm, gesturing to the wide window at the other end of the room, though all Janet could see was star-scattered space. "Your world lies in cinders, Dr. Fraiser. And *I* have wrought that. You call it *apocalypse*, a word with such horrifying weight to you Tau'ri. But your ignorance is astounding, for it has nothing to do with your tales of angels and trumpets. Do you know what such a word means in the language of your ancient Greeks? Your Daniel Jackson could tell you. It means the lifting of a veil, Dr. Fraiser. The uncovering of knowledge. It is *I* who has brought this to your squalid little world. No, Dr. Fraiser, I need no information from you." She leaned over the table, her face inches from Janet's. "I will burn your Earth to the ground and start anew. And you... Oh yes, I have use for you."

"What... use?"

"Worry not, Janet Fraiser. For it is a gift I offer you. Your friends... your SG-1... you wish to see them again, do you not? Then let me grant that wish. All we will need is patience."

She drew her arm from behind her back and it was then that Janet realized what it was that had brought her such searing pain. Hecate held the healing device over her stomach and Janet felt its rays pierce her, and she realized then that there were worse fates than death.

ABOUT THE AUTHORS

Sally Malcolm is the commissioning editor at Fandemonium Books and has overseen the production of more than 50 novels based on STARGATE SG-1, STARGATE ATLANTIS and STARGATE UNIVERSE.

Sally has written **STARGATE SG-1: A Matter of Honor**, **STARGATE SG-1: The Cost of Honor**, **STARGATE ATLANTIS: Rising** (novelization), the novella **STARGATE SG-1: Permafrost**, and, with Laura Harper, she has co-written **STARGATE SG-1: Hostile Ground** (book one of the Apocalypse series). She has also penned four audio dramas for Big Finish Productions: STARGATE SG-1: Gift of the Gods starring Michael Shanks, STARGATE ATLANTIS: Savarna starring Teryl Rothery, STARGATE ATLANTIS: Perchance to Dream starring Paul McGillion, and STARGATE SG-1: An Eye for an Eye starring Michael Shanks, Claudia Black and Cliff Simon.

She also wrote two episodes of the video game STARGATE SG-1: Unleashed which were voiced by Stargate SG-1 stars Richard Dean Anderson, Michael Shanks, Amanda Tapping and Chris Judge.

STARGATE SG-1: Exile is the third novel Sally has co-authored with Laura Harper and the second book in the Apocalypse series.

Laura Harper co-authored **STARGATE SG-1: Hostile Ground**, as well as **STARGATE SG-1: Sunrise** with Sally Malcolm (writing as J.F. Crane). **STARGATE SG-1: Exile** is her third novel for Fandemonium Books.

Laura is currently working on an original novel and book three of the STARGATE SG-1 Apocalypse series.

Stay in touch...
Follow us on Twitter
@StargateNovels

Find us on Facebook at
facebook.com/StargateNovels

Sign up for our newsletter
at StargateNovels.com

THANKS!

STARGATE SG·1   STARGATE ATLANTIS

Original novels based on the hit TV shows **STARGATE SG-1** and **STARGATE ATLANTIS**

Available as e-books from leading online retailers including Amazon, Barnes & Noble and iBooks

Paperback editions available from StargateNovels.com and Amazon.com

If you liked this book, please tell your friends and leave a review on a bookstore website.

STARGATE SG-1 is a trademark of Metro-Goldwyn-Mayer Studios Inc. ©1997-2015 MGM Television Entertainment Inc. and MGM Global Holdings Inc. All Rights Reserved.
STARGATE ATLANTIS is a trademark of Metro-Goldwyn-Mayer Studios Inc. ©2004-2015 MGM Global Holdings Inc. All Rights Reserved.
METRO-GOLDWYN-MAYER is a trademark of Metro-Goldwyn-Mayer Lion Corp. © 2015 Metro-Goldwyn-Mayer Studios Inc. All Rights Reserved.